THE CROCUS LIST

Gavin Lyall was born and educated in Birmingham. For two years he served as an RAF pilot before going up to Cambridge, where he edited *Varsity*, the university newspaper. After working for *Picture Post*, the *Sunday Graphic* and the BBC, he began his first novel, *The Wrong Side of the Sky*, published in 1961. After four years as air correspondent to the *Sunday Times*, he resigned to write books full time.

Gavin Lyall lives in London and is married to Katharine Whitehorn.

Also by Gavin Lyall
in Pan Books

The Wrong Side of the Sky
The Most Dangerous Game
Midnight Plus One
Shooting Script
Venus With Pistol
Blame the Dead
Judas Country
The Secret Servant
The Conduct of Major Maxim

GAVIN LYALL

The Crocus List

Pan Books
London and Sydney

First published 1985 by Hodder and Stoughton Ltd
This edition published 1986 by Pan Books Ltd,
Cavaye Place, London SW10 9PG
9 8 7 6 5 4 3 2 1
© Gavin Lyall 1985
ISBN 0 330 29195 5
Reproduced, printed and bound in Great Britain by
Hazell Watson & Viney Limited,
Member of the BPCC Group,
Aylesbury, Bucks

1

The Duke was dead. The old Duke, last of a generation of Royal Dukes, the one the press claimed was known as the Steel Duke (though they had made up the name themselves) because he had also been a Field Marshal and a real one. The news, coming late on a September Friday, sent a little ripple through the Army. In the Ministry of Defence it brought a few moments of silence: full generals put down their pens and cups and began recalling chance remarks the Old Man had thrown at them when they were mere subalterns, then winced when they realised they would have to put on Blues and remember how to adjust the stars and sashes of their knighthoods for the memorial service. In outer offices the silence was shorter. Brigadiers and colonels who had never known the Duke, and who would be no part of the service anyway, just said: "Yes, I suppose he *was* still alive," and went back to writing applications for jobs in personnel management and fund-raising.

In the London barracks of the Household Division and the Cavalry, and among the Duke's own (now much amalgamated) old regiment on station in Osnabrück, the ripple became a wave of mingled apprehension and pride. They – selected echelons of them – would certainly be part of the service, the most visible part, and rehearsal time was short. The British Army prided itself on its parades even more than on its gallant defeats.

And in the military clubs and the Bishop's Bar at the House of Lords, the news brought a welcome change from silence and an ironclad excuse not to go home to their wives. Some, of nearly the Duke's own age, could remember his first wife – a minor European Royal – whom a few claimed to have known "very well *indeed*" before her

5

marriage. But she had died in a car crash in the wartime blackout, and been replaced by the daughter of a West Country Earl, herself widowed at Dunkirk. She too had died some time ago, and anybody who remembered her better than well properly kept quiet about it. But most of the reminiscences turned affectionately and regretfully on the Duke himself. He had earned his rank, not just played soldiers like some Royals, and there were those who knew *for a fact* that he had been the real brains behind the D-Day landings. After a mission to Moscow he had made a proper study of the Soviet war machine and some said he was the first to realise that the Third World War began the day the Second ended. And his postwar proposals for reforming the regimental system had been remarkable, quite remarkable, although of course the Army had been absolutely right to reject them. The real pity was (they concluded) that the old boy had lived to see the country's defences in such a state, with a timid Prime Minister and coalition Cabinet encouraging the Peace Crusade and seeming to haver over these new Russian proposals for a demilitarised Berlin. Probably what had killed him off, if one did but know it. But he'd had a good innings, and they could show there were still a few who cared by making his memorial service a decent send-off. Provided, of course, that it was held in the proper place and not that bloody great barn over in the City. Still and all, you had to agree that things would never be the same again, and some believed that they hadn't been for some time.

Major Harry Maxim got the news from a chatty guard corporal as he drove out of camp to spend the weekend with his parents, who had looked after his son since his wife's death. It meant nothing to him at all.

2

After Sunday lunch at Maxim's parents the children went into the back garden and chattered maturely about pop groups and skateboarding while the adults went into the kitchen, where Maxim and his sister Brenda fought. Chris, now aged eleven, and his three cousins had come to accept that this was what happened when they met at Littlehampton, but didn't quite admit to themselves that they went outside to escape the clutching sick feeling of hearing their parents behave like tired brats. The grandparents did most of the actual washing up, since there were never enough tea-towels, so probably Maxim and Brenda were only in there because they were scared, like tired brats, that without referees they might go too far.

"Are you telling us," Brenda asked, "that all those soldiers we've got in Berlin couldn't defend the place *anyway*?"

"I don't know why you say *all*," Maxim said; "there's only about thirteen thousand Allied troops: roughly a division. And a hundred miles of perimeter, the Wall. One division can't hold that front."

"Then what on earth are they doing there? Just having a good time at the taxpayers' expense?"

"They are there to stop the Russians just walking in. If they go in, they have to go in shooting."

"And just kill off our soldiers and take over anyway."

Maxim shrugged. "And start off World War Three."

"Do we really want to set up things so that the . . . *anybody*, can start a World War just by accident?"

"They won't walk into West Berlin by accident. But that's what a Standing Army's always been about: to draw a line and say, If you cross that, you've started a real something. So nobody can nibble away with

7

bloodless takeovers. As Hitler did: the Rhineland, Austria, Czechoslovakia."

"And meanwhile, you've got two armies practising to blow each other's countries to bits and getting more and more weapons to do it with. Do you see any end to it?"

"No," Maxim admitted, "but I'm no politician."

"Then why don't you leave it to the politicians?" Brenda asked triumphantly. "Why do you always say they're wrong when they want to talk to the Russians?"

Their mother said from the sink: "Just talking can't do any harm."

"It can if we're doing it unilaterally about Berlin."

"*Unilaterally*," Brenda said. "Of course, that has to be a dirty word in the Army. I bet you even have to go to the loo multilaterally."

"No, that's strictly a Naval tradition."

"Harry!" A disgusted bark from his father.

"Sorry. But it's sitting down without the Americans and French that does the damage. It splits NATO, it splits the agreement on Berlin. And that's what the Russians want, more than any changes in Berlin."

"Of course, if the Americans don't like it, that's all that matters."

"We have a four-power agreement on Berlin – "

"That was forty years ago. More."

Their father said mildly: "It was the Russians who put up the Berlin Wall. They could take it down without talking to anybody."

"Well, they could," Brenda said defensively, then burst out: "So why don't we encourage them? Why can't you see how exciting this could be? For the first time in my life – and yours – we're actually taking a step towards peace. Give Berlin back to the Berliners, make it one city, get the tanks and guns out of the streets – can't you see that some people can be as excited about not having tanks and guns as you are about *having* them? Do you want your Chris to live his whole life waiting for the four-minute warning?"

Their mother said: "I've never seen the point of a warning at all if it's only four minutes. Not that there are any shelters round here, as far as I know."

"Oh, don't worry," Brenda told her. "You'll be safe if

8

you put a paper bag over your head or something daft like that."

"If you're hit by a nuke," Maxim said, "there's nothing you can do. There's nothing you can do if a hand grenade goes off in your pocket, either. But on the fringes of an explosion, any explosion, you *can* do something. Anyway, the four-minute warning's the Worst Possible Case. Tactical warning might be that short. But strategic warning" – he was trying to annoy Brenda by using jargon; if he felt his own temper going, he'd try saying 'just a few megadeaths' in a bored tone – "the Red Army's got its mobilisation time down to forty-eight hours, so probably we'll get that much warning. It could be more."

"Just as long as there's time to appeal to the Dunkirk spirit, put paper bags over our heads and let the Army take over."

"Oh, for God's sake."

Brenda pressed what she saw as an advantage. "There *are* secret plans for the Army – and the police – to take over. They're going to block all the main roads out of cities with machine-guns and – "

"Rubbish."

"Really? Perhaps you just haven't been told. We actually had, well they *tried* to have, one of those farcical Civil Defence exercises up near us, and the Army officers who were supposed to be taking part, they refused, just refused, to do what the town clerk told them."

That hardly surprised Maxim: where the hell did the town clerk fit into the chain of command? But he thought it best not to say that. "Perhaps your town clerk thought it was all a bit of a farce as well. The Army really does know something about survival training, what with Noddy suits and respirators and – "

"What suits?" their mother asked.

"We call them Noddy suits. Protection against fallout and gas . . . I sent you a picture of me in one, on the Porton battle run."

"It made you look like a man from Mars."

"It's supposed to protect you against secondary radiation. So you can move around when everybody else is in shelters – "

9

"And take over." Brenda smiled with quiet triumph.

Their parents had stopped work and were looking at Maxim oddly. It was, he realised, the ingrained British conviction that once a man put on uniform, the next step was for him to Take Over. You might speculate about race memories of Cromwell's New Model Army and even the origins of Magna Carta, but the end result was the way the Army ordered you *out* of uniform the moment you came off-duty. In London, and in no other NATO capital, when an embassy threw a military cocktail party, the rule was that only the hosts wore uniforms; they wouldn't be seen on the streets anyway.

He sighed and put away a handful of teaspoons in the wrong place. It wasn't the fear of a military takeover that annoyed him, but people's blindness to the fact that the Army was recruited from men born and brought up in that same fear. That, and a horror of trying to give orders to people who most likely wouldn't obey them.

"Oh well," he said, "since we'll just about all be in Germany you'll be lucky to find an Army officer with the time to run the country for you."

Brenda's voice stiffened but she stayed calm. "It doesn't look as if *you'll* be in Germany, so maybe you'll get the job. I know: why don't you give us all some saluting practice this afternoon, so we'll have a bit of a start on everybody else? A military dictatorship usually goes in for family favouritism, doesn't it?"

"Saluting won't be required. You can kiss my arse from time to time."

"Harry!" his father exploded. "You can leave that sort of language on the barrack square. I will *not* have it in this house."

Maxim mumbled an apology, avoiding Brenda's eye. Their mother, quite unmoved after thirty years of pretending her children hadn't said what she had clearly heard them say, asked: "But that suit wouldn't stop you being blown up by a bomb, would it? I mean, it isn't made of armour?"

"It's only paper, impregnated with charcoal – "

"Paper!" Brenda laughed delightedly. "You mean even the Army believes that?"

10

"If you're going to survive any *explosion*," Maxim said grimly, "you need a shelter. Or a bit of crisis relocation."

"What's that?" their father asked.

"Being somewhere else at the time."

The chuckles lightened the atmosphere and – luckily – annoyed Brenda.

"There's secret tunnels under all the middle of London," she announced. "With air and water and rations for weeks. Of course, you have to be a Very Important Person to get in, but I expect Harry made some useful friends at Number 10. There was a book about it. The tunnels."

"It doesn't sound too secret if it was in a book," their father said.

"Oh, they didn't mean it to be in a book. They started the tunnels in the last war, against the German bombs, and kept on improving them afterwards."

There was only the encrusted aluminium teapot left on the draining board and Maxim picked it up. "We don't dry that," his mother said; "it takes all the flavour out of it." It was a ritual joke, relying on Maxim always forgetting the teapot didn't get dried.

"The trouble with shelters," he said carefully, "is that you have to be something like a mile down if you're going to be safe right under a 20-megaton ground burst. And what happens to your escape tunnels going back up? Even three miles away you have to be two hundred feet down."

As a retired works manager, their father knew something about the strength of concrete structures. He carefully spread his tea-towel over the radiator to dry and said: "So you'd advise *crisis relocation* instead, would you?" But his joviality was forced.

"Only if you're a VIP, again," Brenda said quickly.

"Are you going to be crisily relocated or whatever they call it?" their mother asked.

"I always carry a strong paper bag with me."

They knew he was dodging the question, but family rules wouldn't let even Brenda probe further. She had to content herself with having winkled out confirmation of one small belief. "So there is going to be 'crisis relocation' for VIPs?"

"If it hadn't been thought of, there wouldn't be a word for it."

"Two words."

"And what are the rest of us supposed to do afterwards?" their mother asked placidly.

"After a nuclear attack or the whole war?"

They looked at him again, and their father said: "Doesn't it come to much the same thing?"

"Not necessarily. The Soviets might opt to take out just London, destroy the government, as an example and to wreck our command structure."

"That," Brenda said, "sounds like quite enough for me. Wouldn't that be the end of it?"

Maxim shrugged.

"You mean to say that with London blown to bits and radiation everywhere *you'd* go on fighting? I do believe you would! Just a little clockwork soldier that refuses to run down!"

" 'It is a typically Hohenzollern idea to believe that it is a crime for a country to defend itself after its army has been destroyed.' "

"Who said that?" Brenda demanded suspiciously.

"Karl Marx, actually."

Rummaging in the bureau drawer for a couple of after-lunch cigars, Maxim's father asked quietly: "Tell me – just as a matter of interest – if the government is destroyed, who decides the war is over? When we . . ." he almost choked on the word: ". . . surrender?"

"It won't be Brenda's town clerk, I can tell you that much. You might say it was up to the individual."

3

"Within six months of a Russian occupation of Britain you'll find Resistance cells and circuits springing up everywhere. I'm quite sure they'll include even such people as trade union activists, the Far Left of the Labour party and so on, most likely our own Trotskyists and Communists. The trouble is, they'll be too late. By then they'll be on the lists, their faces and addresses known. The Russians don't fool themselves, they know they can't hang on to the loyalty of such people. They'll concentrate on keeping just one or two, enough to betray the rest. So the actual, effective, Resistance movement will depend on those who are prepared in advance. Those who can accept it as a real possibility now. That, I hope, means you."

The lecturer paused and coughed heavily but politely into her hand. She smoked too much, although never while giving a lecture and was never tempted to. It simply didn't fit into the rôle of lecturer, and she played her rôles with now-subconscious dedication.

Hardened in backside and mind by years of Army lectures, the nineteen officers in front of her waited patiently.

"That is the whole point of these stay-behind courses," Miss Tuckey gurgled. She cleared her throat and found her lecturing tone again. "Whatever your future postings may be in the service, and whatever jobs you take after you leave the service, there'll always be the chance that some of you will be overrun during a Russian invasion. The intention is that you won't be on any lists: part of your training here will be how to assume new identities or at least give yourself new pasts. Let me assure you of one thing: you won't be alone, although you will certainly feel lonely. Stay-behind groups are far from being a new idea,

13

although the Army hasn't always been as actively involved as it is now. And you will have one advantage that we didn't have in the war: the transistor. Radio sets can now be so small and cheap that it would be unrealistic for anybody to try and ban them. And I'm not talking only about receiving orders: you've no idea how comforting it can be just to listen to a free voice."

She paused, wondering briefly whether to elaborate on that. But they could either imagine it or they couldn't. She no longer expected them to see, within the stocky well-dressed matron with groomed grey hair and fashionable glasses, the tired, tense girl who had hunched over the illegal radio in a Lyonnais farmhouse. The morning when she learned that the organiser of the Tabernacle circuit had been taken in a Milice trap and she was now the leader. Forty-eight hours was the time they were told to hold out under torture; after that, you assumed the Gestapo would know everything, so in that time you had to change everything. Warn others to go into hiding, find new places to cache weapons and explosives, new bases for action . . . Now, forty years later, she was doing much the same thing, not out of any nostalgia for the Great Days, but from a simple conviction that such days had not passed. If anybody questioned this, she suggested they count how many references to guerillas, terrorists and liberation armies they could find in that day's copy of *The Times*.

She coughed again, this time just to explain the pause, and went on. "You should see yourselves as essentially an *urban* Resistance movement. It follows that we are assuming there will still be cities, that the fabric of British society will still remain. If we are a nuclear wasteland, then the Russians aren't likely to be interested in taking us over. It also follows that the occupying force will work through the existing structures of that society, not try to change everything overnight. They just couldn't do it. They'll do what the Germans did in Europe: exercise control through some form of national parliament, the existing civil service, local government, the police, postal and broadcasting systems, the distributive trades and so on. And it's there, in those same channels, that you will sabotage their efforts and try and exert your own control. It's no good setting up Resistance armies in Wales – or here." She made an elegant gesture at the glimpse of moorland in one corner of the window behind her. "You'll simply be ignored. You must go to them, not wait for them to come to you. And you'll find them in the cities, in the key positions that exist today.

"There also already exists the framework you'll need for recruitment and training. I want you to take out your pens and write down all the unofficial non-statutory organisations that you have some personal connection with, or even just knowledge of. In three minutes, please, starting now."

There was a bit of old-fashioned school-marm in Miss Dorothy Tuckey. She stood beaming with confidence as they glanced at each other, puzzled, then began to write slowly, but faster and faster.

. . . the Regimental Sailing Club, Maxim wrote; the Littlehampton and District Model Railway Society; the Royal United Services Institute (was that statutory, though?); my mother's Thursday lunchtime club; my old school association; Camden Ratepayers' Association; the Darts Club at the Hare and Hounds; the Church of England (well, why not?); Military Book Society . . .

Everybody was still writing, or pausing for furious thought, when Miss Tuckey called time. She made no move to collect the papers.

"All those," she said, "are potentially subversive organisations." She rode on over their instinctive amusement. "They are all groups of people with some shared interest or commitment, and therefore a basis of mutual trust. They all have a centralised structure and some sort of a base, even if it's only a temporary or part-time one, and existing lines of communication. And don't forget the amount of further education that goes on in the civilian world. Think of all the local authority night schools, all the summer schools run by industry and the unions, all of those are ready-made training schemes. You can't abolish them without weakening the whole structure of an industrial society, and it would be an enormous job to take them over or infiltrate them all with informers. By the way, did anybody write down the readership of *Sappho* or *Gay News*?"

She joined in their laughter; nobody put up his hand.

"I'm glad to hear it. But quite seriously, don't dismiss homosexuals as unreliable or distasteful. Most of them have just the experience of leading secret, double lives that you lack. Moscow knows all about that. When they were recruiting among the Apostles at Cambridge before the war, they weren't blackmailing those people. They were just picking up young men who had been self-taught secret agents ever since puberty. Who already had a grudge against the existing society because it wouldn't accept them for what they were."

"What about the Church?" someone asked. "I mean any church?" Maxim was glad somebody had pre-empted that question; he was trying, because that was part of the course's teaching, to be as anonymous as possible.

"Ye-es," Miss Tuckey began hesitantly. "The problem is that Moscow has always taken religion very seriously – I mean as a rival. The clergy would certainly be on the lists. But you're right in one way: any religion – Christian, Jewish, Muslim, Hindu – has a background of subversion. They were all underground at one time. And religious belief can be a great solace in loneliness; I dare say some of you know that already."

Glancing covertly around, Maxim saw a few quickly restrained nods. A Resistance war might be lonely in the long run, but on a raw battlefield loneliness could strike in the brief snap of a bullet's flight – even if you were clutching the hand of the next man along. He had done that, too.

"Did anyone write down the Family?" Miss Tuckey asked. "Don't think Moscow doesn't know about that, either. It can be the most dangerous, subversive organisation of all."

Chris? Maxim wondered. Brenda? – yes, she'd join up within months, and Chris immediately . . . Dear God, don't let it happen. Let the tanks and guns be enough, even the nukes, let *me* be enough, just don't let it come to this. He was beginning to see that a secret war would be the most total of all.

★

16

After lunch they paced the clipped grass of the ramparts overlooking the grey waters of the firth. The barracks had been built for the garrison of the fortress surrounding them, set on a low spit of land where the channel narrowed and French ships would be exposed to cannon fire as they picked their way in to supply a second Jacobite rising. Over two hundred years later the sandstone walls stood untouched by anything but Scottish winds and the incised graffiti of recruits who had gone on to die at Corunna and Waterloo, Balaclava and Lucknow, the Somme and Alamein. This of course gave exactly the sort of romantic continuity the Army loves, so it seemed likely to keep the Fort swept, mown and whitewashed for another two hundred years, although no longer for a full garrison. It had now become a useful back room for training courses that needed more secrecy than space.

None of the nineteen was supposed to know who each other were, which obviously couldn't always work but helped establish an atmosphere. The group itself was named – Garibaldi – rather than numbered, which would have suggested how many courses had gone through before them. They all wore plain barrack dress, the only badge being a self-chosen codename, and Maxim already felt uneasy about being 'Jabberwock'. It sounded frivolous, and gave away that he'd read *Alice*. Three of the others had chosen Shakespearean names and he wished he'd blended with them, however much he doubted that 'Coriolanus' had actually read himself. He also wished he wasn't already sure what rank most of the others were, and to what corps or regiment they belonged. What had they learnt about him, putting his life in their hands for the KGB thumbscrew to squeeze out?

Secrecy is the condition for action; trust is the means for it, an earnest Int Corps instructor had told them on their first-night briefing. Maxim had duly pondered that, and come to the conclusion that, in the Army, it meant nothing new.

Miss Tuckey had been cornered by half a dozen of the others in the angle of one of the bastions, and Maxim drifted over. They had got her on to the topic of assassination.

"But couldn't you use it to provoke reprisals, to get

people worked up about the occupation?" That was 'Gremlin' (also a Major, but with the bounce of recent promotion and the smug Calvinism of a Gunner).

"Oh, don't you worry" – Miss Tuckey had to use her classroom voice against the wind – "an occupying power always behaves badly enough without any prompting. If you cause more reprisals the population will probably blame you for making things worse."

"Would you say that it was never a good idea, then?" 'Heracles' asked (not quite Guards, Green Jackets maybe).

"Not never, but the circumstances have to be very special. You have to be very aware of the profit and loss." She paused and pushed her flapping silk scarf down into her golfing jacket. "Have you ever heard of Philippe Henriot? He was the Vichy French Minister of Information and a broadcaster. A very prominent collaborator. The Resistance got him in Paris in early 1944. That didn't cause much trouble because he was only French, and it probably did a lot to put off other collaborators. The one that people really argue about was Heydrich; you've heard of him?"

"SS, number two to Himmler." 'Gremlin' again.

"That's right. And for counter-intelligence he was a lot better than Himmler; London ordered him killed because he was tracking down our networks. That was in Czechoslovakia in 1942. After that, the SS shot about three thousand people; it was why they destroyed the village of Lidice. Now, you can argue that Heydrich would have done as much as that himself, if he'd lived. He really was a most vile man. But if only they could have made his death seem like an accident we'd have been spared all that and still had him out of the way."

"It wouldn't be easy."

"You're right, it wouldn't. These people are always heavily guarded and their movements are kept secret. But do you see the difference between the two? Henriot had to be seen to be assassinated, as an example – but it could have been any collaborator of equal prominence. With Heydrich we had to get *that man*, that cog out of the machine, but it would have been better to make it seem by chance. You do really need great awareness with assassination."

Maxim sensed the discontent, almost disappointment, in those around him. Miss Tuckey was also looking round the group and grinning mischievously and he suddenly saw why. They had come up here to learn techniques and she was trying to teach them attitudes. They wanted to know about sabotage, booby-traps and silent killing. She wanted them to learn silent living.

"Never mind," she said cheerily, "you've got this afternoon on the range, haven't you? You'll enjoy yourselves there."

And indeed they did, enthusiastically returning to tangibles with the study of those foreign weapons most likely to be available to guerillas: Russian and American. They learned, stripped, reassembled and finally fired the AK-47, AKM and M16 rifles, plus one precious example of the new AK-74, then on to the PKM and M60 machine-guns and lastly to the short range for the M3A1 submachine-gun and a clutch of pistols including the Makarov. They ended with bruised shoulders and scratched hands, greasy, soaked in the smell of gunfire and yelling through their deafness, but feeling like real soldiers again and having given away a lot about their backgrounds. Maxim spotted only one other who already knew the weapons as well as he did, but assumed he was spotted in return; although he had made deliberately bad groups with the guns he knew best, it was impossible to be wilfully stupid with a loaded weapon.

In their private mess, the Intelligence Officer had just handed out a 'Secret' folder of news the press wasn't supposed to know, or Int Corps' interpretation of things the press had got wrong. He hovered watchfully as they passed it around. The stories in Continental papers about the Archbishop of Canterbury's relationships with choirboys had been backtracked to a small Italian magazine, a known starting-point for KGB disinformation. It was, Int Corps concluded with a sniff, a crude and hasty reaction to the Archbishop's speech supporting the status quo in West Berlin: Moscow over-reacting to religion yet again.

The commander of the Soviet air division in Afghanistan

had been replaced following the shooting down of the Iranian airliner; it was now believed the airliner could have been hijacked by left-wing Iranians who were trying to escape to Russia.

A Blowpipe anti-aircraft missile, part of a batch en route to Thailand, had gone missing. Int Corps thought it was more likely to be the IRA than Moscow.

"Bang goes one of our choppers in Armagh," observed 'Bluebeard' (a Captain, probably an Engineer).

"*If* they hit it." That was 'Gremlin' again.

"I thought it was rather accurate?" Maxim provoked innocently.

"It's as good as the training. *We* put our chaps through seventeen hundred simulated firings before they get to the real thing." 'Gremlin' blithely confirmed that he was a Gunner. "You start getting worried when they pinch a simulator as well."

"That's a relief." The Int Corps officer caught Maxim's eye and smiled; Maxim tried to look friendly but puzzled.

4

Maxim's sister had been quite right in claiming that the Army has secret plans should there be a nuclear attack on Britain. That is hardly surprising: the military is expected to have plans for every possibility and, naturally, such plans are kept secret. But the slant of the orders might have surprised even Brenda – or perhaps confirmed her worst convictions.

Like most people, she had assumed that the Army is ultimately controlled by Parliament, just like the Post Office and pub opening times. It is not, not quite. Look at the Army List and you will see that the Commander in Chief is the Monarch (the same is true of the Navy and Air Force). The reasons go back to Parliaments who wanted no responsibility for an Army after they had seen what Cromwell did with his, but the fact remains three centuries later the Army's allegiance is to the Crown and the – unwritten – British constitution, and if the Army ever thought that Parliament was behaving unconstitutionally . . .

Of course, it won't come to that. But the point is that the Army needs no Parliamentary approval to plan for a duty that antedates even politics by several million years: survival. Any idea of 'taking over' when Parliament is radioactive rubble is largely irrelevant. The Army does not want the job of running Britain; it simply wants to survive.

For a start, there is no question of blocking the main roads out of London and other cities. There might be some point in keeping such roads open, but that is accepted as impossible. If millions of car-owners decide they will be incinerated if they stay put, then no threat of machine-gunning them will make any difference. They will block the roads for themselves, so the Army looks elsewhere for its own survival.

The embryo of that survival is the Gold List: the key personnel – almost all military and almost all men – from the Chiefs of Staff and their Secretariat, the Joint Planning Staff, Joint Intelligence Staff, Joint Admin/Logistics Staff and equivalents from each armed service. Given enough warning, the Gold List will quietly melt away from London by road, in small groups. Hardly anybody will notice: they are not public figures.

But if there is not enough advance warning, then Operation Playpen will begin. Playpen is (or will be) an area of roughly one and a half square miles in central London. It is bounded on the east and south by the river, and completed by a line running along the King's Road, Grosvenor Place and The Mall, the main bastions of its perimeter being Chelsea Hospital, Buckingham Palace and the Old Admiralty and War Office buildings at the top of Whitehall. Londoners are accustomed to a military presence, usually ceremonial, but seldom stop to think just how concentrated that presence is. Playpen encompasses the Chelsea, Duke of York's and Wellington barracks, with the Hyde Park Household Cavalry barracks just a few hundred metres outside the perimeter; in all, purpose-built accommodation for nearly four thousand troops and much of their equipment, and that ignores the military hospitals and several smaller Army establishments inside the ring.

However, the Playpen planners do not count on four thousand troops or anything like that number. The whole point of the operation is that it can be run by the minimum: Playforce, comprising just one infantry battalion and a few special units, or less than a thousand men in total. More would be wasteful of time, and probably the men themselves. In fact, the boundaries of Playpen might well be the same even if it included no barracks at all; it's just nice that it works out that way. For what really matters is that Playpen holds three easily defended helicopter Pickup Zones: Everest, Peacock and Famish.

'Easily defended' is the key when deploying a small force. The open stretches of Hyde Park would be easier for the helicopters themselves, but in the Worst Possible Case – which is what Playpen is all about – it could be rushed not only by panic-stricken mobs but interdicted by fire from sabotage groups. Those also have to be allowed for. So the three chosen PZs all have existing defences.

Everest is the garden of Buckingham Palace, surrounded by walls and Palace buildings. Peacock is Horse Guards Parade, protected on three sides by government offices and the fourth, St James's Park, easily swept by covering fire. The grounds of the old soldiers' home at Chelsea Hospital, Famish, also have only one open side: the road and the river immediately beyond, again easily covered by defensive fire. There is a fourth, back-up Zone codenamed Tallyman: the playing fields of Westminster School in Vincent Square. But although there are two Army establishments within a hundred yards or so, the grass rectangle is only protected by a wire mesh fence and surrounded by exclusively civilian buildings. (Unless you count the Rochester Row police station, which the Army doesn't. Brenda had also been right in saying that the police had secret orders as well, but the Army politely refuses to plan on the assumption that the police can adapt to a war footing in a matter of minutes. Playpen simply ignores the existence of the police.)

The Operation is a three-stage one. When the armed services go on Alert, Playforce is automatically brought to four hours' readiness (four hours is officially the Army's maximum readiness state; in practice, Playforce is expected to be ready to move at half an hour's warning). Simultaneously, all helicopters belonging to the RAF at Odiham, the Queen's Flight at Benson, the Army Air Corps at Middle Wallop and the experimental squadron at Boscombe Down – all within sixty miles of London – will be grounded. Their fuel will be topped up, all loads and extraneous equipment (one of those phrases the planners love because it sounds so precise) slung out, and no maintenance work done except to make unserviceable machines flyable. There might then be fifty helicopters available, or as few as twenty-five: it depends on whether the emergency has built slowly enough for the formed squadrons to leave for their war stations in Germany. The Lists allow for this: some people are on Standby for survival.

If the second stage is ordered – it never has been, yet –

the helicopters will take off and stage into RAF Northolt, just eleven miles from Whitehall. It is acknowledged that this move will be a 'public' one, so there will no longer be any point in keeping Playforce off the streets. However, most troops will not actually dismount from their trucks except for the PZ control and fire support units, who are supposed to behave 'unobtrusively' or as unobtrusively as men in combat dress setting up machine-guns in top windows can behave.

At this point the Lists will be alerted. The Gold List will probably stay at their desks and telephones, since all they have to do is cross Whitehall to Peacock, which can be done by tunnel. Even the Chiefs of Staff can hardly give orders to the Purple List – Royal and political – leaving from Everest; all they can do is make sure the route from Parliament Square to the Palace is kept clear, and since it passes Wellington Barracks this shouldn't be difficult. Only the Silver List of NATO ambassadors and whoever they choose to complete their small parties will be advised to move, at orderly speeds along prearranged routes, to Famish. Playforce patrols will assist if necessary, and inevitably in the case of the Greeks, isolated out in their Holland Park embassy; the Directorate of Crisis Relocation would be happy to see Greece carry out its annual threat to quit NATO. But in fact, the DCR doesn't take the Silver List with too much seriousness: it is just an unavoidable quid pro quo for the planned survival of British ambassadors (and their military attachés, of course) in Bonn, Paris, Rome and so forth.

Since there is no way in which the actual pickup can be rehearsed, the annex to Playforce orders handling this lacks something in precision. But it is really up to the officers on the spot, all of whom have completed (as Maxim recently had) helicopter direction courses in how to lay out beacons, group people into loads and emplane them, assign bump-and-straggler points . . . The main point the annex makes is that the Zones will continue to be defended until the last helicopter has begun its rooftop sprint for the theoretical safety that begins thirty miles away. Nobody in Playforce knows where the helicopters will go, just that they are too valuable to risk sending back.

They are well-thought-out, clearly detailed orders which a professional soldier can find pleasure in studying, even if he is one of those to stay behind in London. In a retreat, at least a successful retreat, some always have to stay behind; its success depends on them. But if one were a real nit-picking student of military orders, one might have asked: "Supposing the President of the USA is attending a memorial service in London at such a time?"

5

The advance party from the White House had landed on the embassy car pool like footsore locusts. Looking at the mass of dark Granadas with their D and X plates jamming St James's Palace courtyard, George Harbinger had commented to Ferrebee that if the ambassador himself was going anywhere today, he must be jogging there. Anticipating the crush, George himself had walked over from Defence, certainly not jogged. Like murder ("And I imagine it must be *very* like murder") he believed that jogging needed means, motive and opportunity, and whenever opportunity offered, his well-rounded figure gave him an insurmountable lack of means and motive.

"Though if it wasn't for the exercise," he went on, "I can't see why on earth they wanted me over here. Didn't understand a word of it."

"You added tone, George," Ferrebee assured him.

"Hmm. Well, at least we've established the President's spending an hour with the kitchen Cabinet. Don't know how much damage you can undo in that time, but . . . When's the OD meeting now?"

"Not my field, George. But I understand it's to be late Friday, after the President leaves. Papers in by first thing Wednesday."

"Why the rush?" George grumbled. "I'm the last person to invite the public into the business of governing itself, but in this case . . ."

"Perhaps somebody Up There wants to appear to be crisp and decisive in world affairs. D'you mind if we change the subject?"

"Putting a Little Englander in as Foreign Sec – "

"George." It was a breach of protocol to criticise another civil servant's minister quite so bluntly.

"Sorry." George stared gloomily across the cars squirming free of the pack in brief clouds of steam from their cold exhaust pipes; on the bright October morning he was already resolutely sunk in a November mood. "You managed to sound very knowledgeable about helicopters in there."

"Lucky I was, with a Presidential visit." Ferrebee was a big, loose-jointed man, with the handsomeness of an ageing cowboy film star savaged by the fire-scars on one side of his face that had ended his Naval career. "If the chopper hadn't existed, the White House would have had to invent it. I must away."

The pack had almost dispersed, leaving the lone Foreign Office Rover in the early corner and Ferrebee's bagman already holding the door open. He walked across the courtyard that became a lone prairie (or the deck of an aircraft carrier?) under his feet, pausing to light a cigarette halfway. George turned slowly to see why he had the impression that somebody was waiting in the shadowed doorway behind him.

The tall American pounced, grabbing his hand and forearm in a politically experienced handshake. "George! How're you doing? You look great – and I mean that dimensionally." He tapped George's waistcoat and laughed freely.

"Well, Clay. I thought in there that you'd forgotten your old classmates."

"In there? I was just trying to stay awake and look like I understood what those Secret Service guys were going on about. I only got off the plane three hours back." The conference had been dominated by the demands of the White House Protective Detail which would bodyguard the President; George and Clay Culliman had barely acknowledged each other although they had been intermittent friends for twenty years and more. "Look, would you expect me to let on I knew any Limeys *personally*? There's a little thing called job security at the White House, or maybe I mean there isn't."

George's gloom began to melt in memories. They had met during his year at Princeton, when Culliman was a graduate law student, frankly, as frankly as only ambitious

27

young Americans can be, torn between an odyssey in politics and the oak-panelled security of the law. But America had solved that one already, allowing the campaign trail to wind also through oak-panelled territory, although Culliman had found there were more rides offered to loyalists than candidates. Now his wagon had climbed the ultimate hill, albeit only from the inside, which meant there would be no crowd to catch him if he fell. Merely a big Chicago law firm patiently waiting to list an ex-White House aide among its partners.

George had always liked Clay, and had never tried to disentangle that from the thought that he would one day prove useful. He was content to assume that Culliman felt the same about him, particularly if this was the day.

"Hey, if you're walking back to Defence, may I stroll along?"

"Be my guest." Today might indeed be the day; Culliman, he now noticed, had sent on his briefcase with someone more junior.

"I like London in the fall," Culliman prattled on. "Not so many Americans." When he grinned, his mouth opened mostly upwards, showing big front teeth. "I just don't think of London as a tourist city, though I guess there'll be plenty coming to watch the big parade. Are you going to the service?"

"Me? Not a chance, with the whole touring company of European Royals looking for a free lunch at the Palace. The old boy was related to half of them by his first marriage. Didn't the President know him, in the war?"

"I don't think you could say he knew him, exactly. They were on one of the planning committees together before the D-Day landings. When the President was in the Army Air Forces. Be kind of tacky to make too much of that."

"To say nothing of what it would do to the Chicago vote."

"Right." Culliman grinned again and, as George instinctively turned left in St James's Park, gently steered him straight ahead towards the lake and the long way round. They fell easily into the strolling park gait, not in step because Culliman was six inches the taller. With his slight academic stoop, short dark hair and long wrists dangling from the oyster-white raincoat, he looked as if he had never left the campus. But the coarsened skin speckled with tiny ruptured veins and the jetlagged wary eyes were from the campaign trail; they must reach Washington very tired men, George thought.

"I guess this must be where you shoot all those spy movies. You know? – when your people have gotten a secret to discuss they put on their black derbies and swing their umbrellas . . ."

"Very appropriate," George hinted.

But Culliman went on squinting up into the tall plane trees whose leaves were just beginning to crisp in the autumn chill. "You'd think the Soviets would've seen those movies and planted directional mikes in all those trees . . . but maybe all they'd pick up would be show-biz gossip . . . Am I right, you handle security at the Department?"

"In broad terms, on the policy side. And intelligence, whenever one can find it. Supposed to be strictly military, but . . ."

"I'd say this had to be a military affair, I don't know that your Scotland Yard could really handle it . . . What concerns me is the strategic aspect of the President's visit." Seeing George's blank frown, he added: "Nuclear decapitation."

"Ah. Ah yes." Put that way, it was something that had already crossed George's mind, and desk. The President's decision to accept a routine invitation to the memorial service had taken them all by surprise, and spurred a number of other heads of state suddenly to find a blank space in their diaries. With only a few days to adjust their thinking, the London authorities would now have most of the free world's political leaders (and military, of course, with the old Duke's background; there'd be brass hats twinkling under every seat in the house) gathered in a space where a single missile . . . Nuclear decapitation was an outlandish idea, but it was there in the lexicon of Dire Contingencies, and for every Contingency there had to be a Plan.

"What sort of thing did you have in mind?" he asked carefully.

"Well now, we're aware of your crisis relocation scheme. We'd be hoping that the potential evacuation of the President could be kind of grafted on to that. But the final decision to, ah, go, would have to rest with our own people, relying on our own assessment of the indications."

"At affairs of this nature the Lists are reshuffled – as far as they can be – to cope with visiting Persons of Special Importance. And the degree of preparedness would naturally be enhanced." George slipped naturally into the jargon that gift-wraps non-commitment. "However, the US position has never been precisely clarified . . ."

"Sure." Culliman smiled. "I know something about that, too." The American embassy was the biggest in Britain; moreover, there were big Naval and Air Staffs based in or near London. And the USA not only preferred its own view of the 'indications' but also had the helicopters to act on that view: at Woodbridge in Suffolk, just half an hour away at the top speed of an HH-53C, was the USAF's 67th Aerospace and Rescue Squadron. But the plan for using it in a Playpen situation seemed to change, if not seasonally, then at least with Washington's opinion of its London embassy – which was seasonal enough. By now the Ministry's view was that the embassy could run whatever airlift it liked from the residence in Regent's Park, away from Playpen airspace, while anybody who turned up at Famish could queue for a place.

"How I see it now," Culliman went on smoothly, "is that since we've gotten the go-ahead to land the President's helicopter on the Horse Guards Parade, it's only the distance between there and the Abbey that we have to worry about."

"Less than half a mile."

"Right. So he comes down to the Abbey in the usual limo. It's there we assume will be the critical time: everybody in one place for just over an hour, the timings all fixed and everyone knowing about them. So it's just that half-mile, less, back to the helicopter if the indications say Go. That's where the President would be grateful for your assistance."

"Any help I can give – but it's an Army job. I'll have to

30

sell it to the sixth floor somehow. Still, I think they'd be prepared to go a fair distance if there's a chance of your President talking some backbone into the Cabinet over Berlin."

"The President's meeting with the Prime Minister will be only a courtesy call," Culliman said diplomatically.

"Well, if he doesn't *courteously* try to talk some sense into the old fool before the OD Committee meets on Berlin, then God help us all." George's lack of discretion, even loyalty, was opportunistic but deliberate for all that. He wanted the White House to know that the Ministry of Defence at least was totally opposed to any unilateral talks on Berlin.

"The, ah, OD Committee?"

"Overseas and Defence. One of those Cabinet committees that aren't even supposed to exist. Theoretically it's part of the Cabinet, the PM chairs it, so it can reach a decision and hand it to the full Cabinet as a fait accompli."

After a moment, Culliman said thoughtfully: "I guess the President will be aware of this."

"They've held the meeting over until after the service and everybody's gone home," George said, determinedly topping up the President's awareness. "Friday afternoon."

"Is there any, ah, talk of *negotiation*?" The word fell like a broken icicle in the mild morning. For forty years the Allies had been prepared to *discuss* Berlin whenever the Russians felt inclined, but never to *negotiate*. To some, but perhaps no longer to enough, the word meant 'sell-out'.

George shrugged. "When do unilateral talks become negotiation? The old fool's got an attack of statesmanship, always worst when it hits late in life, like measles. Sees a statue of himself in Parliament Square, the man who bridged the East-West gulf, the great Peacemaker."

"Were you still at Number 10 when he came in?"

"For about five minutes." George had been a senior Private Secretary to the old Prime Minister, a man of shrewd judgement, as proven by his decision to take George with him from the Ministry of Defence when the top job beckoned. "Then I was hove out into the cold cold night and only the kindly MoD saved me from a pauper's grave."

For a moment Culliman took that seriously, then a glance at George's style of dress restored the rumour that George was, at least potentially, one of the richest men in the British Civil Service. "So, will you be talking to your people about the, ah, potential evacuation?"

"Will you be using the President's own cars?" They, of course, were being flown in as well, just ahead of the main party.

"That's kind of the key to the business. Those cars are good tough ones, but you can fix a whole lot of Kevlar and armoured glass on a Lincoln and, at the baseline, it's still a Lincoln. I want to tell you, if I was sitting in the Kremlin and planning to start a new war by dumping a strike on London, I wouldn't want any chance of missing the Big One. No chance at all. I'd have the word out to the hard-assed boys to stop anything that looked like the President getting away. And those boys would be experts, really trained. I don't mean anybody on your Scotland Yard lists. Or ours," he added politely.

"I'm sure they'd be there," George agreed. "So you want us to lay on what? Armoured personnel carriers?"

"That kind of thing. With an armed escort."

George stopped in his tracks and let his view lift from the squabbling wildfowl on the lake to the modest Whitehall skyline and its flagpoles. He had to take this seriously. It had begun once at Sarajevo, another time at Gleiwitz, now a forgotten name on the German–Polish border, and it could begin again here.

"That's as far as our thinking goes at this time," Culliman prompted.

"It's an Army matter, all right. The Met couldn't handle that."

"The, ah, Met?"

"Metropolitan Police, Scotland Yard. Well, at *this* time my thoughts go as far as pouring myself a modest drink. Care to come up to the office and join me?"

He was pleased to see a flicker of apprehension on Culliman's face.

"Hold on, George, we're not back at the Colonial now, and I'm jetlagged to hell . . . But if you have a little Scotch . . ."

"I have a lot of Scotch. And I may need most of it before I lay this in front of the DCR."

The Directorate of Crisis Relocation was staffed in the main – and it was a very small staff – by Retired Officers. This is not rare in posts concerning security and intelligence. You get men with training and experience but no longer distracted by ambition, who can concentrate on one narrow task and do it for far longer than a still-serving officer who might move on after only two years, so above all you get continuity. Of course, you also get occasional bursts of bad temper.

"APCs? He wants us to send a column of *armour* charging up Whitehall in the middle of the service?"

"Only if the indications say Go. It's very unlikely to happen, but then, we hope the whole of CR is unlikely."

"What indications? Have they got hold of something they haven't been telling us?"

"No, I don't think there's anything new at all. They're just covering themselves." George knew his own capacity to the fluid ounce, and had reached the DCR office in a well-planned state of mellow soothingness.

"Won't we be getting the same *indications* that they will? If we decide it's time for Playpen, isn't that good enough?" The Deputy Director glowered at George over his gold-rimmed spectacles, some way yet from feeling soothed. He was a retired Major-General in an RO1 post, equivalent to a serving colonel, and he did the real work in the Directorate, issuing orders that began "I am instructed by . . ." a series of come-and-go Directors. He also had an ulcer.

"You know how they are," George said winningly; "they haul in tons of communications kit wherever the President goes, and if we don't squawk at that we can't really object to them using it for its intended purpose. And I dare say they get their satellite read-outs a little earlier than we do."

The DDCR grunted. "But they're rather forcing our hand. Just suppose the President decides to haul ass – do they still say that? You're more up to date on America than I am. They all seem anally fixated to me, calling aeroplanes 'big-assed birds' and telling you 'Get your ass out of here.'"

"Whereas we'd say politely Fuck Off."

"Hmm . . . But suppose he does decide to go in the middle of the service? Aren't we forced to do the same? – just to show solidarity, save their face?"

"A matter for the Defence Staff. I don't know if they feel forced by the Americans . . . and we had foreseen the possibility for ourselves." Indeed, stage one of Playpen – helicopters grounded, London troops on Alert – was planned to come into force twenty-four hours before the service began.

"We obviously can't stop them," the DDCR brooded, making invisible doodles with the blunt end of his pen; "it's the whole business of *helping* them . . ."

"I imagine we can manage it more tactfully than having them import a company of Marines." Tact was always a tactful word to invoke. "And laying out the winged carpet seems a small price for what he'll be doing over here. He'll be meeting the inner Cabinet – "

"Like blowing a bugle at a tin of dog food. What else?"

"Doing the Guildhall speech, and the next day he's giving the word to their Air Force people at Lakenheath. He's sure to cover Berlin; it'll get plenty of space. It's all good for the Cause: we do want him to come."

The DDCR looked up sharply. "Did they say that? – that he won't come unless he gets his APCs?"

"Not in so many words . . . but one can see their point of view. Trying times." He sighed.

"Yes . . . My God, suppose the Met makes a bog of it and he just gets bumped off by some local loony. What I'd really like to see is our chaps handling the whole security side: some of those police *marksmen*, as they call them, don't fire more than thirty rounds a year . . . All right then, I'll draw up an order for the Director's signature . . . But when you say it can be just an addendum to Playpen, I don't like shuffling Playforce around. It's one operation that can only work if everybody sticks rigidly to his task. If we start changing those tasks now . . ."

"Form a special unit," George said promptly. "The

President's group won't be more than seven, just a single vehicle. But better to have three – say, Saracens, you can borrow them off the TA – and no more than thirty men. Only a platoon – "

"George – "

"The obvious people would be the SAS, but it might be even better to get bods just back from Northern Ireland. They're more used to Saracens and street – "

"*George!*" There was a moment of heavy silence while George wondered if he hadn't over-mellowed himself. The DDCR took off his glasses and squeezed the bridge of his nose; he had a lined yellowish face and moved stiffly in his chair. "George . . . if you really want to give orders to soldiers why didn't you stay in the Army?"

Long ago in the days of National Service, George had spent two busy but carefree years in a Dragoon Guards regiment before going to Oxford.

"I thought I might be more use on the outside," he said humbly.

"I think so, too. So if you don't mind leaving a few of the mundane details to us . . . Where I need your help is fending off any flak from the political side. D'you expect any? What about the Foreign Office?"

"We've got a standing remit to lay on an anti-terrorist alert on these sort of affairs, we can wrap it up in amongst that. No, I don't think we should tell the FO, they'd probably prefer not to know. Then they can say it was just us playing favourites when the French President finds out we hadn't laid on a submarine for him. Not that he's going to find out," George added quickly. "Not unless the worst happens and he can always file a complaint with St Peter as he goes in."

"Nice to think there'll be a brown envelope waiting for us on the Far Side; gives one a sense of continuity." The DDCR leant carefully back in his chair. "Good. I'll leave that to you. But we've still got to find somebody from Playforce to act as OC. Can't leave it all to the platoon commander. Somebody with the full Playforce briefing, and if we're doing it properly, he should have stay-behind training as well."

"If I might make a suggestion . . . ?"

"*George* . . ." A warning growl, then: "Oh bloody hell, go on then."

"Chap who's joined you quite recently but I don't think he's got a posting yet. A Major – that would be what you'd want, I imagine. And he's got a fair bit of experience working independently."

"Maxim, I suppose you mean. I wondered when you'd bring him up. Don't you think you've done enough to blight that poor man's career already? I was looking through his 'P' file the other day: the time when he was with you at Number 10 is just about *blank*. He never saw his reporting officer more than once a month and never told him anything then. All the chap could report was that Maxim seemed very security-conscious."

"There's worse things."

"Quite. But there's those, too. Rumours. Goings-on. He's got a reputation for being a bit hasty with a gun . . ." He grunted. "Funny Army when that tells against a man, but : . . Having his wife killed didn't help, either."

"You can't blame him for some terrorist bomb."

"Of course not. But if you really want to do something for him, find him some nice sensible girl close to his own age and get him settled down for a bit."

"I'm not marrying Harry off to some deb who's half horse and the arse end at the top."

"You're getting as fixated as the Americans. No, I don't mean anybody particularly County, he's the wrong regiment for that anyway. Just a steady mature girl – "

"Military or Whitehall parents, maybe a little money of her own . . ."

"Just so. Have you got anybody in mind? That's a good half of the reason he got a London posting again: give him a chance to meet somebody. A Playforce job isn't an arduous one once you've settled in. And I don't imagine he's the type to go wasting his time jiving in discos or whatever."

"He likes Duke Ellington."

"Who?"

"Sorry. Phase One, then: get Harry married."

"I only mention it because you seem to have so much

time for other people's affairs. The Army is actually doing its best to advance your friend's career."

"Is he likely to get a battalion?"

The DDCR sighed. He should never have let the conversation go this far. But it was no secret that a major in his mid-to-late thirties was at the cross-roads of his career. The next step, to command of a battalion – and preferably his own, the one he had joined twenty years before – was the biggest in an infantry officer's life. Many would retire fulfilled and die happy with that memory alone; most never made it. They might become lieutenant-colonels a few years later, but only in staff postings. They would never lead a fighting unit again.

Oh well: "You know his background as well as I do. Not having got to Staff College, and those tours in the SAS – all good work, but he's been away from his battalion too long. They don't know him and he doesn't know them. And you know what I mean about being married. The CO's wife's an absolutely vital person, particularly overseas. All these seventeen-year-old frippets that soldiers marry these days, never been abroad before, trying to bring up babies where they don't know a word of the language. . . . Your Annette would have been first class; you should have stayed in. Might even have stopped you coming to work dressed like a bookie."

George's usual style of dress was a light grey check, expensively tailored but nonetheless Highly Unsuitable for the MoD, where the order of this and every day was a dark blue pinstripe. Given the defiant individuality of regimental dress – something the old Duke might have done something about if he'd had his way – Army officers never looked more uniform than in plain clothes.

The DDCR gave a little satisfied smile as George instinctively sucked in his stomach. "Very well: he probably *is* the best man for the job. I'll get him detached from his course tonight. After Number 10, I don't suppose there's much they can be teaching him about dirty tricks."

6

The sun came up cold and colourless in a sky so polished by the night's rain and wind that you would still be able to feel the stars at midday. That gave the DDCR an uneasy naked feeling as he was driven through the fenced-off streets of central London, already buzzing with police and Army vehicles and dotted with TV trucks, surrounded by early spectators who would gawp at their equipment until the real procession passed. So clear a sky meant enemy aircraft, at least when you were in defence, and the DDCR was feeling defensive and jittery with old memories of doing the rounds of his outposts at dawn.

That was silly, because if the enemy came it would be in eyeless missiles that cared nothing for weather. And even the thought that it was perfect for helicopters didn't cheer him, because it was also perfect for shooting them down. His determined gloom only lifted when they turned through the archway to Dean's Yard behind the Abbey, and into the bustle of the workaday Army. The tall buildings enclosing the Yard had held back the dawn and the blaze of headlights – the Army was being as spendthrift as usual with its batteries – darkened the sky again. Parked just to his left against the glowing red-gold creeper on the old walls were three Saracen armoured personnel carriers. Squat and blunt-headed like wheeled elephants, they were a familiar and comforting sight. Less comforting were the patches of white with bright red crosses on each carrier.

The DDCR erupted out of his car. "Who the bloody hell authorised those crosses? Who's in command here?" His voice had forgotten his retirement.

A soldier stepped forward from a group around the nearest Saracen and saluted. "I wouldn't touch the paint, sir: it's still wet."

"Maxim?"

"Sir."

"Are those blasted crosses your idea?"

"Sir."

The DDCR glared through the headlights. Harry Maxim was not-quite-tall and, from the way he moved, slim under the loose combat dress and unbuttoned flak jacket. The DDCR should know his age – thirty-seven, was it? The thin almost concave face looked older in the harsh light, with deep lines running down from the nose past the polite, deferential, smile.

The deference wasn't appeasing. "You can't go putting red crosses on armed vehicles, man! You know the rules!"

"Ambulances have an easier job through crowds, sir. And it might muddle somebody who was going to shoot."

The DDCR made a growling noise, but Maxim had a point there. And he must remember that the Americans weren't going to stampede without very good reason. If the missiles were being primed now, who would read the Geneva Convention over the rubble?

"Oh, all right, then. If anybody else asks, tell 'em we ordered it." Still disgruntled, he noticed the unfamiliar submachine-gun slung from Maxim's shoulder. "And where did you get that thing?"

"Friends, sir."

The DDCR growled again. When soldiers were readied for action they always put on non-regulation boots or adjusted their equipment in personal ways. The wise commander didn't nit-pick; you just had to trust to their experience, common sense – and even 'friends' at, he guessed, the SAS depot off Sloane Square.

"All right. Is everything set up here?"

"Their Secret Service have got a CP established in the Deanery. That's just through the arch there and to the left." Beyond the Saracens a tall archway, mostly filled in with ornamental ironwork, led to a tunnel ending, after thirty yards, in the gloomy light of the Abbey Cloisters. "If they get the word to go, they'll hustle the President out through the Cloisters and up here, we shove him into the number 2 vehicle and take off."

"Where are you going to be?"

"Rear, sir, in number 3. With just a couple of chaps; we'll act as pickup in case the number 2 gets stopped."

"Good. Make sure the drivers wear respirators; if this actually happens God knows what they'll throw at you. Smoke, gas, I don't know. You might try to make the President put one on, too . . ."

The Platoon Sergeant came up with a crisp salute and a mug of tea. Normally the DDCR would have drunk coffee at this time of day, but it would have tasted quite wrong in this scene. He sipped and talked; the sunlight crept down the wall behind him and the headlights were switched off. Radios crackled as they were netted and signallers grumbled at the buildings around them; men tossed down cigarette ends and were told by indignant corporals to pick them up, because this was Holy Ground.

". . . and you'd better run up the engines every half-hour to – oh blast it! I'm getting as bad as your friend George Harbinger, meddling in details that aren't my business. Have you heard anything from him recently?"

"He gave me a ring a couple of weeks ago, to ask how I was getting on."

"What did you tell him?"

"I said I was getting on fine, sir."

"And how was life at Number 10?"

"Very interesting, sir."

The DDCR looked at Maxim carefully. "All right, Harry, I don't have to know everything." He sighed and took a last look at the reassuring sight of camouflaged figures crumpled comfortably as cats on impossible niches of the steel Saracens, then turned to his car and the huge lonely possibilities that waited in his office.

"I would it were bed-time, Hal, and all well. Haven't had a chance to say that since I had a sergeant called Harry at the Rhine. *Henry the Fourth Part One*, just before the battle of Shrewsbury." From the extra politeness in Maxim's smile he saw the explanation had been unnecessary. "But I bet you don't remember the line that comes next: 'Why, thou owest God a death.' Put like that, it doesn't seem too much of a debt . . . You'll have to keep the vehicles here until around 2400: we'll let you know. And I expect the Yeomanry would like them back without the fancy paintwork. I'm sure your *friends* can rustle up a few pints of turps. Good luck, Major."

As the morning wore on a mutter like surf drifted in through Dean's Arch from the growing crowds. The Yard itself became busy with policemen, American Secret Servicemen and occasional clerics. This aspect of security was nothing to do with Maxim, but he soon realised that it was his job to fend off such people with a salute and some reassuring small-talk, leaving the platoon undisturbed. After one churchman had stopped and goggled openly at his submachine-gun, he told Lieutenant Forrest – OC the platoon – to get all weapons out of sight and drape something over the machine-guns that had been mounted in the Saracens' little turrets.

At ten o'clock the Abbey bells, half muffled, began a slow peal. A Secret Serviceman had attached himself to them, wearing an earplug for his walkie-talkie, and reported to Maxim: "Lawman is airborne." A moment later he got the same message from a radio operator in the third Saracen. Forrest, who obviously had more money than responsibilities, had brought along a tiny colour TV set that one of the signallers had set up on the bonnet of a Land-Rover and was constantly tuning. Abruptly it cut to show the wavery shapes of two helicopters grazing the London skyline.

"Always four pressmen in the back-up helio," the Secret Serviceman explained. "Call the bastards the Death Watch. You can figure out why." He smiled without humour. Younger than Maxim, he wore a thin fawn suit and open raincoat in the cool air, but there was a stipple of sweat on his forehead and Maxim could guess at why the hairline had already receded so far. He knew the stress of bodyguard work himself, but nothing like the months and years of watching over the world's most likely target. I wonder if they last for years? he thought, and tried to make his own smile an encouraging one.

"Lawman is on the ground." And very soon after: "Lawman is in the limo and moving."

"Drivers and gunners," Forrest ordered, and they

climbed nimbly into the Saracens. Then: "Ready!" and there was a rattle as weapons were cocked. Suddenly they seemed to have the wide Yard to themselves; outside, the cheering came in bursts, drowning the steady thump of the marching bands. It gave a sense of being in the back kitchen while the Grand Ball went on upstairs, but something in Maxim's character made him enjoy that. He would always prefer to stand in the shadows backstage watching how the scenery was shifted and the actors braced themselves for an entrance than sit out front and see nothing but the play.

Forrest made conducting movements with his hands, spreading those who wouldn't be in the Saracens to cover the Arch and windows around the Yard, in case some sabotage squad knew about the getaway plan. It was an experienced, well-drilled platoon, and Maxim would only have spoiled their rhythm by trying to help.

"Lawman is at the Abbey . . . getting out of the limo . . ." The Secret Serviceman's gaze roved the rooftops and his left hand brushed his mouth nervously, but he seemed pleased at the loudest cheer yet.

"Lawman is in the Abbey . . ." The Secret Serviceman relaxed as the responsibility shifted to the soldiers. They waited, very still in the cool shadow of their corner of the Yard, through the roar and music as the Royal Family arrived and the hush when the service began.

Clay Culliman and a USAF Colonel in uniform, carrying a slim briefcase, walked through the Arch and quickly past towards the Deanery. Culliman's face seemed vaguely familiar to Maxim, though he couldn't recall the name, but he recognised what was in the briefcase: the 'codes', whatever that meant, that enabled the President to trigger the USA's own nuclear forces. He realised with a jolt that he was within yards of one of the two great power centres of the world; for this hour, it wasn't the Kremlin and the White House, it was the Kremlin and *here*.

Instinctively he began watching the sky. If it came, would he see anything? One plunging spark, one rip of vapour trail, before the flash dissolved him?

"I just hope *something* bleeding happens," one of the soldiers said, and was told to *shut up* by his mates before anybody more senior could say it. Maxim woke up to the Abbey choir, chanting unsynchronised from the TV and the loudspeakers relaying the service to the streets outside, and knew the men were getting over-tense. They were taking their mood from him, as they were supposed to, and he scowled at his idiocy in gazing at the sky; hadn't he learnt *anything* in the last nineteen years? If only he still smoked he could hand round cigarettes, try to wind down the atmosphere.

Forrest did it for him. "Right – half of you out for a stretch and a drag. Corporal Monro, Clarke, Higgs . . ." The soldiers moved and Forrest glanced a reproof at Maxim, who accepted it with a sad nod and forced himself to stand relaxed, watching the TV.

"Clever little things, these," the signaller said, doggedly twiddling to cure the unstable picture, "but it don't stand a chance, not really. The high-frequency stuff that's being pumped out round here . . . Not just TV, but did you see what the Yanks have got next door?" He jerked his head at the Deanery. "The kit they've got . . . You can pick up the handset in there and a voice comes right on: 'White House, Washington,' and you say: 'White House, London here' – wherever the President goes, that's the White House as well – when they open the door of his plane, first thing a bloke runs down the steps with a white handset and sticks it on a little stand thing, so the President's always supposed to be – "

Forrest said: "If you'd shut up, we might be able to hear something even if you have screwed up the picture. And if it doesn't work back in my room I'll have your bollocks."

"It's all satellites," the signaller went on. "He's just narked at me because I could've got him one of these half the price he paid."

"Fell off the back of a rickshaw," Forrest said sourly.

Culliman came out from the archway, peeling the cellophane from a small cigar, and Maxim drifted to head him off from the platoon.

Culliman introduced himself, adding: "One of the President's aides. We do appreciate you arranging all of this" – he gestured at the Saracens – "and the red crosses, that's a nice touch."

43

"Thank you."

"Think they'll come?" Culliman glanced at the sky, too. "You've got all the comm. kit."

"Yeh . . . we're in contact with everybody and everything, and we still stand around and smoke too much. No – they won't come. But don't quote me. The Soviets don't move when we're watching. When we blink, they move. May I see where the President will be travelling, if . . . ?"

"Certainly."

Maxim introduced Forrest and they all went and gazed solemnly in through the rear doors of the second Saracen at two soldiers who stared back with truculent smiles. The sill was nearly three feet off the ground and the inside was just high enough for a man to sit upright on the hard seats running down each side. They had cleared out some of the less relevant equipment, including the girlie magazines normally stored in the seat lockers, but nothing could change the Saracen's very basic nature. Like every armoured vehicle, it was a simple idea built of gritty armour plate and rough welds that had then been doodled over with fire ports, escape hatches, observation slits, smoke dischargers and periscopes, each item with its own crude strength and adding to the final look of detailed brutality.

Culliman slapped one of the heavy doors and seemed to find it reassuring. "It won't do the President's back any good, but I guess some of the airplanes he flew fitted closer."

Hovering in his motherly role, the Platoon Sergeant ventured: "Good to have a military man as President again, sir."

Culliman looked at him. "I guess so, Sergeant. Thank you." But as he walked away, he added to Maxim: "But in my book, it's a lot better that we've got one who reads European history. This is sure as hell where it all starts – whatever it is."

"Is the President going to Bonn?" Maxim asked politely.

"Probably not. Paris, sure. But we're advancing Bonn."

After a blank moment, Maxim realised that an advance party was looking at the problems of a German visit.

"Did you ever serve in Berlin, Major?"

"I've been there, but never on a posting."

"So you've seen their Wall? Sounds good, offering to tear it down, doesn't it? Demilitarise, get the tanks off the streets. I'd have liked it better if the bastards hadn't played the usual game plan, put the message in on a Saturday morning. So we have to start running all over, getting a real translation, hauling guys off golf courses – so the Soviets get the whole weekend to themselves, all of the Sunday papers, and we can't say one official damn thing until Monday. Yes, I'd like it better if they didn't piss on your shoes when they give an invitation to a party. Have you ever met a guy called George Harbinger?"

"I worked with him at Number 10 for a while."

"Oh yeah." A long-drawn sound. "Yes. You moved on, too. George talked about you, I'm sorry I didn't make the connection. Yes, glad to have you running things; I'd better . . ."

He grinned, shook hands warmly, but only moved as far as the Secret Serviceman by the archway. The faint roar of 'God Save the Queen' filtered from the TV set and the signaller finally stopped trying to tune it and stood to attention. Giving one last, pointless, glance at the sky, Maxim did much the same but was glad to see that most of the soldiers didn't.

The anthem ended, and a bugler from the Duke's old regiment sounded the Last Post – a reminder that it was a soldier, no matter how Royal, that was being commemorated. Maxim caught Forrest's eye, willing him *Wait, don't relax, above all, don't blink*.

The Air Force Colonel and briefcase came out from the Deanery and joined Culliman, waiting for the Secret Serviceman's message. The choir sang 'O God, Our Help in Ages Past' as the Queen and Royal Family led the way out.

"Lawman is moving . . ."

Shots.

The soldiers froze for an instant, then shattered into action, clattering aboard the Saracens, crouching with raised weapons and drowning Forrest's unnecessary orders. The TV commentator shouted but was lost in the uproar from the Abbey and the picture blurred as the camera

45

swung wildly. Then somebody's equipment snagged the aerial and the set smashed to the ground.

The Saracens' engines blared (one, two, three, Maxim counted; all started first time. Good). He waited until the scene had stabilised, then picked up the submachine-gun and walked over to Culliman, the Colonel and the Secret Serviceman, who had their heads together and were shouting at each other through the engines' rumble.

"Lawman's okay, okay . . . not hit . . . he's holding there . . ."

Maxim leant in. "The Queen?"

The Secret Serviceman stared at him blankly, then bent his head and squinted as he listened on his earplug. "*No . . . I don't know who got it . . . not her . . .*"

Maxim looked back at the platoon, then stepped into the cool dim archway abruptly cutting out much of the rumble and shouting. He looked back again and the three Americans were running – but past the Saracens, to Dean's Arch and the President's waiting cars. Maxim walked on, across the entrance to the Deanery and its little quadrangle. Ahead, somebody moved in the far Cloister. Just a dark, skirted figure hurrying to the right, away from the Abbey. Maxim pulled out the telescoping butt-stock of his gun, cocked it, and ran.

His rubber-soled boots gave just a faint echo from the vaulted Cloister roof. At the end, the Dark Cloister led off to the right; crouching, Maxim peeked round. It was a rough, whitewashed tunnel with feeble iron-framed lamps glowing on the walls. The far end was blocked by a solid but temporary-looking barrier, cutting off the Abbey buildings from the school.

To his left, near the entrance to the Chapter House, a policeman, an inspector, appeared. "Did anybody come past you?" Maxim called.

"No, the shooting was in . . ." The inspector gestured at the Abbey. He was fairly elderly and seemed rather uncertain. Maxim waved him back and jumped to the far side of the tunnel, then started along it.

A door on his side, locked. Again on his side, grey reflected light from a short archway that led into the tiny Infirmary Court, a miniature of the Cloisters. He had explored this far before the DDCR came visiting. Now he had to turn that corner again.

He braced for the breath-stopping shock of a bullet as he stepped quickly across the archway, saw the figure again and brought down the gun to the aim, knowing once more the forgotten sense of being two men, one with trigger finger tensed, the other standing aside, assessing and giving orders. He hoped to hell he both got it right.

Maxim was still in combat kit when he reached the DDCR's office, although he had left his flak jacket somewhere in Dean's Yard and the police had borrowed – after a High Mass of paperwork – the submachine-gun for some meaningless forensic tests. It was a small spartan room with nothing on the pale green walls but a calendar and what might have been a large map hidden by padlocked cupboard doors.

Four men sat around the table in front of the desk: the DDCR, George Harbinger, a bulky middle-aged Lieutenant-Colonel from the Legal Corps and Ferrebee from the Foreign Office. The DDCR introduced Maxim and ushered him to the spare seat. The legal Colonel looked bland, Ferrebee grim.

"You must have had quite a time of it with the rozzers." The DDCR tried to be reassuring. "Cup of tea? Coffee?"

"Nothing, thank you, sir." Maxim managed not to slump in his chair which, being built to the Army dictum that a sore backside makes for prompt decision-taking, wouldn't have allowed it anyway.

"Or a drop of Scotch? I think it's about that time, and past it – and it's George's Scotch anyway, stout fellow."

"Well . . ." The thought was tempting but the long day wasn't likely to end here.

"He'd like a Scotch," the DDCR decided. "In fact, we'd all like a Scotch." He brought a water jug from his desk.

"I know defence spending's been cut," George grumbled, "but if I'm to take over the whole Army's mess bills . . ." But he had come prepared, with a set of silver cups to match the big flask in his briefcase.

They drank without more than nods, and after the first gulp Maxim realised how much he had needed it – and that he'd better sip from now on; the DDCR was watching him covertly. "So you told them what happened – several times, I don't doubt. I'm afraid you're going to have to tell us as well – and have you got a copy of your statement to the police? Good man."

One result of Northern Ireland was that the Army was very familiar with its responsibilities and rights after an 'incident' – more so than the Metropolitan Police, Maxim had discovered. He passed the statement to the DDCR who glanced at it, then handed it to the Colonel.

George, who had also gulped at his Scotch, was already refilling his cup. "I'm sorry I got you into all this, Harry – "

"You did *not* get him into all this," the DDCR said firmly. "You are still not in the chain of command."

"Nice to have so many people ready to share the responsibility," the Colonel said cheerfully. Ferrebee's glare made it clear he was not one of the share-takers.

So Maxim recited the story yet again. And a recitation was what it had become, recalling a sequence of events that now seemed, with repetition, as inevitable as a stanza of verse or the clock ticking away the minute – it had been no more – from his first sighting of the dark figure to the explosion.

When he had finished, the Colonel looked for permission from the DDCR and asked: "Did the police say anything implying that you might have used more than the minimum force necessary?"

"They asked why I'd fired."

"And you told them," the Colonel consulted the report, "that the man had a grenade with the pin pulled." He looked up. "And you thought he was going to throw it at you?"

Maxim took a sip before answering. "Yes, I thought that at the time . . . but now, I think he was trying to commit suicide."

There was a sharp silence. Then the DDCR barked: "Why?"

"He took out the grenade – he had it in a pocket in his cassock, I think – and called something like: 'You'll get hurt.' I saw the lever go and I shot him. I think I hit him in the stomach or a bit higher. He dropped the grenade, and then he seemed to throw himself on it. He must have got his hands on it. It blew his hands and face off."

He found he was clenching his own hands in an attitude of prayer, pulled them loose and reached for the last of his whisky. George promptly poured him another.

"That must be speculation," the Colonel murmured. "What matters is the interpretation a trained soldier, acting under orders, would put on a situation – "

"*Did* your orders include chasing shadowy figures through the Cloisters?" Ferrebee demanded, his voice rough as the scar tissue on his face. "Or were you supposed to stay with the Saracens in Dean's Yard – which you were supposed to be commanding? Or is there something else about which my Office was not kept fully informed?"

George smiled. "James is a *leetle* distressed that his Office – *the* Office, I beg your pardon – doesn't seem to have grasped the extent of the security laid on for the President."

"But not laid on for the twenty-something other heads of state and prime ministers of friendly nations. *Your* Department doesn't have to explain that to them."

George shrugged. "Just point out that it was the President who got shot at, not them. QED."

Ferrebee clasped his hands – one also fire-scarred – on the table. "In Norwegian, too."

Maxim coughed politely and caught the DDCR's eye. "Could I know what did happen in the Abbey, sir? The police didn't – "

"You don't know?"

"No, sir."

"Good Lord. I suppose they didn't want to influence you . . . Well: there were three shots from a Russian AK-47 rifle, they found that at the firing point. Up on a ledge behind some television lights in the South Transept. It had jammed, apparently, or he'd probably have massacred the whole . . . Well, he killed Paul Barling, Junior Minister in Mr Ferrebee's Office, nobody else, but several got wounded. I believe most of it was chips of stone from the pillars."

"It must be rather frightful," George said contentedly, "for a politician to be killed by mistake for someone else. The final humiliation."

"Your taste really is rather poor, George," Ferrebee said stiffly. "I will put it down to the time of day. I'd better get back to the Office. I hope – I would like to say trust – that we shall be kept informed of any developments." He loped out, leaving the small room seeming spacious.

George went on calmly: "A ricochet hit the Norwegian Chief of Staff in the arm – that's what Jim was talking about – and another nicked Lady Micheldever in the back-side. Mind, it would be difficult to miss a target that size, even in the Abbey."

The DDCR gave A Look. "*I* would put it down to the drink."

"That was exactly what Jim meant."

The legal Colonel said thoughtfully: "It would be a pity to build up enmity in the Foreign Office . . . How influential is Mr Ferrebee?"

"Not very, thank God," the DDCR said. "He's more or less their travel agent, arranges diplomatic visits - ours there, theirs here. Not exactly at the top of the tree, considering he must be close to retirement."

"Comes of joining the Office late," George explained. "Makes it seem your second choice, and the Office is second to none, least of all in self-esteem. Jim started out to be an admiral."

The Colonel touched the side of his own face. "Was that . . . ah, erm?"

"He crashed a plane on a carrier, and I gather it didn't do his eyesight much good either. Blind eyes have gone out since Nelson's day. Personally, I'd've said that anybody who tries to land aeroplanes on ships is barmy enough to be an admiral, whether he can see where he's going or not."

The DDCR clearly felt this wasn't in the best of taste, either, but a lifetime in the Army had persuaded him that the Navy could look after itself. "So, now, where have we got to?"

"A Russian rifle," Maxim suggested.

That brought a freeze. Then George shrugged and

said: "All right, let's get it on the table: was it Kilo Golf Bravo?"

It was the latest Whitehall jargon to call intelligence organisations by their initials in radio code. It didn't prove you knew anything new about them, but not to use it proved you knew nothing at all.

The DDCR sighed. "This is your side, George. It could be just some loony who got hold of a Russian weapon – now why do I say that?" He examined his own instincts. "I suppose I don't *want* it to be the Bravoes. Felt just the same way when Kennedy got killed. But we have to face facts . . ."

"When we have the facts," the Colonel suggested. "I imagine this is something the police and Security are bearing in mind. The identity of the would-be assassin, once established, might help."

The DDCR took the reproof gratefully. "Fine. Leave it to George and his creepy-crawlie friends. Are we happy otherwise?"

The Colonel lifted Maxim's statement and put it down again. "I think this shows that Major Maxim acted quite reasonably, but . . . Where can you be contacted, Major?"

"I've got a billet at Wellington Barracks tonight, sir."

The DDCR said: "I don't much like you going back there – except you'll have to change out of that kit, of course. Your name's not supposed to be released, but the mess'll be full of gossip and speculation . . ."

George said: "I can put him up at Albany. Bags of room."

The DDCR frowned. In one way it was an ideal solution, but: "I don't want you two sitting up all night rehashing this and clouding Harry's mind with *theories*."

"Fear naught. We'll talk nothing but women and shop, no politics. If we get cracking now, we even have time for a bite before the fuzz want Harry back again."

"What for?"

"Whatever happened to the fiend at the Abbey, he's now a faceless one. Harry could be the only man to identify his face, once they've got their photo files sifted."

The Colonel nodded. He had anticipated that, too. He stood up, sweeping papers into his briefcase. "May I ask – do you have a lawyer, Major?"

Maxim hadn't seen a solicitor since the last dreary paperwork after Jenny's death. "I suppose so . . ."

"A lawyer?" the DDCR demanded. "What's he want a *lawyer* for?"

The Colonel and George glanced at each other, and Maxim felt he was missing something.

"Nothing, I hope," the Colonel said blandly. "But, just in case . . ."

Annette Harbinger knew Maxim had seen her moment of apprehension on recognising him, so she smiled ruefully and put her head on one side in a gesture he always found enchanting. "I'm so sorry, Harry – it's just that you always seem to pop up when there's bad news. I know you had nothing to do with today's . . ." and then she saw from George's expression that that was wrong, too. "Oh, *dear* . . ."

"It's not his fault, it's his *job*," George said. "We're putting him up for the night, slightly incognito. There's nobody else coming, is there?" George prided himself on never knowing what was happening in his private life: that way, it couldn't distract him or make him leave work early in order to be in time for it.

"Just the Defence Staff and their wives. No, darling, there's nobody coming. Is this going to be men only, gossipy women confined to the kitchen?"

"No, if we knew any secrets we'd be a lot better off . . ." George threw his topcoat on to a chair and reached for the decanter.

They talked families and schools – or rather, Annette and Maxim did – around one end of the vast table in the gloomy dark-panelled dining-room. For eighty years the eldest Harbinger sons had lived in Albany while waiting to inherit the family acres in Gloucestershire. There were not quite as many acres as George's colleagues alleged – as he pointed out, no one above the rank of Assistant Secretary thinks in less than tens of thousands of anything – but quite enough to spawn such envious exaggerations. The envy was, perhaps, less for the acreage than the independence it gave George; it infuriated people to think that a man so outspoken could never come to a Bad End or the Ministry of Agriculture. That he already had a set of rooms in that private backwater just ten minutes' stroll from Whitehall only made it worse. Their consolation might have been the thought of George living with great-grandmother Harbinger's choice of baronial panelling and immoveable mahogany furniture – if they had believed George had any more visual taste than a goat.

"Have you heard from Agnes recently?" Annette asked Maxim as she poured his coffee.

"Not for a while. She seems to be liking Washington, but she can't say much about her work there . . ." Agnes Algar had also been part of the old Prime Minister's inner circle at Number 10, as liaison officer with the Security Service. Now she was doing much the same job in the Washington embassy, liaising with, presumably, the FBI and CIA. "And I've been on courses I couldn't say much about, the letters just sort of . . ."

"You ought to have married that girl, Harry," George announced. "Somebody should, anyway. Woman reaches her mid-thirties without a husband, she turns sour, starts wearing clothes too old for her. Can't be much good in a liaison job: you need tact and awareness for that."

Tact? *Awareness?* Annette kept a smile on her clenched teeth and dreamt briefly of George with a coffee cup rammed down his throat. Maxim put on his polite smile. He had seen nothing in Annette's own tactfulness – nothing more, that is, than the usual wish of every married woman he knew to get him remarried as soon as possible.

George looked at his watch and stood up. "I want to catch the nine o'clock news on TV. They won't have anything new, but they'll be running everything they've got from the Abbey."

"Can we record it?" Maxim asked.

"*You* might be able to; it takes me half an hour to set up that blasted thing and then it usually gets the wrong programme. They ought to give away a ten-year-old child with every video machine. And every other sort of machine they're swamping us with these days."

Maxim fiddled the video recorder into life while they watched. Since the BBC hadn't been allowed into the Cloisters for any later footage, they were reduced to running the moment of the shots three times. But the Queen had just reached the Abbey doorway when the first shot sounded, so by then the director had switched to his outside cameras and commentator. It had taken three seconds or more to realise the shots were inside, and to switch back there, and longer before a camera steadied on the scurrying, crouching mob that had been the congregation. By then, the shooting had stopped.

"Poor sods," George said. "There you have the flower – faded, mayhap, but the flower nonetheless – of the free world's Royalty, statesmen and men at arms. Between them they must have ordered more shots fired than the world's had hot dinners, and now somebody's blasted off near them. Poor wee cow'rin', tim'rous buggers." But he sounded genuinely sympathetic.

They watched armed police struggling through the crowd, then the camera spotted and zoomed in on the huddle and overturned chairs where Paul Barling had collapsed. It was difficult to see, from that angle, how close the shots had come to the President's party. And, fixed high on either side of the Nave, no camera could peer round to the firing point above the South Transept. They kept the recording going, however, just to hear the distant snap of Maxim's own shot and then the thud of the grenade.

"Just under four seconds," Maxim said, looking up from his wristwatch.

"Four-and-a-half-second fuse in the grenade," George guessed knowledgeably. "Does that tell you what type it – "

But the BBC already knew: an obsolete Russian type, so the fragments proved. Moreover, the only item found on the body had been a London street guide with two telephone numbers scrawled in it. They had proved to be the unlisted private numbers of two Second Secretaries at the Russian embassy.

"Good Lord," George said.

Fresh from Miss Tuckey's lectures at the Fort, Maxim

cringed at the incompetence of it. The news item ended with a reporter mouthing earnest platitudes against a background of Scotland Yard's revolving sign. George switched off.

"It didn't tell us why the weapon jammed," Maxim said.

"Do they jam easily?"

"Not those AKs, no."

"Well, thank God it did." The phone rang in another room and they said nothing until Annette came and called Maxim out. He returned already putting on his car-coat. "You were right. The Yard wants me to go and view their pin-up boys."

"Bad luck. They all look like mad axe-men."

"I've seen some of them before. I don't know when I'll be – "

"We'll keep a mug of cocoa burning in the window for you."

When Maxim had gone, George went into his tiny study and prowled restlessly. It was something of a relief to be working with Harry again – but had he dragged the man into another smudgy episode for his 'P' file? (Never mind what the DDCR said, George automatically assumed all credit and blame.) Some other men might not have come out of it alive, there was that, but others might have paused longer before getting involved . . . He glanced hungrily at the phone and had to remember he was no longer at Number 10, no longer had an ex officio finger to poke into every pie . . . And, blast it, did he want a whisky and soda or a glass of the port?

The phone had given barely a ping before he snatched it up. It was Sprague from the Home Office, and if George had just a couple of minutes, truly no longer, then . . . George went to warn Annette, who loathed Sprague. But it decided one thing for him: the port.

8

Norman Sprague's correctness seemed entirely individual, as if he were obeying some Queen's Regulations for the Home Office that he alone had written and read. He was slim, unaged and with the same perfect sheen to his hair and shoes; his suit was dark, double-breasted and old-fashioned by a precise degree; he had a rosebud in his buttonhole and his tie was Old Harrovian.

"George, a little bird tells me you have a most interesting house guest. Don't keep him all to yourself, that would be too unkind. You must produce him immediately."

"He's round at the Yard, looking at mug shots. Glass of port?"

Sprague glanced intently at the decanter, then relaxed. "Of course, this is one house where one doesn't need to be tactful about the port. You keep an exquisite cellar, lucky man. I'd love a sip. Perhaps it's just as well your friend isn't here, one can be more relaxed without the rude mechanicals."

He selected the best chair – George's own – so naturally, just as he assumed that George would bring his glass across to him, that there could be no resentment. It was simply his due as one of that small and invaluable band of Whitehall old ladies, all male except (in Annette's opinion) Sprague himself, who knew almost everything and everybody and hid most of it while seeming to babble all.

"Confusion to our enemies – " Sprague sipped. "Quite delicious – whoever they may turn out to be. George, we have a little problem after today's *événements*. My Minister is going to have to Make A Statement, and at the moment he can barely remember his own name. He was *there*, did you realise, and the thought that his own dear skin might have been punctured has quite unmanned him. Too pitiful for words. Never mind, it keeps him out of the way while we prepare a helpful submission which he really can't get wrong, unless he reads it upside down. I thought of being 'thorough' and 'relentless', and perhaps we might even 'spare no effort'. I think he'd like that, don't you? – once he's looked up what 'effort' means."

"Had you thought of it being 'this dastardly act'?"

"How could I have missed it? Thank you, George, I knew I could rely on you. He'll love it, I can hear him saying it now – and for weeks to come. Then the PM will express Utmost Confidence – which he may even feel, God knows why – and that will be that. But not, alas, the end for us."

"A Steering Committee for the investigation?"

"Inevitable." Sprague shook his head sagely. "Not to produce anything publishable, that's been accepted *sans demur*, but just to give the PM a day-to-day picture of what's happening, which one trusts won't be."

"Who's chairing it?"

"Rodney Kirkland, we're safe there. Retired admirals add a certain gravitas and he won't understand a word of what's going on. Then most likely Tony Sladen from the Cabinet Office, some assistant commissioner from the Met, we'll have to have the D-G of Five – and the Home Office, that's to be little me. One couldn't very well dodge. But on the whole, quite cosy and, one might say, even steerable."

"Also notably lacking proper representation from Defence," George said grimly.

"George, that's what I *said*. Admiral Roddy was frightfully huffed. Where did I think he'd been all his life? Well, with sailors one would prefer not to speculate. Oh no, he'd been at Defence since the first bow and arrow, their interests perfectly safe in his hands – what could one say?"

"It's an Army matter if it's anything."

"Quite. But the Army's rôle in the whole affair must be a central issue. What your man's orders were, possibly whether he exceeded them – I make no judgements yet –

certainly if it was *advisable* for him to fire off a high-velocity something, causing the culprit to blow himself up."

"Harry believes the man committed suicide with that grenade."

"Yes, so I understand." Sprague's expression was one of faintly pleased regret, as if he had heard that some distant and disliked cousin had lost his job. "*So* difficult to prove. And the precise task of your man at the Abbey – "

"He was commanding an anti-terrorist unit."

"Ah, but was he? Naturally the Committee will do its utmost to ensure that no other task is mentioned publicly, but that raises the question: if he were on anti-terrorist duties, why did he not prevent the terrorist reaching the Abbey in the first place? You see my dilemma."

George saw, all right. Also that it was no more Sprague's dilemma than Sprague thought it was. "The Army had no more than a platoon there; the Met must have had God-knows-how-many coppers around."

"No doubt. The Met – Sir William himself – must bear their due share of responsibility. Indeed, it was Sir William who took it on himself to release the news of the grenade being Russian and those telephone numbers. Not on my Office's advice, I can assure you. But another indication that we don't control the London police. They've managed very cleverly not to be under anybody's direct control for all these years. Self-made orphans: they can't choose a mother now, when they need a skirt to hide behind. I fear for Sir William, I truly do."

"And you wanted the Russian angle suppressed?"

Sprague winced. "Not *suppressed*, George, of course not. But does one want such things *bandied about* before the Committee has had time to produce a definitive version of events? Surely it is the first duty of the Committee to discourage wild speculation. What, after all, does the evidence amount to? Russian weapons, easily available I believe; those telephone numbers – unlisted, as you were about to remind me, but not unascertainable – and an unidentified corpse. No hint of anyone else being involved at all. Might I beg of you just one more drop of this heavenly vintage?"

George got up and refilled the glasses. "They're no further forward on the identification?"

"Not unless your colleague is picking him out of the rogues' gallery at this moment, which one doubts. Such people are unlikely to be common criminals. Thank you so much, you're too kind. Nothing on the body except that street guide, and as for fingerprints and dental records, I believe they're having trouble finding enough teeth or fingers. This is extraordinarily delectable; it wouldn't be one of the '48s, would it? Not a Taylor, surely? You lucky man, George."

"You don't think the unmarked clothes, empty pockets, that could be all of a piece with him destroying his identity by blowing his face off? To protect somebody else?"

"It is difficult," Sprague said judiciously, "to see that phrased in a Committee report. That he hid his identity, no question. But one could see that as the attitude of the lonely psychopath, a man who has sunk his identity in destroying the American President – perhaps any American President – planning meticulously through the years, collecting the wherewithal . . . the gun was quite an old one, they tell me; the grenade, too."

"He can't have counted on the Abbey. American Presidents don't drop in there every Thursday. And how did he plan a way in?"

"It's virtually a public place, George, and has been for seven hundred years. You can take tours, find whole libraries written about it – to be fair to Sir William, security there must be a nightmare. The Church of England is quite as lax in such matters as the Royal Family. I'm not saying I want to see the dear Archbish preaching heavenly bliss in a flak jacket, but . . . No, all quite within the compass of one twisted mind. This is purely a personal opinion – but infinitely less damaging, at this time, than unfounded speculation about foreign involvement."

Reluctantly, George had to agree with the common sense of that. "But even if we circle the Whitehall wagons, we're going to have the whole American nation shooting flaming arrows at us when tomorrow's papers come out. After all, we did nearly get their President bumped off."

"American Presidents are always being shot at; they

probably get to like it, it does wonders for them in the opinion polls. Yes, the media will have a field day, but each under orders to find a unique interpretation of events, so the public will end up thoroughly confused as usual. Thank heaven a free press can't afford unanimity.

"But" – Sprague leant forward and became confidential – "if the White House or Capitol Hill starts getting uppity, there are Certain Steps we can take there. I am going to tell you something, since you've been so understanding and probably because you've got me tipsy on your priceless nectar" – George was sure Sprague had never been drunk in his adult life – "but I want your solemn promise it won't go an inch further, not even a Common Market millimetre. Agreed? It concerns the Reznichenko Memorandum. Can you cast your mind as far back as last month's headlines?"

George nodded slowly, reassembling the events in his mind. The Peace Crusade had overreached its funds and couldn't pay a printer's bill. Somebody had promptly paid the amount, in cash, to the Crusade's bank account. Sighs of relief all round, not least from the printer.

But then the 'Memorandum' had surfaced, seeming to prove that Lord Ettington, one of the Crusade's most prominent committee-men, had met with Reznichenko of the Russian embassy on the evening before the pay-in – an evening when Ettington should have been on the platform of a Crusade public meeting. Denying the obvious implication, the Crusade had turned up the credit slip accompanying the cash: it was signed Ettington. Denying that, Ettington had proved he hadn't withdrawn such a sum from his own account. Tactically, that had been a mistake, as had been his claim that he had missed the meeting because of a stomach upset.

After several days of Moscow denial ('a typical CIA plot'), press speculation and confusion in the Crusade, Ettington had revised his story: he had spent the evening with a lady whose name had been the last attribute he was interested in.

"Has somebody found the prostitute?" George asked.

"Oh no, there never was one. But quite a clever alibi: everybody loves to believe the worst, and it's usually true when it concerns Ettington's private parts. Really they're the most public part of the man; he's so *indiscriminate*." Sprague paused for a delicate shudder. "No, the truth is worse (or better): on the evening in question, me Lord was in dalliance vile with the wife of the Secretary of the Crusade – knowing the poor cuckolded Sec was anchored at the Euston Road meeting. You see the beauty of it now? If he admits the truth – and the lady will deny it, obviously – then he was merely using the Crusade to pursue his foul desires and has to resign as a cad and bounder, losing his only foothold in public life. So he has to let the plot stand and drag the Crusade down with him – and (we have our sources) some of their committee really do think he did a deal with Reznichenko."

George thought about it. "Somebody must have been keeping tabs on Ettington to know where he really was. Don't tell me it – "

"It *was*, George: our own dear Security Service. Habit, I suppose, they've been watching Crusade members for so long. It certainly wasn't their new Director-General who authorised it, not now the Cabinet's virtually joined the Crusade en masse. And I disclose no secrets when I say it was *not* the D-G who brought it to us. But now the interesting speculation is who was truly at the root of it? Who was also following Ettington that night, to know he would be somewhere he daren't admit to – and doing it well enough not to be spotted by Security's watchers? Who could fake the Memorandum – Russian typewriter, the right paper, Reznichenko's signature, Ettington's – who has resources like that? And who profits by branding our Peace Crusade as Moscow-financed?"

George moved uneasily in his chair.

"You wouldn't suggest our own Intelligence Service?" Sprague said gently. "You certainly wouldn't suggest Army Intelligence. But you might, as the only other candidate, be forced to suggest the CIA. However much you hate to agree with Moscow, as one does oneself, they have to be right sometimes: dear Charlie's Indians are *so* activist. But you see what this means, George: *destabilisation*. Treating us as if we were some little banana republic. The President traipsing around Europe with a Revivalist sermon in one hand and poisoning the water-holes with the other – "

"If he knew."

"None so guilty as those who choose not to know; he has to answer for Charlie's Indians *if* we should respond to any Washington criticism of the Abbey – and the part my Office played in the security there – by Revealing All about CIA interference in our domestic affairs."

"Is this your Minister speaking?" George asked, surprised.

"The *Minister*, George?" Sprague was genuinely shocked. "You're being positively virginal; you don't suppose we've told the *Minister* about this. As soon shout it from the rooftops."

"But he has to answer for you in the end," George said dryly.

"Oh poof." Sprague shrugged the thought away. "The Minister will be fully briefed as and when he needs to be. *I* don't want an Anglo-American rumpus, nobody less, but nobody could accuse me of starting it."

Sprague leant back, smiling with the deepest sympathy as George realised the now-seamless circle that bound them together. "But of course," he continued, "none of this need happen at all. My Steering Committee exists – will exist, from tomorrow – to ensure that it doesn't. All I ask from you, George, is your usual understanding and co-operation. A whisper of regret from your Department about the security lapses at the Abbey, a gracious acknowledgement from the Army that there might have been some slight error by a certain officer . . . a hint of Taking Steps . . . I know you'll manage it most beautifully. We are the last of the few, George, those who really understand these matters. And that includes your quite sublime port."

Sprague insisted on saying good-night to Annette. They found her in the kitchen, drinking tea with Maxim.

Sprague was delighted to meet him. "Major Maxim, I believe. No, don't get up, you must have had a quite dreadful day. George and I were just sympathising. And did you have any luck with the Yard's beauty competition? Ah, I was afraid not. It must be nice to be working with George again, I hear you did quite splendidly at Number 10. Dearest Annette, can I apologise enough for ruining one of your rare domestic evenings? One of these days you must . . ."

When he had gone, Annette fixed her dark bright eyes on George and said: "Well?"

George dropped into a kitchen chair, shaking his head slowly. "I think I got raped in there."

"Oh? And did you lie back and enjoy it?"

"I learnt something . . . And we do have a real problem . . ."

"That man," Annette said, "makes me feel lice crawling up inside my skirt."

Maxim said: "He knew who I was."

"He's Home Office. The police know, he knows. He doesn't gossip – unless it suits his book."

Annette said: "It sounds as if you were gossiping in there. His Office is responsible for security, isn't it? Did you very kindly offer to share some of the blame with him?"

"It isn't as simple as that – "

"Or did you finish the whole decanter and decide to blame Harry instead?"

"There's no question of that. Just – "

"I'm bloody well sure there isn't." She smiled sweetly. "I'm going to bed."

Maxim watched George shake the teapot, decide against it, wander to a cupboard and look hopelessly into it, find a glass, run it full of cold water and sip. Whatever he did, he avoided Maxim's eye.

Finally he said: "Harry . . . when you went chasing after the . . . whoever-he-was, was it absolutely necessary?"

"It seemed like a good idea at the time." Maxim's smile was still polite, but a little bleak.

"Yes . . . And when you say he *threw* himself on the grenade – he did really do that?"

"You weren't there, George." Maxim leant back, his eyes closed, his voice quiet and very, very tired. "You've never been there."

9

The morning papers were all that Sprague had predicted. Maxim found it odd – and seductively pleasant – to walk from Albany to Horse Guards Avenue through the early morning crowd and know that he was the one of the two 'mystery men' referred to, albeit far the less important one. It was automatically assumed that the unnamed soldier had been part of an SAS unit, which helpfully diverted attention from Forrest's platoon, the Saracens, and their real task. But most of the headlines focussed on Russian weapons and telephone numbers, of an assassin's bullet that had missed the President by inches and the Queen by as little as fifty yards.

On inside pages, previous assassinations and attempts were rehashed, police security methods dissected – and left that way – and Paul Barling's short career reviewed. He had been relatively young, and a new ministerial appointment, so hardly anybody had an obituary of him on file: the results were largely culled from *Who's Who* and a few library clippings, so that the same anecdotes and quotes cropped up in every paper, however different their conclusions. Maxim learnt that Barling's knowledge of the Soviet Union had made him a Kremlin lackey or, alternatively, that it had made him one of the few sane voices for balanced détente in Europe. All agreed he had been no dynamic speechmaker, but had been made a junior minister because his intellectual grasp of East-West problems had earned him respect in back-bench discussion groups.

But – as Sprague had also predicted – the President had come out of it very well. His coolness under fire – "I've been shot at before" – and a dismissive quote about "It could be just some freako; we have them, too" had focused attention on the Guildhall speech he had made that evening, calling for solidarity in NATO and a united stand on Berlin. There would be happy faces in the Ministry of Defence, Maxim assumed.

However, not in the DCR's offices. The Deputy Director was already at his desk, if he had ever left it, looking haggard and yellow. "Morning. I won't offer you coffee, you can get yourself some, you're attached to this office until further notice. There's a desk a couple of doors down. It's going to be one of those days. *Bloody* politicians all think they're Churchill and won't decide anything until after dinner. Now there's going to be a *Steering Committee* for the investigation, whatever that means.

"And there's trouble on the sixth floor: it isn't going to be as simple as we thought, now they're worrying whether you exceeded your orders. I thought you were there to stop people killing the President and you shot somebody who'd tried, but . . . I don't know. Maybe you'd have done better to stick with the Saracens and let the coppers cock it up for themselves. *I* don't think their marksmen could hit a bear's arse if they were close enough to bugger it, but I suppose it was still their job . . . The Committee may want you this afternoon . . . Are you happy staying with George another night or two? – assuming he's still on. Where *is* he? I don't suppose he was even up when you left. *Bloody* civil servants."

Maxim didn't see George until just after twelve, although presumably he had been up and even in the building for some time before. He threw open the door with a cry of: "Where's me seeing-eye dog? Ah, there you are. Sun's over the yard-arm, barman's arm withering from inaction. Come on, chop-chop."

It was an old battle-cry from Number 10, but the two other Playforce officers in the room watched astonished – although they knew George already – as Maxim got up and collected his coat with a wry smile and faint protest: "I'm supposed to be holding myself available for – "

"I know all about that: they want you over at the Cabinet Office at four. The DD's coming to lunch with us." George closed the door behind them and dropped his voice. "Call it a rehearsal. He doesn't really approve, that's why he's coming along, but whatever he says *you* hang on my every word and you'll die a Chelsea Pensioner yet."

The three of them took a taxi heading – to the surprise of two of them – over Waterloo Bridge and along to the National Theatre. The DDCR glared at the rough concrete and glass façade suspiciously. "What the devil are we doing here?"

"Never very busy at lunchtime and it won't be crawling with Cabinet Office spies like any club you could think of. Food isn't exactly gourmet, but . . ."

"One thing we can be sure of," the DDCR muttered, "it's got a booze licence."

"Quite correct." George pushed the door open. "All right if we glance at a couple of pictures first? Bit of high blood pressure helps the digestion."

The Lyttelton Circle Gallery had an exhibition of about two dozen paintings hung on freestanding pegboard screens under small spotlights. George viewed them at a canter, making two or three notes in his diary. The pictures were splashy acrylics, bright and formless, but in places the colours seemed muddied.

"Duty done." George shut his diary. "Annette's been badgering me for a month to get down here and it's the last day. Drinks are only one floor up."

"Kettleburn," the DDCR said, looking at the exhibition poster. "Never heard of him."

"He's living with Annette's young sister. Hence the duty factor."

"Well, let's hope he's some good in bed."

"I'm going to have to be just a *leetle* more cultural than that when my opinion gets sought."

"You could call them a load of dog droppings, only perhaps the RSPCA would sue you." The thought of George being browbeaten by Annette had cheered the DDCR up. "What does Harry think?"

"Unglyptic," Maxim suggested.

"What?"

"I came across it the other day. It's something that sculpture shouldn't be, so perhaps it's something that paintings should be."

"This is the last time," George said heavily, "that I drag a couple of unlettered military oafs around – "

"Mention Jackson Pollock and Hoffman," the DDCR said. "Then tell him a proper abstract expressionist doesn't have second thoughts and start reworking his colours so much. Where's this lunch?"

George led up the stairs, cursing himself for having forgotten yet again that a bluff military attitude can be the most deceptive front in Whitehall.

"What is this Steering Committee actually going to do?" the DDCR wanted to know.

"Technically, they're there to oversee the investigation and keep the Prime Minister informed on a day-to-day basis. In practice, they're to ensure a politically happy ending, make sure there are no loose ends which the ungodly might pull on and cause unravelling in high places. They'll interview a few key witnesses like Harry, but the real work's being done by the police and Security. All rushing round measuring the unmeasurable, scrutinising the inscrutable, defiling the files – and all hoping to come up with nothing . . . You look doubtful, Harry."

He reached to pour more wine; Maxim held his hand over his half-empty glass. The Lyttelton Buffet wasn't ideal for a secure conversation – the round white tables were bunched too close together – but they had chosen one in what passed for a corner of the shapeless room, and it was early enough for nobody to have taken a table next to them. And as George had predicted, nobody from the Cabinet Office would have been tempted south of the river by the rather tame chicken curry or the savoury pie, even with as much free pickle as he had piled on it.

"Harry, suppose I were to say to you that once or twice in the history of our noble police force, known to be the envy of all nations, there has been a crime which caused such a public outcry for a solution that somebody went out and found the likeliest culprit, fitted the evidence neatly around him – and everybody else lived happily ever after. Would you believe that?"

"I would," Maxim said unemotionally.

"Then why can't you believe it works both ways? Here we have a public outcry, albeit silent, for no conspiracy. I don't give a damn what the papers say. Most people feel just the way we did last night" – he nodded at the DDCR – " 'Just let it be some loony.' It's a comforting feeling; maybe it goes back to the idea that madmen are touched by God, so nobody's to *blame* for all this. Best of all, it should keep the Americans cool – God knows they've got their share of armed fruitcakes – and that's the most important thing for our Department. As for the Home Office and Security and the police, well, political assassins are something they're supposed to know about – ahead of the act. They'll happily settle for some lone nutter as well.

"Now, given that sort of pressure not to find a conspiracy, don't you think a conspiracy might just not be found?"

He sipped his wine and said, almost to himself: "It isn't corruption. Nobody gets anything for himself – except maybe a quiet life. It's just politicians, civil servants, police and all getting together to give the public what it wants. A rare and rather beautiful event, really."

"How will they get over the Russian connection?" Maxim asked.

George shrugged. "I don't have to remind you that the AK-47 dates from 1947: how many millions, tens of millions, have they built since then? I doubt they know themselves, let alone where they've all got to. I don't subscribe to the theory that the Bravoes are all supermen, it's too big an organisation for that, but I doubt they'd send a man to kill the President with a Russian rifle, Russian grenade, Russian telephone numbers – and stupid enough to miss besides."

Maxim nodded. "But that doesn't prove he was working alone. The fact that he made himself unrecognisable –"

"Except for Russian weapons and telephone numbers. No face, no hands, but those. Personally, I would sooner destroy a couple of telephone numbers than blow off my head – and any serious intelligence organisation in the world agrees with me. They simply don't send people on missions which depend on suicide to protect their cover.

Some people take their L-pills, some don't. The point is, you can't be sure how people will behave at that final, very private, frontier crossing."

The DDCR looked suspiciously at the level in George's wine-glass.

"All right," Maxim said. "Then some fringe terrorist group, fanatical . . ."

"There is nothing we can prove. Not today. Perhaps not until somebody turns up the identity of the man at the Abbey. But the Steering Committee *is* today. I just want to get you through that, and I want you to do it by telling them what you *know*, and nothing else. Yes sir, No sir, and Don't know sir – remember that one particularly. Then we may be able to strike some de facto deal: we don't push for a conspiracy, which we can't prove, if they go easy on the security aspect, at least as far as the Army's concerned. The Army," he repeated, playing to Maxim's weakness – or strength.

Maxim recognised that. He glanced at the DDCR, who said nothing. "If that's all, I think I'll walk back over the footbridge. Get a breath of fresh air." His face was calm and blank.

When he had gone, the DDCR made a grunting, sniffing noise and said: "Rather an interesting chap. Not sure I'd want an Army full of him, but . . ."

"Quite." George looked around at the small bar in one corner. "I think I'll have a spot of something to neutralise the coffee. For you? Not even a brandy? Yes, our Harry does try to do the Right Thing from time to time. Terrifying, isn't it?"

70

10

The conference room – one of many in the Cabinet Office on the corner of Downing Street – was an elegant reminder that the building had originally been designed by William Kent for the true lords of Whitehall, neither spiritual nor temporal, but Treasury. It was a quiet, unhurried room smelling of scorched dust from the recently turned-on heating; high-ceilinged, with white-painted panelling above the carved chair rail, and Maxim was seated with his back to a tall grey marble fireplace.

Of the six others seated around the green baize table-top littered with files, diagrams and tea cups, he had met three before: Sir Anthony Sladen, rigid and refined as the surroundings, which were his home ground; the new Director-General of MI5, an academic lawyer with brief wartime experience of code-breaking who had been appointed to appease Parliament and, it seemed, enrage George Harbinger; and Sprague himself, radiating friendliness as fresh as the rosebud in his buttonhole.

"So you aren't any longer suggesting that Person X threw himself on the grenade, then, Major?" The Chairman, Admiral Kirkland, was lean and thin of neck, with a sharp aristocratic face that seemed fleshless under its loose skin.

"No, sir, I just mentioned it as a possibility. I thought he came forward further than I'd expected in the circumstances."

"The circumstances?" The Admiral blinked, puzzled.

"I'd shot him."

"Ah, of course."

Because of the strict hierarchical placing, Maxim sat next across a corner of the table from the Assistant Commissioner from the Metropolitan Police, a man

71

who looked like a perfectly barbered gorilla, contrasting strongly with the well-bred faces around the table. He asked abruptly: "Have you shot many men before this?"

Admiral Kirkland said: "Good God," but let the question stand.

"Some." Maxim wondered whether to try and count back, then added a tentative inspiration: "And I've seen quite a number of people hit by small-arms fire in operational situations. If they're not moving already, they tend to crumple or stagger to keep their balance."

Had he tried to be too helpful? But the glances and feeling around the table had swung against the AC. Policemen, Maxim was coming to realise, were seen in Cabinet Office circles as co-existent but certainly not equal.

Admiral Kirkland said: "Quite. What I'd say from my own experience. Don't expect we'll ever clear that point up."

The AC opened his mouth for another question, then turned a page of Maxim's statement instead. "Now, halfway down page 2, you met the inspector in the East Cloister. Where had he come from?"

"I don't know. There's several . . ." Maxim checked himself in time. "He was a bit further up the Cloister, towards the Abbey." Several members glanced at the big ground plan of the Abbey buildings which lay in the middle of the table, speckled with tiny coloured markers and pencil tracks. Maxim had already charted his own movements on it.

"How far from you?"

"Six – no, more, eight or ten feet."

"What did he say?"

"I said to him – I can't remember the exact words, but – "

"Just go ahead," Admiral Kirkland assured him. "Give us the sense of it."

"I asked if anybody had come past him and he said No, and then he said the shooting had been inside. The Abbey."

"What did he do then?"

"I don't know. I went the other way, into the Dark Cloister, after Person X."

"You didn't see him again after the explosion?"

Maxim thought. "Not to remember. There were quite a lot of people around immediately after that."

"Would you describe the inspector, please?"

Puzzled, Maxim tried to dredge back the hasty glimpse. "A bit shorter than me, say five-ten . . . older, fiftyish . . . just a bit of short grey hair over his ears . . . I think a thin face, a moustache . . . The rest was his uniform."

"You're sure he was an inspector?"

"The two pips on his shoulders."

"Did you notice his number?"

"He didn't have a number." Inspectors didn't.

"Yes, I'm sorry . . . How long would you say you spent with him?"

"Hardly any time at all. Just long enough to say what we said."

"How long would that be?"

"I don't know . . . three, four seconds?"

"You were looking at him the whole time?"

"No. I was trying to watch down the Dark Cloister."

"So you perhaps saw him for . . . one second?"

"It might have been that."

"One second." The AC broke off and thumbed through a neat stack of papers, reaching without looking for a cigarette from an open packet on the table, lighting it with a throwaway lighter. All the time that *one second* hung in the air dissolving slower than his first breath of smoke. The Committee glanced at Maxim and away again, all except Sprague who smiled throughout with rich sympathy. The AC grunted, drew out a paper and skimmed it.

"Sir Roderick" – he looked up at the chairman – "we had three inspectors covering that area, by which I mean the Deanery, the Revestry and the door at the west end of the North Cloister. Two are in their thirties, one just forty: we prefer to have the younger men on these security jobs. None of them reports having seen or spoken to Major Maxim between the shooting in the Abbey and the explosion. I spoke to them all myself. Oh, none of them has a moustache, either."

Emotions swept through Maxim as quick as heartbeats: disbelief, annoyance, apprehension and then, to his own surprise, relief. He said: "You've got a fake copper, then. And a conspiracy. Just put on a uniform and walk in carrying a clip-board."

"Was he carrying a clip-board?" That was the dry, disinterested voice of the D-G from five, at the far end of the table.

"Yes, sir, he was. I remember now."

"You remember now. Good." The D-G took up the questioning. "And what did this man, this *fake copper*, actually do?"

"Well, he . . . didn't really do anything."

"Did he call a warning to the Person X?"

"No, sir."

"Or try to misdirect you away from him?"

"Well, there wasn't much point . . . No."

"Or try to impede you in any way?"

"No."

"You wouldn't say that this *fake copper*, whom you saw for one second – approximately – was of much constructive help to any conspiracy, then?" The D-G was speaking to a distant corner of the ceiling and sounded very bored.

"No, sir."

I blew it, Maxim thought.

11

"Yes, on the whole, it would appear that you did," George said equably. "A phoney copper *is* a new dimension . . . the trouble is, it rather forces an issue that we'd all been hoping to avoid. It proves either that there was a conspiracy, or that you're a fantasist. Not much middle ground for us to do any deals over, now."

"If we could find the copper . . ."

"Quite. But don't expect any help from the police if they don't believe he exists – and they'd rather he *didn't* exist, seeing what he proves about their security."

"How's the Army going to come out of it now?"

"I shall need to think about that . . . They may see the easiest way as taking some responsibility for the security aspect . . ."

"Would it help if I resigned my commission right now?"

"Dear me, no. It would be the height of presumption for the sacrificial lamb to ruin the ceremony by committing suicide first, and you would probably, and rightly, find yourself reincarnated in the Royal Air Force. Anyway, why choose self-pity when there's still the option of alcoholic beverages? Have another?"

"Thanks. I think I will."

"You will? You must be in a bad way." George collected the glasses and got up. "Don't get carried away by the atmosphere in here and do the Decent Thing. You know how I hate drinking alone."

Maxim smiled wanly. Boodle's was just one of he didn't know how many clubs, institutions and associations George belonged to – probably George didn't know himself – and that early in the evening they had the big drawing-room to themselves. With its tall ceiling, sombre colours and the undergrowth of dark leather Chesterfields, armchairs and small tables, it could well have been the anteroom of a well-born regiment at the turn of the century. Or perhaps a film producer's idea of one, and in such films somebody always placed a loaded revolver in the table drawer and left the disgraced officer alone . . .

There was a final edition of the *Standard* in the rack: the President had flown direct to Paris from Lakenheath air base, but the front page picture was the drawing of Person X that Maxim had helped a police artist construct. Releasing that showed that other lines of inquiry had failed, and Maxim wasn't too sure even he would recognise the man from the drawing. It was just a squarish, middle-aged face with thinning hair and no pronounced features. Moreover, it looked somehow coarser than his brief memory, and he hadn't been able to explain just how. He suspected the artist put a hint of criminality into all his faces; it would be difficult not to, after so many years at it.

George who usually managed to be a few hours ahead of the public – although never as far ahead as Sprague – had seen the picture already. "Aged between forty-five and sixty (extraordinary they can't do better than that), probably sedentary life, appendicitis scar, non-smoker . . . The trouble is, that anybody who thinks 'That looks like old Fred' isn't going to think of old Fred as shooting people in the Abbey. We're not dealing with the criminal class. Maybe in a month or two they'll connect it up with some Missing Persons report, but . . . By the way, I saw the report on the rifle. It hadn't jammed, just got a dud round up the spout. So he could've cleared it just by working the action: instead, he dropped it and ran. Any comment?"

Maxim considered. "He'd fired three aimed shots already, and it would take him a couple of seconds to work the action and get his aim back . . . We saw on television how people were ducking. No, I should think he'd lost his chance by then."

"So he behaved quite reasonably in running?"

"Probably." Maxim squinted at George, wary about being invited into yet more speculation.

"The primer in the cartridge had fired, the main charge hadn't. Does that tell us anything?"

"It happens. If it was old ammunition and hadn't been stored properly . . ."

"It *was* old ammunition, like the gun, like the grenade. Now let me ask you something: could you fix a cartridge so that that happened?"

"Are you suggesting somebody sabotaged the ammunition?"

"I'm asking you a straight question: how would you do it?"

Maxim considered, cautiously. "The simplest way would be to pull the cartridge apart, take out the propellant, and fire the primer, then tap it with a hammer and nail. Then put it all together again."

"Excellent! And the nail mark wouldn't show under the firing pin mark later. I hadn't thought of that." Grinning with excitement, George took a large swallow of his drink. "So what you're telling me is that the gun could have been rigged to fire only three shots, then stop, by putting a dud cartridge fourth. And it would be near impossible to prove afterwards."

"*I'm* telling you?" Maxim gaped. "I'm not telling you a blind thing. All this is your bright idea."

"But a good wheeze nonetheless."

"Hold on. If I wanted to sabotage that shooting, I could have doctored the first three rounds. The *first* shot's the most important, it's going to be the best aimed, I mean not the *fourth* . . ."

"But suppose Person X had doctored it himself? – and the first shot had done all he'd really wanted to do? – kill Paul Barling? Then a couple to give himself a margin, in case the first missed, which he fired off against a pillar near the President, then the gun jams on cue and he runs. How about that?"

The thought snapped into perfect focus in Maxim's mind. "With the President and everybody around, nobody would think of Barling as the target. They assume it's a mistake and there's no political blowback. Yes, I like that."

Now George was looking astonished. "You do, do you? It's nice to be agreed with, but wasn't that a little fast for a simple soldier?"

Maxim smiled. "It was something an instructor up at the Fort was talking about: arranging assassinations to look accidental. No reprisals."

"You'd say it was a widely accepted practice, then?"

"In a not-very-wide circle, yes. But why Barling? He wasn't very important, was he?"

"That could be why; if it were somebody more important there'd be bound to be suspicions it was intended. But somebody had to be killed to prove how callous the Bravoes are – if the whole thing was planned to smear the KGB. Sprague told me about something last night, another thing that could be a smear on the Bravoes. He assumed Charlie's Indians were behind it, but . . . I stayed up thinking, then did a little paperwork today."

"Are you saying the Abbey was just part of a pattern?"

"It might be, just might – and that does make your fake copper more real. Less likely to be a one-man affair . . . but I'm not really an expert on these things, and I don't think you are, either. And we'll have to move canny on this, with the Steering Committee resolutely steering in the opposite direction . . . This instructor at the Fort: was he military or civilian?"

"Civilian, and a she. Miss Tuckey, Dorothy Tuckey."

"Ah yes." George had, of course, heard of her.

12

The reception at the American Ambassador's residence had been planned as a cheery thank-you for making the President's visit so smooth and uneventful. It was now doomed to be as cheery as watching a chess match in the rain. Probably like George himself, most of the guests had first decided to stay away, then decided that would look bad, and finally that perhaps things would seem brighter after the fifth drink. Certainly this theory was being given every chance.

George grabbed the one full glass off a tray and looked round for cover. In one corner there was a television personality wearing a television personality shirt, just in case you couldn't place the face; another corner was full of political lords, faded or bloated according to their own tastes. Then, thankfully, he saw Scott-Scobie of the Foreign Office wedged on a sofa between an American songwriter and a woman in gold Lurex scales that turned her into a gilded lizard. Scott-Scobie caught George's eye and smiled desperately.

"I told him," the songwriter was saying, "'Why are you putting the accents in the wrong places in my lyrics?' So he said, 'Okay, I'll change them.' Just like that."

"He never did breathe right," the woman said.

Scott-Scobie muttered an apology and heaved himself upright; he was mid-forties, plump and pink with curly dark hair and usually known as 'Swinging S-S', but there was no swing in him tonight. He drained his glass. "Welcome to the funeral of the Special Relationship."

George looked around for a tray. "What're you drinking?"

"Everything. And it doesn't seem to make a whit of difference. Have you ever noticed that? – colds and misery seem to sop up alcohol, leaving you stone cold sober. Scientific fact. Why didn't I run away to Australia as a lad?"

"You wouldn't have liked it: it's got Australians in it."

"Into each life some Australians must fall. Anyway, they'll probably be the only allies we've got by the end of the year, being too far away to have heard of Berlin."

The reminder settled on George like a wet overcoat. "Did they go ahead with the OD Committee then?"

"They did," Scott-Scobie said grimly. "We're going to talk to the Russians. Unilaterally."

"Lord." George made a two-handed grab at a scurrying tray. "I thought they might have postponed it, with Barling not yet in his grave . . ."

"He wasn't part of the OD Committee." Scott-Scobie gulped and then peered into his glass to see what he was gulping. "And do please remember I've said nothing."

"What's the next move?"

"My lips are sealed. If they weren't, I might tell you that a Russian delegation will arrive here disguised as caviare salesmen to work out the preliminaries, then there'll be some sort of crash conference in Helsinki or Vienna. My side's been pleading to go slow, bury it in the Geneva talks – damn it, the Russians will play along. They've got half of what they want just by an agreement to talk. Splits us off from" – he flapped a loose hand at the room, the Americans, the French, the West German Minister-Counsellor explaining British education to a Dutch Admiral – "all of them. But the PM wants some signed paper to wave at the House and prove he's got a diplomatic breakthrough even if it only says Peace In Our Time in Russkie. Oh well, maybe somebody'll assassinate the delegation when it gets here."

"Scottie, don't *say* such things."

"No, I suppose it wouldn't be for the best. So you'd better see to it that nothing happens."

"Security details are not my province," George protested, recalling just how much, together with Culliman, he had made it his province. But my God, he thought, if Barling really had been the target, could the visiting Russians be next? He shuddered.

There was a sudden hush in the big, crowded room. The Ambassador and his wife had come in from receiving guests in the hall and the crowd was parting in front of them as for Royalty – although mainly because nobody wanted to talk to him. However resolutely one chattered of the weather and education, the sole topic of the evening was written in haggard lines down the Ambassador's pale face.

Then two elderly women stepped bravely forward – American, from the determination to look their best at any age which set them so far apart from the comfortable dowdiness of the British wives. The crowd relaxed into babble again, but the reshuffle had revealed their corner to James Ferrebee, who was broad-shouldering his way towards them. George didn't much want to meet Ferrebee again so soon.

But Scott-Scobie had decided that the only way to be rid of his misery was to pass it on. "Evening, James. We were just discussing whether or not to let Persons Unknown bump off your visiting Russkies. Got them all flight-planned and booked into the best haunts of capitalism?"

Ferrebee glowered down at them. "We were rather hoping that the visit could be handled without help from the cocktail party circuit. And that MoD won't be taking precautions against an American strike on London whilst they're here."

George hunched his shoulders and mumbled into his glass.

"And the Primate's trip?" Scott-Scobie went on cheerily. "That's all lined up?"

"The what?" George asked.

"Don't you read your *Church Times*?"

"Of course I don't."

"You should, George, you should. Your spiritual life must be sadly empty if you don't know who's just been appointed vicar of Sodbury-in-the-Wold. Nor, apparently, that the Archbishop of Canterbury has a long-standing commitment to preach in Berlin on All Saints' Day. He speaks good German, doesn't he, Jim?"

Ferrebee nodded. "He'll be addressing the Berlin Senate, too."

"Splendid. And knowing the old boy's views, I wouldn't be surprised if he slipped in a few words about sticking together on their fair city. A ray of hope yet."

"It'll doubtless be widely reported in the *Church Times*," George grumped.

"It'll get splashed in the Berlin papers," Ferrebee said tartly. "Ours will have to carry something."

"And in *Pravda*," Scott-Scobie added. "They take our church leaders seriously. *They* spread that nasty story about the ArchB and choirboys."

George looked from one to other of them. "Does your Minister approve of this?"

"Good Lord, no," Scott-Scobie grinned. "Our Master thinks it's a quite frightful idea. But we're doing what we can: James here is going over with him. Unofficially, of course – he's taking a few days' leave – but we can still hope that our Jim's well-known diplomatic talents will persuade the ArchB to tone down his remarks a little."

If Ferrebee had any outstanding talent for diplomacy, he had kept it hidden from George – and, to judge by his career, from the Foreign Office itself. But now even he was wearing a bleak smile to match Scott-Scobie's grin.

George shrugged. "Well, if your Minister really thinks that . . ."

"Who knows what our Minister thinks? More to the point, he hasn't been in the job long enough to know who half of us are, let alone what *we* might think. He's just happy that one of his loyal servants will be on hand."

Ferrebee said: "I was going anyway. I have an old friend who's chief pilot for Brentwood Systems; they run a Jetstream and think it would be good public relations to fly the Archbishop over in something like comfort. With his arthritis he can't really take ordinary airline seating."

"Who can?" Scott-Scobie asked. "Those European flights have become positively conjugal. I must say I wouldn't mind you laying on a private plane for me one of these days, James."

"I think I might be well into retirement before you develop arthritis, let alone any religious convictions." Ferrebee's voice had become austere.

"Well, there you have it, George. ArchB denounces

Berlin betrayal, Foreign Sec Sees The Light, reconvenes the OD Committee for prayer meeting and reversal of its decision. Hallelujah, brothers, hallelujah."

Ferrebee was looking down at Scott-Scobie as if he were a blocked lavatory. "There was a time when a statement by the Primate of All England on the morality of a given foreign policy was, *had* to be, taken seriously."

"There was a time," Scott-Scobie said, suddenly morose, "when the word of an Englishman meant something. It meant that, no matter what he'd said, he'd act in his own best interests. It doesn't even mean that, now. Berlin today, Sodbury-in-the-Wold tomorrow. I think I'll become a drunk like George."

George couldn't even summon up the spirit to feel offended.

13

Old pilots, ones who first trained on slow propeller-engined aircraft, cannot watch the countryside flowing past a train or car window without subconsciously evaluating fields for an emergency landing: length, slope, obstructions on approach, surface . . . It is much the same for career soldiers: to Maxim, the low steep Cotswold hills with their clumps of woodland were close-combat country, difficult for tanks and air reconnaissance, needing tight control to attack. It reminded him of the north bank of the Marne, around Château Thierry and Belleau Wood where the German advance of 1918 had been fought to a halt and the American Marines had left one of the most impressive cemeteries of the war. Battles in such country-side would always leave impressive cemeteries; you got too close to take prisoners.

Miss Dorothy Tuckey's 'cottage' – an honorary title in the Cotswolds just as 'Colonel' is in Texas – sat in a web of low walls like roots of the building spreading above ground. Just across one wall were the trimmed yews and squat tower of a church, so perhaps it had originally been built for the verger. Like the village beyond and everything they had passed for the last ten miles, it was made of local limestone, grey-yellow as if the bleak sky had seeped into the stone the moment it had been cut from the earth. Indeed, given the mossy sway-backed roof and baize-green lawns, the sky was the only thing that saved the cottage from looking as charming as a kitten in a basket; George had pronounced the gusty showers as "typical Cotswold weather" before they had cleared London.

The figure in the front garden was very different from the Miss Tuckey Maxim remembered at the Fort. Squat

84

and booted, an old anorak rucked up above a wide trouser seat and the hood pulled lopsidedly over her tall curls, she was eyeing the flowerbeds with the grim resolve of a drill corporal meeting a recruit platoon.

"Mr Harbinger?" Spectacles and teeth glinted damply under the hood. "I won't try to shake hands. It's such a mess, I haven't even started on the bulbs . . . Hello, I've met you before." She beamed at Maxim. "You were on course at the Fort. Jabberwock, wasn't it?"

George introduced Maxim properly, then stood in the drizzle to enthuse over the roses while Maxim, who hadn't touched a garden since the age of six, shuffled his feet on the flagged path. It pleased Miss Tuckey, but he was glad when she took them inside and made tea.

"Now what brings the War House out here on a Saturday afternoon?"

George coughed and said gruffly, "I'd like you to be quite sure who I am" – he handed over his MoD pass – "and I'm going to sound a bit pompous and mention the Official Secrets Acts – "

"Oh yes, I have to sign a declaration every time the Army takes me on for another job. I think I've got the gist of them by now."

"Good. But I want to emphasise the need-to-know principle and ask you not to discuss this business with anybody except myself. Not even Harry here, if you can't get me. And if nothing more comes of it, perhaps you'd just forget we were ever here . . . I'm sorry to sound melodramatic."

Miss Tuckey laughed a blast of cigarette smoke. "I've spent most of my life getting mixed up in things that sound melodramatic from the outside. Carry on."

But it wasn't that easy for George. He took a thin sheaf of badly typed – by himself – papers from his briefcase and shuffled them as if reluctant to let them go. He had, although he would have snorted at the idea, a civil servant's fundamental fear of seeming ridiculous. It might have been his subconscious self, being more honest, who had insisted on Maxim giving up a day with his son to come and make sure he went through with this.

"I've got résumés of . . . ah, *happenings*, spread over the last two months which I'd like you to look at. See if you can give an opinion on whether they're related."

"Happenings?" She leant to take the papers but George clung on to them. "In my sort of field? Do you mean acts of sabotage?"

"Er . . . could I just say 'covert acts'? The word 'destabilisation' has been mentioned . . ."

"A carpet-bag word these days, Mr Harbinger. If you only have a list of *happenings* – is that the latest Whitehall word? – it's likely to be very incomplete. I don't mean that unkindly: destabilisation is usually a very wide affair, trying to change a whole climate of opinion, and you use as many methods as you can. You spread rumours that somebody is too old for the job – as a faction seems to be doing about a certain church-warden in this village, although they'd be horrified to think they were using the tactics of the more activist intelligence agencies."

"But not only rumours?"

"Oh no. That's just one element. At the other end of the spectrum, terrorism is also destabilising: blackmailing a government into changing a policy, or destroying the government by showing it can't maintain law and order. Are your happenings doing that?"

"Ah – no."

Miss Tuckey pondered. "I'm not too sure how much help I can be . . . I preach Resistance against illegal governments; destabilisation is a way of putting *in* an illegal government. Of course, there may be some overlap of basic techniques in the field of secret behaviour . . . Well, I can but try."

But George stayed clutching the papers. "If you could just . . . see if there appears to be any pattern, any direction . . ."

Miss Tuckey raised her eyebrows above her elegant glasses. "Surely, if any pattern of events were directed against the State, it would be for the Security Service to make a judgement?"

George snorted. "Not with that old blatherskite in command. And that's really why I didn't want to become too official at this point . . ." Since he found it difficult to be unofficial without sounding more official than usual, he almost added 'in time' but stopped himself, in time. "So if you'd be kind enough . . . ?"

At last he let go of the papers.

Once you have a low-ceilinged rambling room with a big fireplace and leaded windows, it would probably look 'cosy' if you furnished it with one of Security's ICL2980 computer banks. As it was, Miss Tuckey had left the furnishing to time: the room seemed to have been filled by inheritance, travel, and the need for things to put things in and on. George was wallowing on a shapeless chintz sofa, while Maxim sat in a 'modern' Danish chair that looked more out of date after twenty years than did the Regency table under the window – a north window, to protect the rosewood top from the sun – where Miss Tuckey spread out the papers. She lit another cigarette and called over her shoulder: "Help yourself to more tea, please."

George made one polite wriggle like a beached whale and let Maxim pour, then wander round to look at the pictures and books. There were lots of both, by now covering all but a few per cent of the yellowing wallpaper so that redecorating the room was virtually impossible. There were engravings of French châteaux, water-colours of the Holy Land and Scotland in the style of travelling clerics and maiden aunts, and photographs in whatever frames happened to fit them: a college graduation group, portraits of men and women in 1945 uniforms, other small groups in more modern plain clothes.

"You've included the Reznichenko Memorandum," Miss Tuckey commented. "Do you have any . . . *particular* reason for that?"

"I'd prefer if you'd just judge for yourself," George said politely, "from what shows above the surface."

Neither in the photographs nor the books did Miss Tuckey make the least attempt to hide her interest in irregular warfare, but upon reflection, why should she? She had impressed on them at the Fort that the more people who knew the rules of secret war, the more would be good at it. She wanted a country ready to rise, invisibly, in arms. The books included Orlov, Che Guevara, the IRA handbook, M.R.D. Foot, Miksche, three by Miss

Tuckey herself . . . Maxim took down a small American paperback about ambushing semi-armoured cars; it was remarkably frank stuff.

"The trouble is, most of our best people didn't write books." He realised she was talking to him. "They were terribly dedicated; the moment the war was over – or they thought it was – they threw themselves into making the peace work. Became teachers, missionaries, New Town planners; they believed in things. You really had to; it got too lonely otherwise." She coughed heartily and sat down opposite George.

"Let me say this," she began carefully; "that I cannot see, from these incidents and anything I've noticed for myself, that there is any destabilisation campaign directed against the government. If anything is going on, it's directed against one aspect of government policy: relations with the Soviets and the Warsaw Pact countries. It may be even narrower than that.

"Normally, one only wants to change one or two aspects of a government's policy, but one attacks on the broadest front possible. Suggest that its health programme lets babies die, that its ministers are building beach-houses with money diverted from slum clearance, that its generals buy too many tanks that they can't maintain. Now, all these things may be true – they often are – but one really only cares that the government is getting too cosy with Moscow or, from the other side, Washington. But you launch your covert attacks on all these other points because everybody knows that babies and slum clearance are good, beach-houses and tanks bad – people who may have only the haziest idea of where Moscow and Washington are or what they mean. And of course, this has the added advantage of concealing your true reason for wanting that government overthrown.

"That is very important. The objective of a Resistance movement is plain. You try to keep its members secret, but want everybody to believe that they're lurking behind every door. A destabilisation campaign has its best chance if it cannot be proven that it is going on at all. Am I really telling you anything new, Mr Harbinger?"

George smiled reflexively. "You're putting it with, shall

I say? – rather more honesty than one usually finds in this field. How does this apply to this present situation? *Is* there a present situation?"

With obvious reluctance, Miss Tuckey shuffled the papers into two piles. "Don't you have computers for just this sort of thing? Analysing events and finding patterns?"

"Oh yes: you wait six months for somebody to write it a programme, feed in the data and quick as a flash you have a gas bill for a million pounds and twopence."

Miss Tuckey grinned and held out the two clutches of paper. "Those I think back up your theory; these I rather doubt."

George flicked through the Yes pile. "You've decided in favour of the Reznichenko Memorandum, then."

"Well, you know, Moscow really ought to be able to get money into organisations more subtly than that – but that's the one thing they can't say in their own defence. It would have needed some professional skills, and some inside knowledge of Lord Ettington's behaviour which I don't have. Perhaps you do."

George just smiled at that. "And the shooting at the Abbey."

"Well . . . when somebody takes the trouble – and skill – to get past a security cordon and fires off a rifle at, what would it be? – forty yards?"

"Nearer thirty," Maxim said.

"And hits somebody in the heart, then I'm bound to wonder if he didn't intend to do that all along. I think I was talking about that up at the Fort."

Maxim nodded.

"And the KGB should be able to do better, just as with the Reznichenko Memorandum. But – and everybody goes around saying that the press always gets the facts wrong – here the facts were a Russian rifle, grenade and the telephone numbers. Those facts weren't wrong, though I'm pretty sure the inference was. You have the KGB looking very active at a time when, I would have thought, it would be trying to stay out of the limelight – in this country, at least. But a lot of people in a lot of pubs are going to be saying: But if they didn't actually arrange it, they must have given them the weapons and telephone numbers. It was a good smear."

George shuffled the papers for a moment. "But you don't think they tried to smear the KGB by planting that story about the Archbishop and the choirboys?"

"Because that made the KGB look clumsy – in our sophisticated eyes? No, it's another example of what I've been saying. A lot of European, Catholic, peasants are sitting around in their cafés saying they could well believe it of a leader of a Church which, to them, is a heresy. On the balance of trade, Mr Harbinger, I think the KGB would count that a successful smear. And how do you penetrate the KGB's disinformation line? I doubt if even our friends at Langley could pull that off."

George grunted and shuffled on. "But you accept that somebody could have been behind Westerman's performance at the Church House disarmament conference?"

"You chose all these examples," Miss Tuckey pointed out. "All I'd say there is that it's no great trick to make a man seem drunk if you know he'll take a drink before going on to the platform. You need access to his drink – but it was presumably in a crowded room – and a little chemistry, but one man in the right place could do it."

"It was a great show," George remembered, chuckling. "I heard a private tape of it. One felt he rather lost the Methodist vote when he called the Bishops a bunch of limp old pricks . . . I do apologise."

But Miss Tuckey rocked with laughter. Maxim had expected her to wobble – she had enough figure for it – but she must have been very tightly corseted.

George put the papers face down on the sofa, so Maxim gave up the attempt to read over his shoulder and gazed across at another collection of photographs on the opposite wall.

"So," George said; "on the balance of this trade . . . ?"

"Oh Lord." Miss Tuckey slumped back and fingered her pursed lips. "We have two prominent anti-NATO campaigners made to look like traitors or fools, two apparent instances of the KGB interfering clumsily in our affairs . . . all a bit fortuitous. Yes, I have to say there's something going on, but . . ."

"But?"

"It's all very small-scale. A true, broad-front destabil-isation campaign would take a lot of men, money and organisation. Even if you limited it to undermining the government's soft policy on Russia in Europe, I'd still expect a back-up of pro-NATO articles planted in the press, lecturers offering their services free on the circuit (and nobody's approached me), nasty rumours about our ministers floated in the Continental papers . . . all needing a lot of organisation, a lot of money."

"Like Charlie India Alpha."

"Indeed. The CIA's the only people who could take it on – and it's the only way that they'd do it. They do throw money and men at a problem. But that suggests to me that they aren't behind this. Perhaps thirty years ago, when they were just getting started with the old wartime OSS people and not much funding . . . Oh, but not now. Anyway, we keep talking about the right people in the right places. Those would all have to be British, just to have the access."

"These people don't sound like a bunch of amateurs."

"No, there's some training and knowledge there, and they have the right toys: Russian typewriter, rifle, grenade and so on. But no back-up to broaden the attack." She lit a cigarette and blew a blast of smoke towards the ceiling beams. "Tell me, Mr Harbinger, do you think these people are winning?"

George went very still except for a perplexed blinking. "No-o . . . from where I stand I don't think they've influenced the Cabinet in any significant way, not on its policy towards Russia . . ."

"Then perhaps that isn't what they're trying to do. Perhaps that *is* their broad front, and they're trying to achieve something narrower within that. They may well have anticipated that somebody, like yourself, would see a pattern after a time, and they wouldn't want that pattern to give away their true, more limited objective. Cover within cover. If you bury your diamonds in the back garden, you put your amethysts above them and rhine-stones above those – and hope people will stop digging too soon."

George clasped his hands and frowned at them. "Can you suggest . . . ?"

"After a few minutes' study of half a dozen *happenings*? You flatter me."

"Then . . . we have a bunch of people, not amateurs, not Charlie's Indians, but with the right toys and training . . . Can you suggest who – ?"

"Definitely not." Very quick and clear. "You came to me and asked if I, with my background, could see a pattern. I've given you as honest an answer as I can, and perhaps a little more, but all I'm doing is sitting here theorising in a Cotswold village. To start guessing at names is a very different matter."

"I didn't get as far as mentioning names."

"You were going to, Mr Harbinger," she smiled. "You were going to."

George stared at his brogues, turning his feet inward to study the flecks of Cotswold mud he had picked up between the car and the cottage. "This visit is unofficial, as I said, and we're only dealing with theories and patterns, as I think you said. But" – he looked up suddenly – "if anything further happens to make this less theoretical, I'd like you to remember what these people are doing: working against our system of government. I'm not asking what you think of our current Prime Minister and Cabinet; it's the system that's being threatened. Two people are dead already, at the Abbey. Harry had to shoot one of them." Miss Tuckey flicked her glance at Maxim, but her quiet smile stayed unchanged.

"So" – George heaved himself to his feet with a grunt – "if I come back more officially, I would be grateful, most grateful, for any names you might guess at. And thank you for your hospitality, most kind . . ."

Taking a sudden chance, Maxim asked; "If there's anything we might have forgotten, could we give you a ring later on? Will you be in?"

George stared at him suspiciously. Miss Tuckey said: "Well, if you . . . but really I don't think I can say any more. I've given you my theory and that's all I deal in these days. Nobody's going to trust an old woman living alone out here with any facts."

Maxim guessed that was directed more at George than himself, but persisted: "You know how there's always something, some small thing . . ."

"Certainly, if you like – only do remember this isn't a secure line. I shall be going out for about an hour after dinner, just a parochial committee meeting, but . . ."

"Thank you very much. If we call, we'll make sure it's in doubletalk. And before I go, might I use your loo?"

"For God's sake put a tourniquet on it," George muttered, impatient to be off. But he had to wait, and then again at the front door when Maxim suddenly started reminiscing about his unfinished course at the Fort.

Driving back up the village street, George jerked annoyed looks at Maxim, who was studying the map. "What got into you there? I thought you were going to ask her for a date, next. Falling for older women's one thing, but there has to be a cut-off point."

"Where can we buy a camera around here?"

"A *camera*? Do you want to go back and take snapshots of her? In her gardening boots and nothing else, perhaps. Dear God, there has to be a law against people like you. No great-grandmother's going to be safe . . ."

"Yes, I want to go back. But not until she's out. One of the photos on her wall: it's got the fake cop from the Abbey in it."

George didn't say anything silly like 'Are you sure?'; he just drove half a mile in silence, then asked: "Why didn't you get some sort of warning to me? I was babbling on – "

"I didn't spot it until we'd nearly finished. And – I wasn't sure how you'd react."

"After twenty-something years in Whitehall I can dissemble my true feelings with reasonable adequacy."

Maxim said stolidly: "What about this camera? We can't get into Oxford before the shops shut. How about Bourton-on-the-Water? I seem to know the name."

"One of the prettiest tourist traps in England. Garden gnomes and home-made cakes. Garden gnomes *eating* home-made cakes."

"Sounds a likely place to sell cameras, then. Turn right when you reach the A424."

"Just to get things clear, you're proposing to break and enter the aforesaid cottage?"

"Proving that fake copper exists is rather important to me."

"Yes, yes, I do see . . . and I suppose you want me to hold your torch and spare jemmy?"

"Up to you, but now you mention it, I'll need some tools. What sort of kit d'you have in this car?"

"How should I know? Whatever you get with a Rover, unless somebody's pinched them."

Maxim knew that George, essentially a countryman, was more familiar with tools and machinery than he cared to remember in his London orbit. But he could also believe that George hadn't bothered to examine the tool kit of his new car. "Well, I should be able to pick up a pair of pliers in this Bourton place you speak so highly of."

"God Almighty."

Maxim smiled comfortingly. "Don't worry. I'm sure Annette'll wait for you."

"After jail, or Bourton-on-the-Water?"

14

They drove back out of Bourton in the gloomy, still gusty dusk, but even in that light the village, sprawled around a shallow stream criss-crossed with toy bridges, had an undeniable if rather practised charm. And even in that season it was bustling with foreign tourists in foreign-tourist hats. "They ought to be buying jars of Cotswold mud and water," George grumbled. "Shake 'em up like those snowstorm globes to remind them of their holiday in Merry England . . . Does it have to be tonight? I mean, we could go back in a few days and I could distract her while you . . ."

It was cold feet, but probably only on behalf of the ministry, the government, the whole structure that George derided and had committed his life to. Senior civil servants just could not be caught burgling cottages; Army officers had, perhaps, a more flexible public image.

"The picture might not still be there in a few days," Maxim said patiently. "If she's involved herself, we've tipped her off. If she guesses somebody she knows is involved – and she must know the fake cop in the picture – she could tip them off. And start covering up for them. And this evening, at least we know she's out. But I can do this by myself."

"No, if you're in, I'm in. I started all this." That at least was an attitude that owed almost nothing to the Civil Service. Then, afraid he might have sounded gallant, George added: "Somebody's got to make sure your military instinct for loot doesn't take over."

Working on George's local knowledge – his father's home was less than an hour's drive away – they planned to reach Miss Tuckey's cottage at half past eight, when the other committee members would have had time to digest and drive in from the countryside. "These committees don't have the local roadsweeper on them. Did you get all the kit for your nefarious trade?"

"I think so. And a better camera than I'd expected." It was a 35mm affair, even if a rather simplified one, with a built-in flash. There had even been a cassette of fairly slow black-and-white film.

They had one drink – Maxim had never seen anyone order a triple Scotch before – and went on to eat at a roadside café. It had a bright plastic deep-fried atmosphere and menu but the alternative, as Maxim had pointed out, was a long slow dinner at some hotel where they would have made themselves conspicuous by not, repeat not, ordering a couple of bottles of wine.

"The Reznichenko Memorandum," he asked cautiously. "Is there anything I could be told about it?"

George thought, shrugged, and said: "Sprague told me in deepest confidence, but . . . It's a fake, all right. Five was tailing Ettington that night and he never met Reznichenko."

"Well, if Security's in on that, couldn't they be finding the same pattern that you have?"

"The Old Guard there, they might – but their new D-G's told them to lay off organisations like the Peace Crusade, so how can they admit they've found a pattern? That's why the only person they dared talk to was Sprague. So I wouldn't hold your breath for them to move."

"Well, there's still us."

"So it would seem. You're eating that stuff as if it were *food*." He was staring at Maxim's plate with real puzzlement; his own was still half-full. Roadside diners were not George's environment.

Back in the car, Maxim said: "I don't think I've ever heard you make anything but complaints about food. The Whitehall canteens, your clubs, any restaurants we've been in . . ."

"You've never heard me complain about Annette's cooking."

"I've never heard you say anything nice about it."

"Well, she knows it's good. How are you – we – going to do this?"

"The front door's a Banham lock, I don't fancy my chances with that, but the kitchen door's just an ordinary job and a couple of bolts. She doesn't use the top one, it's jammed with paint, and I loosened the saddle on the other when I was pretending to have a piss. You know," he added thoughtfully, "if she's keeping any secrets in that place, she's not trying very hard, with a back-door lock like that. It should be easy."

"I'm glad more people don't take that view."

"Have you ever been burgled?"

"Not in Albany, but in Hertfordshire, yes."

"Did they pick their way in neatly?"

"The devil they did, they broke about every – "

"Exactly. If you're going to strip a house anyway, why do a neat job on the lock first? Lock-picking's almost entirely an intelligence trade by now. Can you pull in at the next lay-by?"

They stopped on a straight stretch of upland road, blatantly obvious, and since there was a can of oil in the boot Maxim opened the bonnet to give them a cover story of the oil warning light having come on. The car itself, a new Rover 3500, was far from memorable in Gloucestershire; it was probably the only British saloon a local landowner would think of owning.

He had bought three large tins of pilchards. He took off their opener keys and, with gloved thumb and a pair of heavy pliers, bent the ends with the tin-opening slot to right angles. With a small hacksaw he cut the bent ends to fractionally different lengths.

"I could have used nails," he explained, "but if you get one thick enough it's a bugger to bend without a vice. And then you probably have to file a flat side on it: a real picklock's square-sectioned. This should give a bit more grip on the bolt."

"I hope this is an inborn talent and not something you learnt at the taxpayers' expense. You don't think she'll suspect something? Just by the coincidence of time: we visit her, the same evening, she's burgled."

"The whole idea is she *won't* know she's been done. I could get in far easier by just busting a window."

"Sorry," George said humbly. "In Whitehall one gets

too reliant on the old school tie to open doors for one."

Although it must have been over a hundred years old, the cottage was still on the edge of the village simply because there was no building land beyond it. The back garden ended at a short steep scarp falling away to a small stream crossed only by a footbridge. On the other side of the stream there was a collection of farm buildings, but they linked to a different road further down. Maxim bypassed the village completely, map-reading George up a third road above the farm and they left the car there, with perhaps a quarter-mile walk down into the valley and up again to the cottage.

The night sky was still clouded, picking up just a hint of the glow from the street lights that silhouetted the church, trees and houses on the opposite crest. They climbed one wall, to get away from the car, and waited for their eyes and ears to tune themselves to the darkness. They heard, and then stopped hearing, the wind breathing in the trees overhead and the stream rustling in the valley. The silence grew very quiet and the occasional noises very loud, and they began to belong. Maxim touched George's arm and they moved carefully down the slope and, well upstream from the farm, stepped into the stinging cold water.

Maxim scouted the cottage to make sure it was empty, then helped George over the corner of the dry-stone wall, where it seemed strongest, and guided him under a face-high clothes-line strung across the little lawn. The kitchen door was much younger than the cottage, with two frosted glass panels in the top half.

He tried two of the pilchard keys in the lock and put one away immediately. He kept on with the other, probing and turning gently, feeling the movement. The Intelligence Corps instructor who had taught him the trade would have had such a lock open with one twist, but Maxim was out of practice and the lock was old and arthritic.

"Torch."

George fumbled out the little pinhole torch and watched as Maxim delicately smeared a film of shoe polish on the end of his key, then probed again and immediately withdrew it to study the marks on the polish. He did that several times until he had established the depth to reach the lock and bolt and, he now knew, a single spring-loaded tumbler holding it in place. Depth is half the game in lock-picking; the other half is getting enough leverage for the turn, since even a proper pick has no shaft going right through to rest on the end ward like a real key. He took out the pliers, settled the pilchard key firmly in their jaws, pushed it to a precise distance into the keyhole, and turned. For a moment he wasn't sure if the sudden give and click was the lock opening or the key breaking, but then the door almost unbalanced him by swinging open. He froze.

But no sound came from inside the house and the lights, as he'd already checked, were all off. He eased the door right open so it wouldn't swing and slam.

"She didn't use the bolt," he whispered. "I needn't have bothered. Take off your shoes and socks: we don't want to leave wet prints all over."

"I'll freeze."

"Tough. Off."

"I remember now why I left the Army," George muttered through clenched teeth. "It was pigs of majors like you."

They left their shoes and socks outside. Maxim shut the door behind them, then fixed the loosened bolt saddle firmly with Superglue.

There was an unguarded wood fire flickering in the room where they had sat with Miss Tuckey, throwing deceptive shadows that stretched and shrank quickly on the walls. All the curtains were already drawn. George had wisely slipped into a pattern of complete obedience, and moved silently around the room to establish aiming points with the torch on the pictures Maxim indicated. Shooting at a slight angle to avoid the flash reflecting from the picture glass, and cheating on the film speed setting because he was so close to the wall, Maxim took three pictures of the man he had seen at the Abbey, and one of every other recent-looking group or portrait. It all went very quickly and smoothly, and he still had half the film left.

He ran the torch over the shelves, cabinets, table drawers, but there were no more photographs and no obvious photo albums. Upstairs? It didn't seem likely: the first floor was in the roof itself, with sloping outside walls and few places to hang pictures. The tiny beam of light flickered over the telephone – and back. It was in its cradle, but the mouthpiece end looked crooked. He lifted it carefully and got no dial tone, then saw the plungers were taped down. He unscrewed the mouthpiece, which had been hastily jammed on and caught by the thread. By then he wasn't surprised at what he found.

"What is it?" George breathed in his ear.

Maxim said nothing. He laid the telephone and torch back on the table, then probed delicately with the end of a penknife. Inside a minute, he had the substitute microphone and its extra wires in his hand.

"Okay," he said softly.

"Was it being put in or taken out?"

"Don't know. But they hadn't finished." He looked around the flickering shadows from the firelight. "I'm going upstairs."

"Harry, let's just get out of here." He had to say it; he knew it wouldn't make any difference. Maxim put the camera down, picked up a poker from the hearth and started for the stairway.

The stairs creaked, even where he placed his feet carefully at the wall side, and the ludicrous self-portrait of himself as a householder, properly armed with a poker, going *upstairs* to hunt burglars made him stop to tauten his thoughts. He reached the top charged with a cold, dangerous instinct, as he needed.

Street lighting seeped into the tiny landing from an open door, so at least some curtains were undrawn and he daren't use the torch. The open door might be an invitation, but he didn't want to turn his back to it. He planted one foot carefully to stop the door being swung in his face, and took a breath of air that was wrongly warm and sour. Then the door moved.

It jerked his foot, banged his knee and was yanked back open. He jabbed the poker at chest height of a moving figure and then his eyes were stung closed with pain.

He threw himself forward, touched and held an arm, was hit in the stomach but clung on, dropping the poker and hauling the man to him. The man clasped him, foolishly, because in Maxim's blindness contact was safest. He jerked his arms loose and reached for the head, trying to blink the searing pain from his eyes. He couldn't; in his double darkness, he had no choice. He killed the man.

In the gasping aftermath, he had no idea of where he was, nor how much noise he had made. It must have been a lot. His blind hands found the still-open door and then there was George, very close, whispering: "Harry, what happened, are you all right?"

"I'm blinded. Where's a wash-basin?"

"Christ . . ."

Maxim swamped his eyes with water, time and again, dulling the pain except when he tried to see. It was better to keep his eyes closed.

George was back at his shoulder. "How is it? What was it?"

"Chilli powder, I think." Some of the water had stung Maxim's lips and tongue.

"You know he's dead?"

"Sorry. I didn't know if he was armed or . . . Who was he?"

"God, I don't know. Come on, I'll help – "

"Get his wallet. Something."

"Harry, d'you know what they've done to *her*?"

"What?"

"She – she's dead anyway. Come *on*."

"Get his wallet."

George had himself once been a soldier. He didn't tell himself that, since he was no longer on speaking terms with himself, he just obeyed an order and rummaged through the man's pockets as if he were checking a suit going to the cleaners'. Then swabbed the wash-basin clean, guided Maxim downstairs and found their shoes and socks, moving with a numb efficiency that abstracted him from the terrors of his imagination. The last minute had left him naked in a desert of infinite horror. He would live for ever with the torchlight glimpse of a wide-eyed corpse dribbling blood from a broken neck, and see Miss

Tuckey's eyes above the gag that smelled of vomit and was stained with more blood from, he had to realise, a deliberately bitten tongue . . .

From the ramparts of Whitehall he had got no glimpse of such realities of the secret world, no hint from the sanitised prose of intelligence reports. And if that showed how high the ramparts were, they seemed immeasurably higher from the outside. They would never accept him back. Career, family, home – all had been ruined in a few seconds. He found himself making imploring promises to God, then retreated into hating himself, and Maxim of course.

"Take the picture," Maxim ordered, still blind.

"What?"

"The photograph on the wall, *the* one. Take it. It won't matter now."

What could anything matter now? And then they were in the sanctuary – however temporary – of the wide cool night.

15

He started the car by letting it run downhill – Maxim had insisted they park so that there would be no give-away noise of the starter – and drove steadily for several miles. Almost as steadily, he told Maxim of what had happened to Miss Tuckey.

"Sounds as if she killed herself, then," Maxim deduced.

"She was handcuffed . . ."

"Who was the man?"

They were out on the anonymous A40; George pulled into a lay-by and gingerly fingered through the wallet with renewed twinges of horror. There was only money and a driving licence.

"Oldrich Praeger," he read. "Address in SW16, he must be . . . thirty-four," working out the age from the licence expiry date at age seventy. "Have been," he added gloomily.

"We can get it chased up, but it's probably one they hand out to anybody about the right age when they're on the job." Having no photograph, a driving licence is thin proof of identity. "All it tells us is he must've had a foreign accent, for them to give him a name like that. I should have got you to photograph him," he added. George came close to retching.

When he'd swallowed he said: "The police will find him. And then . . ."

"D'you really think so?" Maxim turned his red-rimmed eyes at George, winced with pain even at the feeble car light, and shut them again. "Those boys are going to go back. They've got a lot of clearing up to do – more than they expect, now. But the police won't find a thing unless we call them."

"Harry – you *killed* that man!"

"I've said I was sorry – "

"*Sorry?* We were there illegally, we broke in, when they find that out they'll . . ." But the future horror was too big for words.

"George, they aren't going to find out a thing if we don't tip them off. Don't you see who we're up against? Your Kilo Golf Bravoes."

The truth was that George hadn't been thinking about anything except himself. Maxim's assumption came as a relief – and a very obvious fact. He had wondered how the KGB would react to the Reznichenko Memorandum; now he saw they must have been analysing the pattern long before it had occurred to him. The Abbey would simply have stamped PROVEN on their file.

Maxim was well ahead in his thinking. "They must have bugged her for the same reason we went to see her: she was somebody unofficial but experienced in underground work – *They'd* know they were up against some British group, not the CIA. Perhaps they bugged a dozen other people as well, but they'd only hear you and me talking about naming names on her bug. It's probably one that picks up conversations in the room as well as just on the phone, but I can show it to the boys at – "

"*Harry*" – impossibly, yet further darkness had dawned on the total blackness of George's conscience – "then we led them to her. *We got her killed!*"

Exasperated, Maxim opened his eyes and glared through the pain. "They're killers. They had her phone bugged before we even thought of going there – and they were never going to leave her alive once they'd started asking her questions; how could they? Just as they couldn't leave that bug in her phone. She did the one thing she could to screw them up by killing herself first. So don't waste that: make an anonymous phone call."

George turned the ignition key, very slowly, and jumped when the engine started. "But – what will the police think happened to . . . *him?*"

"Who cares?" Maxim sat back, closing his eyes against his ineffective tears.

George came out of the call box sounding shaken and pensive. "I told them it was a murder and all they wanted to know was my name . . . Does holding a handkerchief over the mouthpiece really disguise your voice?"

"I shouldn't think so, but – "

"They always do it in films."

"You're not a public figure, nobody knows your voice. What did they *say*?"

"They wanted more details and I said it was a murder, dammit, and why didn't they do something about it, and he said 'Another of those,' and . . . well, they *must* do something. Mustn't they?"

"It's Saturday night, they probably get a lot of hoax calls from drunks." Maxim wished he had made the call himself, even if George had had to look up and dial the number for him. But the police would *have* to react – wouldn't they?

George was in no mood to hang around: he wanted to be back in the safety – illusory though it might be – of the big city, with a drink in his hand. He had some memory of having promised God to give up drinking, but God hadn't turned the clock back, so that didn't count any more. He skimmed Oxford on the bypass and settled to a steady seventy mph on the M40.

As London got nearer, his confidence trickled back. "Do you think they got anything out of her?" he asked.

"Names? No; she wouldn't commit suicide *after* talking. But we didn't get them either."

The thought damped George down for a few miles; then he asked: "How are the eyes?"

"Getting better."

"Chilli – a new weapon, for them."

Maxim just grunted. He was assuming that the spice had come from Miss Tuckey's kitchen, a makeshift to arm 'Praeger' while the others went to get a van or just new instructions, since they wouldn't have planned on removing a body. On leaving her dead, yes, but a whiff from a cyanide gun would have brought an automatic verdict of heart failure on a stout, elderly smoker.

The chilli also meant that Praeger had been just a wire man, with orders *not* to kill anybody who came at him, just blind them and run. That seemed obvious, now he had had time to think. He hoped George wasn't thinking the same thought.

But George was looking further forward. "With her background, it'll be referred to Special Branch and Five . . . and that fiddled telephone . . . and Praeger without any background – we should have left his wallet, but they'll trace something about him anyway – and then we can admit we went to see her – *once* – and what we talked about, and there we are."

"It'll all blow wide open – in a very narrow, quiet way." Maxim was fairly familiar with Whitehall by now.

"Just so. Even the present Cabinet won't want to admit it's had right-wing desperadoes running around interrupting the even tenor of its betrayals. No, there are Ways and Means, and whether by way or by mean, those persons will be traced and told to cease and desist. Or be charged with Barling's murder. It must go that way – mustn't it?"

Only it didn't. The local police had had a busy evening, with an exceptional number of hoax calls that led them to non-existent road accidents, drunken brawls and even – a touch that showed a nice appreciation of British susceptibilities – a rabid dog on the loose. George's murder call had sounded the phoniest of the lot; it had certainly been the most amateurish. A single policeman finally arrived to try the doors – all locked – and ask if the neighbours had heard anything suspicious. They hadn't. Not until Miss Tuckey had missed next morning's service did a neighbour with a key go in to see if she was all right.

By then the house was tidy – and empty. Miss Tuckey's car was gone, and so were some of her clothes and suitcases. She did go away a lot, but normally told somebody first, so it was odd. Eventually the police were called back, but they found nothing. The telephone was in one piece, there were no bloodstains, no signs of what they still call 'foul play' as if somebody had been kicked behind the referee's back. There might have been a rug and a sheet missing from the bedroom, a picture gone from the wall, an incomplete rack of spice jars. But imperfection and incompleteness are normalcy; sheets get torn, rugs stained and sent for cleaning, pictures need reframing, spice jars break on stone floors. The police agreed that her disappearance was odd, even suspicious, but oddness and suspicion are on every breath a policeman takes – and meanwhile, their offices are stacked with files of unquestionably real and still unsolved crimes. So the vicar signed a missing person report to be added to the dozens of others filed that day all over the country and that, until something else happened, would be that.

16

"The Army ought to start asking questions when she doesn't turn up for the next course at the Fort," George said hopefully. "And she must have relatives and friends. With her special background *somebody* must get suspicious. And if not, I'll see if I can think of an excuse to try and contact her myself."

"If the bodies never turn up," Maxim said, "and I assume they won't, I can't think what else there is to find."

It was like a Monday at a football club, with Saturday's umpteen-nil defeat to be analysed, and an injury list that promised worse to come. Knowing George despised soccer, Maxim didn't mention the thought, and in any case, George's feelings were more complex than his own. No evidence of two deaths meant no evidence of his involvement in them. In saving themselves, the Bravoes had saved George as well, although only from the consequences, not the horror. So perhaps God had turned the clock back, in a very God-like way. It wasn't, George felt, quite enough for him to renew any promises about alcohol.

Maxim just wanted to know where the battle lines now stood so that they could make new plans.

"I could try going back to the Steering Committee," he said, "and simply tell them what's happened. You needn't be mentioned; all my own work."

"I know you mean that, Harry," George sighed. "But as you say, what's to be found? Certainly nothing that proves a conspiracy. You'd simply be committing suicide: you're either a killer or some fruitcake who thinks he's a killer, and neither wanted in today's modern Army, thank you." He glanced to see how Maxim had taken the word 'killer', but saw only the usual polite smile.

George lifted a stack of the day's and Sunday's papers – none mentioned Miss Tuckey – and dropped them on the floor. "All right. Concentrate on the second man at the Abbey: call him Person Y. Where are we?"

Maxim opened his briefcase on the desk. "I got the photographs."

"Printed already? That's quick."

"Friends. They also looked at the bug from her phone. It's a new model, they were quite excited. And it was most likely picking us up in her room, as well as calls."

George was sifting through the snapshot-sized photographs Maxim had taken, identifying portraits of several people concerned with Resistance or Intelligence, and mostly now dead. Then he turned to the big original of the man Maxim remembered from the Abbey. It was actually of two men, smiling into the camera against a chunky city skyline. And now it was out of its glass frame, he could make out a faded signature at the bottom:

Jay Keyserling, St Louis, 1968.

"Good God, we're home and dry."

Maxim shook his head. "Wrong man. We want the other one."

"How d'you know?" George peered closer. Of the two men, one was, in indefinable but unmistakable details, American; the other, by seeming 'normal', was clearly British. The American was wearing a lapel badge, big enough for his own name and some other word. George, who didn't need glasses (as he kept telling people), reached for his magnifying glass.

"That's Keyserling," Maxim said. "The other word's CCOAC."

"Never heard of it." George glared at the picture. The Briton would, presumably, have also been issued with a name-badge, but with a British horror of self-advertisement had taken it off the moment he could. Blast his idiot Britishness.

"Some sort of business convention, fairly respectable – if you can have such a thing," he ruminated. The well-fitting lightweight suits were too expensive for academics yet too fashionable for government officials, and the ties were soberly striped. "In Saint Lewis, 1968."

"Is that how you pronounce it?" Maxim was surprised, having spent much of his life listening to various versions of what most people called 'The S'n Looey Blues'.

"Yes, and loud and clear on the Saint or they'll give you a ticket for Cincinnati, and it could be months before your next of kin were informed." He ruminated a while longer. "You're sure this man, the Brit – ?"

"As sure as I can be. He's younger, there, but I'd think that man would be around fifty now. About right."

"So we've got an identification on the wrong man, but it's the only path through the mire. Can you follow it up? He's probably a prosperous American businessman, prosperous enough to go to international conventions: try all the American and international reference books in our library, then the London Library. You're not a member, are you? I'll give them a tinkle. But don't approach their embassy yet . . .

"Of course," he added, "our Brit may not have known Miss Tuckey at all, since Keyserling signed this photo to her."

"Why not just send a picture of himself? Keyserling looks as if he could afford it. I think the Brit belongs, somehow."

"Yes . . . and I suppose, if the picture wasn't printed until after he'd gone home, Keyserling would send it anyway. So, action this day."

"Mind you," Maxim said, "I could go back to her cottage and have a second snoop, taking my time. There might be – "

"Harry, you are not to go near that cottage, not even *think* of going near it – and I can read your thoughts by now. They are a hell-broth of ideas to provoke coronaries and hair loss in middle-aged civil servants. Why don't you take up a hobby with a purely personal risk, like parachuting . . . Ah, sorry." He had forgotten Maxim's Special Air Service background.

"I've done thirty-two jumps and never quite got over the feeling that it would be better to arrive by chauffeur-driven Rolls."

"I thought it was supposed to be very exhilarating, once the 'chute opened."

"It is," Maxim agreed. "If you think of the only alternative."

Keyserling, Jay Pedersen, banker; b. Jefferson City Miss., Mar 1 1912; s. Frank Elmer and Ingrid . . . Maxim copied it all out, just in case, but without much hope because it ended: d. Jan 7 1979.

"So he was only sixty-six when God called in the loan," George commented, reading through it. "It's that Midwestern winter as does it; I was there in February once, I nearly turned up my toes then except they'd have snapped off . . . still, it's nice to have a banker dying early." George's brother-in-law banked. "Local bank, Navy commission in the war, Pacific, executive at First Chicago, back to home state at St Louis, rising to President of Merchants and Trappers (State) Bank, a pillar of the Bogie Club, the Board of Civic Progress and the Episcopalian Church . . . He seems about as straightforward a citizen as ever foreclosed on a widow and fifteen orphans, not a hint of creepy-crawliness, no European connections, not even any gaps." George was adept at reading entries in directories, official lists and Who's Whos from many countries which tried to skip the most interesting parts of a subject's life. "Good Lord, he wrote books, too: *Foreign Debt: A Pauper's Promise*, not exactly a snappy title, but it sounds as if he saw something the New York banks didn't, and *The Credit of Faith*."

"That one was published over here, Parados Press, 1965. They dug up an old catalogue reference to it: it seems to be that honest banking practice and churchgoing come to the same thing, ungodly Marxism leads to phoney exchange rates."

"You're paraphrasing, I assume. Well, well – a banker who can read and write, yet. I suppose the Midwest would be where you might still find one. And it does tie up: I uncovered CCOAC in your absence."

He had eventually decided to ask Security's registry and its computers for a trace, muddling the trail by getting a colleague to send the request for him and burying it in a list of acronyms, as if they had been collected over a period of time. The prompt reply showed just how little Security now had to do: CCOAC translated as Churchgoers Concerned About Communism, a one-off conference held in May 1968. Initial funding had come from local businessmen, and delegates – mostly businessmen themselves – from a dozen countries had paid their own air fares and hotel bills.

"But claimed it off tax later, no doubt," George said sourly.

The conference had no covert political purpose, Security believed, even if one presidential and several senatorial hopefuls had demonstrated their statesmanliness from the platform.

"In other words," George interpreted, "they couldn't trace any CIA funding. But there probably wasn't any; in the Midwest you wouldn't need it. But where does it get us? This CCOAC makes it more likely that Person Y was involved in the things we think he was involved in, but . . ."

"We still don't know who he is."

"Quite, and exactly. Probably a British businessman with enough money to go romping off to America on some tax-deductible crusade – heavens, you weren't anybody in the Sixties if you couldn't do that twice a year."

"We also know he's a churchgoer, or was then. Miss Tuckey was involved in church work. Person X at the Abbey was dressed as a cleric . . ."

"What *are* you suggesting?"

"Nothing. Or . . . maybe there's a crusade going on, as you said. Believers make good soldiers. Miss Tuckey said they made good agents. Does Security have a list of British delegates to CCOAC?"

"No. This is all they had on it. Why bother? These people certainly weren't on Moscow's payroll." He brooded, glanced at his wristwatch, then poured more coffee from a big silver-plated flask which he had installed himself. The room, which looked over the Embankment side of the building, was a mix of his own and Civil Service furnishings. The desk and carpet were his badges of rank and he hadn't presumed, nor even thought, to change them. But the drinks cabinet, the expensive desk chair – "A civil servant's only assets are the strength of his back and backside; I am not having my career fore-shortened by Her Majesty's fiscal indifference to spinal problems" – and the bits and pieces on the desk were George's imports. They included an ugly marble pen-stand, presented by the retiring Prime Minister, which George never used but displayed as proud evidence of the biggest mistake a civil servant can achieve: becoming too identified with a political figure.

He stared moodily at the photograph, at the thin face with its moustache and big ears smiling out at an un-imaginable future. Or had it been so unimaginable? Was Person Y even then planning to take up secret arms against a sea of predictable troubles? No, it was just a photograph. But – "Could this man have done something to stop you reaching Person X? You must have turned your back on him."

"I thought he was a policeman."

"Quite. But could he have tried something?"

"That's what the Committee couldn't swallow."

"I can see their point. And Person X could have taken a shot at you."

"He'd dropped his rifle in the Abbey."

"He could have had a pistol as well: sensible precaution. Or really have thrown that grenade at you."

"Not a chance. I was covering him with – "

"Harry, he was not *expecting* to meet a superman like you. My point is, neither of them even tried. X just shouted something about you getting hurt. If that wasn't a threat, it was a Jolly Decent Thing To Do, seeing as how he was about to blow himself up. You see what I'm getting at? They wanted to kill one person in the Abbey, to shock everybody, but do as little more damage as possible."

He clasped his hands in among his chins and glowered at the desk top. Behind him, the rain trickling down the window made wavery verticals behind the strict horizon-tals of the venetian blind. "There must be a list of CCOAC delegates somewhere in St Louis. I'll think what I can do about that; I don't want to go back to Security, or through Six . . . when you come down to it, how do we

113

know some of the Old Guard in those places aren't involved in this *bloody* attempt to run the country from the shadows? I don't like the government we've got, but nobody voted for men with rifles in the Abbey." He sat very still and spoke with quiet ferocity. "*And* they've let the Bravoes in, given them a potential scandal that . . . I don't know what. But we're a small country, now: we can't afford big mistakes."

Maxim was smiling and nodding politely. "Anybody could be involved. Going to Miss Tuckey was a risk, but – "

"D'you think she . . . ?"

"Very much doubt it. She was too obvious, with her lectures and books – and what access did she have? No official standing. Probably a few friends in high places, but it would be better to recruit them instead. No, I think she thought she could guess at somebody who might be involved – like Person Y – but nothing more."

"Unless it was cover."

"Double cover."

"I know: rhinestones over amethysts over diamonds." George had lapsed into determined gloom. "That way, you end by staring through a telescope poked up your own – "

"The most she might have done," Maxim said soothingly, "would be to give them training in techniques. She couldn't have been supplying Russian weapons, typewriter, unlisted phone numbers – oh, were those two Second Secretaries on the No-go-Alone List?"

There was, had to be, a discreet list circulated naming those (mainly) Soviet Bloc officials in London with whom it was *highly inadvisable* to have a solo drink or dinner. Maxim hadn't seen an update of the list since leaving Number 10.

"They were on it," George grunted.

"How would she get hold of the KGB's local order of battle? No, whoever gave them the kit could give them the training to go with it. These people have got good contacts – but with whom?"

"You're getting grammatical." George sat looking like a frog who has no idea where his next fly is coming from.

114

"All right. You get back to the Playforce office and look busy. I'll think whether I have any cousins in St Louis."

Maxim got slowly to his feet, his thoughtful face sending a shiver through George, because that look usually meant he might be going to *do* something. "You took a recording of the TV replay at the Abbey, didn't you?"

"It was you working that blasted machine."

"Can I come back with you and play it over – or borrow it?" On Saturday, Maxim had moved back into Wellington Barracks; he was supposed to be looking for a new flat to go with his London posting.

"Of course. I've got a meeting at four, should be through by half five."

Maxim half turned away, then decided he'd better say his piece anyway. "Would you mind if I followed you back – just to try and see if anybody else is trying to? I'm not very good at that sort of thing, but . . . one thing we do know is that the Bravoes know we're involved. I mean we George Harbinger and Harry Maxim."

17

As far as Maxim could see, nobody followed George through the fading damp light back to Albany, although there was no way to be sure and less way of knowing if he was followed himself, not over such a short and crowded distance. He caught George up at the porter's lodge and they walked together up the Ropewalk.

"Security here could be good," Maxim said tentatively.

"Apart from once having a porter who was a burglar, I think it is. The back gate's kept closed these days, so there's only the one way in and I have to tell the porter the name of anybody who's coming – you know that."

"Even when you're throwing a big party?"

"Well, not then, no, just to warn him I'm expecting guests . . . I see what you mean." It takes only one leak to sink a ship, one gate to let in a Trojan horse. George was frowning in thought as they clattered up the prison-like stone steps to his set.

Annette greeted George with cheery concern and Maxim with, he thought, some coolness behind the immediate offer of dinner. Suddenly he could imagine George on the Sunday after that Saturday evening at the cottage, exhausted by nightmares, pacing the rooms and jumping whenever the phone rang. As a good wife, Annette would have blamed it, whatever *it* was, on Maxim. Rightly so, he thought sadly, and I'm going to make it worse.

He said: "Thank you, no, I'm just picking up a book George promised me."

"And a quick jar," George called from the cloakroom. "Go on in, Harry, help yourself, you know where."

"I'll get some ice." Annette vanished.

Alone in the big drawing-room, where Annette's choice of bright fabrics had fought hardest, albeit still without winning, against her dead in-laws' passion for dark-panelled gloom, Maxim went straight to the telephone. It was the same old-fashioned type as Miss Tuckey's, and he unscrewed the mouthpiece carefully but found nothing extra inside. Looking around, he remembered it was difficult to plant bugs actually inside panelling, but even his half-trained eye could see that the elaborate cornices and mouldings gave a myriad opportunities to a good wire man.

Annette came back, shining with suspicious goodwill. "You haven't got yourself anything yet, Harry. It's usually Scotch, isn't it? Water and ice?"

He took the glass, although he disliked iced drinks after the brief British summer, and asked: "Had a busy day?"

She ignored that. Glancing over her shoulder, she whispered: "What *happened* on Saturday night? George came in looking like *death*. Can you tell me what it was?"

"Misunderstanding, all cleared up now," he said, and her look told him how much use that reply had been.

"I *see*," she said, smiling lopsidedly. "You *are* getting into our little Whitehall ways, Harry. Oh well," gaily now, "these things blow over. Have I had a busy day? I made it seem like one. I got out to the shops this afternoon, and have you noticed they're into Christmas *already*? Two and a half months ahead. The Americans do it much better, having Thanksgiving to space it out so they only have a month of Christmas, though they do seem to let their elections creep back, just as we do with football . . ."

George bustled in, rubbing his hands. "A drink, a drink, my kingdom for . . ." He gave Annette a piece of paper and put his finger to his lips. Annette stared, but took it silently while George clanked and prattled over the tray of bottles. "Had a good day, sweetie? Harry, the book, I was forgetting, it's over there . . ." He pointed to a rack of video tapes. "Dig it out for yourself, will you? It's quite good on D'Urbino and Speckle particularly, if you were ever thinking of going back to that monograph."

"One of these days, when I've got the time." Maxim found the tape of the Abbey shooting. Annette passed the paper back to George, her eyes wide.

"Of course, what I'm really interested in," Maxim went on, "is where D'Urbino got *his* ideas from." He looked at the paper George held out. "Was he really the innovator they make out? I'm not trying to run him down, but . . ."

He read:

The place could be bugged. Did anybody get in here today?

Annette had written:

Somebody lost his way going to a lunch party at the Metcalfes', but I didn't let him in. I was out for 2 hours from about 2.30.

Still talking about the designer of Antwerp's city walls, Maxim reached and scribbled:

Exploration, then penetration.

"I've got an idea," George said. "Why don't we take Harry out to dinner at the club? As long as he stops talking fortresses. Or we can get that over with while you change – right?"

With silent frightened eyes, Annette went to the bedroom.

The cliché image of London clubs being full of government officials muttering Top Secrets over the cold steak-and-kidney pie had, Maxim was coming to see, not only a lot of truth but also a lot of sense. The essence of a club is that it is select and private; you cannot be followed in there. A club servant might be taking Moscow gold, so perhaps one should not share secrets with them, and so might another club member – but since he is likely to be a government official as well, you already have a far bigger problem than just his being a member of your club. As to planting electronic bugs, you would need an ant colony of them and an army of listeners before you could be reasonably sure of covering every room in London where George Harbinger might whisper an indiscretion.

"I'll put in a request for them to check out Albany," George grumbled, "but it takes months to get them to do your office, never mind your home. I've been trying to get routine security stepped up, but you come right up against the lords of the wallet: who's going to pay for it? I've got another meeting tomorrow, but . . ."

"George, are they really doing this to us?" Annette demanded. "In our own home? It's absolutely hateful."

"There's a war on. Or *they* are determined there should be."

"But why now? You're not even in Downing Street any more." She glanced quickly at Maxim, then back to George. "Or is this something to do with last Saturday?"

George shivered. "Let's say it could be."

"Oh." She stared into the dregs of her gin and tonic. "If that was all to do with *them*, I don't mind so much. That's a bit silly, isn't it? I just thought it might be something, well, personal and rather awful. But I expect you'll tell me, one of these days."

"One of these days," George promised, and they smiled quickly at each other, isolating Maxim in a twinge of envy. People who have been married, apparently happily, for a long time can make you feel an outsider with just one private glance.

George went to make sure there was a table for dinner; Annette said: "I'm so sorry I acted the way I did with you . . . somehow I'd got to blaming you, you know how it is . . ."

"It could have been my fault. Some of it."

"No, I'm sure you were doing your best." With a sharp memory of the darkened cottage, Maxim wondered: my best? My most direct, but perhaps not my best. "I do trust George completely," Annette went on, "I just have to, with his work and so much he can't tell me, but when he came back in that state, I just couldn't help . . . I don't know if I was thinking about Another Woman, but if George was being blackmailed about something like . . . and he'd taken you along because you were tough and . . . you see the silly fantasies I get into when I'm alone?"

"It was nothing like that," Maxim said with huge relief.

"I suppose I read too many thrillers, but in the end I'd convinced myself you'd got too tough and killed somebody and George was mixed up in that!" She laughed cheerily.

"Ha, *ha*," Maxim agreed feebly.

★

Back at the Barracks, Maxim had to wait until after midnight before he had the officers' mess video machine to himself. He ran through the sequence of the shots, listening carefully and timing the spacing with the seconds hand of his watch. Then he picked up a long poker from the fireplace and held it like a rifle when he played the tape again. At each shot he jerked the 'rifle' up, as the recoil would kick it, then re-aimed as fast as he could.

"So you've finally lost your last marble," a voice said from the far end of the room. It was the duty officer, prowling with a cup of tea in his hand. Shamefaced, Maxim twirled the poker casually.

"It's that SAS training," the duty officer went on. "Learning to live on seaweed and beetles. Bound to have an effect. Can I help by uttering a strangled cry and falling at your feet? Anything for one of the Army's élite."

"Piss off," Maxim suggested.

"Or have I stumbled on the trials of the Regiment's new secret weapon? Fear not, my lips are sealed. Gad, I never realised what Total War really meant until this moment . . ."

Maxim left him cackling and slopping his tea with mirth. In his room he unpacked the little portable typewriter that had once been Jenny's, and stared at a blank paper until his embarrassment had faded. Then he began to tap:

'1. The range from the firing point to where the rounds impacted was between 35 metres (the shot that hit Barling) and 30 metres (the ones that hit the pillar) . . .'

Twenty minutes later he had reached paragraph 9 when a voice from the next room told him that if he were typing anything other than his bloody resignation he should bloody well do it at a more civilised bloody hour. It sounded a senior voice; Maxim went to bed.

18

"All very competent," George said, "though I don't find any significance in the intervals between the shots – but what does it all prove?"

"That they wanted to kill Barling. Himself. Not just smear the KGB by making them seem callously careless in their shooting. The pause after the first shot, making sure they'd killed him, which isn't easy to do with a heart shot, but they couldn't go for the head because the sight line wouldn't fit with shooting at the President's head — "

"Harry, *please*." George put his head in his hands. "Anything you say, except just don't say it this early in the day."

"Why Barling?" Maxim asked bluntly.

George waved a hand vaguely. "He was an expert on Russian affairs – as much of an expert as MPs get to be on anything – and they made him a junior minister to add credibility to their soft-line policy. He couldn't speak against that policy once he'd accepted a government post."

"Where did he stand on Berlin?"

"Why Berlin?" George asked suspiciously.

"Miss Tuckey told us to look for a narrow objective within a broader attack. Berlin seems the most immediate. Are we going to demilitarise our Zone there?"

"This is not your concern, Harry."

"The government can give one of two answers to the Russians: we'll talk about Berlin, or we won't talk. After two months we haven't said we won't talk. What the hell sort of secret d'you think you're keeping? The time and place of the talks, I'd say."

"I don't know about that," George grumped.

"Then I hope these people don't know, either, although they seem to know a lot. They smeared Ettington, they drugged Westerman, they killed Barling: I call that escalation. I think they're getting desperate, and Berlin seems the likeliest cause. We can't defend on a broad front, George, not just two of us. We have to find the next point of attack and be there first."

"I do hate this remorseless military logic, particularly when – as usual – it is based on an incomplete knowledge of the facts."

"Any general would like to postpone his battles for forty years until the historians can tell him what to do. But he's usually short of time as well as information, same as us. What difference could Barling's death make to Berlin?"

George sighed. "I may just be able to tell you after his funeral."

"Neither death, nor life, nor angels, nor principalities, nor powers, nor things present, nor things to come, nor height, nor depth, nor any other creature, shall be able to separate us from the love of God . . ."

"Romans 8," Sprague whispered. "I believe Barling was quite a devout man. By Parliamentary standards."

"Quite," George said, as the coffin wobbled past his ear. "And we haven't had anything tactless about the Lord gave, and the Lord hath taken away, since your Committee hasn't apportioned the blame yet. Book of Job, I believe."

"One, possibly verse twenty-one," Sprague topped him easily.

The coffin reached the catafalque as the minister finished his intonation: "Let not your heart be troubled: ye believe in God, believe also in me. In my Father's house are many mansions."

"And doctrinally at least," Sprague murmured as they sat down, "the Church of England has a seat by the fire in every one."

The crematorium chapel was a large, modern redbrick structure with pews varnished to a garish yellow. It was crowded, despite its size, for Mrs Barling had made no effort to keep it private, and there were TV crews on the driveway outside. A lady, George thought sombrely, with a fine appreciation of the political timescale: come the inevitable memorial service in three weeks' time, people would already be asking 'Barling? Who was he? Oh yes, *him.*'

122

"I held my tongue, and spake nothing: I kept silence, yea, even from good words; but it was pain and grief to me," the minister droned, his voice thin in the unfamiliar acoustics. "My heart was hot within me, and while I was thus musing the fire kindled: and at the last I spake with my tongue . . ."

"I do believe that the widow Barling," Sprague whispered, "is trying to tell us something. She must have chosen this psalm. Why not the dear old 23rd? – at least a decent bit of poetry. But of course he never did speak with his tongue, nor ever would have done if he wanted to hang on to his job. They almost never do . . . is this the moment, George, to tell you something of uttermost Top Secrecy?"

". . . and verily every man living is altogether vanity," the minister went on.

"Something the Committee has not yet *quite* decided," Sprague murmured, thumbing through his hymn book, "but I believe will come to accept shortly. If our dear departed were *not* going to speak out against the Berlin talks, as seemed altogether likely, suppose – I must say suppose – that some deranged mind decided to eliminate *him*, under the guise of a Muscovite attempt on the dear President? Consider that for a moment, George." He raised a satisfied, bright-eyed smile towards the pulpit.

"Good *Lord*," George said, bowing his head.

Sprague's smile got even brighter. "If one thinks about it, the President makes an ideal stalking horse. Nobody else could possibly be the target. But, viewed in tranquillity, that is pure theory, so another theory is equally tenable. Think on it, George."

"Why Barling, though?"

"It frees his followers in the House. He would have voted with the government, they would have voted with him. Now we have twenty-five Members, it could be more, floating free and liable to vote their consciences. A frightening thought, for a coalition government. However, there are no signs of a foreign policy debate being forced at the moment, and one rather doubts there will be unless something dramatic happens, so one might say the assassin failed . . ."

"You still believe it was just one man?"

"What other evidence? That mythical policeman whom your Major saw for just one second, as he admitted? Amen," he added, in perfect time with the congregation. "No, the lone psychopath, all quite within the compass of one warped brain."

"And now a right-wing brain, which must sit nicely with our Masters."

"You know me better than that, George," Sprague reproved from the corner of his mouth. "And what conspirators were you favouring? Charlie's Indians? I won't deny *that* might find favour with our Masters." Sprague rose, bright-eyed and smiling pleasantly, to sing the hymn.

"Of course," he said, sitting down again, "it would have been so much easier if we had the assassin alive and on trial. But your Major, alas . . ."

". . . while we look not at the things which are seen, but at the things which are not seen: for the things which are seen are temporal; but the things which are not seen are eternal . . ."

"So like our dear friends from the secret services," Sprague observed. "Concerning which, one hears a whisper that the Secret Service, the White House Protective Detail, is holding a little affair called an After Action Study. Presumably to find out what went wrong in the Abbey."

"Standard procedure," George suggested.

"Doubtless. And far better than any Congressional inquiry or suchlike; I gather it's a totally private proceeding. But since it didn't happen on their home ground, they will be requesting witnesses from where it did happen. You do follow me?" Said reprovingly, because George looked as if he might have been following the lesson.

"Yes . . . they'll want some of our people. You aren't thinking of refusing?"

"Of course not. Once the request becomes official, we shall send somebody from the very *highest* level of my Office, nothing less."

"But not anybody who actually knows what happened."

"But who does really know? Surely this is where the Committee comes into its own. When we have resolved the matter, we shall be in a position to give them all the reassurance they can ask. And reassurance is what it comes down to: security remains a national responsibility. They can't ask for more than that we have reviewed and reformed our procedures."

"For we must all appear before the judgment seat of Christ," the minister warned them; "that every one may receive the things done in his body, according to that he hath done, whether it be good or bad."

"Reassurance," George agreed glumly.

"The President was not, after all, harmed. Nor were a dozen other heads of state who are not, I think, going to request witnesses for an After Action Study." Sprague turned the last word into a throat-clearing noise, because the minister had finished just ahead of him.

With a jerk, the coffin began trundling on its conveyor belt towards the curtains and the waiting flame. It was, as always, a moment of terrible sorrow and, because of the creaking conveyor, cringing banality.

" . . . the soul of our brother departed, and we commit his body to be consumed by fire," the minister gabbled, trying to keep pace with the vanishing coffin; "ashes to ashes, dust to dust . . ."

In the moment of silence before the organ started and the congregation began to move, somebody sobbed loudly. It was a lonely world-wide, world-deep sound.

"So where," Sprague asked, "might it not all end?"

So far, the autumn had brought gales, soft bright days left over from summer, misty still days, windy showery ones and now a fine drizzle. Even the weather's become a bloody coalition, George grumbled to himself as he watched the politicians edging in front of the TV cameras and the civil servants edging away.

Sprague summed up: "So, we can be united in this as all things? Everything to be handled through the Committee? Bless you, George, for being, as ever, so understanding . . ." He drifted away towards his Minister's car. Sprague never drove himself, but was never short of a lift.

Walking towards his own car, George passed James Ferrebee, gulping at a cigarette behind a pillar. "Back to the pit-head?" he suggested.

Ferrebee jumped at the offer. "My Master offered my

seat to Mrs Barling. Quite right and proper, but I didn't fancy trying to scrounge a lift from a back-bencher." Ferrebee's status was not that of Sprague.

As they drove out, the next funeral cortège was coming up the drive. "Production line business," Ferrebee commented. "But, given a place like that, I thought it went well. Barling himself would have approved."

"He was a devout man, I gather."

"I believe so."

"Only he wasn't going to resign on our Russian policy – like Berlin?"

"He talked about it, but . . . when you finally reach a position where you might get something done, you usually tell yourself that you can do more by staying, trying to soften the effects of a policy than walking out and being replaced by somebody who gobbles up the policy flavour-of-the-month. Civil servants as well as politicians."

"Power tends to castrate, absolute power makes you forget you ever had them, as with our current ministers." Feeling Ferrebee's cool glance, George hurried on: "I hear the Americans are going to invite witnesses over for a post-mortem on the Abbey. Have you heard that?"

"No." Ferrebee stared suspiciously. "Was that Norman Sprague? I saw you two had your heads bowed and I was pretty sure it wasn't religious devotion. That man's a private transatlantic cable."

"Many would subscribe towards sinking him to the ocean bed. But I assume he was telling me that they'll ask for Harry Maxim, and the Committee would rather he didn't go."

"Sprague can't tell the Army what to do."

"No, but there are policy matters, I shall probably be consulted . . ."

"Do you want him to go?"

"The Americans aren't going to be impressed by somebody from Sprague's Committee who wasn't within miles of the Abbey telling them Not to worry old boy, the Redcoats have muddled through again, can't recall the details but just take my word for it . . . If they want Harry, I want him to go. We've got some fences to mend in Washington."

"I gather he was suggesting a conspiracy theory to the Steering Committee. If that doesn't fit with the Committee's findings – and we must be letting Washington have those eventually – will that really patch things up?"

George noted that Sprague – it would only be Sprague – had been leaking a version of Maxim's performance at the Committee. "I think Harry learnt a lesson there, and I could teach him a few more before he goes . . . I wonder, now: Sprague may have been a bit too clever in tipping me off. Suppose, when the White House Detail asks for Harry, it isn't to give *evidence*, but advice? Everybody's flattered to give advice; be churlish to refuse. Suppose I gave Clay Culliman a tinkle on a secure line and suggested that?"

Ferrebee lit another cigarette. "If you think you can out-deviate Sprague, then I doubt my Office will raise any objections. Only – don't let him *shoot* anybody over there, will you? It could be counter-productive."

"I'll search him myself at the security check." George was already phrasing his call to Culliman; perhaps the request should be for Maxim to 'make himself available' to the Study group, a suggestion of staying several days, give the chap a chance to see Washington in the fall . . . and make a quick trip to St Louis and back.

"But I don't get to fly Concorde?" Maxim asked.

"Correct. You do not get to fly Concorde." The Deputy Director of Crisis Relocation peered sternly over his spectacles. "You go on the regular RAF VC-10 from Brize Norton. They run a perfectly good . . . well, they probably can't miss something the size of America. You've never been there before? You should enjoy Washington. See if you can get our people to introduce you to a few American officers; broaden your mind. Only don't come home with the idea that the solution to every military problem is the *helicopter*."

"No, sir. It's artillery."

The DDCR, who had begun his career in the Artillery, became even more suspicious. "Correct again. Why don't you tell that to the RAF and see where they make you sit?"

19

Long-distance travel is a fever dream where time and mood slip out of control, leaving one unexpectedly early or late, delighted or depressed, until a mosaic of tiny things builds a flat earth beneath you again. Things like understanding the coins in your hand and the meaningless greeting of a shop-girl, like predicting the traffic behaviour and using a telephone without reading the instructions.

World-seasoned traveller that he thought himself, Maxim sat glumly watching the dawn over the Washington skyline, having woken far too early and dry-mouthed from the air-conditioning in the aircraft and now the hotel. He had already drunk all the ginger ale and soda from the room refrigerator, and was now sipping the tonic water, which tasted hideously medicinal. Outside, it looked like becoming a warm, sunny day, which increased his alienation after the British autumn. It emphasised that he was not only far west of London, but far south as well, on a latitude with Sicily and southern Spain. Later, he would go out and stroll the city before his noon date at the Smithsonian and the afternoon meeting with the Secret Service.

Abruptly, as with all cities and their tight schedules, the street below was jammed with cars and Maxim assumed the coffee shop on the ground floor would be open. In fact, it had been open for some time already, as had half a dozen other places within easy walk, because America believes in man's inalienable right to eat whenever he is awake. On a brief evening stroll, Maxim had also noticed a few tourists who had clearly solved the problem of eating whilst asleep; it is an oddity of America that only tourists are truly fat, never the locals.

The ceremony at the Smithsonian Air and Space Museum was for the presentation of an old Spitfire that had been hauled out of an English lake and identified as belonging to 71 Squadron, the first of the Eagle squadrons formed from American volunteers back in 1940. Restored and re-painted in RAF workshops, it was being formally handed over – together with glasses of champagne, Bourbon or Scotch – by the Ambassador's wife in front of a small and mainly military audience. That was why the Liaison Office, looking to make some gesture of welcome, had invited Maxim. Agnes Algar was there because she had asked.

She freely admitted, although only to herself, that this was because Maxim would be there. She did not quite admit that was why she wore her best summer suit, and indeed had it rush-cleaned for the event. It had, after all, needed cleaning, and there wouldn't be many more chances to wear it that autumn, so . . . and anyway, why shouldn't she look her best for once?

There hadn't been time to get Maxim's name on the usual notice of forthcoming visitors to the embassy; she had been signalled by the Security Service, who shared the Steering Committee's deep distrust of the visit and wanted her to debrief him after his meeting.

"Well, if it comes to that, I don't exactly trust the dear boy myself," she had remarked to her mother, who was winding up a short visit en route to stay with some Canadian cousins. "He has that Attila the Hun touch which rarely goes over big in diplomatic circles."

"I thought you rather liked him, when you were at Number 10?"

"Oh yes. I dare say even Attila had his moments."

"I'm sorry I won't meet him. At one time, I thought that you and he . . ." There was a delicate relentlessness with which Mrs Algar pursued the main task of any mother with a long-unmarried daughter.

"Mother dear, he is *Army*. Can you see *me* as an Army Wife?"

"I don't know . . . You always seem to pick rather *dashing* men. I mean Graham with his yachts, and David was a test pilot, wasn't he?"

"Graham was a snake." Said very grimly. "And David was another."

"Oh yes," her mother had said with a smile of – surprisingly – reminiscence; "the dashing types usually are, in the end."

After the ceremony, Agnes and Maxim walked through other halls of the museum, where she displayed more knowledge of the aeroplanes and nearly as much of the rockets as Maxim – essentially a personal-weapons infantryman – could offer.

"So what do you think of Washington after – what? eighteen or twenty hours?"

Maxim smiled and considered. "Green, and white, and wide and dusty."

"They're certainly tearing things down and putting them up at the moment. Nothing more than that?"

"It sounds a bit daft, but . . . it looks like the capital of America. Like they'd want it to look."

"Yes – the Founding Fathers, and L'Enfant, did a pretty good job." She stopped, looking up at a rocket: a towering metal redwood that had never flown because the ones that flew were junk scattered across the Gulf of Mexico. "They do things whole-heartedly, over here. Even if it's some idea like building a restaurant like a ship. They make it *look* like a ship, with waiters like pirates singing shanties into your clam chowder. We'd get scared half the way through and back off and just stick a few ship pictures round the walls. It's good to see you again, old sport, although the reason could be more auspicious. I wondered if it was you when we first got news of the Abbey – no insult, just that some people get picked for some jobs. How's George liking life back at MoD? Not drinking too much more than too much?"

"He's ticking over. It's nice to see you, too." Perhaps it was the estrangement of Washington, perhaps that he hadn't expected Agnes at the Smithsonian, but it had been a surprising thrill to see the familiar smile in the crowd. Although not all that familiar: her oval face was leaner now, her light ginger hair cut shorter and more clearly styled. It might be something about blending with the efficient American women he had seen around the city, or it might be a feeling of exile. She smoked more than she

130

had done before, too, lighting a cigarette with real hunger when they came out into the sunlight.

"Well, you'll be seeing more of me. Ycu know I'm debriefing you this afternoon? Maybe you'll feel like a drink after that. I'd like to hear what you've been up to."

"Certainly. Happy to." But there was a flat wariness in his voice, and she didn't push it. But I was right about him being up to something, she thought.

20

The 'Secret Service' in America began, and continues, as a branch of the Treasury hunting down counterfeiters, largely by undercover means. Since it was the only nation-wide law enforcement agency when McKinley got killed in 1901 – making three presidential assassinations in forty years – it was the only group that could easily take on the job of bodyguarding future presidents. So it was not to the White House but the Treasury Building next door that the embassy car delivered Maxim at three o'clock that afternoon.

He remembered a big, elegant room – whose, he never learnt – with wide-spaced deep leather chairs that created a literally laid-back atmosphere, rather than one hunched over a table. Only the agent from Dean's Yard, the one person Maxim recognised, was leaning forward and looking eager among his seniors. A middle-aged woman silently traced his movements on a large-scale map board; there were photographs of the Yard and the Cloisters pinned up there, as well.

The questioning was polite and leisured, but thorough. Then one of them asked: "Can you tell us what the Rules of Engagement were for your task, Major?"

"Generally, that I had to be convinced any person posed a risk – and to give a warning before I fired."

"Did you give a warning, then?"

"I think I shouted something."

There was a momentary pause. An older, more senior, questioner asked: "Did your superiors accept that?"

"I suppose so."

The first one came back: "Did the police inspector you talked to confirm that?"

Maxim took a deep breath. He had offered George the

idea of trying to leave Person Y out altogether, but George had been firm: the Secret Service would spot any gaps.

"I think I'd better say that the Steering Committee didn't seem to believe I saw an inspector. The police say they can't identify him. It was all happening rather quickly, and by now I'm getting a little unsure myself." That was strictly his own idea, to try and cover any hesitations while he hid the trail that led to Miss Tuckey and the picture on her wall.

He sensed a mixed reaction of sympathy and severity. "Sure," the first interrogator went on, "but you are a career soldier, trained to be at your best when things are popping – right? And trained to identify uniforms and rank insignia straight off?"

"I wish I'd made that point to the Committee."

They smiled politely. "I guess it was just your British modesty. But if we can assume the police inspector really existed – you did hear him speak? Was his voice straight-up English?"

"He only said a few words," Maxim said slowly, trying to remember. "All I can say is, he didn't sound odd for a London police inspector."

"Could he have been American?"

That startled Maxim. "He didn't sound American." What the hell were they getting at? But there was an American connection, in St Louis 1968. He fought the idea down; they were recording him – quite openly – and would presumably analyse the tape for changes in his voice pattern afterwards. He clung to bafflement.

The older man explained softly: "The President has more enemies in the United States than he does in England. That's what we assume, anyhow."

Maxim nodded, hoping his relief didn't show – or record. A ripple of glances round the room and the older man said: "I guess that about wraps it up, then." He stood up. "Thank you kindly for coming over to help us out. We do appreciate it. We didn't get around to any of that 'advice' you were going to give us, but . . ." and they all laughed.

"Are you doing anything else while you're over here, Major?" the other one asked.

It was the oldest trick in the book: lighten the atmosphere, stir in a few laughs – and throw the fast ball.

"Looking around Washington," Maxim said evenly. "And I might run up to New York for the day."

They were all over him with friendly, jokey advice. "If you get talking to any New Yorkers, they'll tell what a lousy dirty city it is, all full of crime and weirdos and garbage. I'm telling you, Major, the one thing you don't do is agree with them. Or they'll push you under a subway train or force-feed you kiwi fruit, whatever the new thing is this week. Take care, now."

But have I taken enough care already? Maxim wondered.

Agnes's office in the Rotunda, the wartime annex built beside the embassy, was a rather different place. Maxim would have known it for a British government office no matter where in the world he met it: small, neon-lit, with a hodge-podge of cheap furniture and painted to look scruffy even when it was surgically clean. A room that British civil servants moan about but defend the way New Yorkers do New York, because it shows how unique they are in coping so splendidly in such surroundings. If that doesn't make you feel humble, you must naturally be so humble that the hell with you anyway.

"Sit down, Harry," Agnes waved at him. "Any wires sticking out of the chair are strictly HMG's parsimony, nothing to do with your heartbeat or perspiration rate. You can tell us all the lies you like. You've met Colonel Lomax, I think? He's sitting in on behalf of MoD, the Army and because he'll have to walk the dog if he gets home early."

"My daughter from dancing class, actually," Lomax said with a tight smile. He was a small, neat man with curly grey hair who had met Maxim at the airport.

"We agreed it would be simplest if you only had to say your party piece once – once more, I mean," Agnes went on briskly. "We'd like to hear everything, but particularly what questions the lads in the Gucci shoulder holsters asked."

It was like eating the same meal at every mealtime.

The restaurant changed, as did the maître d', but he still watched like a hawk and swooped with a pained query if you didn't savour every mouthful or tried to hide a tough end of meat under your lettuce. And never a cigar at the end because there never was, quite, an end.

When Maxim hoped he had finished, Lomax glanced at Agnes, then said: "They brought up the Rules of Engagement business, then? I don't see how it concerns them."

Agnes answered before Maxim could think of anything. "Question of our Harry's vulnerability. Is he looking to clear himself? I fancy that's what bothers them about a possible American end: whether Harry's going to do any investigation of his own ideas over here."

"Why should he? What ideas?"

Agnes smiled. "Why and what indeed? If there was somebody dolled up as a copper at the Abbey, you've got a conspiracy, and it's only if there was a conspiracy that the Secret Service is really interested, because that means there's at least one bod floating loose who presumably still wants to kill the President. If we believe Harry, then there *was* a conspiracy. But since the alternative is that he's just a banana-brain who makes things up, he's got a natural bias towards proving a conspiracy – hasn't he? What should we conclude, Jerry?"

The question turned off Lomax's interest like a tap that realises it had flooded itself into deep water. "Good Lord, we're just required to report what he told them, no question of . . ." But there was doubt in his voice. He looked quickly at his watch. "It looks as if I'll make that damned dancing class after all. Harry, if you're still around, we must . . ."

When he had gone, Agnes lit a cigarette, slumped in her chair and grinned broadly at Maxim. "Well, are we a little banana-brain after all?"

"Thanks for bringing it up."

"It's what the Steering Committee's trying to prove, isn't it? And knowing you, I doubt very much you're standing still for it. So let's hear what jolly japes you and George have been up to since then."

Maxim considered. "What are you going to tell your Service?"

135

"I can't make any promises."

"Okay. Let's see, now. I spent that Sunday at Little-hampton; on the Monday I dined at one of George's clubs – "

"Bugger you, Harry Maxim. I want to know what you've done."

He nodded placidly. Anger didn't suit her friendly snub face, making her seem out of place in that aloofly cut suit – and he realised he was mentally taking it off her. He nodded once more and tried to remember that this was, dammit, the British embassy.

"I told the D-G of your Service what I thought, once. At the Steering Committee."

"That old fart."

"May I quote you?"

A snap glance of fury, then a tired little laugh. "Yes, it has come to that, I suppose. So you're out on a limb. And I bet you're further out than anybody realises. I know you, chum. And George, too. But what do I tell my Service?" She took time to think about that, then lifted the telephone. "Algar. I'm off now, going downtown. I'll check in – okay?" She looked back at Maxim. "You heard me. Off-duty. Let's have that drink."

"No," Maxim persisted. "You either tell your Service or you don't."

She stood up, reaching for the desk lamp. "You like your orders cut and dried. Well, I don't blame you, after . . . All right: from here on you're totally off the record. Do you believe me?"

"Yes."

"Or one day . . . I wouldn't want you for an enemy, Harry. You take loyalty seriously. God help me, I hope I still do" – she clicked off the light – "where I can still find it. I'm beginning to need that drink."

They sat in thick wickerwork chairs on an open balcony atop one of the older hotels, close to the floodlit shaft of the Washington Monument. Beyond it, the mild night sky was busy with lights arrowing down into National airport and jinking up away from it, following the curls of the river so that if one fell, it would fall into that. Agnes had brought him there for the view, but it was impossible not to watch just the aircraft lights, perhaps macabrely hoping one would lose its grip. They reminded him of what the city was really about, more so than the near-deserted streets below, dominated by monuments and government buildings that themselves became monuments after dark.

Agnes listened carefully and without interruption except to clarify a name or time. They were halfway through their second round of drinks when he finished; she leaned away so that – sitting beside him – she could peer back at him through the dimness. "Golly, you do live, don't you? Those you run into may not, but you soldier on. Literally."

"Do you believe all this?"

She gave that only a moment's thought. "A lot of it's still guesswork by you and George, but the rest, yes. If something like that were going to happen, now would be the time. And you say my Service doesn't believe it?"

"George didn't want to put the business at the cottage to them, you can see why, and it's pretty clear they don't want to believe in a conspiracy anyway, even when they knew about the Reznichenko Memorandum."

"That smelled bad even from here, but now you say they had proof it was phoney and didn't tell the Home Sec? That means they didn't even tell the D-G. My God, it's come to that pitch already. This is the sort of thing my mob is supposed to be ironing out and they daren't admit they've even been involved – except by whispering to people like Sprague. *Sprague*."

"You know him?"

"Met him." She snatched a gulp of her drink and banged the glass on her teeth. "And the Bravoes seem to believe it . . . They shouldn't *have* a team like that in Britain, acting so openly. It shows how safe they feel; six months ago they wouldn't have dared . . . And I believe you when you say you killed one of them. I might not have believed it if you'd said you hadn't."

"The world is full of people I haven't killed."

"So far. And you had George along with you on that? Poor man. His blood pressure must be stratospheric. But the Bravoes aren't going to like that, you know. There's no rules in our business, but there's more or less a convention that we don't kill each other. Once that gets started, you don't know where it could end."

"They must have been planning to kill Miss Tuckey."

"Oh yes, they've killed people in Britain before. Usually their own defectors and so on . . . but outsiders, not professionals. I know it sounds crazy to you, but that's the convention. At the moment. Now you've broken it . . . well, let's hope they count Miss Tuckey as a pro and call it quits. If not, you could be a target."

"Just me?"

"Just you. You're thinking of your boy? No. That's more or less another convention – and they don't want to send you berserk, doing God-knows-what more damage. It'll be you personally, but nothing personal, if you see what I mean. Just getting across the message that 'Oi, there's a convention about these things, remember? Now we've squared it up, we can start again from scratch.' I should keep your back to the wall."

"I'll try and remember."

Looking at his face, calm in the faint glow of the awning lights, Agnes felt a flush of exasperation at failing to get her message across. In fact, Maxim had listened and believed: she knew far more of that world than he did. But his own world had stretched to the hinterland of the Gulf states, where a mixture of religion, politics and blood feuds made death a beginning rather than an end. There were families and organisations out there which had sworn to kill him far less cleanly than the KGB would, and he had learned to live with that. Not exactly with courage, which is a wasting asset, but with a soldier's fatalism that if it happens, it will be tomorrow and not today.

"All right," Agnes said resignedly, "so what it boils down to is that, despite your assurances to the White House Protective Detail, you're sneaking off to do a little sleuthing on your own?"

"If we can identify this Person Y . . . it seems the only thing to do."

"Sure. But you'd better do it carefully. Grow a long-lost cousin in Missouri, or something. Have you booked anything? Then don't until I've done a little looking up.

I'm supposed to be just liaison, and the climate isn't good for that. But a list like that can't be anything secret . . . Did George suggest you got me mixed up in all this?"

Maxim smiled and shrugged. "He suggested I contact you. But I would have done anyway."

"However, not just for my big blue eyes and tiny morals? And what's he going to be doing meanwhile?"

"Nothing out of the ordinary, I hope."

21

As it turned out, George had not had to stir up the matter of Miss Tuckey himself. It arrived at his desk, as he had privately hoped, simply because he was the long-stop for security/intelligence matters that nobody else wanted to field. It had not been the Army which first noticed her disappearance, but an old Resistance colleague. Forty years after the event, the survivors were a sociable group with their own small London club and a way of closing ranks that, in wartime, had needed to be desperately widespread. The file brought with it a twinge of now-familiar guilt and a covering note from Army Intelligence: *Will you please try and persuade the creepy-crawlies that we have neither the facilities nor any reason to investigate this lady's apparent disappearance. Even if she fails to turn up for her next set of lectures there is nothing we can do but not pay her.* Sir Bruce had a low opinion of civilian intelligence officers.

The usual 'open end' at MI6 was a small bird of a man whose telephone voice sounded permanently pained. "My dear George, *we* haven't any interest in the woman, missing or not. If the Army doesn't care what happens to its lecturers then that's no skin off *our* nose. As you know perfectly well, and I'm sure they do, too, *we* can't mount any active investigation in this country" – just as if six had never done such a thing. "*We* only got involved because we're being badgered by one of our ex's, an old friend of hers, I believe. They were in the Resistance together, that sort of thing. We took him on after the war, when we were a bit short-handed. He retired some time ago; had a stroke, I understand." The sentence ended on a high, uninterested note.

"What's he worried about?" George asked.

There was a pause; there almost always was when you asked a question of the Secret Intelligence Service. After twenty years, George still couldn't decide whether they spent the time thinking or it was just to show they needn't really answer anything.

"You've got our note? That's really all we know. She vanished, it was reported to the police, they couldn't find anything criminally suspicious. We at least went to the trouble of asking them."

"Is he going to make a fuss?"

Pause. Then the voice said distantly: "He certainly should know better. But he was rather . . . *wartime*."

"If he had any idea of what she was doing for us, MoD doesn't want it spread around. Would it help if I go and lend him a sympathetic ear?"

This time, the voice after the pause might, by MI6 standards, have been described as faintly eager. "If you really feel like doing that, George, by all means. I've got his address around here somewhere. It could be the best thing, might even do some good."

Clenching his teeth, George had to remind himself that he had now got just the endorsement he wanted.

Edward Marriage, Secret Intelligence Service (retired) managed a small boat-hire yard on the Thames below Oxford. There were five boats moored to the shored-up bank, all with names beginning *Duke*, hung with bright blue fenders that hadn't saved them from long scratches and stains. Behind, in a tilting wooden boathouse, a youth with cropped hair was tinkering with a partly stripped engine. The place smelt of oil, paint, damp and slow failure, and Marriage himself sat with his back to it in the cold sunshine, looking across to the willows and alders of the far bank and the fields beyond. It was very still, with the landscape painted in shades of smoke.

They drank tea out of mugs labelled Captain and Bosun brought by his wife, who was small, bright-eyed and determinedly busy. The stroke had left Marriage hunched and rigid; he turned his head slowly and his smile had become a lopsided leer. His legs were wrapped in a tartan rug and he was fortressed by small tables, stools, a frame to help lever himself upright. George had an old kitchen chair brought from the boatshed.

"We never met," Marriage said carefully. "I got my Little Problem before you became involved in our side. You were at Number 10? But you aren't there now?" However carefully he spoke, he still released a little dribble from the stiff side of his mouth and wiped it away with a routine gesture of his left hand. His right hand was permanently supported by a strap around his neck.

"No, I'm back at MoD, security and intelligence, on the pol side. That was why Miss Tuckey's file came across my desk."

"Yes . . . are you allowed to tell me anything about her?"

"I was rather hoping you could tell me. I'm afraid she's just a name to me."

Marriage took a moment to assemble his thoughts. "I don't get out much, just sit here pecking out letters to old friends" – there was a portable typewriter on one of the tables – "and she was coming to tea last Monday. Liz had it all ready – but she didn't show up. That's not like Dot, I felt if she'd been called away she'd have got word to me somehow so . . . so that's why I rang the Firm. Of course, I hardly know anybody there, not now . . ."

The file had shown that Miss Tuckey had had no official connection with the Intelligence Service since turning down a backroom job there in 1946, the year Marriage himself had joined them. After losing most of its wartime recruits back to the universities and the law, the Service was determined to maintain its new influence, in Whitehall if not the world. The gap was filled with people who had learnt something about intelligence and too much (in the Service's view) about weaponry in the Resistance schools of the Special Operations Executive. But they remained second-class citizens as the Service restocked itself with young men of the right background from Oxford and Cambridge. After all, with the sunset of Empire and most departmental requests becoming for economic intelligence, you need trained minds who understood international banking, surely George could see *that*? So the Resistance-trained amateurs were gradually shunted to filing jobs or forgotten overseas stations where they needed do nothing but show an invisible flag and curl a lip at the way the CIA did the real work.

George asked: "Did she say anything about her job?"

"Oh no. Dot never would. But I knew she was giving a series of lectures somewhere, and they weren't being reported, and there's only one thing you'd ask Dot to lecture on, so . . ." The mouth did its best to become a wry smile. "I just guessed you were getting interested in the old Winter Garden stuff . . ."

"Winter Garden?"

Marriage's smile became slightly superior. "Before your time, of course. And that was the Americans." He called them *Amurricanes*, in a heavy stage accent that came over as an envious sneer.

"An American Resistance movement?"

Mrs Marriage came up tentatively along the line of boats, making sure she caught her husband's good eye before she moved into their circle of secrecy. She wore a faded anorak over her long cardigan. "I'm just popping into town to pick up a parcel from the station. It could be the parts John was wanting. Can I make you some more tea before I go?"

"No. We're both swimming in tea, we're both sinking in tea." Marriage's tone became abrupt and petulant.

She just smiled. "All right, dear. And shall I see when the garage can take in the car? The clutch really does need – "

"There's nothing wrong with the clutch. It's the way you drive it."

"It's snatching. I really think it's getting dangerous."

"It's the way you drive it."

"I'll see what the garage says. Don't get cold out here. Get Mr Harbinger to help you if – "

"Mr Harbinger's got better things to do than help an old cripple around. I'm not getting cold."

"Very well, dear." She smiled at George and walked briskly away.

"I don't know why I'm so bloody to her," Marriage grumbled, "except that she *tolerates* me. God knows I got enough of that in the Service." They heard the car start at the third try and roar jerkily up the track behind the boathouse, leaving a faint cloud of blue smoke drifting around the corner.

"I should have asked you if you wanted more tea," Marriage said, suddenly remorseful. "But perhaps you wouldn't mind something a bit stronger? There's a bottle of vodka in the cupboard over the desk in there. It's all I can offer, but if you felt like pouring us a couple, then topping it up with water . . . Liz doesn't like me having a snort before sundown."

For once in his life, George would have been ready to forego a drink. But there was a gentle desperation in Marriage's crooked face, and his hand crawled on the rug like a dying spider. "Don't worry about me," he said. "Half my brain cells are dead tissue anyway, so a few more won't make much odds. She can't count *them*."

Did one more matter? The man was already living beyond sundown, George told himself. "Actually, I happen to have a flask of Scotch on me, just in case I broke down on the road . . ." He tried to force the joviality that was usually so easy. Marriage watched as George filled two of his silver cups, refusing water with it.

"It's good to taste the real thing for once; that vodka's mostly water by now." He poured the neat whisky into the corner of his mouth and wriggled with slow, painful relief. George's drink tasted of shame, but he needed it too, by now.

"The American Resistance movement," George prompted delicately. "Was that Winter Garden?"

"In the early Fifties, we all started setting up Resistance networks again, all over Europe, when it looked as if the Soviets were going to come west on the next train. The Air Force was particularly interested: escape routes for aircrew and so on. The Americans took it very seriously; of course, it was the Company by then." If Marriage knew the current jargon for the CIA, he didn't bother with it. "And they'd learnt a fair bit in the war, with their OSS – Office of Strategic Services, same as our SOE. I know they were collecting recordings of all the national songs, so they could set up a Radio Free Norway or Denmark or Italy somewhere, after . . ."

"And a Radio Free Britain?"

"Oh yes. The trouble was, we could believe in the Continent being overrun again, but we couldn't face up to it happening here. So the *Amurricanes* wanted to do it, and we let them."

"An American network in Britain."

"Probably quite a good one, too. My Service wanted me to try and penetrate it, just on general grounds, but I told them: the whole point is not to have their names on our files, all ready for the Soviets to take over. But I spent a few bob buying drinks for a couple of old OSS types who'd turned up in their London station and they took pity on me and let drop the codename: Winter Garden. And flower names for the different groups. At least that's what they told me, it could be sheer bull. But it was before they went in for all the cryptonyms and digraphs and five-letter codes because that's what computers like . . ."

A lone motor-cruiser rumbled upstream, tidily cluttered, steered by an elderly man with a black labrador sitting on the cockpit seat behind him. He waved and Marriage lifted his cup slowly in return.

"One of yours?" George asked politely.

"Private. Did you think this was a poor country? Hah. Just go and count the private boats up and down the river. Most of 'em don't get used more than a few hours in the year. A poor country."

The boat left a wake that rocked the long drifts of dead leaves on the water and slapped against the quay below them. Marriage finished his drink and put the cup down very obviously.

My God, George thought, cringing, he wants me to kill off more of that fossilised brain. And I'm going to do it, so that he might, just might, tell me something useful. Have I been sending people out to do this? Mind, he excused himself quickly, this is exceptional, quite exceptional. *And* difficult. Even a trained interrogator would have a problem here . . .

Thus excused, he poured the drinks. "Did Miss Tuckey have anything to do with that? Help them recruit or . . . ?"

"But then she'd have their lists, wouldn't she? And they wouldn't want that, any more than they wanted the Firm to have them. Once you've got a list, you can drag in the whole network. That's what I'm worried about: if your people are . . . working along those lines again, and Dot's been helping out, somebody might think she'd got *your* lists. An old lady living alone in the country, you do see . . ."

George did, and yearned to tell him the Army had thought of it, that Maxim had mentioned how they worked under codenames, then wondered if the Army should tell Moscow that, too – and realised that he was after a list, as well.

Marriage misinterpreted his hesitation and said querulously: "Dot really didn't tell me a thing, nothing. I was just guessing. I don't want you to – "

"Of course not," George soothed him. "I appreciate your concern." And that at least is true, he thought, because if I were a crippled old man living on an early pension filtered through the Secret Vote – and thus controllable – I wouldn't want any whisper of indiscretion getting back to the Service. And probably you're in hock to the Service's banking friends (the Service always had banking friends) for this boatyard, too. They'll never foreclose, because they want you to die in debt. Controllable.

"Getting back to Winter Garden," George said confidently, no longer needing to invoke Miss Tuckey, "you might say it's up my street. What sort of training did they get?"

"Radio, cyphers, handling explosives, the sort of thing we got at Wanborough in the old days."

"Weapons?"

"I doubt most of them would need it; everybody did national service in those days, some would have been in the war."

"They didn't issue any weapons?"

Marriage looked at him oddly, wilting George's confidence. "Our people made it pretty clear there were enough guns still floating loose from the war and getting into the wrong hands. We did make them promise No Guns."

"D'you think they stuck to it?"

"You know, I rather think they did. Probably not for

146

the right reasons. A Resistance group should use enemy weapons, or stuff that can take enemy ammo – and the Company just didn't have enough Russian gear then, in the early Fifties. Now they could do you a boatload right off the shelf, nothing down and nothing to pay if you shoot 'em in the right direction."

"Would there have been any training in destabilisation?" George had thought carefully about risking that word. But one thing he was sure he had learnt was that Marriage was no part of any conspiracy, had indeed no useful friends left. That was why he was reduced to talking to George Harbinger.

"Destabilisation? God, no. You can't destabilise an occupying army, you've got to blow the buggers up. All that came later, when the Company reached the big time."

"Sorry. And you think Winter Garden's all withered away now."

"Just think about it. They wouldn't have been recruiting schoolboys: they'd want mature people, organisers, types with a sense of responsibility and a bit of gloom, kids and a mortgage. You need to be pretty gloomy to think of Resistance in peacetime, don't you? So they'd have been picking people in their thirties then, now they'd be in their sixties. Past it, except for running safe houses. Dead of heart attacks, crippled old men like me. It's long past, now.

"As much as anything, it was the Company that changed," he mused into his cup, beginning to slobber the whisky now. "They got more confident – more money, too, of course. Not just giving radio sets to bank clerks, they were giving bank accounts to politicians. They didn't want to wait and react, they wanted the Other Side to react to them. *That's* when they began the destabilisation thing . . . but Winter Garden, no that's long past."

22

George could have cabled Maxim, but that would have meant a cypher clerk at each end reading the material, and a letter by diplomatic bag would have taken at least thirty-six hours. So he settled for a secure telephone call, indifferent to what that would do to Maxim's reputation among the Defence Staff at the embassy. Until then they had treated him with a mixture of sympathy as a man caught up, by line of duty, in a political imbroglio, and suspicion at what he might do to make things worse. A long secret call from a Ministry of Defence civilian locked the pendulum on the side of suspicion.

Colonel Lomax contrived to bump into him as he left the booth. "Harry, I don't know what that was all about, and I'm not asking, but can I beg one thing of you? Unless you've got a clear order through the proper channels, please don't *do* anything over here. I don't think London realises just how touchy things were even before the shooting at the Abbey. With the Peace Crusade and the Berlin business, we've got so many fences to mend already that we just can't afford another broken strand. So be a good chap and just look at the sights, do a little shopping, try to get to a football game . . ."

"And of course, I do feel bad about it," Maxim confessed to Agnes a few minutes later. "They must have a rough time of it at the moment . . ."

"Let 'em sweat a bit; Washington's a key career posting for most of them, it can't all be cherry blossom and cocktails. So what did George have to say?"

Maxim told her. She ended up shaking her head in slow disbelief. "It's too facile an explanation: blame everything on the CIA. And it still isn't their scale of operation; they'd do it big or not at all."

"All right, but . . . these people have got connections with somebody. The training – "

"Out of books."

"Not a Russian rifle, grenade and typewriter, not out of books. It's just the sort of kit Charlie would have been supplying. Who else could do it?"

Agnes stood up slowly, stretched her back, lit a cigarette and sat down again, frowning thoughtfully. "Winter Garden was before my time, but I did hear about it in my training. And there was a move to set it up again in the late Sixties, but that got sat on. Do you know about the UKUSA agreement? That was when they first created Central Intelligence over here. It's all classified, but what it amounts to is that we won't play the Great Game over here and they won't play it in the UK. So we invoked that agreement, and Charlie said Winter Garden had set a precedent and we said No it hadn't, it had just been a Cold War expedient and those days were over. My own mob was right at the front of the fuss: we didn't want any more secret organisations on our patch."

"Could they have gone ahead and set it up anyway?"

"No. They could never have done anything wide-scale without us knowing – and a Resistance movement has to be wide-scale to be any use. You must have learnt something about this in recent months?" She said it with a sly smile; he hadn't mentioned any of his own stay-behind training.

"Would you remember who was involved from Charlie at the time?"

"Why?"

"George read me over a list of CIA personnel who were in London in the late Sixties – "

"A list? He's barmy. It must be like a telephone book: their London station's the biggest they've got, there would have been hundreds coming through . . ."

Maxim silently handed over his notes.

Agnes read them through, then said more calmly: "Well, he does seem to have got the top people . . . I met most of these . . . Bodey, but he's dead, now; Kilmartin was strictly an analyst, wouldn't have been involved . . . I think Foulque resigned way back . . . Magill, yes, old Mighty Mo, I remember *him*. But he retired, too; they're just about all gone, the old team.

"Mo would know something about it," Agnes went on thoughtfully. "He was OSS, then in London at the time of Winter Garden, then he came back in the mid-Sixties. A real player, that man; could charm the pants right off a girl."

"Did he?" Maxim asked innocently.

"No . . . but it might be worth talking over old times with him. He's got a law office in New York; a lot of the old team were lawyers. He must be sixty-something now . . . yes, I think I'll give him a call. D'you feel like a shopping trip to New York? Everybody ought to get a bite of the Big Apple."

In a way, it was a waste of the cover story Maxim had been kiting for his trip to St Louis, but if it was a step forward . . .

October is the cocktail month in Washington; the British embassy can be throwing three parties a week, and with the Liaison Office's yen to keep Maxim busy, he inevitably found himself sipping deep-frozen Scotch with a wing-commander from the Office.

"How on earth," he wondered aloud, "does anybody stay sober in this city?"

"Iron willpower and a stainless-steel liver." The RAF man peered into his empty glass, trying to decide which to rely on. "And the last man on his feet gets the extra hundred mil in foreign aid. No" – he nodded at the babbling drawing-room behind them – "this is just froth. The real business gets done at working lunches and small dinner parties. When they start feeding you, you'll know you're somebody. Ah, I spy a presidential aide: that makes the evening A Success." A small crowd had knotted at the door where the Ambassador was greeting guests. "Clay Culliman, you've heard of him?"

"I met him," Maxim said, stupidly slipping in a bit of inter-service one-upmanship.

"*Did* you, now? – Where?"

"The President's visit to London."

"Of course. Yes, you were the chap at the Abbey." His round pink face beamed. "That's something to tell my wife. We couldn't get a babysitter, so I was expecting a cold TV dinner thrown at my head when I rolled back. Now I can say I've been mixing with both the noble and the notorious. You won't mind being that, for the sake of a fellow warrior in the cold drinks war? I think I can risk one more, in that case. Nothing for you?" He ambled off towards the nearest tray.

Disgusted by his own conceit, Maxim drifted out to the steps down to the lawn – the night was still warm enough for the big windows to be open – flanked by two huge, discreetly floodlit magnolia trees. A few couples and small groups were there already, muttering and sipping in the half-shadows, but Maxim stayed clear, drowning his sorrow in darkness.

I wish I could be *doing* something, moving, he thought, with an infantryman's loathing of being pinned down in a known position.

Beyond the silhouette of the trees, flat black against the glow of Georgetown, lay Dumbarton Oaks, site of the 1944 conference that had shaped the United Nations. Or maybe those trees *were* Dumbarton Oaks, and he had a momentary vision of the free world's foreign ministers sitting like Robin Hood's gang around a flickering campfire, greasy lumps of venison in their fingers, arguing about who should be permanent members of the Security Council.

But no, Dumbarton Oaks must also be a mansion or conference centre, and the vision faded, leaving an ember of a smile as he turned to find another drink.

His way was blocked by the Ambassador and Culliman, talking politely about gardens as they came through the french windows. Culliman glanced at Maxim, did a double-take, and stretched out his hand. "It's Major . . . ah . . ."

"Maxim," before the Ambassador had to admit he couldn't remember, either.

"Sure, we met . . . yeh, just before things got exciting. Good to see you. You'll be over for the After Action Study. Kind of you to come."

"No trouble."

"George keeping fit?" Culliman chuckled at the idea; the Ambassador murmured something and backed into the room. "I guess you'll be getting back for the Soviet visit, now."

"The which?"

"You haven't caught up with tonight's news? Yeh, I know how it is when you're travelling. It'll be all in the *Post* tomorrow. Your government's invited a Soviet delegation to talk about Berlin next week. All the details, place of meeting, flight times, everything."

"Did we announce all *that*?"

"Doesn't make your job any easier, huh? No, it wasn't announced: it leaked. It's good to know ours isn't the only State Department with too many back doors." There was a hard edge on Culliman's tone.

"I doubt I'd be involved," Maxim said slowly, thinking fast. "The President's unit was a one-off thing . . ."

"Well, I guess once we hear it officially, I'll be drafting a note saying we don't think it's a frightfully spiffing idea." He grinned and shook Maxim's hand again. "Hope to be seeing you, Major."

Maxim trailed into the room behind him, vaguely looking for a fresh drink and finding Agnes instead, who had been more than vaguely looking for him. "Mixing in White House circles, are we, Harry? What changes in American policy can we hope for as a result of your high-level talks?"

"He was telling me about the Russian visit."

"Oh yes." Agnes's face became grim. "I just got that myself. Good old Britain: not only doing the wrong thing but unable to keep it secret. Great start to a party." Looking around, Maxim saw the Ambassador already making defensive gestures to a couple of guests. He also caught a number of covert glances at himself: was that what a few moment's conversation with a presidential aide did for you in this town?

"Let's get out of here," he said irritably.

"An old line, but welcome nonetheless. No, Jerry, you can't have him – " to Colonel Lomax, who was waiting to pounce. "Harry's carrying my books home from school

152

today. And he's taking me shopping in New York tomorrow. Christmas is coming and he thinks I ought to know about some little joints called Tiffany's and Bloomingdale's. Is that all right with your Office? He can't pawn his ticket home if he's flying Riff-RAF airlines . . .

"He had the look of somebody about to invite you home to cold chicken and salad with a mug of real warm English beer," she continued as they walked the long black-and-white-tiled corridor. "Don't bump into those pillars, they're fakes, they don't really support anything except an illusion of Empire . . . Yes, I spoke to Mo Magill, he'll see us tomorrow morning, we'll fly up on the shuttle, I don't know what we'll get, but . . . and I've got a line into St Louis: there's a thing called the Western Manuscripts collection at UMSL – ghastly word, but they use it themselves, it means University of Missouri-St Louis – that latches on to the papers of operations like CCOAC, and they've got them. Can you imitate an academic? – like not washing or changing your shirt for the next few days . . . ?"

Her car was utterly undistinguished, a distinction that would not please its makers, but suited Agnes's instinct to choose the average and inconspicuous. Maxim had noticed how she had adopted certain American phrases and mannerisms as well, not because she was trying to pass as an American, but just to blend into the background. That was something an infantryman could understand.

"The Russian visit," he said. "What do you make of this leak?"

"Have you thought how many departments would know anyway? Number 10, the FO, my mob, Defence probably, and the Met. It doesn't have to be your Abbey activists."

"Somebody might have let slip something, they wouldn't have let loose every detail."

"True . . . Were you thinking that broadcasting it was another piece of the pattern?"

"Could be. And it does show these people are well connected. Security for the Russians had better be good."

"D'you think it'll be you again?"

"I don't think I'm our favourite guard detail commander, right now."

"But you'd do it."

"I'd do what I was told."

"And maybe a little bit more . . . I wonder if those idiots realise just how much they frighten you and me . . . people who support a system because, in the end, the answers have to come through the system. Throw out the rule of law and you throw out the string that'll lead you back out of the maze. Live or dead, the Minotaur's won. D'you know what I'm talking about?"

"Greek legend, among other things."

"And all on two glasses of Diplomatic white wine. You must have an intoxicating presence, Harry. And while we're on the subject of law and order, were you planning to go West under your own name?"

"I was going to ask: if I make a return trip in one day, no hotel, I could buy an airline ticket for cash and give any name I like – couldn't I?"

"They might ask for some identification: in this country, the man who carries cash is guilty until proven innocent. However, I can do you one unused Canadian passport and a Saskatchewan driving licence, not even one previous little-old-lady owner. Canadians don't need a US visa."

"I see," Maxim said thoughtfully. "And how does that fit into the UKUSA agreement?"

"Imperfectly. But very occasionally we used to get somebody who wanted to talk to us and had good reason not to talk to the Feds or Charlie, and the simplest thing was to slip him into Canada and cite the Old-Commonwealth-Pals Act. However, our current D-G's stopped all that, so you might as well use it before the date-stamp runs out."

23

The bar/restaurant near Union Station was dolled up to look like an English pub and doing it better than most London pubs did, to Maxim's traditionalist eye. In his view, London pubs were trying to be either video game arcades or sets for Oscar Wilde plays.

"They sometimes have jazz here in the evenings," Agnes chattered, "although I don't know if it's up to your standards. Oscar Peterson was in town the other week, I read – you like him, don't you? Pity you weren't here, I could have rustled up a ticket or two and you could have explained the finer nuances. Does jazz have finer nuances?"

Maxim thought briefly about a pun on Ray Nance, then just smiled into his beer: in a pub he felt duty bound to drink beer, although it certainly wasn't English ("With all those lovely vitamins floating around in it, damn it, you can *see* them," as a fellow officer newly back from the USA had put it).

"So you met our dear D-G at the Steering Committee," she went on. "Isn't he loveable? Just what we've always wanted, an academic international lawyer running Security. Can't think why we've stuck so long with people who knew something about the job."

She stabbed out her cigarette and lit another. She had plunked her pack with the lighter on top of the bar, as if she were planning to smoke the lot before she moved on. It was another American gesture, though far fewer Americans do it in these cancer-conscious days.

"There is a 1952 directive that's never been superseded," she said deliberately. "The Service should, and I quote: 'be kept absolutely free from any political bias or influence', unquote. A pretty thought, and what it really means is

Try, brothers, Try. You can't draw a hard line between international and national politics, not these days. Political influence is what the Other Side wants, as much as anything, and you've got to meet it in that arena. But we did try, damn it. We knew what lay down any other road: a political scandal that made it worthwhile for Parliament to get involved in Security. That's what happened with Charlie's Indians. They'll never get away from Capitol Hill now, and they'll have to keep playing politics just to protect themselves.

"So we tried – and we got a political appointment anyway. Now we're part of government policy, which happens to be hear no evil, see no evil . . . one bloody monkey's enough if he's in the top job." She snapped her cigarette in her fingers and burnt her knuckle. "I'm getting all bitter and twisted: you'd better feed me. I just don't have many people I can say these things to."

"You didn't say it around the Service?"

"Why d'you think I'm in Washington? It's a nice place, but my job's in London. Oh well: it could have been Gibraltar."

The eating at least was American, at a tiny corner table lit by a single candle in a jar. Agnes chose quiche, Maxim hadn't been in Washington long enough to tire of seafood, so he took crab. On a small stage at the far end, a man with a neat beard began tuning a Spanish guitar to the piano.

After a while, Maxim asked: "Why should this chap Magill tell us anything tomorrow?"

"I don't know that he will: but he was in High Places at the right times, so it's worth trying the Good Old Times routine . . ." But just why am I doing this? she wondered. Yes, I believe those people exist and they frighten me and I want them destroyed. But I'm sticking my neck out: one squeak from the FBI that I'm breaching the UKUSA agreement and my own Service will swing the big axe . . . Pity about Agnes Algar, could have gone a long way in the Service, but went charging off on some unauthorised stunt in America, typically female in the end, trying to save the career of some soldier who'd got himself . . .

Is *that* why I'm doing this? For Harry?

She glanced cautiously at him, munching his crab in the candlelight. He had a calm lean face, never to be called handsome, and if he looked up he would put on his quick protective smile, to say Don't ask about me, I'm all right, talk about somebody else . . .

You're not all right, chum. I know that much about you. But in this one you're *right*, and that makes me right, too, without having to decide just why I'm doing this, and perhaps doing more than I'll ever get around to telling you.

"Why did Magill leave the CIA?" Maxim asked. "Was it just retirement?"

Good old Harry: let's get back to facts. "No, he left early. I don't know quite when, some time in the Seventies. It was a bad time for Charlie's Indians: the White House cavalry was charging through the reservation every second day. First Nixon purged them to get the spotlight off himself, then Ford had a go and Carter ran his own massacree. At one point they dropped seven hundred men – *seven hundred* – think what that does for morale. Think what it could do to security. I think Mo left in the middle of all that. I imagine he just saw the writing on the wall and didn't like their spelling."

Maxim had finished his crab and was pushing bits of salad around his plate, trying to identify them in the dimness, and listening with half-turned head to a tenor saxophonist who had joined the guitar to swap phrases of the Beale Street Blues.

Agnes watched with amusement as his interest quickened or faded with each phrase. When the number ended, he clapped in a careful way, unconsciously trying to say exactly what he felt about it. The other diners, who mostly hadn't been listening, just clapped.

"Not so good, hey?" she asked.

"A bit slick. Too many notes from the tenor, but . . ."

"You'd better be a Canadian who knows about jazz. And forgive me asking an indelicate question, but how are you off for money – on the whole trip? I don't imagine the Army's too generous."

"I've got my own credit cards. And George gave me a

157

big lump in traveller's cheques. He said money was one problem I didn't have to have."

"Good for him. But he's got it so that it hurts. However, they're all signed Maxim, right? You'll have to cash in some and then buy more signed . . . We haven't got a name for you yet. How about Winterbotham? I've always wanted to know a Winterbotham."

"I'm damned if I have."

"Good: you'll remember it. Think of all those dreadful jokes you suffered at school. Alan James? I think that'll do: Alan James Winterbotham, this is your new life. Practise a signature – and initials."

Maxim found a radish on his plate and ate it. His expression changed. "That was a strawberry. D'you serve *strawberries* with crab here?"

"Live a little, or at least die quietly."

24

The ride down Northern Boulevard from La Guardia airport to the Queensboro bridge may not be the best way to see New York for the first time, although Maxim caught glimpses of its towers jolting towards them over the grey horizon. But does anybody see New York for the first time these days? Most people have been familiar with its skyline since they were old enough to focus on a TV screen. They may feel New York for the first time, because its fast-dealing busyness is something the screen doesn't catch, and may smell it for the first time, if they come in high summer, but one of the great first sights of the world is gone for ever.

Magill's offices were towards the top of a modest tower on midtown Madison. They were kept waiting for just a couple of minutes – "While Mr Magill completes a call" – in a cool-warm windowless reception area soundproofed so that even the loudest complaint about a bill would come out as a hushed croak, then ushered through into an office that was almost straight from Charles Dickens.

Agnes stood and looked around, then caught Maxim's thought by saying: "What, no rolltop desk? Cheap, Mo, cheap," and Magill came out from behind his flat-topped mahogany desk with a shout of laughter and hugged her and patted her bottom.

He was a big man, everything about him was big, shoulders, chest, nose, eyes and ears, everything except his near-flat stomach and his hair, which had faded on top and grown to wise-looking grey tufts over his ears.

"Rolltops?" he shouted over Agnes's shoulder. "This is genuine Sheraton, sweetie, except the asshole never made a piece in his life, on account he was into franchising ahead of anybody except the Pope. How're you doing?" – this to

Maxim, over Agnes's shoulder, stretching out a big hand – "you must be Major Harry Maxim. Sit down, children, d'you want to get married or divorced or just sue each other? Have some coffee." He poured it from a Victorian coffee pot waiting on a hotplate and launched into a description of a case he'd just won, punctuated by blasts of laughter and big gestures.

Maxim sipped his coffee and glanced covertly round the room, at the shelves of leather-bound legal volumes, a row of Spy's legal cartoons, framed degrees and photographs of Magill as a young soldier and, he guessed, General 'Wild Bill' Donovan, the founder of US intelligence.

". . . the guy called me the minute he got back to his office, and he said: 'Mo, do you agree with me that judge was as wet as hell?' and I said: 'If you so say, but he was sure swimming in the right pool.'" He rocked his swivel chair back with more laughter. "Okay then, what can I really do for you? – or did you just want to talk about old times?"

"Just that, Mo," Agnes said. She was sitting in the main client's chair, wearing a dark brown suit with a faint orange check and clutching a huge floppy handbag in her lap. "Just old times. Something's come out of the woodwork . . . D'you remember Winter Garden?"

"Sure I do, but you don't. You weren't even born then."

"Just barely. But I heard about it in training. Would anybody still have lists of those people, Mo?"

"Jeez, no. I never had lists myself. All that stuff, you just don't have lists. Washington wanted them, we said the hell, the whole thing is busted if you have lists. We gave them codenames and radio frequencies, they never got lists out of us. All this is long gone; long, long gone."

"Well . . ." Agnes seemed momentarily lost; Maxim did nothing except sit still and watch, as Agnes had told him to. She fumbled a cigarette from her bag and lit it. "Well . . . did you ever arm these people?"

Agnes's head was down over her cigarette; it was Maxim who caught the moment of stillness in Magill's big restless body.

"Arms? Never, no way at all. This was then, we were

160

indenting for paperclips one by one in those days. We just didn't have arms." He laughed abruptly, an afterthought.

"Good, that clears that one up. So it can't be the old Winter Garden crop."

Magill smiled. "I still don't know what you're talking about."

"I suppose I'd better tell, just in case you've got any thoughts. Things have been happening in the UK. You must have read about the Reznichenko Memorandum? Somebody faked it: Russian typewriter, letter heading, Reznichenko's signature – all backed up by a first-class tail job. Then somebody got a leading anti-NATO speaker drugged and he blew an important speech." Agnes was putting all her cards on the table; " – and then there was the Abbey. Somebody took a shot, not at the President, they could have killed him easily, but knocked off a man who could have swung thirty votes in favour of a Berlin settlement. That was with a Russian rifle; then he blew himself up with a Russian grenade. How does all that grab you?"

"Your people will think all that stuff ties up together, hey?"

"It's a pattern, Mo."

Magill put his elbows on his desk, clasping the dainty china cup in front of his mouth with both hands. He wore a plain white shirt as fresh as new snow, tiny gold cufflinks and a polka-dot tie. There was no sign of his jacket, but there was a second door to the room, so probably he had a private bathroom and clothes closet as well.

"I don't know anything except what I read in the papers, but from what I do read, your government can't see this pattern."

"Governments? When did you start caring what *governments* can and can't see?"

Magill grinned behind his cup. "Getting old, I guess. But your Service wants to get it all sorted and gift-wrapped for them? Or is it just you? and the unknown soldier here."

"Harry? He was heading up the President's getaway operation at the Abbey. He shot the chap who did the shooting."

Magill gave Maxim a steady, searching look, and Maxim smiled self-consciously back. "Over here for the After Action Study, hey?"

"Was that in the papers?" Agnes asked innocently.

Magill gave another shout of laughter. "Okay . . . but I'll tell you what I think, sweetie. I don't think your new Director-General knows anything about this. I don't even think he's the sort of guy who'd want to know anything about this. And I further think you're working all on your ownsome on this and that's why you've come to good old Uncle Mo instead of going to the boys at Langley. Am I right?"

Agnes's smile was small but seemingly frank and cheerful. "The boys at Langley don't do much talking to us just at the moment. And suppose I did get through, all they'd say is it's nothing to do with them, they weren't even in the Company at that time – and how many of them were?"

"If you're worried about Winter Garden, there's nobody left who had any status around *that* time, sure. But I'm telling you, forget Winter Garden. It's long gone – we didn't give them arms, we didn't give them the sort of training you're talking about. And they're old men like me, now. Forget it."

"There was some talk of replanting it, in the late Sixties, when you were back in London. That I do remember."

"But maybe you also recall how your Service dumped all over us on that one? Hell, the first time we met, you were bringing in some by-hand-of-bearer letter telling us we were trying to depose the monarchy, devalue the pound and make the natives play baseball instead of cricket. I recall that. Great days, great days."

"I do remember. But actually" – Agnes's voice became pure Oxford (the university, not the town) – "that was just Track One, wasn't it? – cover, in case we noticed anything on Track Two, which was a small destabilisation group. The right training, the right arms, everything that's coming to the surface now. Were you running that, Mo? – or who?"

In his own gaping reaction, Maxim almost missed Magill's. This time the lawyer didn't freeze, he wavered.

Between denying Agnes's guesswork and denying his own responsibility, as she had intended. And now, small and neat, she overrode the big man behind his own – undoubtedly genuine eighteenth-century – desk as he opened his mouth to reply.

"Don't say anything for the moment, Mo. Just let's look to see if we can make a case, all right? Those were the days when the Company was really into the Track One, Track Two stuff, cover within cover, mostly to fool Capitol Hill, I dare say, but other governments too, and all to hide destabilisation. That was something you were *right* into at that time: Africa, Chile, South-East Asia – so why not Europe? We were all set up for it in Britain: a Labour government, anti-nuclear movement, swinging along on borrowed money with Carnaby Street and the Beatles – they were going to bring World Peace all by themselves – fat, dumb and happy. But your Company could see the writing on the wall, even my Service didn't like the way things were going. They were positively glad when the Russians went into Prague: it reminded people . . . But, Mo, don't snow me that the Company didn't see all that and start a Track Two behind the comeback of Winter Garden."

She was speaking quietly but fast, and pausing for breath in the wrong places, the way politicians do when they fear interruption.

"Well, that's the case, anyway: whether it would stand up in court, you're the lawyer, you'd know better than I – but we're not talking about courts and proof, just leaks and public opinion. Because when my government does see the pattern – you're quite right, they don't want to see it right now, and my D-G isn't helping them – but when these people do the next thing, and it'll have to be something big – they're up against a deadline on Berlin, they've already escalated it from forged documents to drugging people to shooting them, God knows what comes next – well, when something new happens, the lone psychopath theory will be dead, dead, dead. And then what? Who are they going to blame next? – Moscow Centre? I'll tell you something, Mo, my government isn't in the business of blaming Moscow Centre right now. I think it would prefer to blame somebody who's already responsible – as you'll know if you really do read the papers – for every dead dog and blocked drain right across the world. The Company."

There was a silence, then Magill heaved a grunt of laughter out of his big chest. "And you think it really is the Company?"

"What I think won't matter by then. It'll be what my government thinks."

"And you want to be first in line to give it them."

"Let's say I don't want to be last in line, not if it's what they want anyway. I'm a career-oriented girl. Oh, and there's one thing I didn't tell you: Moscow Centre's on to the pattern. Not surprising, really, since they know they didn't do these things. Harry ran across their tracks the other day; he killed one of them, but he's a bit like that. Career-oriented, you know."

Magill looked hard at Maxim. "That didn't make the papers."

"No," Agnes said, "and I don't think anybody can prove it. Did you ever meet a Miss Tuckey?"

"Dot Tuckey? Sure, she'd been with you, SOE. I didn't know her then, only later."

"They got to her, too. You tell him, Harry."

Maxim told him. Only he left out – as Agnes had instructed – any mention of CCOAC and St Louis.

Magill listened, then said: "Jeez. You are deep into bear country, Major. Did you tell him?" This to Agnes.

"I told him. You can see how worried I got him."

"Yes . . . so where do you want to go from here?"

"What I really want is for us to reach these people before Moscow does: there's no argument about who *they'll* want to pin it on. And after that – nothing. Silence. Blaming it on the Company would be just a fallback – you wouldn't believe me if I said I wasn't thinking of that, but you might believe me if I say we'd prefer the good old British way: that nothing happened and there's no blame at all. The psychopath theory can cover the Abbey, and for the rest" – she shrugged – "we can make sure there's no proof. Moscow's got nothing but bodies and they aren't going to dig them up to prove us wrong. But if we're to

164

handle it this way, it's got to be fast and we need every lead you can give us."

Magill leant back, rocking gently in his chair. "You've grown up, sweetie. You've got style. I'm truly sorry we never got to work together . . . Now let me tell you where I stand. I've got no official connection with the Company any more, but it's still useful. Even if I wanted to try and screw them, I'd be stupid: it would lose me clients and money both. So I tell you what I'll do: I'll look into a couple things, maybe call somebody – can you get back here after lunch? I'll clear my desk, anything I've got for you I'll tell you privately. Excuse me, Major, but I don't know you or your security clearance. This way, if anybody asks, I may have talked to an agent from British Security. That much I can carry. Okay?"

Going down in the lift, which was uncrowded because it was still early for lunch, Maxim said: "*I* think he just wants to put his hand on your knee – in a purely uncle-ly fashion."

"Why, Major Maxim, I didn't know you cared. But I'm a big girl now." Her face was controlled and serious.

"How d'you think we're doing?"

"Let's walk a bit."

They walked uptown on Madison, which quickly loses its advertising-agency and legal-eagle gloss in that direction, with a chill wind in their faces. A mere two hundred miles from Washington had brought them into a different season, although it was obviously the first hint of real autumn in New York: around them, others were hurrying because they were too thinly dressed, or tugging at coats and gloves that were unfamiliar and awkward after half a year at the back of the closet. Maxim felt smug in his thick car-coat for the first time in America.

"Well, at least we established how it all started," he said. "Were you guessing at that Track Two business?"

"More or less. But Charlie's Indians" – she had avoided the British jargon with Magill, Maxim had noticed – "are a big outfit, and big outfits tend to behave in patterns. It was worth trying. Yes, we got that far, but we didn't get any names, not yet. Are you hungry?"

165

"So-so."

"I don't feel like anywhere too swank. Do you mind missing Delmonico's on your first visit to New York?"

They missed Delmonico's by only a few blocks geographically but far more gastronomically – or so Maxim assumed, since he also assumed that Delmonico's didn't specialise in hamburgers and tuna sandwiches for the decorators working on the shop next door. But he felt securely anonymous jammed in a corner against the steamed-up front window, and perhaps that was what Agnes wanted.

"The trouble is," she muttered through her sandwich, "that we don't really have the leverage I was trying to imply. Mo may just not care what gets said about the Company – it's all the new team now – as long as he isn't caught saying it himself. And if he gets blamed for some dirty work that got started fifteen years ago – and I doubt he was directly responsible; he was too senior, then – how much does it hurt him now? His clients must know he's ex-Company, and like it. It suggests good Washington connections, as he said, and a certain fluidity of ethics, as he didn't say. Clients do like winning."

"He must still want the whole thing stopped."

She raised her eyebrows. "I wish I agreed with you. Look at it this way: Track Two is now doing just what it was set up to do, in just the situation they foresaw: a weak British government getting too close to Moscow. If Mo liked the idea then, why shouldn't he like it now?"

Maxim chewed thoughtfully on something he had decided to eat rather than take out and look at; he had chosen the hamburger. "Do you think the CIA could still be running it, then?"

"No, the old reasoning still holds. If Charlie had triggered it, there'd have been a big back-up of propaganda and so on. I think the British end somehow managed to start itself up – though I'm damned if I see how."

"What's the problem?"

"Because that's exactly what Charlie wouldn't want them to do: start anything without a clear directive from over here. And there's only one sure way to do that: recruit and train them individually, or in pairs, but never let any one of them see the whole list."

"So somebody must have got hold of the list."

"That could be our strongest point: that things are running out of control. But it depends on how much control the Company *wants* to have now . . ."

"Not just a list, though," Maxim went on. "They got hold of a cache of arms and other kit. That sounds like a base, somewhere. They wouldn't issue those things individually, I'd think. I mean, if one of them steps under a bus and you start valuing his estate for probate, Ullo, ullo, ullo, how much is a case of Russian grenades worth?"

Agnes grinned quickly. But Maxim was most likely right. Spreading such immediately incriminating material around was more risky than one truly safe house. "It's something we'd like to know, all right."

"You could ask."

Agnes was about to say scathingly 'Ask how?' but caught herself in time. "So now you go and tramp the streets changing your traveller's cheques into cash and then into traveller's cheques signed Winterbotham. Spread it around the banks – have you got both passports? Clever fellow. Think up a story why you've got cash and want cheques but *don't* tell it until they drag it out of you. Sign of guilt. What the hell business is it of theirs? You're innocent, remember."

25

This time there was no waiting at the reception desk; Agnes carefully avoided the girl's eye as she was shown straight through to Magill's office.

The door to the inner room was open and Mo was standing watching a newscast on a TV set in the far corner, sipping from a cut-glass tumbler.

"Hi, sweetie, like a drink?" He mixed her a dry martini from a collection of decanters on a silver tray – nothing so arriviste as a drinks cupboard or private bar – set on a small table. The other furniture was a couple of wing chairs, a single-ended Victorian chaise-longue and a fruitwood dressing-table. The room was decorated in quiet tabby-cat colours, with style – and a purpose. She sipped her drink.

"I did some thinking," Mo said, "and I figured I didn't need to call DC after all. Maybe I should tell you about one man. D'you want to hear?"

"I'm all ears."

"Not all, sweetie, not all." They sat in the wing chairs. "It goes back to the old OSS days and the crusade we were running against Hitler, along with your SOE and Dot Tuckey and people like that. Like Arnie Tatham. Did you ever meet with him?"

"The name sounds . . . Didn't he get killed by Italian terrorists?"

"Right. I first met with Arnie, it must've been '44, I didn't get to know him well then, but he came out of that with one hell of a name as a field man. He was a natural, you find them sometimes, if you're lucky, and from the damnedest backgrounds. Most anywhere except where you'd go looking. Like Arnie: his old man was rector of an Episcopalian church in small-town Illinois. I think his mother died when he was young and he grew up with more books than friends, maybe more Shakespeare than Mark Twain. I guess if there hadn't been the war, Arnie would be a professor at some small college writing monographs on how many times Hamlet called Ophelia 'a dumb broad'."

"*Mo* . . ."

But Magill was already grinning to himself. "Okay – but did you ever reread *Hamlet* as power politics, destabilisation, covert operations?"

"And assassination."

"Plenty of it. Rosencrantz and Guildenstern would be working for The Mob, these days. And did you wonder how an Elizabethan audience would take all of that? I'd say they loved it – and they understood it. If that was what you did to keep control, that was what was needed."

"So Tatham became a top field man by reading Shakespeare. And was he running Track Two?"

"He set it up, I just ran interference for him, trying to keep your people looking the wrong way with talk about opening up Winter Garden again. I guess it worked, too – until you figured it out." Agnes noted the sly flattery and smiled. "But if you're going to ask me did I know who he recruited, no I didn't. I never wanted to."

Agnes absorbed that and found that she believed it: Mo had been thirty years in intelligence work, which trains up a determination not to know some things quite as strong as the desire to know others. "And Tatham got himself killed in Italy – what? four, five years ago?"

"Right. He retired over there: his marriage had gone, and so had his daughter's" – and so had Magill's first marriage, she knew: marriages in the secret world had a high casualty rate – "and she went over to keep house for him." He took her glass and freshened their drinks. "Then some asshole of a journalist printed a story that he was still working for the Company and a couple of weeks later the Red Brigade snatched both of them. It was the usual stuff: demands for money and release of terrorist prisoners . . . I don't know how much pressure we put on for the police to get off their butts and do something. I wasn't with the Company any more, and Arnie didn't have much in the way of friends left in DC, so . . . Anyhow, they killed him. In front of his daughter; they made her take pictures of his body . . . Then the cops did do something, but I don't know if it was a tip-off or dumb luck: they raided some farmhouse up in Tuscany and found her still alive. They charged some people with the murder, a year later. It was that big show trial, everybody charged with everything, the Bologna train station bombing, Moro's murder, you remember it . . . I don't recall if they got a conviction for Arnie. What did it matter?"

Agnes sipped her drink, assuming that Magill was watching her face for signs of disappointment. "That sounds like the end of the story, then."

"That's the end of it, sure. What I haven't told you yet is the beginning. When the war ended, the OSS was busted up: they hung on to a few units – there was a whole alphabet soup of SI, SSU, X-2, CIG, for a time – but most of us just went home to build a brave new world with law books and Shakespeare. We figured the United Nations could handle the rest.

"So then it started over." He stood up, ticking off the events with his glass against the fingers of his left hand. "The Soviet takeovers in Czechoslovakia, Hungary, Poland. The Berlin blockade. First Soviet nuclear test. Mao in China. The Korean war. And when we could see some of these coming, we didn't have the resources, the agencies, to head it off. That's when Central Intelligence really got started."

"A new crusade?" Agnes said quietly.

"I guess we saw it that way: I did, for sure. That's why I came back when they called. But I'd say a crusade was something you came home from, for Arnie it was a way of life. He was a believer. Not a preacher, just a quiet believer. You know one of the things he believed in? He believed in England – well, Episcopalian is your Church of England, and I think his grandfather was an immigrant back around the end of the century.

"Now when I say he believed in England, I don't mean your thatched cottages and warm beer, he didn't think the place was *cute*, not just his grandfather's birthplace. I wonder if Arnie even bothered to go there. No, he thought of England as Magna Carta and Shakespeare and

Churchill and Milton and the rule of law – a lot of great ideas and ideals that maybe you were going to just crumple and throw away." He had been pacing the room with slow, majestic energy, ending by peering down through the venetian blind at Madison below. "That's what made him a natural for Crocus."

"Crocus?"

After a moment, Magill said: "Yes. We called it that, so if it leaked out it would get mixed up with the old Winter Garden names." He sounded annoyed at himself for letting that slip, and Agnes wondered how much was genuine: the codename, the slip, the annoyance. You had to think like that with Magill. Tatham might have been a natural, but Magill had been the achiever in the secret world.

He went on flatly: "So I fixed things for him – he was posted to Germany; we didn't want him in London having to ride the cocktail circuit." That was standard practice: where possible, you ran a group in one country from a nearby one. Most Soviet espionage in the USA was directed from Canada and Mexico. "But he came through London when . . . when he needed to."

"And you never saw the Crocus List?"

"Like I say."

"But somebody at Langley saw it. If the time came, they'd be directing operations from there and they'd want to know just who they were directing, where they were placed in British society – everything. And somebody must have taken over when Tatham resigned."

Magill shook his head slowly. "No . . . I didn't tell you how he left, yet. It was just after Nixon fired Dick Helms and was dumping all over the Company to get us to take the rap for Watergate, and Congress was hearing words like assassination and setting up committees and . . . like everybody was pissing into our bathtub and hoping to stir up a U-boat. At one time it looked like everything we'd done in twenty years was going to be spread out on the table – and that included setting up a group to destabilise our closest ally, if it got needed. Now, do you think anybody who wasn't already tied in to that wanted to get tied in, at that time?"

Shaking his big head slowly, he lowered himself on to the chaise-longue and sat back carefully. "I said, I said it to Arnie, we had two choices: that file on the committee table, or Crocus had never happened and surely wasn't happening now. If we tried to keep it alive, we had an open flank: some guy trying to save his own ass by telling them: 'Jeez, if you think I did bad things, just look at what Magill and Tatham were doing in London.' Arnie was ready to take that risk, but I wasn't: I'd been the one at London station. I told him, either that file went up the Hill, maybe with the list he'd recruited, or it all went in the shredder."

"Not much of a choice," Agnes said.

"No, I had him by the balls. It wasn't the only operation that went into the shredder at that time – you could figure that for yourself. So, Arnie went to London and closed it off, wiped our prints off everything, and I shut down the Langley end. And from then on, it had never happened. Only, he never spoke to me again. He'd been all set to save England and I'd stopped him. He put in his resignation, took out his pension contributions and walked."

"But with the Crocus List in his head."

Magill turned the heavy glass in his hand, studying the reflections on his drink. "I'd assume he couldn't forget it if he wanted to. It would only be ten names, maybe. Arnie didn't think that big was beautiful, he believed small was secure – and Crocus had to be secure; the blowback potential was massive. Natch, if the operation had gotten the go-code, that List would only have been part of it. The big push would be diplomatic propaganda, screwing the pound sterling on the money markets . . . mugging the Mother of Parliaments would've been quite a job." He smiled lopsidedly.

"Only now, your Crocus List is trying it all on its ownsome."

"Not mine, sweetie, nor the Company's neither. I told you: it never happened."

"Why did you leave the Company, Mo?"

The big man sighed heavily. "Maybe I'd stopped believing, started wondering if things couldn't have been just a bit different. Maybe I'm just saying I wish we hadn't done the things that went wrong – old men think like that, kid themselves along. You can't regret everything. So . . . I hung in there another year, shredding a few more files, saying maybe it was time I went back to the law, and when I got this offer . . . I took my medal and they all cried. And I cried for Arnie, because he'd trusted me." He sighed again. "Sweetie, you are looking at an old moose who just can't figure out where he took the wrong trail, and he'll never get back up that hill again. Maybe I should just've stayed here and untangled Mrs Wertenheimer's fight with her landlord. That, I could've got right."

Despite herself, Agnes smiled with real warmth at the old crocodile – Magill was never a moose – shedding genuine crocodile tears. She believed in most of what he'd been saying; she had no idea of how much he believed himself.

Magill put on a brave, wry smile. "And how's about you? Is there still a crusade out there someplace?"

"Perhaps. Perhaps I'm on one now . . . I like to think so."

He reached and took her hand. "That's what I like about you. You belong to the good times . . . there were some, had to be. Tell me we can still win more than we lose."

"You and me together, Mo? Strictly under the UKUSA agreement?"

He threw his head back with laughter, then hauled her to her feet and hugged her to him. "I should've thought of invoking that long since. Yes, you and me."

Her body had stiffened for a moment, but she made herself relax and huddle against him. This was why she was there; this, and something more . . . "Why, *Mister* Magill," she reacted with over-prim innocence.

"You and me," he repeated, smiling reassuringly. "The ones who understand crusades. D'you want . . . ?" He nodded at a door that must be the bathroom.

"Won't be a minute." She took her big shapeless hand-bag with her. She was unsurprised to find a long silk bathrobe, neither masculine nor feminine, hanging on the back of the door. When she had undressed and put it on, without catching her own eye in the mirror, she went back to the other room and dumped the handbag on top of the dressing-table. As an afterthought, she routed in it to find her cigarettes and lighter, leaving it sloppily open.

Afterwards, she sat in one of the chairs and lit a cigarette, still in the bathrobe; Magill seemed to like his women never quite naked. He stayed stretched on the chaise-longue.

"Fix yourself another drink, sweetie."

"No thanks. It's either too early or too late."

"Never too late . . . didn't we just prove that?" He chuckled contentedly. "We should have got together a long time ago, when I wasn't an old man."

"You aren't old, Mo," she reassured him.

"Not with you, maybe . . ."

There had to be something left on the sideboard for her: she had earned it. But she was going to have to ask for it.

"Mo – where did the Crocus List get its training?"

"Germany. We had so many military establishments over there, the Company had its own place, Camp King close off Frankfurt, I guess most of it would have been there. Good practice for them getting there: fly to Paris, make contact with somebody who gives them a new pass-port, find your own way to Frankfurt."

"They must have done some in Britain."

"I guess." Magill stretched lazily. "Arnie would've fixed it."

"And a base to store weapons and stuff. *That's* something you must have known about. It would have had to be protected by some sort of front for the gold chain to run through."

Magill just said: "Long time ago. All shredded and wiped clean."

"Then how did it self-start?"

"Just a clutch of Britons getting together in a pub, nothing to do with Langley."

"Except for what you've told me."

"We've been socialising. You came up to socialise, we socialised."

Agnes clenched her teeth, recognising a dead end. "And what happened to Tatham's daughter?"

174

"Sure, her . . . last I heard, she was living in the old family house in Illinois. Matson, Illinois."

"Did she go back to the name Tatham?"

"No, I think she stayed with her married name. Hall. Clare Hall."

That was too easy; Agnes was immediately suspicious.

Magill went on: "You could write her. Tell you what: I'll give her a call and say you'll be writing, okay?"

"I might even drop in and see her."

"Well now, about that . . . with the UKUSA agreement and all . . . You just write her."

"While time goes by."

"Sweetie, I wouldn't want for you to get in a hassle with our government. That wouldn't help a career-oriented girl at all."

"*Damn* it, Mo, this is happening *now*. Something your God-fearing Arnie Tatham set up and is happening *now*. Because somehow that List got away. *How?*"

"I shredded it myself, without looking at it. You look great when you're mad."

That made Agnes even madder, because she knew her friendly snub-nosed face couldn't cope with anger. She grabbed her handbag and went through to the bathroom.

When she got back she had put on not just her clothes but the cheerful little-girl smile that suited her far better.

"I'll be away."

Magill was mostly dressed, too. "Be seeing you, sweetie. Next time you're in town, don't forget old Mo."

"Never." She reached and pecked his cheek.

"Off to find your soldier friend?"

"That's right."

"Seems a nice boy."

Thank you, Mo, she thought: that'll do nicely. She had hoped to end on a note of pure hatred.

26

She was meeting Maxim at Pennsylvania Station, to take the Amtrak Metroliner back to Washington. For no special reason except that it was something new to show him, and it avoided the long grind out to the airport, the brief shuttle flight, and another cab queue. Airlines were brisk morning things; in the afternoon, you drifted home by train.

She bought first-class tickets and still had half an hour to spare. She found a phone booth in the shapeless concourse and called Magill's office.

"Sweetie, what can I do for you that I didn't already? If there's anything I forgot, put it down to old age and I'll try and remember next time." If there was any post-coital tristesse about Mighty Mo Magill, his lifetime in covert operations hid it well.

"Couple of small things. How secure is this line?"

A momentary pause, then: "Hold on," and humming silence. He could have been warning his receptionist off the line or switching off – or on – a recording device. She didn't care either way.

"All secure. Shoot."

"I've been thinking, Mo. I'd still like the name of the front for the Crocus List."

"Long gone, I told you."

"I'd still like it. If you can't remember it, look it up and give me a call in Washington this evening. You've got my number?"

"You sound kind of imperative, sweetie. Could there be any reason for this?" The old crocodile was smelling hook, not bait.

"We were peeped, Mo."

"No. No way at all."

"Mo, I'll tell you something, now. Your Company – my Service, too – got itself into video and pin lenses and ultra-violet light, all wires and electricity. I never could understand electricity: it bites you. So I just staggered along with good old photography. I found this sweet little man who fixed up a non-reflex 35 for me, slowed down the motor wind so it wouldn't make a sound, fixed in a timer to take a shot every thirty seconds. Oh yes, and a filter to make it like the cap of my handcream tube looking out of my handbag and on the dressing-table. It's a lovely dressing-table, that, Mo. I want you to know how much I appreciate your dressing-table."

She turned to smile benevolently at the scurrying passengers behind her. There was a rare pleasure in black-mailing somebody, privately, from so public a place.

"You're in those pictures, too."

"That's right, Mo. They wouldn't do me any good with my Service, I grant you that."

"Attempt to blackmail an ex-Company man."

"You're so right. The whole thing could catch fire, all over the front pages, Crocus List and all. But I'm on a crusade – " As professionals, they were cutting a lot of corners. He hadn't suggested the film might not come out, although she couldn't have had time to develop it yet, and she wasn't working through a 'friend' sent round to sym-pathise with him, deplore the whole thing and assure him it could be stopped if he'd only tell that terrible woman one little thing . . . " – And since I'm not married or anything, I thought I'd stick to the personal angle. I assume even your second wife would be used to this sort of thing by now, but I looked you up: you've got a boy and a girl, both around college age, and – "

"You lousy little whore!" Then she knew she'd won.

When he'd calmed down, she said: "If whores don't get no respect, they should at least get paid the rate for the job."

"Jesus. Okay, then, call me in – make it fifteen minutes."

But it was a long and lonely quarter of an hour. Was there any way he could have traced her call, or picked up background noise and was now rushing downtown in a wild attempt to snatch the film from her? She stayed at the back of a shop until it was time to come out cautiously and find an unoccupied phone again.

Magill was still at his desk. "A limited liability company called Anglam Gateway."

"Registered office?"

"Taplin, Green and Keeley, solicitors at Lincoln's Inn."

"Did they provide the directors?"

"A Mr Wainwright and a Mr Nightingale."

"Great. Thank you, Mo. And the other thing – now I think about it, don't call Clare Hall in Matson. In fact, don't call anybody, don't do anything. Just work on Mrs Wertenheimer's problems with her landlord."

"Am I going to get that film, undeveloped?"

"Mo, you're too respectable to look at such things. As long as nothing happens, nothing will happen – okay? The good old British way. Be seeing you. Or not."

It was too late to ring Defence – early evening in London by now – but Maxim had given her the number of one of George's military clubs and she left the name of Anglam Gateway and its solicitors with the secretary there. There was a certain reassurance in hearing the calm voice three thousand miles away scrawl the message down and ask politely: "May I say who – ? Miss Algar. A-L-G-A-R. Thank you, Madam, I'll make sure he is informed . . ."

Then she rang Information, asking for the number of Clare Hall in Matson, Illinois, just to establish that it was real. After that, she practised her cheery-little-girl act to allay any of Maxim's suspicions, which of course he wouldn't have anyway. When he arrived, he was doing much the same thing, since he wasn't as naïve about the values of the secret world as she assumed: assuring himself there was nothing to suspect and being careful not to find any signs of it. Anyway, there was soon the train to look at.

He liked trains. An airliner is an airliner, anywhere in the world, but a train is part of the landscape. Sadly, the Metroliner had lost confidence in being a train and wanted to be an airliner instead: the coaches were rounded like a fuselage, there were airliner seats with fold-down tables from the seatback in front, even a company magazine at each place. Maxim found himself reaching for the non-existent seatbelt.

First class meant Amclub: everything on Amtrak was

Am: Amcoach, Amcafé, an effect slightly undermined if you recalled Batman and his Batmobile, Batcopter and even Batrope. Maxim wondered if they would serve Amsandwiches.

The air-conditioning roared softly and they got their first drinks as they came out of the tunnel and on to the New Jersey marshes, where gulls circled the refuse dumps among a forest of concrete stilts carrying the highways south. Any big city has a dirty hem to its outskirts.

Agnes told him what she had learnt. Condensed, it sounded very little for an afternoon's talking, but simultaneously it was a surprising amount from a man who had started the day denying everything. Both ways sounded bad to Agnes herself.

"D'you think this is the real info?" Maxim asked.

"I don't think he's trying to kid us," Agnes said, rather more grimly than she had intended. "I think he feels guilty about his old buddy Tatham and doesn't want to interrupt his posthumous triumph, the Crocus List. At the same time, he knows a lot of this is going to get known by the people who matter and he doesn't want to be the man who hindered the investigation. He wants us to get there, but too late. A lawyer's solution."

"Crocus List." Maxim tasted the phrase. It was good to put a name – totally meaningless though it was – to two faces he had seen so briefly. "Ten, you said."

"Less, by now, I should think. After fifteen years, some may have emigrated, died . . . would all of them spring to the colours when called?"

Maxim brooded for a time. "We should have the CCOAC list tomorrow."

"Yes . . . but don't expect too much from that. Tatham wouldn't have recruited the whole Crocus List from that. One or two, maybe, and I'm damned if I see how we'll identify them in a hurry, but . . . ."

"I'll cable it straight to George and see what he can make of it. If we can just identify Person Y . . . I'd rather like to get home and talk to him myself."

"Harry, sticking a bucket over some citizen's head and beating it with a broomstick is not going to advance your career."

"Seeing imaginary policemen at moments of stress isn't doing it much good, either."

Agnes pondered for a while. "Matson can't be too far from St Louis. Illinois is just across the river and turn left . . ."

"I could stay overnight and drop in on her." They had planned his St Louis trip as a one-day event.

"I wish I could go myself, but if she complains and London hears about it, they'll put a stop on me doing anything. She may not say a word, but – it's another base to be touched."

"All right."

"If you're away for a night . . . I'd better start building you an alibi around Washington. Would you mind if it leaked out that we were having an affair?"

After a moment, Maxim said: "No, not at all."

"Just a *teensy* bit quicker next time, Harry. A certain enthusiasm lends conviction in these matters." But her own light-heartedness made her feel tawdry. She badly needed another drink, but Maxim hadn't finished his first, yet. She lit a cigarette instead. "I could check us into a motel out of town, you give the number to the Liaison Office, I'll give it to my office, and hope their nasty little minds think that's all that's going on."

They were both quiet for a long time, both thinking much the same thing: was such a pretence a way of beginning, or would it destroy the might-have-been? And both concluded, with an inner shrug, that it was the right thing for the job in hand; anything else could wait.

The train ambled out of the flat New Jersey landscape where the towns had a shapeless, unrooted look like a child's model village that must be cleared away by suppertime. Beyond Philadelphia, the farmland became vaguely English in the fading light, with neat fields and little clumps of trees at the corners. A claret-jacketed waiter served them a warmed-up airline meal with little bottles of wine.

"One thing you won't have out there," Agnes said, "is a credit card for Winterbotham. That makes you a very third-rate citizen indeed, but that's how they think of Canadians anyway. The snag is, it means you can't rent a car: they insist on a credit card for that nowadays, so you're going to see America by bus."

A man in a dark suit across the aisle had been working on business papers since New York. At Philadelphia he had been joined by two others in what was obviously a preplanned meeting, since the moment dinner was cleared away and a new round of gin and diet tonics ordered, they began a miniature board meeting. Apart from learning something about front-end loaded deals and arbitrageurs, Maxim found it restored his faith in American trains. They might try to look like aeroplanes, but at least there were still smart waiters serving drinks to tycoons as they shuffled papers where the noughts ran off the edge of the page, building a case to be argued to some Washington agency the next day.

He murmured some of this to Agnes.

"Poor security," she said unromantically. "The government could save itself billions by hiring a few wide-eared gents to ride these trains and find out what new rip-offs are being planned. Probably a violation of umpteen civil rights, but . . .

"Actually," she went on quietly, "there's a point in there. People let their guard slip when they're travelling; they'll tell you things they wouldn't say to a neighbour they've known for years. Probably something to do with it being a finite relationship, but . . . Sorry, you probably learnt all that on the Ashford course."

"It was a long time ago."

"Just what *did* they teach you there?"

"Oh, techniques of surveillance, when you're sitting alone in a car you move into the passenger seat, make it look as if you're waiting for the driver to come back . . . the trouble is, I never got a posting where I had to use it."

"If you're going on to Matson, you might find a bit of it useful. One person alone can't do much, but perhaps . . . Would you like an hour or so's refresher course when we get back to town?"

"Fine."

"All right. I'd better go to the embassy to check if anything's actually happened today. There's a bar on the north side of M Street, just before . . ."

27

Maxim made sure he got there well ahead of Agnes. ("Give yourself time to reconnoitre the Subject's area and known haunts.") It was a sprawling split-level place where you could take on board anything from a glass of beer to a four-course dinner plus the right wines at each course, and with about as much choice about where to sit: at tables in the middle, at booths and alcoves at the sides, on the bar stools, on other stools up against long shelves. It had a friendly dark-panelled atmosphere with brisk service, and most of the diners and winers were around Maxim's age. Well, so was Agnes; it was probably her local, being only a few blocks from her Georgetown address.

Maxim took one quick drink at the bar, went on back to the toilets ("Establish whether there are any other exits") and then chose a stool against the wall with a beer and the *Washington Post*. ("Generally, choose a position towards the back of a bar or pub. Make sure you have something to read; a single person doing nothing but drink and smoke looks suspicious.")

He spotted the Subject the moment she came in. She had changed her clothes – as he had himself, in a sprint through his hotel – to a pale coffee-cream skirt and russet blouse under a hip-length waterproof jacket. ("Study the Subject's clothing to anticipate how it could be changed quickly: a reversible coat, a hat that could be stuffed into a handbag or pocket.") The jacket could be reversible, a different pattern on the inside, but there was no hat and the bag she carried was tiny, by Agnes's standards.

If she saw him, he didn't see that she saw him. And from the way the staff greeted her, she was obviously a regular there; she had to chat to several before taking a glass of wine to a booth towards the front, out of Maxim's sight. So probably she had spotted him.

But he was still covering the door and to move his seat apparently just for the sake of moving would seem suspicious – and it occurred to him that Washington DC would be full of people who knew the surveillance trade, that tonight a lot of people would be running genuine surveillances. Perhaps in here.

The lively Georgetown faces suddenly looked like masks.

There was one lone man at the back of the bar, forty-fivish, reading a newspaper – but a real surveillance should be done by at least three people, the A-B-C method, although not all would come into a bar, perhaps only one . . . He shook himself out of a spiral of suspicion and isolation. ("It is normal to feel self-conscious and conspicuous on your first few times in the field; do not let this distract you from the Subject.") And the Subject was moving.

He took his glass back to the bar, glancing at his wristwatch as a reason for not buying another, said good-night and ambled towards the street. At the door, Agnes suddenly turned round and came back.

Maxim was sure his amble had become a rigid march, but he kept going. ("If forced to come face to face with the Subject, avoid catching the Subject's eye.") He went on out.

When Agnes had retrieved the paperback book she had 'forgotten' in her booth and reached the street, Maxim was standing a few yards away, studying the map in a pocket guide of Washington. She waited for a gap in the traffic and scurried across the road. Maxim began strolling on the original side, perhaps fifteen metres back.

He was surprised at how light and lively M Street still was in the middle of the evening. Not just bars and restaurants – and there were plenty of those – but most of the shops were still open: you could still buy a winter outfit, birthday card, book or a pressure cooker, and lots of people were doing so. The crowd gave him cover, but gave it to Agnes, too.

She was varying her pace, moving briskly, then strolling ("Find an average pace between the Subject's two extremes") and carrying her light-coloured jacket over her arm. The slope down to Rock Creek began to steepen and the shops thinned out as they moved away from the centre. Agnes dived into one of the last, a pharmacist's with tall free-standing shelves.

Maxim kept going. ("Follow the Subject into a big department store, but never into a small shop.") In daylight, he could have used a shop window as a mirror to watch the pharmacist's across the road, but lit windows were no use, and who stands staring into dark ones? When he reached an angle where he could watch the shop-front without being seen from inside it, he stopped and consulted his guide book again.

Time passed, in very low gear. Georgetown conversation swirled around him:

"I'm telling you, that was a great party, really great . . ."

"I'm talking about the 700 series . . ."

"I'll take you to some place quieter . . ."

Maxim noted that he should start any remark in Georgetown with the pronoun 'I'. Meanwhile, people went in and out of the pharmacy, but only two women of conceivably Agnes's age: one very tall and striding in a long ethnic-of-somewhere skirt, the other short and waddling, flat-heeled, long blonde hair, dark jacket and beret and a huge shoulder bag.

Compelled to move at last, he crossed over and glanced casually into the pharmacist's as he passed. No Subject in view. He studied a restaurant menu a few doors along, feeling confused, and angry at his confusion.

("If the Subject appears to have been lost by accident, continue in the direction the Subject was proceeding.") But this Subject hadn't lost him by accident: she had brushed him off within minutes, in less than a quarter-mile of straight well-lit street. He was going to be a star turn out West, by himself.

Then he knew where she was – or would be, moments after he committed himself in one direction: behind him. By trade she was a hunter.

His one hope was to head for the small area of streets and alleys he had explored around the bar-restaurant before going inside (". . . reconnoitre the Subject's area . . .''). His own trade included the quick memorising of landscape and cityscape, and at one corner there was an L-shaped alley that cut off the building on the corner itself, giving an alternative route to making a left turn on the streets.

He lengthened rather than quickened his pace – difficult to detect from behind – stepped into the alley and sprinted as hard as he could. It was hardly wider than a car, and somebody had parked a van halfway along. He brushed past it and ran stooping round the corner of the L, where the only light was fixed high up on a wall. He kept running up to the cross-street, turned right back towards M, slowing but glancing at his watch to excuse a half-jog.

Right again on M, completing the four sides of a small square, and right into the first leg of the alley again. It would be too much to hope to sneak up on Agnes peering around the corner under the alley light, but – but a man was doing just that.

Ducking to put the van between them, Maxim ran crouching, his soft-soled shoes making the barest patter on the rough but, thank God, dry paving. As he slipped past the van, the man disappeared round the corner.

Maxim caught him three strides up the second alley.

The man heard or sensed him at the last moment and turned with his hands coming up to a fighting stance, but Maxim feinted through them and hit him low in the stomach. The man collapsed against the wall and slid down it, making gurgling noises. Up ahead, cars and people moved undisturbed on the bright street at the top of the alley; Maxim had time to search the man's pockets – and then suddenly he hadn't.

A clatter of steps and another man swung under the alley light, pistol in hand and coming to the aim. Maxim ducked behind the first man, who was hauling back his breath in short gasps. For a moment there was deadlock, then Maxim remembered his dark sunglasses case and took it out, aiming like a gun. The second man ducked back around the corner and Maxim backed off, crouching and aiming, until he was within a few metres of the cross-street.

He was twenty fast metres along it when a cockney voice said: "'Ullo, sailor, watcher doin' ternight?"

It was the waddling blonde in the beret from the pharmacist's, and under that, Agnes. He grabbed her arm and started towards the lights of the corner. "Did you know there were two blokes behind us?"

"No, I . . ." She shut up and matched his pace. Nobody came out of the alley. They crossed M Street and kept going, and in a doorway she snatched off the wig and beret and rammed them into the shoulder bag that had been expanded from the purse she had been carrying before. "Damn, and I was being so clever fooling you, I never looked behind. What happened?"

"I thumped one of them, then another turned up with a gun. I left."

"Did you kill him?"

"Of course not."

"Sorry, I never know with you."

"At least we know they've caught up with me."

"The Bravoes? It could be, doesn't have to be. Your chums in the Treasury, the Secret Service, *they* could be behind you. They were interested in whether you were going to start investigating anything over here . . . let's cross." She hustled him to the far side of the street.

"With a gun?"

"For God's sake, the Secret Service carries guns like credit cards, every enforcement agency does."

"Where are we going?" They were getting away from the busyness and bright lights.

"Just my car."

They drove slowly around the streets of old houses, now cramped by lines of parked cars. "But it could be Them," Agnes conceded. "If they're after you, all it needs is a telephone call to your parents: 'A question about your son's camera insurance, could you put me in touch?' 'Sorry, he'll be back from America in a few days' – bingo. Washington's the place to start, and the embassy only uses two hotels here. See how easy my job can be?"

"Frankly, no."

"Okay. I pulled a dirty trick on you in the pharmacy. I

took too many risks, putting on the wig and beret and changing my shoes. You did fine up until then. *I* screwed it up by not noticing somebody behind *me*. They probably thought you'd added me as a convoy."

("When it appears that the Suspect has somebody following them to detect any followers, ignore the Suspect and follow the follower instead.")

"But," Agnes decided, "even if it was the Secret Service, we don't want them knowing you're off to St Louis and points West any more than we want the Bravoes . . . Can you travel with what you've got?"

"Ye-es." Maxim trusted neither his passport – now two passports – nor any money to the hotel room or safe. "I'd need to buy a toothbrush and a shirt – "

"So buy 'em. I'll pack a bag at my place and we can make that motel alibi real."

28

Agnes made no pretence of escaping any following car by 'accident'. Being a skilled driver, particularly in towns, was part of her job, but the only skill she displayed that evening was in not actually hitting anything. After making unsignalled turns and abrupt lane changes through Chevy Chase and Bethesda, she blasted to a highly illegal speed south on the Beltway, ducked off it, rejoined a few miles along and finally came down to a leisurely cruise through the Virginia countryside.

Maxim knew her driving well enough to be relaxed about it, and spent his time folding and refolding a road map. Finally Agnes said: "Do *stop* it, Harry. *I* know where we are. Just trust me."

"It isn't that. I just hate not being able to put my finger on a map and say, 'I'm there.'"

"Oh Lord. I suppose that's the soldier in you."

"Be thankful I'm not a Gunner: I'd've brought my theodolite along and surveyed us down to the inch every five minutes."

"A small mercy, I suppose. Where we are, however, is south-west of Alexandria. From here it's a pretty direct route back to National Airport tomorrow. Happy now?"

"Yes." But she noticed he didn't put the map away until he'd located himself precisely.

They registered as Mr and Mrs Alan J. Winterbotham, although the motel clerk was more interested in the car's licence plate.

"That's America for you," Agnes said, shaking out her hastily packed clothes. "If you aren't on wheels, you must be on the skids. Some states even issue a non-driver's licence: it actually says This Is Not A Driver's Licence,

188

because you need something for identification. I thought you handled that well, Mr Winterbotham. Anybody would think you'd spent your life checking unmarried ladies into motels."

Maxim looked back expressionless, knowing she was babbling from nervousness, knowing his own stolid attitude was nervousness, too. The motel was made up of separate cabins, wide-spaced and private among trees – but more to the point, the cabin had its own phone extension and twin beds.

"I'm going to have a bath," Agnes announced. "You'd better ring your hotel and leave this number there. If Jerry Lomax or anybody tries to get hold of you . . . I'll ring my office in the morning."

She spent a long time in the bathroom. When she came back in her long nightdress, Maxim was in the bed by the window, bare-shouldered and riffling through a handful of motel pamphlets.

She hopped into her own bed. "Are you reading?"

"This stuff?"

She snapped off the light between the beds and lay listening to the night. It was quiet except for the murmur of the highway a mile off. After a time, she said: "You did all right, back there . . . followed the rules."

"I didn't follow you very far."

"I told you: I took a risk. Sorry. I just wanted to make the point that the rules aren't everything . . . it's an attitude. If you're going to be Winterbotham out there, think about him. Not just job, address, past history – get into the habit of thinking Why am I *here*? Where have I come from? Where am I going next? Have a reasonable answer ready at every point, but don't be too quick to explain yourself. Sorry, I'm lecturing." She fumbled for her cigarettes and lit one. In the brief flare of the lighter she saw he was lying back, hands clasped under his head, staring at the ceiling.

"Go ahead."

"I may as well . . . Forget anything you've heard or read about 'living the part'. It can't be done, and if it could, it wouldn't be any use. If you play innocent and unnoticing too well, you won't attract suspicion, but you won't notice anything, either. Act the part and know you're acting it – and that *they* don't know.

"That's really the key. You've got to love that idea, really love it: *they don't know*. Relish it, wallow in it. Let it give an extra colour, spice, dimension, to everything you do. At the bad moments, don't look back and think, Well, at least I'm a major in the British Army. And don't look forward to a time when you can tell somebody all about it. You've got to live in the moment, and the way to do that is to think *they don't know* and really enjoy it. The only way. Believe me."

Halfway through, her voice had become an echo, disorientating Maxim until his memory came to rest in a stone-walled lecture room with the Scottish wind rattling the windows. "Did somebody tell you that, once?"

"A Miss Dorothy Tuckey, on my first training course. A long time ago."

"I didn't know you'd met her."

"She taught me how to react and not to react. The least I could do when you told me . . . An unknown grave, I suppose. She might have thought that was appropriate."

After a time, Maxim asked: "Did you ever live that sort of life? – for any length of time?"

Agnes took her own time deciding to answer. The glow of her cigarette briefly outlined her snub-nosed profile against the dark wall. "Yes . . . right at the beginning, before my face got known. I got myself a job as typist and general dogsbody on a small magazine we thought was being financed from Moscow. We didn't care about the magazine, we just wanted to trace back the gold chain, see who handled it. After a time they used me as a courier: everybody else on the staff thought they were being watched. They were quite right, too, by then."

"How long did it last?"

"Eighteen months, about. Living and working with those people, eating and drinking with them, and the only taste I learnt to like was *they don't know*." The taste, relearnt that afternoon in New York, was still in her mouth.

"What happened in the end?"

"Nothing special. It just got too obvious that nobody bought the magazine so Moscow hauled in the chain. Or perhaps I made a mistake: you can see which I'd rather believe. The magazine folded and we all got drunk on Bulgarian wine and I made a speech about going out to penetrate the government and cut the arteries of the police state right at its heart – you need Bulgarian wine to say things like that, it makes me faint to think of it now. And the next day – well, nearly – the Service put me on the list as an Administration Trainee.

"I suppose we got a few more names on a few more files, learnt a bit about Moscow's accountancy procedures. And I learnt a lot – mostly about myself . . . about giving everything but keeping something back because you'll have to start giving again tomorrow. Is there some secret You inside that rather activist exterior?"

"I don't know . . . I don't think there was; you live a very open life in the Army, the secrets aren't personal ones . . . I suppose I used to think the worst that could happen was that I got killed. Just Lights Out and somebody else's problem from then on. Now . . . it's getting a lot more complicated. The Army can teach you to handle anything – except loneliness."

She breathed the last gasp of smoke towards the ceiling and stubbed out her cigarette. "Do you want to come into my bed, Harry?"

"Yes."

"Promise me one thing: don't say you love me."

From then on, everything went dreadfully and completely wrong. Perhaps it was too small a bed, because it had to hold the ghosts of Mo Magill and Jenny, Maxim's dead wife, as well. And perhaps they were hoping for an innocence that was long past both of them . . . It went wrong.

Sitting weeping in the bathroom, Agnes demanded of herself how she could have been so responsive to every whim of Magill's mood, and so dull but demanding and clumsy with Maxim . . . When she went back he was asleep, or pretending to be, in his own bed.

In the dawn, grey with sea mist, she drove him to the airport.

29

Meanwhile, back at the Ministry of Defence, George was not back at the Ministry. Something sudden had come up concerning the family fortunes, and he had to consult his solicitors: it was the one excuse that his seniors, being closer to retirement and thus deeply concerned with land values and capital transfer taxes, accepted with sympathy.

George actually did spend the morning with solicitors, although not his own. Taplin, Green and Keeley – or their ghosts, since none of those names now survived in the list of partners – had offices on the south side of New Square, a corridor with an uneven floor under the carpeting and doorways that had subsided to odd angles. Mr Nightingale's room was the third along to the right.

"I rather think," Mr Nightingale said, "that I was at school with your uncle, C. A. Harbinger. Would that be right?"

"Really? Uncle Charles? Yes, indeed." George had chosen to ask for Mr Nightingale because he had already established that connection.

"First-class cricketer. I'm sorry he missed his Blue, but Oxford was very strong in those years . . . How's he keeping?" When last heard of, Uncle Charles had been keeping a Malaysian girl less than half his age in a Vancouver penthouse, but George managed to recall some less interesting small-talk, and like winged seeds the conversation spiralled delicately down to business.

"We don't actually act for you, do we?" Mr Nightingale asked politely.

"I'm sorry to say you don't, one feels bound by tradition . . . This is quite unofficial, but" – hoping that would be interpreted as 'almost official' – "it does concern my work at the Ministry, security and intelligence on the pol side . . ." Mr Nightingale had been a wartime soldier in a fairly respectable regiment (George's opinion, as an ex-cavalryman) and while he had filled out to a pink-and-white chubbiness, he still wore a small military moustache that had stayed loyally ginger as a reminder of the Desert campaign.

George continued with deliberate diffidence: "It's all rather confidential, I know of course you'll respect that; the problem is rather whether you feel you can disclose anything from your side without an official request from Security, and I'm sure you'll understand why we'd rather avoid that at this stage . . ."

"If it concerns one of my clients, you must appreciate my position is quite clear."

"I really don't know whether it does or not . . . May I simply go ahead and ask?"

"By all means."

"I believe you were once a director of a small company called Anglam Gateway Ltd?"

"Oh yes, that . . . we wound that up ten years ago, at least."

"Can you tell me anything about it?"

Mr Nightingale considered. "There was nothing confidential about it: it was a bright idea some Americans had for setting up training courses – that sort of thing – for their businessmen and other people coming over to Britain for the first time. You spent a week in the countryside being lectured on British business practices, company law, how to address a Duke . . . all sorts of things like that. It did quite well, for a time."

"What happened eventually?"

"I think the American end decided to, ah, quit while they were ahead. There was a trend for the multi-national corporations to set up their own courses, on a European rather than purely British basis . . . We were totally dependent on the American end to send us the, ah, trainees. It was essential to recruit them over there, before they arrived; if they found it was getting too expensive to advertise and recruit, well, that was that."

"And you were a nominee shareholder and director."

"Ye-es, I think you could certainly assume that. The
c.l.—9

problems of American citizens being directors of British companies . . ."

So Anglam had been, effectively, entirely in American hands: they sent the trainees, probably nominated the lecturers, and when the time came could quietly pull out, pleading changes in the American scene which the British directors couldn't challenge. George veered away from the obvious next question, which he was sure Mr Nightingale wouldn't answer.

"Did the company itself own any property?"

"Oh yes. It rented an office in Knightsbridge for a while, and actually bought a house in Tunbridge Wells. We sold that when we picked up another house down near Eastbourne. A more secluded place, very pleasant. I actually gave a few lectures there myself, on company law. Always had a most pleasant time."

"And that was sold when the company was wound up?"

"Certainly."

"Do you happen to know who bought the properties? Turnbridge Wells and Eastbourne?"

A slight frown crinkled just above Mr Nightingale's gold-rimmed spectacles. The Uncle Charles connection was wearing thin. "I imagine we still have the conveyancing documents down among the cobwebs somewhere . . ."

George said: "Well, I dare say I could find out from the Land Registry."

Mr Nightingale beamed with gentle superiority. "I'm afraid you couldn't, you know. You need the permission of the owner to go in for a title search, so you'd have to know the owner first. You mentioned security: I can assure you that one of the most secure things in British life is who owns what property. It's been said, although I wouldn't say it for myself, that the lack of pressure for change stems from the Royal Family's landholdings. A remarkable amount of it is alleged to be held through nominees. If the true title to land were fully disclosed, it might prove that Her Majesty really was the richest lady in the world, which would be, I'm sure you agree" – he smiled at George over his spectacles – "rather vulgar."

George smouldered quietly.

"Of course," Mr Nightingale added, "you could always go and park a caravan on the grounds. The true owner or owners would have to reveal themselves by going to court to have it removed. A lengthy process, and perhaps you don't have a caravan . . ." Mr Nightingale was enjoying himself.

"The Americans themselves" – George opted to risk it – "for whom you were acting . . . can you . . . ?"

"I'm afraid not. Not without a very good reason. You said something about a security aspect . . ."

"Yes. It's quite possible that Anglam was a front organisation." George decided to plunge; he had already given away too much if Mr Nightingale himself was one of the List, but George didn't think he was, simply because he had been too easy to find.

"A front? For what?" Mr Nightingale was no longer amused.

"We came on the name through a retired CIA man in America; let me put it that way."

"There is a very serious allegation inherent in that."

"Yes," George said carefully. "Hence my quite unofficial approach. Let me say that I would imagine the courses were genuine for most of the time, but on occasional weekends, perhaps, they taught something rather different."

There was a long silence, apart from the creaking of Mr Nightingale's chair as he swung a few degrees either way, frowning down at his desk top. At last he said: "You have no proof of this?"

"And we're unlikely to get any. If it was a front, it was designed precisely to block any such proof, with nominees and cut-outs unto the seventh generation. But I'm not really concerned with your Americans of ten years ago. They're water under the bridge, and if it was murky water . . ." He shrugged. "I'm only interested if any aspect of Anglam still lives on."

"It was totally wound up."

"Yes . . . but the properties still, presumably, stand. It's just conceivable that one or other of those houses was passed on to another organisation . . . A long shot, but the only lead I seem to have."

"Are you implying that something is still, ah, going on?"

"Something is certainly going on. *Where* it's going on . . ."

Mr Nightingale considered. "The reputation of my firm, no matter how innocent our connection . . . Tell me, Mr Harbinger, how do you envisage this, ah, matter being concluded?"

"Very quietly," George said firmly. "The very last thing my Department wants is any overt scandal with a CIA connection."

"Quite. Indeed, quite. Let me see, now . . . I could dig up those documents . . . I seem to recall we dealt through local estate agents, and knowing the properties personally, I might well have recommended them to you, as a prospective buyer . . . Dear me," he smiled wanly; "I seem to be becoming quite conspiratorial."

30

When it was late enough for the embassy to be fully staffed, Agnes called to say she probably wouldn't be in, but could perhaps be contacted at the motel number. Now, if the Liaison Office had got the same number from Maxim, then the embassy gossip vine had to be more security-minded than she believed possible for it not to come to one conclusion.

And how close and how far wrong they will be, she thought numbly.

The morning crawled past. St Louis would be a nearly two-hour flight, and then getting to the university and making polite conversation . . . She drove out for an early lunch at a small diner down the road and was back at the cabin by half past twelve. That was when time really started to drag.

She wished she had brought a bottle of gin with her, even a bottle of wine, but now the only place she could find one was a state liquor store, and while the clerk would know of one, sitting with a bottle waiting for the phone to ring wasn't her own image of herself. Anyway, she'd been drinking too much, of late. She was also running out of cigarettes. But she'd been smoking too much, as well. Pull yourself together, girl.

She lit another one.

I'm not the type to get lonely, she thought. It's a relief to get away by myself for once. She switched on the electric kettle and made a cup of instant coffee flavoured with powdered milk and artificial sweetener. At least the water must be real, she hoped. She spilt it when the phone rang.

"Alan J. Winterbotham."

"Hi, there. How was the flight?" She didn't care if the relief showed.

"Routine. Sorry I've been a time. I've just sent a cable to the club: list of delegates expected for the next week's visit – does that sound okay? The convention was quite a thing, it seems."

"Any mention of Tatham?"

"No." He sounded surprised. "D'you think he was there?"

"I would have been, doing his job. It would need the personal touch." Tatham the believer, recruiter of believers. Yes, he would have been there – but not as Arnold Tatham. "Give me the British names."

He read them over, but Agnes thought she had heard of only two, and one of those now dead.

"If we just get your one," she reassured him, "we're that much further forward. It's up to George now. Are you off to the wilds of Illinois?"

"Wilds is right. It's only two and a half thousand population and one bus a day in each direction. I can't get there tonight: I'll probably spend the night in Springfield and be in something like ten tomorrow. It'll give me time to buy a clean shirt here, anyway."

"Okay, and take care – Alan."

She was going to have to spend a second night at the motel, if only to continue their cover of an 'affair'. My God, if only they knew . . . but nobody will ever know. How could I have got it so wrong when it mattered so much? Magill wasn't the first time I've given my Little All for my job, but that can't mean I can only get it right when . . . With Graham, and David, it had mattered – for a while – and that was fine . . . She let herself drift off to memories of fiercely joyful nights that now . . . that now . . . They'd been *snakes*. Whatever you said about Harry Maxim, he was no snake.

So why couldn't *he* have got it right last night? He was like a schoolboy, never mind that I was behaving like a schoolgirl, I cannot stand a man who can't *cope* with me . . .

Even if I was using him, a time of my choosing, to wash away the guilt . . .

Why couldn't it have gone *right*?

*

In the middle of the afternoon, she rang her office: there was nothing more than a routine acknowledgment of the debriefing report she had sent after Maxim's meeting with the Secret Service. Plus a warning not to let him start doing anything of his own.

Ha! *You* try and stop him, she thought.

But soon – perhaps very soon – I am going to have to lay it on the line, tell them what really has been happening . . . The trouble was, she could prove nothing yet and certainly didn't want her Service approaching Magill direct, for confirmation. Still, she could get started on a draft. She took out her pocket recorder and began dictating.

If somebody had suggested to Agnes that she was not security-minded, she would just have stared at them. Security was her trade, always had been. But, as Maxim had realised the evening before, her training was in hunting, not being hunted. Even in the long-ago undercover work on the weekly magazine, she had always worked with the comforting feeling of being in her own country, with the big battalions immediately behind her. She had never – quite – known what Dorothy Tuckey, and Magill and Tatham had known of the real loneliness of the hunted. Otherwise, she would never have put anything on record in that isolated motel cabin, all ready for Them to snatch when they kicked the door in.

By Hand
Private & Confidential

Dear Mr Harbinger,

Anglam Gateway & its Properties

With the kind assistance of the local estate agencies I have gone some way to tracing the subsequent history of the two properties owned by the above company.

The Tunbridge Wells house was sold, as I believe I told you, when the company acquired the lease on Oxendown House, near Eastbourne. It was purchased by the late Colonel J. R. M. Clarke, and passed to his children on his death seven years ago. Three years ago it was sold to a Dr William Baxter, who lives and operates his surgery there.

Anglam Gateway had only a nineteen-year lease on

Oxendown House, which is part of the Gardener Estates. We sold the residual sixteen years, approx, to a client represented by Harvey Gough & Partners, who soon afterwards resold it by private treaty to a small company whose name I have not yet discovered, with the rumoured intention that it would be turned into a private nursing home.

However, I understand it has since been resold to yet another private company, who appear to have resold the lease to the Estates who in turn sold the farmland to local landowners but rented the house to the company, presumably for a much reduced sum.

I am afraid this is all very complicated and difficult to untangle at short notice, but I hope, nonetheless, that it is of some help.

Please give my best regards to your Uncle Charles;
Yours sincerely,
Donald Nightingale.

George locked the letter away, smiling with grim satisfaction. Practise in peace, Dr Baxter of Tunbridge Wells, he thought; you sound an honest pill-peddler to me. But if that wasn't a second smokescreen settling on Oxendown House as fast as possible after Charlie's Indians had withdrawn their own, then I don't know smoke signals when I smell them.

He would have liked to know who that 'client of Harvey Gough & Partners' had been – Arnold Tatham himself, perhaps, using the pension contributions he had withdrawn on his resignation. Certainly that was as close to a gap in the smokescreen as there had been, when Charlie's Indians were screaming (silently) for a quick sale to sever their connection but before a barricade of shell companies could be erected to take it over . . .

But why had Tatham wanted to keep that house? To keep a base, yes, and what could be an isolated one, surrounded by farmland, yes – but he could have bought some other, without any history. Unless Oxendown had certain special facilities, something not easily transferred . . . He would like to take a look at Oxendown House. He also wished Maxim was back.

31

The East Coast of America is dominated by the big cities: Boston, New York, Philadelphia, Baltimore, Washington all exert such a gravitational pull that the smaller towns are sucked into an orbit of dependency on the nearest city sun. In the Midwest, not even Chicago exerts such influence, and St Louis very little at all. Across the plains on either side of the Mississippi and Missouri, it is as if a giant city planet had exploded, leaving a random scatter of asteroid towns frozen in their wanderings but uncommitted to an urban star.

Never quite random, of course. Some grew up on river crossings, at water-holes on the westward trails, and a remarkable number – Matson included – on the railroads or, thanks to founding fathers with a keen eye for land values, where they deduced the railroads must come. Robert Julius Matson had guessed right: the first train had come through just nine years after the town was founded in 1858, pulling behind it the fertiliser works, the corn mill, the seed-corn warehouse, and with them the quiet prosperity that spawned the first Masonic lodge in 1871, a voluntary fire brigade in '75, the telephone in '84 and the first sewer in 1920. All this – and a lot more – Maxim learnt from a centennial booklet in the town library, just one floor up from the town offices.

Already he had spent an hour wandering around the town – it needed no more time than that – trying to get the feel of the place. This wasn't easy, because it was clearly a private town: self-contained within its white wooden houses that seemed as well-rooted on their green lawns as the tall trees of Elm Street, Pine, Walnut, Chestnut . . . the usual street names of such towns, not unimaginative, just because you built houses like that and named streets like that. If you wanted to be different, you could find a big city at the end of the railroad and be different there. He guessed a lot of young people had: the few faces on the street seemed of retirement age. He realised why when he walked down to where Main Street crossed the railroad tracks and saw the grass-grown rails, the deserted depot and the dusty windows of the empty fertiliser works.

Robert Julius had been right, but only for just over a hundred years. The railroad giveth and the railroad taketh away, and when it stops giving and taking, a lot more stops as well. Maxim stood on the rails and tried to imagine the bustle as a train panted in, of the steam glowing the lamplight at night, of the sense of distance and connection . . . but it was trying to imagine the broken chimes of a clock you never heard.

Nobody had even thought to throw stones through the windows of the fertiliser works.

The *Matson Sentinel* had died, too, just a few years before, and the bound copies of its back numbers were also in the library. Maxim leafed through them because – as he was forced to admit to himself – he had no idea of how to approach Clare Hall. Surrounding himself with local knowledge was a form of entrenchment; if you dig in and stare at a hill you can often persuade yourself you know what's going on behind it. Confidence wins battles; even false confidence has won a few.

(This is not a battle, he reprimanded himself. Alan James Winterbotham does not fight battles.)

The woman librarian finished a murmured telephone call and drifted across. "Are you finding what you wanted?"

"Just pottering," Maxim (Winterbotham) said. "Seeing America by bus on my way home. As far as Minneapolis, anyway. My car busted there."

Her indifference told him he had explained too much (but maybe Canadians, or Winterbothams, did explain too much). "Looking up the town history? It's kind of quiet these days, since the railroad pulled out. Mostly folk retired off the farms around here."

She had the Midwestern accent that is usually called 'flat' because the Midwest doesn't believe that emotional

202

emphasis makes the corn grow taller. Her tall thin elegance was camouflaged by a loose, dark woollen dress and heavy glasses, but restored by her prematurely grey hair – she was about Maxim's age – that was cut in simple elegant sweeps over her ears. Perhaps she was playing the part of a small-town librarian but hoping not to be taken too seriously.

"Anything more you'd like to know, just ask." She drifted away to the shelves, shuffling a book here and there.

County Board Approves Salary Hikes, Maxim learnt, along with Matson Mothers' Club Makes Donation. This is not telling me much about the far side of the hill, he thought. Hold on, now. If Mothers' Club Donation makes the front page, how about Local Rector's Son Kidnapped, Murdered, In Italy?

Since he wasn't sure of the date, it took a little time, but there was no missing it when he found the right volume. It ran across three weekly issues, and was blatantly lifted from the big city papers and radio, but the editorial comment was strictly home town. If any Matson citizen had taken an Italian holiday that year, he would have kept very quiet about it.

He read carefully, starting with the last issue where the facts would be most accurate, and working back. He took no notes – why would Winterbotham bother? – but he had been trained to memorise map references and other details of a mission. The SAS didn't like its people getting captured with pockets full of data. There was, of course, a picture of Arnold Tatham himself, much younger than when he had died, and of his daughter Clare. She, too, was younger and dark-haired – but unmistakably the librarian.

The room seemed very quiet as he closed the volume and selected another and made himself turn its unseen pages for ten more minutes. She was back at the desk when he stood up, stretched elaborately, and said: "Guess I'll get myself a cup of coffee."

"If you're coming back, we close for lunch around half twelve."

The centre of Matson was brick-built, a few buildings rising to three storeys, a few of them whitewashed but the rest left the whisky colour of the local clay. Somehow the roads managed to be the same colour, but several tones lighter. The drug-store, where he had breakfasted late, was around the corner on Walnut Street, a deep dim-lit room with a counter and stools midway down one side, after the racks of magazines and trinkets. He bought a magazine and flipped its pages while he drank the coffee.

Perhaps he had been stupid, but had he actually done any damage? She would recognise him when he made his approach, would know he had been behaving deviously – but he would be straight into devious matters anyway. And the accounts of Tatham's kidnapping and death had been very worthwhile reading. A woman walked in and sat at the middle of the counter – Maxim had chosen the furthest end. She wore a bulky mock-leather jacket of much the same colour as the local brick, a tweed skirt and even in that light, wrap-around sunglasses. Apart from that, she was Agnes Algar.

Maxim felt a moment of total disorientation before he realised that something must have gone badly wrong, that because she had not greeted him he must stay being Winterbotham, that because they were strangers he must make the first move. She had lit a cigarette and was alternating puffs with nibbling on a Danish pastry and sipping coffee. He went and bought a pack of cigarettes from the machine behind him, searched his pockets, then asked: "Could I trouble you for a light, Miss?"

She snapped her lighter. "Can't give it up, either, hey?"

"I've tried." He drew on the first cigarette for eight years, nearly choked, and wheezed: "First today, anyway. Thank you. You don't sound local."

"I'm British, just passing through. You don't sound as if you were a native, either."

"I was born in London, I moved to Canada, oh, twelve years ago. Are you from London?"

"Not by birth, but I worked there. Don't we all?"

The druggist, a bird-like little man in his fifties who longed to repeat his father's reputation as town matchmaker, but had so little chance since the youngsters who hadn't moved out permanently were commuting to bigger towns, was delighted to see two mature strangers getting together over coffee. In his view, friendships made over alcohol – as in the Star Bar around the corner – seldom lasted. He threw his own span into the bridge he saw a-building.

"Now, isn't that a funny thing? – I get two people meeting in a town like this, and wouldn't you know it? – their paths have crossed before. Isn't that a funny thing?"

"London's a big town," Agnes said coolly.

"It sure is, I visited there five years back, with my wife – now, would you know the Bedford Hotel? Wouldn't it be something if you both knew that?"

"I think I used to drink there with a man called George Harbinger," Maxim invented, knowing how George loathed tourist territory. "A fat man. He was something in the Civil Service."

"I don't think I ever heard of him," Agnes said.

The druggist surreptitiously slid Maxim's coffee along the counter, fixing him next to Agnes. "Lady, do you mind my asking if you have an eye problem? With the dark glasses in here, like . . . I could recommend some medication, or – "

"I got mugged," Agnes said bleakly. She pushed the glasses up, giving Maxim a glimpse of the purple bruise under her left eye.

"That is terrible," the druggist pronounced. "I mean truly terrible. It surely wasn't – "

"Not here."

"Terrible. You should get a doctor . . . Mister, you should tell her she should get a doctor."

There was a huge anger welling in Maxim that choked off anything he might have said, a yearning to reach that mugger and snap his arms, which he could do so easily, then kick the helpless manhood out of him . . .

I love her.

He had no idea whether that was a decision or a revelation. It was just a fact, whose origins no longer mattered. He shook his head slowly, to show some reaction, staring past the druggist at the dark handcrafted old shelving, wondering if he should remember every detail of this place, and sadly realising he would only remember the huge can of chilli that appeared on the menu board as Home Made.

"Dreadful," he managed to say.

A customer came past to the pharmacy counter at the back and the druggist said: "Excuse me, folks . . ."

Agnes touched his hand on the counter, quickly and secretly.

"Calm down, Harry. I'm all right. Really."

"Was it Them?"

"Them. They got the Clare Hall address and that you're here; I was drafting a report . . . I should never have put anything on record in that place . . ."

"I led them to you."

"Not you. I think they must have had a bleeper on my car; I never checked, and they'd have taken it away when they caught up – damn it, it's what *I'd* have done: a simple radio bleeper with a magnet, you can stick it on in two seconds. We probably lost them on the Beltway, and they'd been chasing round the Virginia countryside trying to pick me up . . . those things only have a range of about three miles."

"I led them to your car. I should have been there."

"I wished you were – but they'd probably have killed you."

"They could have tried."

"You aren't armed, Harry. And they could try again."

"I wasn't going to ring you until I'd got something to say . . ."

"I know. Would you care to walk me around the block?" The druggist was heading back purposefully.

In fact, they just walked around the corner and got into Agnes's rented car.

"Are you really all right?" Maxim demanded.

"It just shook me up. By now I'm mostly tired, I was driving most of the night. The closest I could get last night was a flight to Chicago."

"What will London say?"

"I'll dream up something for them later. Now, have you contacted Clare Hall yet?"

206

"Well, sort of . . ." Rather shamefacedly, he told about the library.

"At least we know she's not at home," Agnes said. "The Bravoes may not want to go around asking questions, they'll probably just stake out her house. We'll pick her up when she goes for lunch – and we've got something to say, now, even if it's just Run for the hills, lady."

"We've got a little more than that. Reading up about Tatham's death . . ."

32

Clare Hall came out of the library just before twenty to
one. Agnes climbed from the car and walked unhurriedly
across the road to intercept her.

"Mrs Hall? I'm sorry to trouble you, but something's
come up concerning your father's work. I'm from the
British Security Service, I'd be glad if you'd check with
our Washington embassy to confirm that."

Clare Hall stopped and looked around, not at Agnes and
not looking for help, but as if reassuring herself that this
was Matson, Illinois. Then she smiled politely. "Do the
Feds allow you to do this?"

"Strictly speaking, no. But it would have taken longer
to convince them than to come to you direct. I'm afraid
there's a Moscow element interested in the matter as well.
That was entirely my fault."

"I don't understand this one bit. And aren't you over-
playing the part, with those sunglasses?"

Agnes raised them. "That was the Moscow element."

They sat in the car on the south side of the park that
occupied, neatly, one single block on the edge of town
where they had run out of tree names and fallen back on
Roosevelt and Jefferson streets. A few schoolchildren were
throwing a football around the memorial to the dead from
the Great Southern Rebellion. Maxim had never known it
described that way before, but the list – he had seen it
when walking the town earlier – was long enough to
justify any name. It was a shock for an outsider, particularly a soldier, to sense how much more the Civil War
had meant beyond interesting developments in tactics and
weapons.

"The point is," Agnes was saying, "that Moscow now
knows your father set up the Crocus operation."

"Through your mistake," Clare Hall said calmly.

"Quite true. But they must have known one thing that I only just learnt – obviously they'd file and cross-reference anything about an ex-Company man – which is that your father's body was never found. You do see where that leads? Is he really dead? – or is he still running Crocus?"

"I took pictures of him. They made me."

Agnes considered. "Yes, I did hear that. But I think you should have gone for an emotional reaction, there. Said you actually saw him killed, or lying dead. I could take pictures of my own father lying dead, and he's still zapping the greenfly on his roses whenever the rain lifts. A man like your father, with over thirty years of undercover work – well, he could plant a story in the Italian press, fake a kidnapping, tip off the police where to find you, and walk out of the country on a false passport . . . to him, it would practically be routine."

"If you want to believe that, I can't prevent you."

"The problem is that you can't prevent Dzerzhinsky Square believing it as well. Believing the worst is what they're best at. But we can drop you at home and let you wait and see, if you like."

There was a long silence. In the back of the car, Maxim took out his pack of cigarettes and looked at them. Although they were an unfamiliar brand, all the routine motions of shaking one loose and putting it in his mouth seemed totally natural. Could he really have become a smoker again after just one cigarette? No, he couldn't, because he still didn't have a light.

Clare Hall said: "What do you suggest I do?"

"Get out of town," Agnes said crisply. "Stay at some motel, or with a friend, not a relative. And then contact the FBI, I'll back you up, talk to them myself."

Agnes was putting herself out on a limb. Whatever else the FBI said, it was going to say Why didn't you come to us first? Because, Maxim realised, I insisted on going to St Louis for the CCOAC list . . .

"All right," Clare Hall said. "But I have to stop by my house and pack some things and pick up my car."

"Ye-es," Agnes agreed reluctantly. "We may still be ahead of them. They don't give their field men much scope. On something like this, they'd have to check back up the line, it could be as far as Moscow, before they move . . . Harry, will you drive?"

That wasn't to save any masculine pride: she was a better driver than he was, and both knew it. But she wanted to look around, watch for reactions in parked cars that they passed. Unfamiliar with American cars, he got started with a thump from the transmission and a delayed surge of acceleration from the automatic gearbox.

"You introduced him as Alan," Clare Hall said, "and now you call him Harry."

"What are names in our trade?"

"I'd like to know that you're good at your trade. I haven't seen much sign of it yet."

"Just stay alive and you may prove something yet."

Maxim took a corner with a sudden tilt, betrayed by the power steering and soft springing. "Sorry . . . But taking up that point, do you have a gun in the house?"

"I could have," Clare Hall said cautiously.

"A hand gun?"

"Yes."

"Can I borrow it, at least as long as we're with you?"

"You mean you aren't even armed?"

Agnes said: "Your Constitution doesn't say anything about the right of foreigners to bear arms. Is this your street? Circle the block, Harry."

Apart from the central few blocks where the offices, shops and banks stood shoulder to shoulder, Matson was lavishly – Americanly – widespread. The most modest white frame house had, to Maxim's eye, an absurdly large amount of lawn, dotted with bushes and full-grown trees that towered over them. Perhaps it was because the land was so abundant that nobody had put in fences, hedges or walls, as the British would have done immediately to define their territory.

What had been the rector's house was a two-storey wooden building with gables that stuck out at each side under steep roofs, and a long porch with wooden columns.

"I can't see anything," Agnes said. "Back into the drive-way."

In reverse, the car felt like an Army truck, but Maxim got it on to the concrete without scraping the big trees that shaded the house. He took Clare Hall's keys and Agnes moved into the driving seat while he ran, literally ran, through the house. Then he called them in.

"First, could I have that gun?"

It was a Walther 9mm, undoubtedly 'liberated' some time in the war, but still in good condition unless it was one made by slave labour, when grains of sand were said to have been added to increase the wear and tear. No, Maxim thought: if Tatham decided to bring this one home, it would be good. He'd know. There was a sealed box of ammunition dated fifteen years ago. He broke it open, loaded the gun, and felt better.

While Clare Hall packed upstairs, Agnes watched the street through the net curtains of the living-room.

"What do we do now?" Maxim asked quietly.

"Tag along with her as far as we can. She's got to get in touch with her father, if he is still alive. I don't know if there'll be a way I can look over her shoulder, but . . ."

The room still had a heavy, masculine feel to it, lined with old books and formal photographs. Maxim scanned them, but he didn't really expect Tatham to have been fool enough to cover his wall with pictures of the Crocus List recruits.

"D'you think Magill knew Tatham's body was never found?" he asked.

"Another little thing he didn't tell us. The whole Company must have known – but what should they do? There's no point in trying to track him down if they want to forget he ever worked for them. Can you see anywhere she keeps business papers? Here, you watch for a moment."

Glancing over his shoulder, Maxim saw her fiddling at the lock on a bureau drawer. Boards still creaked upstairs as Clare Hall moved about. Outside, the street was empty, and looked as if that was usual. Setting up a surveillance in such a place would be ridiculous: it was a lace-curtain neighbourhood, and behind every curtain was an old couple with nothing better to do than watch what everybody else did. In that, if not much else, Matson was international. Of course, if you were police or FBI you'd flash a badge and join the old lady behind her curtains with your binoculars.

And if you were somebody else you'd flash a gun and end up in the same place: it was a common terrorist tactic to take a family hostage and do their killing from that temporary base. They knew better than to look obvious sitting in parked cars, and probably Moscow knew as much, too. The street still looked empty, and very menacing.

He heard Clare Hall coming downstairs, was aware of Agnes hurriedly stuffing paper into her bag and sliding the bureau drawer gently shut. He beckoned Clare over.

"There's a pickup truck, parked round the side of that house nearly opposite. Do you recognise it? *Don't* touch the curtain."

Agnes was suddenly at his other shoulder. Clare said: "That's the Gleissner house, they maybe have the decorators in."

"It's parked facing out," Agnes whispered. "Most people drive straight in: *we* backed in for a fast getaway. Give them a call, please."

Clare Hall punched a number on the telephone and listened. "They don't answer."

"Try once more, just in case it was a wrong number."

There was still no answer. Agnes said: "I think it would be best if you called the police and said there was something suspicious going on."

"Send some poor deputy up against Moscow Centre?"

Agnes and Maxim glanced at each other. They certainly didn't want a dead policeman to explain away. "I could talk to him before he came over," Agnes said thoughtfully, "tell him what's going on . . ."

"*You're* going on," Clare Hall said. "You brought them here – now you get me out of this."

"In a way, it was your father who brought them here. Harry: what d'you think they're going to do?"

Maxim shrugged. "I assume they'd rather catch us on some lonely road, but do they think that truck can outrun your car?"

"Yes," Agnes said. "Those trucks have damn big engines, and with no load in the back . . . Yes, they'd think they could catch my Snailsprint Special. They could, too." Instinctively, Agnes had chosen an innocuous low-powered model at Chicago airport. She was regretting it now.

"We can just wait here for them, then," Maxim said.

"They could walk *in* here," Clare Hall said.

"I wouldn't mind them trying to get close."

"Harry, could we try and settle something without a shoot-out for once? We'll be here for ever explaining why we're here. And God knows what the embassy . . ."

Maxim looked impassive. Clare Hall said: "My car's faster than yours. We can get through to the garage without them seeing, then unlatch the doors and crash out while – "

"No," Agnes said firmly.

"My God," Clare Hall said, "we can just walk out the back door and keep this house between us and the Gleissner house until – "

"*No.* D'you think Moscow hasn't heard of back doors? It's routine to cover back and front, and they're great ones for routine."

Clare Hall glanced fearfully towards the back of the house. Her jitters were showing; no matter who her father was, the Moscow Bravoes were still something that happened on late-night TV, not in Matson, Illinois.

She rounded on Maxim: "So you're the tough guy, why don't *you* do something?"

"You say there must be somebody at the back?" Maxim said to Agnes. "They've split their force. If I neutralise him or them, then the back way could be open."

Agnes had never been in such a situation before: she had been on the outside, among the watchers of a house, moving two steps back on the rare occasions when the police or people like Maxim had been unleashed to go in, and shrugging sadly that things could not have been settled in a more civilised way. Now she was on the inside, and there was no civilised way out that she could see from there.

What they could see was the watcher himself, around the corner on the cross-street and about a hundred metres on a direct line across the lawn, at the only place where he had a clear view between the shrubs and full-grown trees. He was bending over the open engine of a parked car.

"He wasn't there when we circled the block," Agnes said. "But a hundred to one that motor's in perfect nick."

Maxim was calculating the cover given by the trees and shrubs. "If I can slip out of a side window . . ."

"Are you sure?"

"This is my end of the business."

"All right – but, Harry: try not to neutralise him too hard."

Agnes planted Clare Hall in the kitchen to cover the back while she herself scurried to and from the front, checking on the Gleissner house.

Standing behind Clare for a few moments, Agnes said quietly: "With the effort Moscow's put into this, at short time and long distance, your father seems to get more and more alive."

Clare gave a vague snort.

"Living in England?" Agnes suggested.

"If that's what you want me to say."

"If they do catch you," Agnes went on calmly, "it would be nice if I could warn him that they'll be after him as soon as you're through talking to them. Given their methods, you won't last long."

"I *know* about their methods."

"Really?"

"I worked at Langley in, you'd call it the 'registry', until Dad resigned."

Yet another little something Mo Magill didn't tell me, Agnes thought, hurrying back for a look from the parlour window. All secret services recruit from families – not for nepotism, but just a pious hope that trustworthiness, whatever that was, was genetic.

When she got back, Clare Hall said irritably: "Your *friend's* taking his time."

"I hope so. That way, he's likely to get it right. Why didn't you ring up your old friends at Langley and tell them what's going on here? They'd get something organised pretty quickly."

"It was a long time ago."

"You *know* what your father's doing with that Crocus List, and you just don't want to wreck his little games."

Clare Hall looked at her coldly, downwards, since she was some inches taller. "Get mad at me and I'll paste you one, little girl."

"You and a freshly broken arm."

A watcher merely pretending to fiddle with his car's wiring has to turn his head away at times; the pretence demands it. When he turned back, there was a slim man in a new-looking fawn windcheater shambling across the quiet street and glancing from a paper in his hand to the houses around, obviously seeking an address. The watcher bowed his head into the engine again; he didn't want to be asked.

He wasn't. Maxim said softly: "Do you see where this gun's pointed?"

The watcher straightened slowly, looking down. The automatic was aimed at his crotch from about eighteen inches.

Maxim reached and took the humming CB radio, half-hidden by oily rags, from the engine compartment. "Now shut the bonnet – the hood," he remembered the American word. "And into the car, please."

Later, the watcher would think of all the other moves he might have made – if he had been prepared. He would also remember being taught about those paralysing first seconds after meeting an unexpected and horrible threat. At least he'd be able to say the teaching had been true.

At the front window, Agnes hadn't seen them get into the car. What she heard was the muffled roar of an engine, close, then the garage doors banged open and a silver compact swerved around her own car and hit the road in a squealing turn. She knew Clare Hall must be in the car, but had no idea of what to do about it.

The men in the Gleissner house had no doubts. Two of them were in the truck and it had jumped off by the time she looked back at it. Agnes looked around for her hand-bag, car keys – it was too late.

The compact had swung round the corner, roaring up

past the watcher's car; the truck didn't bother. It charged across the road, bounced up the sidewalk and across the lawn – no hedges or fences – weaving between the bushes and trees.

At first, Maxim didn't know where the silver car had come from, but the style of driving didn't belong on those quiet streets. Then he saw the truck bucketing through the bushes he had crawled among so slowly and started cranking down the window, but the truck was long out of range. And then Agnes came sprinting across the lawn.

She can run, he noticed. Not just hurry with her bottom sloshing from side to side, but *move*.

"Swing around," he ordered. The watcher was in the driving seat, Maxim behind him.

The watcher took his time, fumbling the key, mistaking the gear. He had recovered from his fright. The car reached the far kerb as Agnes arrived. She – and a tap from the gun – moved the watcher to the passenger seat.

There was a distant bang.

Agnes drove off. "Where did they go?"

"Left at the corner." He tapped the watcher again. "Put your seatbelt on, friend. It could save your life."

"I don't know what in hell all this is about – " the watcher began. He had, to Maxim's unAmerican ear, a fairly standard American voice.

"Something to do with what I found in your pocket. Now shut up."

Agnes swung the corner smoothly and accelerated, not wasting a second or an inch, and in a strange car. Then she braked. Ahead and to the right, a puff of black smoke was rolling up above the houses and trees.

"Oh God." She drove on slowly.

The fire was at an intersection, a pyramid of flame and smoke boiling above the interlocked pickup truck and silver car. Already there was a circle of people forming around it, swaying back as the wind toppled the flames towards them. One man was hopefully spraying an extinguisher on the edge of the flame pool; a police siren whooped from the town centre.

Agnes stopped a block away, watching, then turned to

Maxim. He shook his head. "It's over already. Either they got out fast or they didn't get out at all." He had seen burnt-out vehicles, and their occupants, before.

Agnes moved off slowly, keeping north towards the edge of the town. Maxim asked: "What about your car?"

"I'd like it, but it could be a mistake to go back now. Better keep moving."

"Won't they trace you from a hired car?"

"Yes, in time. But they've got a lot to think about already."

After a few minutes and one zigzag they were out on a straight if not wide road between the cornfields strewn with rotting stalks. Agnes speeded up, then abruptly slowed to a stop. She sat there, her head bowed and her shoulders shivering; when she lifted her hands off the wheel, they shook

"God, Harry, I'm sorry . . ."

"Take your time."

"Just . . . you're speaking to somebody, and a minute later she could be . . ."

"I know. And you don't get used to it. Not unless you're the wrong sort of person to start with."

"Your lady friend," the watcher said, "does not have a strong stomach."

The pistol rammed him forward in his seat. "And you don't have a strong neck. I won't kill you in here, but we can take a walk in a cornfield."

After a moment, Agnes slid the car into Drive. "Thank you, Harry. And *you*: you helped, too." She wound up to a fast but safe speed. "What are we going to do with the excess baggage here?"

"D'you want to stop and ask him a few questions?"

"You are kidnapping me," the watcher started, remembering his innocence again.

"I doubt he knows anything we don't already. He's just a pawn."

"The name's Gulev, and he lives in Chicago." Maxim had the contents of Gulev's pockets – which had included a revolver – spread on the back seat.

"Bulgar?" Agnes asked the watcher.

"I am an American citizen. You are committing – "

"I dare say." She drove silently for a few more minutes, then stopped. "All right, Gulev; this is as far as you go."

Maxim saw a sudden dampness on the watcher's forehead.

"Give him back everything," Agnes said, "except the gun and one thing – his driving licence, say. Now listen, Gulev: that licence is proof that we had you and could have killed you – when I show it to your bosses in Washington or London, and I know them better than you do. So you just tell them we didn't bury you in some cornfield in return for them not trying to kill Major Maxim in the future? Have you got that? Good. Have a nice rest of the day."

Maxim got out first and watched Gulev on his first hundred yards back towards Matson, just in case. When he got back in, he asked: "D'you think it'll work?"

"No, frankly."

Maxim smiled. "From the first day I joined the Army, I assumed the Russians wanted to kill me."

"I had to try," Agnes said between clenched teeth.

After a time, Maxim said. "Yes. Thank you."

The Illinois farm country isn't truly flat, as film directors show it (Maxim blamed his disappointment on them) by choosing the few stretches where you could roll a bowling ball from horizon to horizon without losing sight of it. Slow rises and dips unnoticeable to a car's engine pull the skyline closer, and clumps of trees around the still-frequent farmhouses pull it closer still. But it certainly didn't need a map; he put that away.

"Did you find anything useful in her papers? I noticed you pinched a photo of Tatham."

"I got her last batch of telephone bills."

He was unimpressed. "Nothing more?"

Agnes gave him a superior glance. "You don't know American phone bills: they actually tell you something, like what numbers you dialled long-distance. To Britain, for instance."

"Ah. Did she?"

"I think so, but I haven't had time to look carefully. They may not tell us much, she could have been smart enough to let her father call her. You didn't know she was CIA as well, for a time? Just a filing job, I think, but she may have learnt something . . . Not enough to charge out and try to beat the Bravoes at that game . . . damn it, I did *not* know she was going to do that."

"Of course you didn't. But d'you think she was escaping from us or Them?"

After a time, Agnes said: "You're a reassuring person, Harry, but any way you look at it, we got her killed."

"Nothing to do with her father, the CIA, the Crocus List, Moscow? – just us?"

"I know we only reacted – but here we are driving a car hijacked from some Bravo across the Midwest, breaking God-knows-what laws and with two or three people burnt to death back there . . . Is it enough to say we didn't start it all?"

He knew Agnes was going to fear sleep for the next few nights, would be trying to bypass her dreams with drink and pills, and he longed to see her through those nights. But he also knew today's events would tear them apart. If he could say anything, it had to be now.

"Reacting is our job; we aren't supposed to start anything. But if they fire the first shot – "

"That's the Army way, Harry."

"No, the Army way would be to fire back the next thousand and anything else we could lay our hands on. By that standard, I think we've behaved quite politely. But not reacting at all won't make the secret war go away. I think we were stuck with it the moment the world got The Bomb. It didn't stop nations wanting to get their own way, it just made them scared of using their armies. So they shifted to surrogate armies: guerrillas, terrorists, agents they could disown – all well away from The Button. So – here we are."

Agnes slowed the car and looked across at him curiously. "You've been doing some thinking."

"No, mostly just listening to Miss Tuckey." Then he nodded. "Yes, some I thought of for myself. Trying to think about what I'm doing, and why."

"And it may be crooked, but it's the only game in town."

"Oh no. Somewhere across the Elbe there's a Major Ivan Maximovitch who's put as much of his life into his army as I have into mine. And some days – you can't help it – we'd like to know how it would work out. Nothing to do with politics or human rights, just to know which one of us is the best. We'd need a supporting cast of a few hundred thousand, but they're mostly in place already . . . We'd make quite a chapter in history, between us. And *that's* the other game. But" – he lifted the pistol from his lap – "I think I'm safer with just this."

"Put that bloody thing away, we'll be in Springfield in a couple of minutes." If he had done anything towards consoling her, her tone didn't show it.

33

"I didn't identify all of them," Annette told George before he had even had time to order a drink; inevitably, they had met in one of his clubs. "Four are dead anyway, and there's five others I'm not certain about. One of them could be either of two people with the same name, but I've got twenty-two who are alive now unless they've died in the last year or so. How's that?"

"Brilliant. What are you drinking?"

"Anything." Then, remembering that such a careless attitude to alcohol offended George: "Gin and tonic, lemon, no ice. Can I go on?"

"May I see?" George read the St Louis list through carefully, feeling guilty that it took such a neat and thorough piece of paperwork to remind him of how competent a woman he had married. And he could guess at the amount of work it represented: it had been no simple skimming of *Who's Who*, since few businessmen enter those pearly gates without the visa of a knighthood, or at very least, a CBE or CMG. Only four had achieved such distinctions.

Somewhere on that list is Person Y, he thought, glaring at it as if he could make the name shuffle its feet with guilt. But at least there was a pattern: a Church connection (where it showed), a tendency to independence and running their own businesses, although not all were businessmen: one was a university lecturer, another a solicitor. But no Person Y.

Blast.

"What did you say?" Annette was suddenly anxious.

"Nothing, you've done a marvellous job . . . perhaps I can narrow it a bit further." Taking the ages, he thinned the list down to twelve men who were now around the fifty-year mark.

Their drinks arrived and George gobbled more or less silently for a while. Then he said carefully: "I have an American banker from the Midwest sending a signed photograph to an Englishwoman who was involved in the French Resistance. A picture of himself and some Briton, just the two. It's the Brit I want, and he's somewhere on that list. Where's the connection?"

"The American had an affair with the Englishwoman in the war."

"Typically feminine; you've all got pornographic minds. No, he spent the war in the Pacific."

"Then they had an affair after the war. If he's a banker he could afford a European holiday, I should think."

"That still doesn't tell us who the Brit is – and before you start, he's too old to be their love-child. Cleanse your thoughts and start again."

"What else do you know about your American?"

"Nothing much . . . he wrote a couple of books."

"What sort of books?"

"One was a polemic on banking practice, by the title, and the other was about the Red Menace."

"What does your Englishwoman do – since the war?"

With a shiver at talking of Miss Tuckey in the present tense, George said: "Oh . . . gives lectures, writes books – "

"Writes books."

"Everybody writes books, these days . . ." George let his voice trail away. Keyserling had been anti-Communist: Dorothy Tuckey's work on Resistance techniques – seen as a future need – were anti-Communist. So perhaps the photograph was one writer paying homage to another whom he admired? "It still doesn't tell us who the Brit was."

"Another banker? Or another author – no, there isn't one on the list . . . Or a publisher? There's one of them. Could that be the missing link?"

"Most publishers look like missing links . . . But no jumping to conclusions. First we have to know who published Miss . . . Library."

One advantage of London clubs is that at least the older ones maintain good libraries that stay open after the public ones are closed. Miss Tuckey's works had been rather specialised, however, so it was only in the third of George's haunts that they found a couple of her books. The earlier had been published by the Parados Press and printed by Arthur Fluke & Son, Worcester.

"By God," George whispered – the particular library had that leather-bound and unread atmosphere – "I do think we've found him."

According to Annette's notes, Julian Fluke from the CCOAC list had spent a couple of years with a London publisher before joining the family printing firm in Worcester, where he had soon started a small imprint of his own. The books had been marketed through a bigger publisher: that, George knew already, was not rare and even today needed relatively little capital – particularly when you owned a printing works already.

"Isn't Parados some sort of fort?" Annette murmured.

"It's a bit of a fort, the wall you build to stop yourself getting shot in the back. Ha!" Such a name was no coincidence. Parados had specialised in Resistance memoirs and some crusading religious works. But it had published no books since 1970. Shortly afterwards, Julian Fluke had left the family firm and gone to work for HMSO Press, the government printing works in Edinburgh. The latest *Whitaker's Almanack* showed that he was now Deputy Controller, Classified Printing.

George shook his head in slow admiration. After the CCOAC conference there had been two years spent winding down Parados Press – which could have made Fluke too overtly an activist figure – then the retreat to Edinburgh and the gradual penetration of the government institution he would understand best. Now, just about every secret government paper that needed printing would pass under his nose. A true position of trust – and in one way, Fluke's loyalty ran deeper than anybody had guessed.

34

They left Gulev's car at a shopping mall on the outskirts of
St Louis and got a cab out to the airport. They were back
at the Washington embassy around dinner time, but the
messages had got there sooner. Those were stacked in
order of time and mounting hysteria on Agnes's desk. She
flicked wearily through them, then reached for the phone.
"They certainly traced my car . . . Hello?"

Maxim could hear the operator's anguished squawk.

"Never mind that," Agnes said firmly. "I'm not at
home to anybody except London, but you can tell Colonel
Lomax and Mr Giles that I'm back." She put the phone
down. "Giles does the same job for the Other Mob, Six.
You probably haven't met him."

She took the cover off a portable typewriter and began
to type in expert bursts; Maxim remembered her undercover two years as a secretary. He lit a cigarette and
slumped in a corner chair. Without looking up, she said:
"You're getting the habit again fast."

Maxim looked at the cigarette in his hand. "Funny. I
thought I'd be fireproof after eight years."

"You'll fail your next Combat Fitness Test and then
what?"

"Not quite the most pressing of my problems."

"No . . . light me one, would you?"

He put it in her mouth. "Report?"

"I seem already to have reported to Moscow," she said
sourly. "It's about time London got a few words as well."

They could identify Lomax's urgent Rifle Brigade stride
in the corridor well before he slammed through the door.
"Good God, Agnes, what did you – and *you*!" He suddenly saw Maxim. "I told you specifically *not* to – have
you been in Illinois as well? I should have guessed. You can

have no idea of what we – By God, you'll stir up a rerun of the War of 1812 any moment now."

"Jerry," Agnes said wearily, "turn down the heat and come off the boil. I'll have something for you in a minute."

Lomax gave her a vicious glare and subsided in another corner. Just as Agnes finished, Giles came in, tall and aristocratic in evening dress, having been called away from some function. He had almost no hair and a permanently amused expression.

"My dear Agnes, you *have* been enjoying yourself – except for your poor eye. What happened there? You've even got Charlie's Indians speaking to me again, although I won't pass on what they're saying. It seems they'd arranged in Matson to be tipped off if Arnold Tatham's daughter did anything newsworthy, and I suppose getting burnt to death counts as news even in these days. And would this gentleman be Major Maxim? Yes, I've heard of you. Delighted. Edwin Giles." They shook hands.

Agnes handed over her report. "Once encyphered, I shall send that Flash to Snuffbox, recommending a very limited initial distribution."

Giles disentangled a pair of gold-rimmed half-eyes from the silk handkerchief in his breast pocket and perched on the corner of her desk to read it through. Lomax bounced up to try and peer over his shoulder; Giles simply handed him each sheet as he finished it, and at the end waited with his indecipherable smile unchanged.

Lomax said: "This appears to be the work of a diseased mind."

"Two diseased minds, actually," Giles pointed out. "Assuming that Major Maxim endorses it. You do? Thank you."

"We can't let this be signalled," Lomax said.

"I doubt we can stop it. Not short of eliminating Agnes and the Major and burying them under the magnolias. And given their advantage in years, and the tendency to activism revealed in that document, I'm not sure I'd choose to join you in that. We could, however, send our own telegrams expressing our own views."

"My own view is quite clear: fantasy."

"Not all of it, Jerry: by no means all. Taking just today's events, there seems to have been more going on in Matson, Illinois, than even our two young friends here could have achieved unaided. An elderly couple held up in their own house, bullet holes in Mrs Hall's car, a silenced machine-gun in the burnt-out truck beside its burnt-out passenger . . . How do we explain those away? Charlie's Indians seem to accept a Moscow factor, and while they can't officially act in their own country, the FBI isn't going to be caught not seeing Red when Charlie does."

"That's not my business – "

"Exactly . . ."

" – but now I've read this, I have to send something."

"Then why not send Major Maxim? Put him on the first available seat to London, tonight if possible. I have no doubt that the Ambassador will authorise whatever it costs. Most willingly."

"Damn it, I probably should send him back to Illinois . . ."

"But Illinois hasn't asked for him. Only for our Agnes, who has diplomatic immunity, unless the Ambassador chooses to waive it. I've seen nothing public nor private to suggest they know she had a male accomplice (forgive me) let alone who he is. Is your name on record out there, Major?"

"No, but a lot of people saw my face."

"All the more reason to get that face back to London prompter."

Agnes stood up, clenching her jaw to stop her face sliding off its moorings from tiredness and strain. "I want to get this down to the communicators."

"Something you might add," Giles said, "from a private source: that Mrs Hall had her passport with her. In her handbag; it didn't get too badly burnt."

Agnes nodded slowly. "So she was going further than just across a state line. Thank you, Edwin. Would you like a copy of this when I'm through?"

Giles smiled resignedly. "Yes, dear, I suppose I'd better have."

"The more the merrier." She went out.

"And, indeed, the safer," Giles added.

"Do you two usually swap reports?" Lomax asked.

"We represent the same national interest, the spirit of inter-service co-operation . . . The answer is No, we don't, it's most unusual, but so is this situation. Let me advise you, Major, that should you ever come into possession of exclusive information, always share it before reporting back, in the hope that others will report it at the same time. Otherwise, the Top Floor will say: 'If we're only getting this from Major Maxim, it means he's been on the booze and invented it to cover his expenses.' Don't you agree, Jerry?"

"The Army doesn't work quite like that," Lomax said tightly.

"All Top Floors work like that. *In numero veritas*: in numbers, no matter how contrived, there is truth. In a solo report there is only *vino*. Which is why dear Agnes wanted me to have a copy."

"Are you going to send a report yourself?"

"You know, I don't think I have a choice. Not now."

"Are you going to say you believe in this Crocus List thing?"

"That I find it . . . possible. And am making my own discreet inquiries, and so on and so forth. My Service isn't directly concerned with activities within the UK, but one doesn't want to find the bandwagon's done gone."

Maxim asked: "Will the Ambassador waive Agnes's immunity?"

"Normally, he might well – spirit of Anglo-American harmony and all that. But a little discreet circulation of her report in the White House and Langley could have them imploring us *not* to let her make statements to the Illinois police, let alone stand up in court. Jerry, if you're going to get the Major on a plane tonight . . ."

Lomax threw a fierce glance at Maxim and stood up. "London" – he glanced at his watch – "London's fast asleep by now." He strode out.

In the silence, Giles watched Maxim covertly, then coughed and said: "You wouldn't have a cigar on you, Major? I'd been counting on a French colleague with good Cuban connections . . . Never mind." He walked to the window and stared out through the black shapes of the trees, stirring in the wind against the lights of Massachusetts Avenue. "And, of course, I did know Arnold Tatham."

Maxim looked up. "How well?"

"I wonder if anybody knew Arnold well. You could spend an evening chatting to him, having a splendid time, and at the end he wouldn't have told a thing about himself."

"Did you think he might still be alive?"

"Oh, yes, the lack of a body – we're a suspicious lot. But we can't spend our limited budget investigating Charlie's Indians; they're supposed to tell us what they're doing, anyway. And if a man of Arnold's experience wanted to vanish, it would be quite a job . . ."

"Could he have set up and still be running the Crocus List?" Maxim asked bluntly.

Giles winced. "Anybody with Arnold's experience could have set it up, given the backing. But what sort of man would have kept it going after he'd been told to shut it down? – and after he'd left the Reservation?"

"The List wouldn't know it was shut down unless it was told: there wouldn't be a headline in *The Times*. All he'd need to do would be not tell them. Though," Maxim frowned thoughtfully, "sitting there for ten years waiting for nothing . . . it would be nice to get a Christmas card at least."

Giles was nodding and smiling. "You're getting the hang of it, Major. And it could be just that: a Christmas card signed Fred, easily explained away to your wife as that American buyer I met on the Frankfurt trip years back . . . It must always have been a long-term, deep-cover operation. Their job was to get themselves into positions of access and influence. And from Agnes's report, they seem to have succeeded."

He caught Maxim's look and sighed. "Yes, I do seem to be believing it, don't I? Must watch that, when it comes to my own telegram . . . But if such a List existed, this Berlin business would be the time to send it something more than a Christmas card, and Arnold Tatham . . . I said I didn't really know him, but I got to know of some of the things he'd done – most impressive – and perhaps some idea of the man. I'd say he was a very devout man. It is, in purely practical terms, a very useful thing to be. Loneliness is the curse of our trade. If you confide in God, you can be reasonably sure He won't whizz round to the nearest KGB informer the moment you've fallen asleep in a puddle of beer. Have you ever been on a mission in plain clothes – before today?"

"In Ulster, a couple of times."

"Then you know about these things, putting on a new identity and so forth – but more important, taking off your old one. I expect they stripped you naked, they certainly should have done, then searched your clothes for give-aways. A nasty feeling, but very necessary to your own survival. Arnold did far more of that than either of us; in the war they fed them French food and wine for the last twenty-four hours, in case they were captured quickly and made to vomit – a very small cruelty, by Gestapo standards. I have the feeling that Arnold could give up his real self more easily than you or I just because he didn't have to leave God behind with the London bus tickets and coins and tailor's labels."

Maxim waited, and when Giles said nothing more, asked: "So perhaps God told him to keep the Crocus List going when Langley told him to stop it?"

Giles said slowly: "It's always difficult to remember that you aren't working for anything more than the interests of your own country. One would like to be on a crusade, but . . . if God doesn't turn up to head the parade, He's a tricky part to replace."

35

George Harbinger was no fool; he knew he could be walking into trouble at Eastbourne, and had no intention of just vanishing. On the other hand, he was doing something totally unauthorised, bits of which might turn out to be illegal as well. So he could hardly leave a note on the DDCR's desk – or anybody else's – saying Send in the SAS if I don't come out by noon. Difficult.

But having thought along those lines, he realised he could leave a sealed envelope with Annette saying much the same thing. It was a nasty thing to do, because he had to pretend it would be good news. He was used to keeping secrets from her, not deceiving her. But anyway, he'd find the place deserted, and after a bit of snooping around, would ring back and tell her not to open the envelope at noon after all.

Mind, he'd better have some good news to tell her as well, not just that he'd got his head out of the lion's mouth with no more than saliva stains. Well, he'd think about that later.

Oxendown House stood alone, a few miles outside Eastbourne where the coast road swung a mile or more inland clear of the high cliff edge. George overshot it the first time past: it was invisible from the road behind a slight crest – presumably the Oxen Down – at the end of a long track studded with cattle grids and surrounded by pasture land. Quite good land, George's country eye noted, and certainly well drained by the limestone beneath.

The house itself was built on a terrace cut into the Down, facing the sea and bracketed by mature trees. It probably dated from the golden age just before the First

World War, but whether it had been the belle of the ball or the ugly duckling nobody could tell now. So much had been added by way of extensions, dormer windows, garage and outhouses that it had become a dowager slumped over the green sofa of the Down, any thought of good looks forgotten in uncorseted comfort.

The track turned into a curling gravel drive that brought the Rover on to a courtyard of York stone at the back of the house. He stepped out boldly, trying to look as if he were there to buy the house, but nobody came to sell it to him. He wasn't too sure that he would want it anyway: the courtyard, shadowed by tall cedars, had a mossy dampness that might have been charming in summer, but on that day gave George twinges of rheumatism just looking at it.

He then made a mistake. A real buyer might have stood and looked around a bit, but would then have gone and rung the bell beside the french windows under the portico. But since nobody seemed to have heard him arrive, George decided to have a snoop.

The courtyard became a flagged terrace running round one side and the front of the house. From there the land went on down to the distant cliff edge in a shallow valley of lawn and pasture that must have been carved by a stream that had long ago dropped underground in the limestone. That was about all that George could remember of his school geography lessons. Beyond was the grey English Channel and tiny pencil lines that were ships scratching their thin white wakes.

The lawn should have been mown before the end of the summer, he noticed, and turned to see if the frontage of the house had the same slightly run-down look to it.

A man in a khaki ski-mask was pointing a submachine-gun at him.

"Good God," George said, not acting in the least.

"It's Mr Harbinger, isn't it?" the man said in a pleasant English voice. "Come inside, please."

"Damn it, I came here just to look at this property – "

"All the way from the intelligence and security side of MoD. Yes, yes. Don't let's waste any more time. Go inside." He made an impatient gesture with the gun – an

231

old Russian one, not that there are any new Russian submachine-guns. I'm in the right place, George thought, but not in quite the right way.

There were french windows in the long rambling frontage as well. They went through a drawing-room where most of the furniture was dust-sheeted humps and into a large kitchen fitted with restaurant-size cooker, dishwasher and sink. It had been built to cater for twenty or more at a time, but only one corner seemed to be used now. There were a few mugs and a half-full bottle of red wine on the corner of the table, beside a bowl of earth with a few fingertip green shoots.

"D'you like flowers, Mr Harbinger?" the man asked.

"Don't know much about them. Out of doors, I'm a farmer, not a gardener. Daffodils?"

"Crocuses."

"I do believe," the DDCR said, "that it would save my voice and blood pressure if I simply had a tape set up in here so I could press the switch whenever you walked in. It would start: 'What the devil have you been doing now?' In fact, I don't think it would need to say more. That simple question seems to cover your total output . . . Well?"

Maxim smiled uneasily. "Have you seen a report sent over to Security last night, sir?"

"No. Jerry Lomax mentioned it on the phone, in a roundabout way, when he told me he'd deported you. Poor devil, you must have taken years off his life, too; he'd have to be up at four in the morning, Washington time, to make that call. No, I've been trying Security for the last couple of hours but they seem to have pulled up the drawbridge and stuck their heads under the pillows. Do you know what's in it?"

"Sir."

"It sounds as if *you* are, apart from anything else . . . just give me the worst."

"I'd like to get George Harbinger to confirm some points, sir. And he may be able to add some more: I sent him some data from America."

"You did, did you?" the DDCR said coldly. "No

wonder he was so bloody anxious to send you over . . . Well, you'll be lucky to find him. Not in yet as far as I know, and he's hardly been in the last few days, off seeing solicitors and . . . was *that* all to do with this thing?"

"It could have been, sir. May I try and ring his wife?"

The DDCR pushed the phone across the desk. "Go ahead. But be careful, he says he thinks his phone's bugged. Don't know if he's got the DTs or the KGBs . . ."

"I think it probably is bugged, sir." But the Albany phone rang unanswered, bugged or not.

In the silence after Maxim had put back the phone, the DDCR leant carefully back in his chair. "You really meant that about being bugged, Harry?"

"I've run across the Bravoes in this thing, sir. And I took one of their mikes out of somebody else's phone – in this country."

The DDCR absorbed that. "I'm just a civil servant now: no authority over you at all. I assume you're working to somebody I don't know about."

Maxim smiled. "Only George, if anybody."

"Who has no authority over you either in such matters. Harry, it sounds as if you're on a lonely road . . ." He stared at the ceiling beyond Maxim's head. "People on the outside think of the Army as pure woodentops, no thinking allowed, just obey orders as if we were cogwheels inside a washing-machine: warm wash, hot wash, tumble drain, slow spin . . . if it keeps 'em happy to think that way, fine. But then a war comes along and we're expected to be deep-thinking, imaginative, adventurous but caring. Perfect butler turned into the perfect lover . . . Is this just the rambling of any old soldier?"

"It doesn't sound like a civil servant, sir."

"No . . . We're more arrogant than the Civil Service. We don't think anybody could understand us: they're afraid somebody might understand them. The point is, people *don't* understand, particularly about what we mean by orders. They assume they're as simple as hot wash, warm wash; you and I know it's Go and do this by so-and-such hours and report back. We're trying to turn out people who can make their own decisions and choices. With you, we seem to have succeeded."

Maxim fell back on the old Army answer: "Sir."

"Never explain, never complain." The DDCR eyed him with what might have been friendly coolness. "The trouble that daft phrase has got me into. The problem is, people – "

George's assistant poked his head round the door. "I'm terribly sorry, Deputy Director, but I've got Mrs Harbinger on the phone. She's a bit troubled and . . . actually, I rather think she'd like to speak to Major Maxim instead, if you don't mind, she didn't know he was back until I told her he'd just got off the – "

The DDCR picked up the phone. "Transfer the call on Mr Harbinger's line, would you?" He smiled and nodded at the assistant, who melted away. The transfer took time, as usual, so he went on: " – the problem is, people don't understand the second, unstated, half: Do something about it, or live with it. Preferably the first, although the Civil Service – Annette? How are you . . . Yes, you want to speak to Harry, he's here . . ."

Maxim listened and asked quickly: "Where are you speaking from? Okay, fine . . . Give me that address . . ." He scribbled on a pad the DDCR pushed towards him. "No, I'm sure he's all right. I know something about these people, there won't be a problem, but I'll be down there as soon as . . . he'll be all *right*, I'll handle it."

When he had finished, the DDCR said: "Handle what and how? No, don't explain, but has something happened to *George*?"

Maxim took a deep breath. "I think he must have got himself . . . kidnapped. I know it sounds weird, but it's part of this whole thing."

"If you know where, we'd better get the police on to it."

"I'd rather have a go first myself, sir."

The DDCR looked at him. "One day, Harry, with a bit – or a lot – of luck you'll find yourself leading a whole battalion, 680 men at current establishment, and then that road is going to be more lonely than anything you've ever known. Because, for them, by God you've *got* to be right. Tell me something: does all this go back to the Abbey and the fake copper nobody believed in? Yes? Then tell me one thing more: are you doing this to prove you were right, or because it matters to this country?"

Maxim said: "I started trying to find somebody nobody else wanted to find. Now I know it's important."

"All right. I'll give you three hours. If you haven't rung in, I'll have to do something."

George Harbinger was in darkness, the total darkness of a windowless room and probably darker in the mind from knowing it was underground. The lights had been on for a minute or so while the man had handcuffed his left wrist to a water pipe, so George knew he was in a long narrow cellar, roughly walled with breeze blocks, that led out of the small original cellar at the back of the house. He was probably under the slope across the courtyard, with ten or twelve feet of earth above him. Thinking about that didn't help.

It was a timeless place, because the man had taken his watch: George recognised this as a trick to speed the feeling of disorientation that, in time, would leave him so grateful for light and company that he would answer any question. He was a long way from that, he told himself, but in time any man . . . and how much time had passed already? Would Annette have opened the envelope yet? And would anybody believe her? Oh yes: if she thought George was in trouble, she'd get herself believed.

How much time do *they* think they've got? He was pretty sure there was a second man who had stayed out of sight: perhaps somebody who knew George – they had got his name and posting right – and whom George might know. What were they doing? – waiting for him to soften up, or packing up and pulling out? . . . and leaving him here? They wouldn't do that . . . would they?

Why didn't they come and ask some questions? That bowl of crocuses had been a question, in its way, seeing if he reacted. Stupid romantics, sitting around a totem of their codename, probably drinking red wine to toast the future! *Really* . . . The only other question had been who knew he was here. He thought he had handled that quite well. "I have left a sealed envelope naming my whereabouts that is to be opened if I do not ring in by one o'clock," he had said pompously, hoping to be disbelieved. He had just been prodded downstairs to the cellar.

It must be noon now, an hour earlier than he had told them, and the envelope opened and help on its way. He was certain it must be well past noon, but without light and time there are very few certainties . . . except that George needed a drink.

36

Maxim came to Oxendown House in his own way. If they were expecting more visitors – and he had to assume they were – they probably expected the police, charging up the track in cars. Once a policeman gets his aching feet into a car, he is loath to take them out again. So Maxim came from the cliff side.

He wore his 'Cammie' jacket of broken browns and greens (many civilians now wore those, in the country) with gloves to hide his hands and a net scarf stuffed with tufts of grass that he draped over his face as he raised his head, very slowly, into a gorse bush atop the last crest before the valley – a 'combe', as it was known locally – that became a lawn at the top.

The house was about two hundred metres away, its wide front and terrace nicely framed by the spreading cedars. What interested him more was the sprawl of bushes that ran out from the trees on either side of the lawn. If he could reach the nearest of those bushes unseen, he had cover right up to the terrace.

He watched for several minutes but saw no movement; he was in a hurry, but not that much of one, and not now that he had the house almost in his grasp. He lowered his head as slowly as he had raised it and wriggled back down the slope, then took out the Walther and jacked a round into the chamber.

Keeping the chimney-pots of the house in view over the crest, he jogged along the reverse slope, and when another patch of gorse on the crest offered, slid up for another look. The trouble was the bare slope on the far side that led down to the shrubbery. But already he was out of sight from anybody at the dormer windows looking out to the sea, unless a watcher was right up against the glass. He hoped these people were trained to stand well back in the shadow. There was a gable window overlooking his side, but if he moved just a few metres on, there would be the broad trunk of a cedar in line with it.

He crawled along to position the tree carefully, then, keeping his body dead in line with it, wriggled slowly over the top and down the slope, in plain view should anybody walk out on to the terrace.

Then he was among the bushes, picking broken sticks out of his way as he worked towards the corner of the house, watching both front and side. When he touched brickwork he felt, almost as tangibly, the advantage pass to himself. To somebody like Maxim, close was safe.

The front of the house had too many windows, the terrace was too wide, and there he would have the south light behind him. So he moved towards the darker side, keeping right up against the wall, with the pistol and his head twitching in every direction. As he ducked to pass a ground-floor window he heard the muffled buzz-buzz of the telephone, and waited to see if it got answered. It stopped after three rings, and now he had one person at least pinned down somewhere in the middle of the house; he could risk making the next move quickly.

A single-storey outhouse had been built on at that corner, forcing him away from the main house and into the view from the gable window. He slipped around it with the pistol watching the window. Ahead was a newish garage, separated from the outhouse by a shoulder-wide alley floored with rotting leaves.

Distantly, there was a moment of hammering and he paused, puzzled. At the end of the alley, he could see the rear corner of a Land-Rover standing on a courtyard of smeary green stone.

They were going to need that. He crept forward until he could see the whole vehicle: an old hard-topped model with windows all round, and nobody sitting in it. Maxim slid clear of the alley and crouched back against the house wall, covered by a small bush in a rotting tub, and wondered if he could reach the Land-Rover unseen. Ten metres, no more, but ten metres out in the open, under the windows of the house . . .

Somebody walked out of the glass doors a few metres to

his left, heading for the vehicle. Maxim froze: the man was carrying a Russian submachine-gun.

But he wasn't hunting, just carrying the gun one-handed by its pistol grip, perhaps one second away from firing if trouble came his way. He didn't even have that second, with Maxim's pistol pointed at the middle of his back, but this wasn't war. Not quite.

The man walked round the back of the Land-Rover and opened the driver's door. If he were just getting something out of it, then on his return he would be facing the ludicrously small bush in its tub . . . The engine whined and blared, and Maxim ran.

The vehicle had just begun to move when he banged the gun against the window. "Stop right there!"

The gaping face stared back down the pistol barrel, then the Land-Rover jumped off, and in that moment Maxim could have blown the face away. But that was too small a satisfaction for the long road he had travelled. He fired twice through the driver's door, low and forward, and then was knocked aside as the rear end slewed on the mossy stone.

He rolled further and came up aiming, but the Land-Rover wasn't going for the driveway; it swung left and smashed into the bushes flanking the terrace where it stretched round that side of the house.

Maxim reached the corner of the terrace overlooking the lawn just as the Land-Rover broke free of the bushes, and shot twice more, plunging fire through the passenger window towards the driver's legs. He saw glass star and crumble.

The Land-Rover slowed, turned a crawling half-circle across the lawn, and rammed the terrace wall at the far end. Maxim vaulted the balustrade, ran up to the passenger side, yanked open the door and snatched the submachine-gun from the floor. The driver was folded over the wheel. Maxim ducked round the vehicle, so its bulk would shield him from the house windows, and dragged the man out. He gasped as he hit the grass.

There were two bullet wounds: one through the muscles of the right thigh that didn't seem too dangerous, and one in the left knee that was pumping blood steadily.

"Keep your hands spread and still," Maxim ordered, starting on a tourniquet. "Is there anybody else around?"

The man stared blankly, gasping.

"I want to know," Maxim went on, "because if somebody else starts shooting, I shall lose interest in keeping you alive."

"Nobody," the man whispered.

Maxim plugged the wound with lumps of torn handkerchief and began binding it up. "Nobody? Not even a fat friend of mine? – George Harbinger? In his forties?"

"Yes . . . he's all right . . ."

"That is nice. I'll ask you where, in a minute – but what were you going to do with him?"

"Nothing . . . Let him loose . . ."

"Really? Why snatch him in the first place, then?"

The man closed his eyes, looking very pale. Maxim finished rough-patching the wounds, then reached into the Land-Rover and found a coat. He spread it over the man; no point in him dying of shock just yet.

"All right, you'll live if you stay still. Now, where is he?"

The man told him. Maxim searched him as he did so, indiscriminately, turning everything out of the man's pockets and not caring too much about gulps of pain. Among the odd things were a wristwatch and a handcuff key.

Then he took the keys from the Land-Rover, just in case, and also had a quick rummage through the back. It was hastily piled with suitcases, a box of groceries, a typewriter case, some other, larger sort of plastic case, a workchest of heavy-duty electric tools and a small box holding two old-style Russian grenades.

He took the grenades. "I'm glad you forgot to pocket one of these. Soon you must tell me who the gentleman at the Abbey was."

The french windows at the back were unlocked; in fact, one was open, so the man hadn't been pulling out. Perhaps he'd just been going to position the Land-Rover for a getaway. It would have been quite possible to drive down the lawn and then away over the fields while the police came charging up the main track. In ordinary cars, they wouldn't have been able to follow.

Nobody had shot at him, but he wasn't taking anybody's word for it. He scoured the ground floor, kicking open doors and waving the pistol in one direction, the submachine-gun in another, ready to use a grenade if anything seemed too suspicious. Then he reached the bedroom floor. One room was clear, and then he was in a big bedroom overlooking the terrace and lawn – and the moving Land-Rover.

The man was gone: just a dark patch on the lawn beside the coat and wheel ruts showed where he'd lain. Maxim felt in his pockets for the keys, but he still had them. A spare key hidden in some corner of the vehicle? He raised the submachine-gun, but the Land-Rover was already dipping off the edge of the lawn, jolting over the pasture land – and Maxim realised it was unpowered, just rolling downhill. The man had used the slope of the lawn to roll it back until it had speed to swing into a three-point turn and now . . . now it was downhill all the way.

It took one wire fence without check or swerve, and there may have been a second, but it was a long way away and the Land-Rover was just a bobbling black shape. It must have worked up to quite a speed, because it didn't collapse suddenly off the cliff, but vanished smoothly. He didn't hear a thing. But he did wish he'd remembered that Land-Rovers had been invented before steering-column locks.

George ducked his head against the light, blinking helplessly at the dark figure in the doorway. "Get me some water," he croaked. "Before anything else, just get some water."

"No whisky?" Maxim asked.

"Harry! My God, you're back!" He was still helplessly blind before the neon strips that ran down the long cellar.

"If you will go hiding in dark corners, you miss all sorts of news." He undid the handcuffs.

George stayed on his rickety wooden chair, rubbing his left wrist. "They left me some biscuits and water, but I knocked the water over in the dark. What's the time?"

"Oh . . . coming up to three."

"What? I thought it was midnight. They took my watch."

Maxim gave it him back. "How many did you see?"

"One, but he had a ski-mask on. And I think there was another somewhere. How many did you meet?"

"One. He's just driven himself over the cliff in a Land-Rover, but I . . . no, it can wait."

"I didn't hear anything."

"Down here, you wouldn't." The door to the second cellar was remarkably thick, but not heavy. The sound-proofing could hardly be to keep noise *out*, Maxim thought, and he wandered the length of the room. The end wall was just limestone, left as it had been cut, without any facing and now pocked with holes.

"Shooting gallery," he said admiringly. "Neat: no ricochets off limestone, they just go in and stay in. Same thing as Gibraltar: they do all their live firing in the tunnels there."

He helped George, still stiff and cold and perhaps begin-ning to tremble, through the original cellar – the door had been not exactly secret, but behind a panel that Maxim had found already lifted down – and up the steps to the kitchen. He gave him a mug of water. "You'd better ring Annette."

There was a telephone in the drawing-room, but it was dead. When Maxim traced the line to a junction box, it was smashed. He fancied he'd heard that happening. George came in and collapsed on to a sheet-covered chair. "Is my car still here?"

"I doubt it, but I'll check." The only place was the garage. He found the door unlocked and the place empty except for the usual clutter, and a cardboard box in the middle of the floor, as if ready to be taken away. It held a couple of jagged-edged bits of metal that might have been cut from a car body, some old rags stained with dark green paint and there was a general dusting of the same colour on the dusty concrete; somebody had been using a spray gun.

He went back. "You're short one car. It looks as if one of them took it away and dumped it somewhere while the other loaded up the Land-Rover. Then he was going to release you and give himself time to get out of the area while you wandered around trying to find a phone. I think we should start doing that."

"D'you really think they were going to let me go?"

"I think the smashed phone proves it; not much point, otherwise. And once you'd got here, this place was blown as a base. They'd have to expect a follow-up." He looked around longingly in the low, opaque light from the terrace windows. "I'd like to do a proper search, but it would take days. Leave it to Special Branch: we can tip them off from London."

"We can walk into the police station at Eastbourne. Damn it, *I* haven't done anything wrong. I've been *kidnapped*."

"And because you were kidnapped *I* shot somebody who went over the cliff in that Land-Rover. *I'm* not walking into any police station. Now, let's move."

They walked back roughly the way Maxim had come, across the pasture to where he had left his car in a lay-by on the main road. Maxim did his best to demilitarise himself by letting his camouflaged jacket hang open to show the civilian sweater and shirt, but the only pace George could make across that ground didn't look suspicious anyway.

"Do you know," George said thoughtfully, "what was the worst thing about being down there in the dark?"

"Lack of whisky, I should think," Maxim said lightly.

George was silent for a time. Then he said: "Yes. But not just wanting it: feeling how much I needed it. It worried me."

Realising George was serious, Maxim tried to think of something helpful. "You were under a lot of stress. I've never been a prisoner, unarmed, helpless – except in exercise situations. And you can't really fake the real thing."

"Thank you, Harry. But it wasn't that . . ."

"Did they try interrogating you?"

"The one did. He asked how I'd found the house, who else knew, he said nobody would find me there in that place . . . I don't think he was very serious, though. And he didn't stay very long."

"Probably wanted to nip upstairs and check the place wasn't full of coppers, if he was on his own by then."

"Yes . . . it all seems a bit unreal and tame, now. I

suppose they really weren't going to kill me. I mean, that isn't the way they seem to work. I told myself that, in the dark, but I wasn't very convincing." He looked around at the wide green downs, the tattered grey sky and out to the Channel, where a broad blade of sunlight broke through to glitter the surface: " 'Set in the silver sea' . . . he must have been looking south when he wrote that. There's a helicopter."

Maxim had heard it already, its pulsing carried on the wind as it tracked the line of the cliff edge. "Somebody's reported the Land-Rover."

"We'd better keep moving."

"Better if we watched. We're just taking a stroll. You'd stop and watch a helicopter rescue act, wouldn't you?"

They stood there – luckily too far from the cliff for it to be natural for them to hurry down and peer over – as the helicopter swung into the wind and began hovering.

"I didn't know you were coming back," George remembered suddenly.

"It was a bit hurried. Things happened out in Illinois . . ." He told George briefly. The helicopter wavered itself into position, the winchman standing in the open doorway, then sank gradually below the cliff edge.

They walked on towards the road. "So it's finally got into the open," George said. "Well, not the open, with the broad bottoms of the Security Service planted on it, but the whole thing, back to the Abbey and the Reznichenko Memorandum and Tatham himself in 1968 . . . Harry, when we add our experience here today, you know I think we've won? There isn't a committee in Whitehall that can whitewash this lot away."

"If that matters any longer."

"What do you mean by that?"

"They could have done more to cover themselves. Pushed you over a cliff in your own car, driven you away somewhere, anything to give themselves more time . . . I don't think they want much more time. They think they've got enough."

"They can't do anything now without it being obvious it's part of the pattern."

"But do they know that?"

37

George phoned Annette, then the DDCR, from a telephone box in the little village just before Eastbourne, while Maxim sat in the car sorting the dead man's belongings and guessing how long it would take to establish that he had bullet wounds as well as the other problems of being dead. But just empty pockets would be suspicious enough.

"Charles Henderson," he told George, when he got back. "Address in Bath. He's got credit cards, too, so it's probably genuine. He wasn't on the CCOAC list, as I remember." He started the car, then slipped a cassette into the player. After a moment, it launched into a rock number.

He turned down the volume. George glared: "Harry, I didn't think even you liked this syncopated rubbish."

"It's pretty much unsyncopated, really. Almost everything on the beat. Mr Henderson had it in his pocket."

They listened to five minutes of it, George hunched and miserable. Abruptly, it became a sequence of bleeps, then a gabble of electronic noise. With one pause, it lasted about a minute. The rock music started again in mid-track.

Maxim wound the tape back and listened again.

"For all I know," George said, "that could be number one on the Hit Parade."

"I think it's more likely to be a computer program."

"Do they use those things in computers?"

"Normal thing, for the household computer. The trouble is, we don't know what brand of computer."

"They're different?"

"Yes."

"Do you mean these blasted things are supposed to be revolutionising the world and they don't even speak the same language? How d'you know about computers, anyway?"

"I'd like to say it's because I belong to the computerised Army. In fact, it's because Chris has gone crazy about them. I'm going to have to buy him one for Christmas."

Mollified by Maxim's ignorance, George said: "Well, if he knows more about it than you do, why don't we ask him what brand it is? Your parents don't live far from here, do they?"

Crawling around Brighton and through Worthing stretched the thirty-mile journey to over an hour, and it was almost dark when they had picked Chris up from his school and reached the centre of Littlehampton. Or not quite, because it was one of those small towns which had closed off its centre to make a pedestrian precinct; Maxim parked as close as he could, but on a yellow line. Chris's eleven-year-old morality made him draw in his breath with solemn disapproval.

"I know," Maxim said, "but I've been mixing with some corrupting influences. Anyway, Mr Harbinger will pay if we get nicked."

Chris led them straight to a small home-computer shop, and Maxim realised how many Saturday mornings the boy must have spent with his nose pressed to the window. The proprietor, small and elderly, greeted them warmly. Two men – one expensively dressed – with a boy seemed a certain sale.

Maxim held out the cassette. "There's a program on this. Can you tell us what computer it's written for?"

The proprietor's smile faded.

George said: "If you've got the one it fits, I'll buy it."

"No, I will," Maxim corrected.

The proprietor didn't care who won that argument. Chris, however, cared very much. He stood very still, his golden-brown eyes following the discussion, and only reluctantly switching away to watch the proprietor run the cassette into one machine after another.

"I've been meaning to get one for months," George insisted.

"You? You need an instruction book with a pair of scissors."

"I have two daughters," George said with dignity.

"And I intend to see them raised properly on the principles of Kinder, Küche and computing."

"I promised Chris – "

"Daddy." Chris touched his arm: the screen had flashed up a sequence of incomprehensible instructions and the proprietor was beaming.

"Is that all we get?" George demanded.

"No, sir," Chris assured him. "That's just the listing. You have to run it."

"We'll do that at home," Maxim said quickly. "You can make it work?"

The proprietor said: "From the look of the program, you'll need an interface and a joystick as well, sir. I would recommend . . ."

One way and another, the price had doubled by the time they got out of the shop, and Maxim let George pay it. In the car, he asked the disappointed Chris: "Is this the model you'd have chosen for yourself?"

"Well . . . there's nothing *wrong* with it . . . I think I would have preferred . . ." He just hated to see any computer slip away from his grasp, and he was grasping the keyboard of this one very tightly on his knees.

"You can hang on to that until my daughters get back from school," George assured him.

Once inside Maxim's parents' house, they worked as a team. Maxim hauled his father and mother away from the TV to introduce George, whilst Chris started linking the keyboard, transformer, interface, joystick and cassette recorder to the TV screen in a tangle of wires and plugs recruited from all over the house.

With puzzled joviality, Mr Maxim said: "So you've hired Chris, now, have you?"

"It's the age of the *enfant savant*," George said, looking at the mess. "But is my drawing-room going to look like a Tac HQ?"

"Can I offer you a cup of tea, or a drink . . . ?"

"A drink would be absolutely splendid. I've had a rather trying day."

"Make it a big one, Dad," Maxim suggested, not trying to catch George's eye. Perhaps there is a time to reform, and a time not to reform. But he watched surreptitiously as George took his first huge swallow and stood there, letting it flow through him, a transfusion of new life. How many years since George had his first drink of the day after sundown? he wondered.

Chris said: "I'm ready, Daddy." The screen was lit but blank except for a small heading: TAKEOFF WEST R.

Maxim ushered his father into the kitchen. "I'm sorry, Dad, but some of this could be rather secret. We can't help Chris seeing it, but . . . I hope I can tell you one day."

With the three of them alone, Maxim said: "Run it, please."

An irregular line of battlements appeared at the bottom of the screen: perhaps a symbolic city skyline. Low over them, a small aeroplane shape rose, coming towards them but slanting slightly to the left. The screen went blank for a moment; when it cleared, there was a small red dot in the middle of it. The aeroplane carried on steadily and vanished at the top left-hand corner. The screen went blank again, except for TAKEOFF WEST L. It was a mirror image of the other, with the aeroplane rising towards the right.

Chris said: "I think I can make that red spot move . . ."

"Try it."

The screen said TAKEOFF EAST R. The aeroplane rose, slanting left, then began a positive turn even further left – a right turn for the aeroplane. As Chris experimented, the red dot jumped, wavered, crawled towards the aeroplane and had just reached it as the plane finished a half-circle and the screen blanked. The same thing happened with TAKEOFF EAST L, except that the aeroplane slanted to the right, then did the same turn back across the screen. This time, Chris had the red dot over it much earlier.

"It's just one of those games," he said sadly. "You know, where you shoot down aeroplanes."

Maxim ignored George's stare. "Just one of those games," he said. "Sorry, Chris."

With Chris also banished to the kitchen, they sat at one end of the little dining-table, the telephone between them and George's hand creeping towards it, then drawing back as his thoughts blurred again. Beyond the green plush curtains, doors slammed on home-coming cars, a metal garage door creaked open, a child rumbled past on a skateboard.

"We're dealing with a Blowpipe missile," Maxim said, trying to find a point of certainty. "It's the only man-portable one that you can control on to the target. The rest are infra-red, fire-and-forget stuff. Control makes simulation training vital: I met a Gunner who said they did seventeen hundred simulations before they even got near a practice round. And we know a Blowpipe's missing from an export order: they couldn't pinch a simulator as well, so they made up their own."

Perhaps that plastic case in the back of the Land-Rover had been a similar home computer.

"I take your word for all that," George acknowledged. "But it doesn't tell us what aeroplane, nor where. Unless you're having the same horrible thoughts that I am."

"The Russian delegation. They're here, are they? When do they fly out?"

"It's open-ended. When we know when it'll end we'll *try* and keep it secret, but they'll have people popping back and forth to Moscow all the time."

"If it's all vague and ad hoc, it'll be that for the Crocus List, too."

"They don't have to be gunning for a particular Russian group or aircraft. If they hit *any* one it might be enough. It'd certainly be enough for me and most of Western civilisation."

"Let's think about the airport: it must be a specific one, with two parallel runways heading east-west. They're planning to be on a line between the two, firing slightly left or right. But on an east take-off the aeroplane turns 180 degrees to its right . . . Look, there must be some pilots' handbook that gives all this sort of thing. Get on to your office before they all go home."

In the relief of having something to do, George barely noticed that Maxim was giving the orders. He passed them on crisply: " – and never bloody mind what *for*, just *have* it there, on my desk." He put the phone down. "And let us hope we are still dealing in prediction and not history."

38

An Aerad Guide – in fact, several fat loose-leaf volumes of it – was on George's desk. Also waiting was a grey-haired man in a very military suit whom George's assistant introduced as Group-Captain Coulson from NATS. ("National Air Traffic Service," the assistant whispered. "He thinks you may need help.")

George frowned at the idea, smiled at the Groupie, and pushed the guide to Maxim. "See what you can make of it, Harry."

One look told Maxim why they needed Coulson: each airport – formally called an 'aerodrome' – took up at least six pages, some printed on both sides, showing the general layout, ramp areas, SIDs and STARs (whatever they were), ILS, NDB/DME . . . He quietly pushed the volume back, open.

George took a glance. "Good God, it's written in Linear B. I shall never fly again."

"Easy when you know how," Coulson assured him. "Now, what do you want to know?"

Maxim said: "We're looking for an airport with two parallel runways running roughly east-west and you make a 180-degree right turn soon after take-off if you're going east. Sir," he remembered.

Coulson frowned thoughtfully. "You don't usually make a one-eighty so close . . . but sooner or later you've got to turn to get to where you want to go. Where *do* you want to go?"

Maxim looked at George, who shrugged and said: "It could be Russia."

Coulson raised his eyebrows. "Russia's to the east of most places, so you wouldn't need to turn west. Are you sure your airport isn't in China?"

George glowered. "Unlikely. How about the two run-ways?"

"Heathrow, in this country. Charles de Gaulle. Schiphol. Frankfurt. Hannover. Tegel."

"Where?"

"Berlin." The silence was very sudden. Coulson went on: "It's run by the French, their sector, but it's the one commercial flights use. Ours is Gatow, but that's strictly military."

Maxim asked: "If you were taking off east, would you make a 180-degree turn?"

Coulson found the right pages. "Yes, if you wanted to get onto Centre Route 2, but that's the way back to West Germany and London. Right 180-degrees at three thousand feet and not less than three miles from the beacon. If you wanted to go to Russia, you'd go straight ahead over East Berlin, but I don't think anybody ever does that."

George said carefully: "Thank you very much, Group-Captain . . . would you care for a drink? Derek will get you one. I'm most grateful, and I wonder if you could treat this as being rather secret?"

The Groupie gave one last look at Maxim's mixture of combat and civilian dress and went out.

George slumped in his desk chair. "Berlin again. But why? What can they shoot down there?"

"They must want to make it look as if the Russians shot it down."

"They can't be going to blast some airliner. That doesn't sound like their style."

"They're going to blast somebody. You don't shoot to wound with a missile."

George shook his head slowly, then got up and found a copy of the *Standard* on a side table. It was All Saints' Day and the Archbishop of Canterbury's sermon in Berlin was briefly quoted on page 2. Sure enough, he had denounced any unilateral talks on Berlin as "an abdication of care for a brave and beleaguered people . . . Are we to say of Berlin 'I know him not?'" Strong stuff, with a hint in the last paragraph that the Foreign Secretary would have liked to call the Archbishop an Interfering old —, only daren't.

"These buggers," George said, "are planning to shoot down the Archbishop of Canterbury." He sat down. "No, they can't be. It's just not on."

"He'll be flying out of Tegel," Maxim said. "And it fits: Moscow's been trying to smear him, and they shot down that Iranian airliner – they've set themselves up for this. It doesn't have to be perfect, just so long as a lot of people believe it. And if the missile comes from East Germany or East Berlin – "

"A *British* missile."

"There'll be damn little left to prove anything – and that'll get called a Russian fake. Who's going to believe the British shot down the head of their own Church?"

"Exactly: why should these Crocus List people do it?"

Maxim took care with his answer. "I think the whole pattern is sacrifice, not assassination – when they use violence at all. A couple of them have committed suicide; you could say they sacrificed Barling – he was a churchgoer, wasn't he? – when he wasn't going to resign over Berlin, and that freed his group to vote their own way. But they didn't try to kill me at the Abbey or you at the house today. What bigger sacrifice can they make than their own Archbishop?"

"And the pilot of the aeroplane, and Jim Ferrebee, and a few others probably."

"They're on a crusade. And I think they're right at the walls of Jerusalem. At that point, a few civilian casualties might be acceptable sacrifices as well."

George looked at him and growled: "Just a simple soldier."

"They aren't simple soldiers out there. One tries to adapt. But whatever it is, can you just stop the Archbishop flying out of Tegel?"

"That shouldn't be a problem: Jim Ferrebee's out there with him. I can get him to . . . but, Harry, wait a minute: you're saying these Crocus clowns must have smuggled a *missile* into East Germany? They pull out your toenails for trying to take in a copy of *Playboy*."

"They must have it disguised as something else."

"And how? The thing must be . . . how big?"

"With the launcher and sight, four and a half feet and

something over forty pounds. It would have to be in a vehicle. Maybe built into it." He was recalling the odd bits of car-body metal in the garage, the power tools in the Land-Rover . . . "I'd like to know what the police find at the Oxendown House garage."

George instinctively glanced at the telephone. "Yes . . . we've got a little explaining to do . . . But if you're right, suppose these clowns get caught in East Germany? Even at the checkpoint? Think how that would look. Brits with a British missile . . ."

"Somebody had better catch them first. If the police have any ideas about the vehicle, we need to know them."

"I could try going through Security." George sighed. "*Try*."

"You've got to make them accept Agnes's report."

George sighed again.

"Or do nothing and just see what happens next," Maxim offered, smiling as politely as ever.

Glowering, George picked up the telephone. "Find me the Deputy D-G at Security, will you? No, the *Deputy*, I don't want the D-G himself on any account . . . He's Old Guard," he explained to Maxim. "Still has some belief in the Sovbloc threat, though I fear thoughts of his pension loom largest of all . . . Alfred? So sorry to interrupt your dins, but you recall a little morsel that came in from Washington in the early hours? . . . Yes, I do know about it . . . And yes, I know this isn't a secure line, so I thought that if you and I could get together in, say, half an hour? . . . Oh, I'm sorry you don't think so, because I'd like some advice about what to say to the East Sussex police about a little happening down near Eastbourne today . . . Of course I know about that, I was, you might say, involved . . . Yes, I expect he was very dead, although that wasn't my direct doing, but one feels one has a duty to explain things to the constabulary, unless you felt otherwise . . . Ah, good. Half an hour, then? . . . I'll be there."

He put down the phone. "Would the wheels of government turn so smoothly without a regular greasing of blackmail?"

Maxim smiled again. "You might emphasise that the Bravoes are in on this."

"That'll be a little more difficult. Nobody's likely to have identified that burned-out bastard in Illinois . . ."

"You can prove they've bugged your rooms at Albany."

George stared. "I'd like to know how."

"No problem."

39

George put the little microphone, looking like a metallic spider with its stiffly bent wire legs, on the table. "Major Maxim took this out of my telephone in Albany just this evening."

Perhaps he felt a little weight lift, a tiny erasure of guilt, for Miss Tuckey's death, now her microphone was at last in the right hands. The hands, small and thick-veined, belonged to the Deputy Director-General of Security, whom George hadn't seen for some months. He was saddened to see how aged and shaky the man had become since being passed over for the top job. He had opened the meeting by taking two different-coloured pills and George suspected he was checking his pulse when he put his hands in his lap.

"Aye, it's one of Theirs," the Deputy said in a voice softened by tiredness as well as a faint Scots accent. "But he shouldna have taken it out."

George waved that aside. "I asked for my rooms to be swept a week ago. We haven't got time now for fancy work: do you accept the gist of Miss Algar's report – and now the likelihood of an attempt on the Archbishop?"

"I would accept it as a possibility. I think I can promise we will endorse any warning you send to this man – Ferrebee? – in Berlin. For the rest . . ." He glanced through thick pebble lenses at the Assistant-Commissioner from the Met, the sleek heavy whom Maxim had met in Committee. He had picked up the microphone and was twiddling with it.

"Your part in the Eastbourne matter, Mr Harbinger – " he began.

"I was kidnapped at gunpoint."

"Well, then Major Maxim's involvement . . . he seems a

very active gentleman. I would like to know who authorised his use of a firearm."

"Yes, yes, we can worry about that later. What did the local Branch find down there?"

The AC picked up a sheaf of telex messages. "After the body had been recovered from the Land-Rover and found to have gunshot wounds, there was a search done on the house. Yes, there was some evidence that it had been used for terrorist purposes . . . the cellar had been used as a shooting gallery, they picked some Russian bullets out of the walls, but far too soon to say if they match the rifle from the Abbey. Bloodstains on the lawn, 9-mil cartridge cases on the terrace – was that the work of Major Maxim?"

"I was handcuffed to a pipe in the cellar."

"Ah yes . . . and evidence of them converting and respraying a vehicle – "

"That's what we want."

" – most likely a Volkswagen camper, from the bits and pieces left around. They resprayed it dark green and probably cut a big roof hatch and a smaller hole, round, about five inches across."

George blinked, then guessed: "For a stove pipe?" With its short fat body and long tube behind, a Blowpipe launcher could well be disguised as a stove and pipe – then pulled loose and fired through a wide roof hatch. It was a lot more likely than standing on an East German road and blasting the thing off.

The AC just smiled his meaningless gorilla smile. He didn't need to guess at things that were beyond his reach.

"So now do we believe these people are *serious*?" George demanded.

"Aye," the Deputy D-G said wearily. "But I also believe they are out of our territory. If the vehicle is to be in East Germany tomorrow afternoon, it is quite likely there already. Certainly on the Continent, would you not agree?"

"Probably, but what about what's still on your territory? Which could include Arnold Tatham if he's still alive and still directing it, which seems to be an increasing possibility. Have you tracked down the phone numbers Agnes sent you?"

"George," the Deputy D-G said, keeping his hands in his lap, "I think you can take it that they will now be looked into."

"*Now?* After you've had the bloody things for eighteen hours?"

"You just don't appreciate how things have been, these months since . . ." He shook his head slowly.

If George had not appreciated, the clenched painful smile on the old man's face – yet he wasn't ten years older than George – would have told him almost everything that had happened (and not happened) in Security during the last half-year.

"All right . . . but for fifteen years these people have been training, biding their time – and tomorrow looks like being their big day. I want it not to be, and I don't want them to have any more days after that."

"You draft the warning to Berlin, George. The Assistant Commissioner and I will add our endorsements."

"I would need to talk to my superiors before committing us to that," the AC said.

The Deputy D-G didn't look at him. "Take all the time you need – up to, say, fifteen minutes. If the Archbishop does get shot down in flames, it might be advisable to have your Department's name on the telegram predicting this. Whether or not we can do anything about it, I believe it would be advisable."

Thoughtfully, the AC went to find a telephone.

George was late back at Albany, but Annette hadn't been lonely. A team of Security Service sweepers was already at work, fanning their gadgetry at the panelling and dissecting the telephones. Annette was in the small bright kitchen, drinking coffee with the DDCR.

She jumped up and hugged George. "Are you all right? Really all right? Can you tell me . . . ? Never mind, but we can *talk* again, they say, in here, anyway. *Bugger* the KGB!" she shouted cheerfully.

"Did they find anything?"

The DDCR said: "A couple of devices. So far." George felt guiltily pleased that he hadn't been misleading the Security Service after all, and sat down at the table.

"Coffee?" Annette asked, then caught the look on his face. "All right, I'll get it." She went out.

"How did it go?" the DDCR asked.

"We got off a telegram to Ferrebee in Berlin . . ." And, after some pleading by George, the Deputy D-G was trying to persuade the Prime Minister's office to persuade the Intelligence Service's switchboard to persuade their Director-General to fly back from Edinburgh . . . "God knows what he's doing there, but now we can't meet until morning."

"It's a pity the Prime Minister doesn't like you."

"Yes, but it's the only positive thing about him. How's things at the Department of Waste and Warmongering?"

Annette came back with a very large tumbler very full of whisky and water, and George pounced. "Have you eaten anything?"

"I think I had something at Harry's parents' place."

"I'm sure you got *something*, but was it something you chew as well as swallow?"

"I'll have some biscuits and cheese later."

Annette gave him a look and went out again.

"Speaking of Harry," the DDCR said, "well, people *are* speaking of Harry. The East Sussex police, for one of many. The last phone call I got, they were practically suggesting I should have put a citizen's arrest on him. But I think I've got it retrospectively squared that he was authorised to carry a weapon: his CO was my G-2 in Two Armoured . . . We are getting to the point, George, where we need a whole bloody unit devoted to finding out what Major Maxim is doing and then telling him to stop it. And they'd have to be better men than you and me."

"If it hadn't been for him, the Crocus List would never have come to light. Where is he now?"

"I don't know. He left a message for you." It was a sealed envelope. George opened it, read the note and passed it back impassively:

I'll call you from Berlin. Harry.

40

Perhaps, like Merlin, Sprague lived backwards in time: born in the future and ageing with a perfect memory of what was about to happen together with a misty ambition for what lay ahead in the past. That would explain a lot, George reflected. Or perhaps – he re-reflected – one could explain Merlin's magical reputation in the corridors of Camelot by assuming he was the first true civil servant, gifted with an unromantic vision of what people were going to do (rather than what they should) and building his career on that. While poor King Arthur thought he was running the Round Table all by himself.

So George shouldn't have been surprised to find Sprague had invited himself to the little group that met around a Cabinet Office table at dawn, still wearing their almost identical black overcoats because the heating had only just switched itself on.

"I can't quite see," Sprague was saying, "why you sent Major Maxim to Berlin, George."

"I neither sent him nor let him go. He just went."

"Extraordinary how your Department works. I would have thought his name on any passenger list could alert the Other Side, which on the whole we don't – "

"According to our man in Washington," Sir Nicholas said, "this Maxim used a false identity out in the Midwest. He may well have retained it." The Director-General of the Intelligence Service was a spectacled, near-bald man in his late fifties, with the bulk of a football player who has not quite replaced training with dieting.

"*Most* extraordinary," Sprague murmured. "I suppose it would be too much to ask what – if you know – he might be going to *do* there?"

George glowered. "I imagine that rather depends on what Sir Nicholas is offering to do there."

Sir Nicholas raised his eyebrows in mild surprise. "I don't recall making any offers, George."

"I assume you have *assets*, as you call them, in East Germany, East Berlin. How fast can you communicate with them?"

"*Really*, George."

"Let me put it this way: can they get off their backsides fast enough to intercept this Volkswagen van full of Brits and a British missile before it gets nabbed by the VOPOs – and the Bravoes, they'll be there on the double – and those Brits confess to being your agents and whatever else is written out for them to confess to?"

That brought a pause. Sir Anthony Sladen, nominally in charge as the Cabinet Office always was, looked nervously around for candidates. "Does the Security Service have any further information that might . . . I mean . . . ?"

The Deputy D-G moved his old hands slowly across his papers. "Aye . . . we have checked out the British telephone numbers Miss Algar sent us. One is Oxendown House itself – "

"So Arnold Tatham *could* have been there?" George snapped.

"It would be a possibility. The other two numbers are a Church of England hospice in Suffolk and a small *Arts*" – dirty word, that – "dining club off Southampton Row. No, George, we have not kicked down the doors in either of these places. We shall inquire, with full authority, as to who might have been at this end of those calls at a more reasonable hour."

"It would be a large assumption," Sir Nicholas said, "that Arnie Tatham was at all three places."

"Did you know him?" George had noted that 'Arnie'.

"Ahhh . . . I'm not sure I'd say *know* him . . ."

"Everybody seems to say that about him." George got up, pulled off his overcoat and tossed it into a chair. Sprague did the same thing, only more elegantly.

"He was just . . . very good," Sir Nicholas went on thoughtfully. "A dedicated man. One of the few that didn't play the part, he *was* the part. You know, I wonder if you're going to catch Arnie if he doesn't want to be caught. I wouldn't like the job myself."

"Well, he's somewhere over here, running this Crocus List."

"That is implied, but hardly proven, by Miss Algar's report. What she clearly proves is that List's activities have attracted the Bravoes in. Now if *they* can prove what's going on, it would make our government even more apologetic – and acquiescent – towards Moscow."

"What I've been saying all along," George pointed out.

"I dare say. But my point is that it isn't like Arnie to let that happen. The opposite of what he'd recruited the List for."

"Are you saying he may have died in Italy, after all?"

"No-o . . . that was too elegant, a beautiful piece of deception."

"From what one reads," Sladen said, "it does not seem to have deceived the intelligence services of the world, yet nothing has been done, until now, to find him."

"How could one justify the funding?" Sir Nicholas smiled blandly; it was a good face for blandness. "With what object? To prosecute him for living under a false identity? I believe you have to prove a fraudulent intent for that . . . No, I think we've just been waiting to see if Arnie surfaced somewhere. Myself, I personally believe he'd somehow go back to the Church . . ."

"That place in Suffolk?" George glared at the Deputy D-G of Security.

"We'll try, George, we'll try." He turned his wrist slowly to see his watch. "We should be making touch there very soon . . ."

"That apart, however," Sladen said, "there doesn't seem too much to go on. A Volkswagen camper van, but no number plate . . ."

"That's the problem," Sir Nicholas said. "And even if we found it, what could my *assets* do? Talk these people into going home quietly? Push them into the Spree? Risk starting a brawl, even a gunfight, in East Germany? These assets are real people, George, flesh and blood, quite apart from their value to the Service. I want a clear directive if I am to move on this matter."

"The Prime Minister?"

"Yes. If he will acknowledge the threat – "

"That man wouldn't acknowledge a fart in his own bath."

"If you say so . . ."

Sergeant Gower collected Maxim at the Arrivals gate of Tegel – known locally as The Pentagon because the French chose to build the terminal in that rather unsuitable shape. Gower was part of the Intelligence Corps company in the Berlin brigade, and they had met on the Ashford course.

"We got a flash to stop a dark green Volkswagen van at the checkpoint, if it tried to go out," Gower said, "but they didn't have a number. Just that it had a roof hatch and a stove pipe. And I've found which hotel Mr Ferrebee is in. The Archbishop's addressing the Senate this morning then lunching with the Mayor and flying out at 1530."

"Thank you."

"It's not much to go on," Gower said gloomily. "But we'll try." He was a shortish man in his mid-thirties who managed to seem older by his mournful outlook and shambling unmilitary gait. His worn sports jacket and the untidy length of his blonde hair weren't very military, either, but Int Corps didn't always try very hard at such things. Often the opposite.

"A little bird told me that Mr Ferrebee got a telegram through their office here," Gower added.

"Good. Then he'll be in the picture. Can you give me a lift there?"

"Happy to," Gower said sadly, dumping Maxim's bag in the back of an elderly Audi with civilian number plates. "Things have been very quiet since the Soviets put up their proposals. Behaving themselves. Maybe you can do something about that."

The meeting knew Sladen had failed on his mission to Number 10 just from the look on his face as he lowered himself stiffly into his chair. He placed his hands carefully on the edge of the table and pushed fiercely for a moment, his knuckles turning white. Then he relaxed and said: "It was, I think, the Stegosaurus which had one brain in its head and another in its arse, to control the tail. I've always liked the big saurians: they managed to rule the world for about 140 million years, which sets a bench-mark for any civil service. But I've sometimes wondered whether, when the front brain shut its eyes and ears, the arse brain wasn't reduced to swishing around in the dark.

"The PM will sanction no action until he has had more time and fuller information – "

"More *time*!" George exploded.

Sladen held up a hand in so imperial a gesture that George stifled with surprise, because Sladen was stepping not so much out of character as into the one he might once have become. "Gentlemen, we of the arse brain cells are swishing in the dark."

But, George thought sadly, he's got even that wrong, because when nobody leads, we retreat into our little cells and do nothing. Not even swish.

41

Three of them made Ferrebee's hotel room seem crowded.
It was narrow, no more than twice the width of the single
bed, with a window at the end giving an excellent view
of a new office block just a hundred yards away across the
car park. Ferrebee himself sat on the bed, littered with
newspapers, Maxim at the dressing-table alongside, and
Sergeant Gower at the small desk under the window. No
matter how small, a Berlin hotel will always give you
space to lay out your workpapers, just as it will always
find an extra floor for a *Konferenzraum*. It is in business for
business.

"I'm very glad to see you again, Major," Ferrebee said,
"although your presence seldom indicates good news.
Perhaps you can expound on the extraordinary telegram I
got through our office here, early this morning? Signed
by George, the *Deputy* D-G of Security and some Assistant Commissioner from the Met. Assuming they weren't
all bitten by the same mad dog, could you tell me what's
behind it all?"

"It's a rather complicated story," Maxim said, "but
what matters is that we think the threat to the Archbishop
is real. Have you altered his travel arrangements yet?"

"No, not yet. I want to know where you think this
threat will be."

"When the plane overflies East Germany or East Berlin,
depending on the take-off direction. It has to be close: a
Blowpipe missile can't reach very high."

Ferrebee stood up and stalked over Maxim's feet to the
window, leaning past Gower to pull the net curtain aside.
The sky was a cold windswept blue with puffy clouds
trundling towards them over the office building. "It's

264

easterly at the moment, looks as if it should hold. Take-off east, then."

"You could take him out by road, sir," Gower suggested mournfully. "Pick up a flight at Hannover."

"As a last resort," Ferrebee said. "But I don't want to put His Grace to the business of being searched by the Volkspolizei at two checkpoints. It's . . . humiliating, and after yesterday's sermon they aren't going to treat him kindly. I laid on this private flight so that he could get in and out in comfort. He's not a young man, nor a particularly fit one."

Maxim nodded. "Then can you reposition the aircraft to Gatow? I'm sure the RAF would . . ."

"The aircraft isn't here yet. We're supposed to be flying out at three thirty local time, and I don't suppose the aircraft'll be in more than three-quarters of an hour before that. A company may lend you their Jetstream," he explained, "but they take it back between flights. You have to work a company aircraft hard to justify it to the shareholders. All right, I might get it repositioned to Gatow, though that would mean a delay . . . Why don't we just go for a delay? It gets dark early these days: if we hung on until after dark, would your missile be able to hit us then?"

"It'd be difficult – but why not simply wait until I give you the all clear that there's no more danger?"

Ferrebee had been pacing the narrow space beside the bed, with Maxim keeping his feet well under his chair. Now he stopped abruptly. "How can you guarantee that, Major?"

"I can't. But if you don't go until I give the okay . . ."

"What are you going to be *doing*, Major?"

Maxim gazed back, then smiled to soften his look.

Ferrebee said: "Do you know who these people are, then?"

"We've got three names so far. One's dead; yesterday. The other two we haven't found yet – but there's more we don't know about. We do know what van they're probably using, and our people at Checkpoint Charlie have orders to stop it, but it's probably over there already."

"Then what are you going to do?"

Maxim said nothing.

"I do hope, Major, that you are acting under orders."

In no town or city in the world has the British Army (or the American or French) more power than in Berlin. Theoretically, little has changed since 1945 when the city came under Allied military government, so that the Foreign Office can merely advise the General in command what to do next. But a Foreign Office official on leave, shepherding the Archbishop, is less than the mud on an Army boot. Until one gets back to London, of course.

So Maxim just kept on smiling, and not quoting his non-existent orders.

Ferrebee dumped himself back on the bed with a twang of springs. "Very well. I'll do as you *suggest*. But: I don't want any hint of a change in the Archbishop's arrangements to get out. That could lead these . . . these madmen, to change their own plans. And what about when we get back to London? There has to be security there."

"You'll be covered," Maxim assured him. "Security's finally got its boots on with this one. The whole thing should be wound up in a day or so."

"That's something." Ferrebee brooded for a moment. "This is absolutely incredible, you know: assassinating the Archbishop of Canterbury. It hasn't happened in over eight hundred years, Thomas à Becket . . ."

"Murder in the Cathedral," Gower said. "It's been well remembered. I dare say it stirred up a bit of fuss at the time, too."

"It did, Sergeant, it did. Though that wasn't intended."

Maxim stood up. "It's intended now."

"What were you thinking of doing next, Major?" Gower asked as they walked back towards his car.

"I thought I might cross over and look at some parked vehicles in" . . . he glanced at the travelling sky . . . "East Berlin, with this wind."

Gower may have sucked in his breath sharply, but it was lost in the wind that indeed seemed to be holding steady from Siberia, hustling at their backs and flickering dead leaves past them. His voice and face certainly became more mournful. "If you get caught over there, Major – "

"If *they* get caught over there, too . . . We're in a bind."

266

"You wouldn't want to go over in uniform. But I could do you an orange card . . ." In uniform (not that he had one with him) Maxim could go into East Berlin by simply flashing his ID, just as a Russian officer could cross to the West, although the Russian might have more explaining to do to his seniors if he ever went back. An 'orange card' would identify Maxim, under any name he chose, as a civilian British official. However, he didn't want to be anything official at all.

"I think I might stroll across as just a tourist. I've got a Canadian passport that seems to work . . ."

"Have you now?" Gower's professional interest lit up. "I wonder how you found that – it had better be good. Very popular passport, the Canadian one, these days. Marks you down as a big spender but not committed to an American viewpoint, if you follow me."

"Real Canadians also travel."

"I don't blame them," Gower relapsed into gloom. "But you could get searched. It wouldn't look so good if you had anything *useful* on you."

They walked for a time in silence. Gower's training had made him leave his car, which was probably known as belonging to an Int Corps man, some distance from the hotel. The same instinct for invisibility made him stop at a street crossing and wait for the green light, although there was no risk in walking. Berliners are disciplined pedestrians and were being rewarded by gangs of workmen stretching the already wide pavement to make strolling that much easier. Prosperity is the clang of a shovel, Maxim realised, and the shovels had started clanging almost as soon as the guns had stopped in 1945. Prosperity was now all about them: they moved in a canyon of concrete and plate glass that channelled herds of polished cars intent on being the first to catch a jaywalker. It might not be beauty, but it was solid worth.

"I could probably find you something useful," Gower said at last. "And leave it over there for you."

"I've got a little nine-mil something already, though it could use a few more rounds. Now, if I could find that on the other side . . ."

*

267

The meeting went on simply because nobody wanted to be the one to suggest it had ended already. The tabletop was littered with signals and coffee cups and the room quite warm, even fuggy, although nobody was smoking. We smell like old men, George concluded gloomily.

"Could we not," the Deputy D-G from Security suggested diffidently, "appeal to Charlie's Indians, as we seem to call them now, for help? They have a more activist reputation and presumably more assets in East Germany than we can afford. It would not be the first time, after all . . ."

Everybody drew back fractionally, as if he had loosed a cockroach in the middle of the table. Then all leant forward again, because they could take such things.

Sir Nicholas pursed his lips. "If they weren't involved already, they'd be delighted to step in and show us how it should be done. But as they *are* involved, they're trying to distance themselves as much as possible. They know whom our masters will blame if it becomes a debacle."

"Not without justification," Norman Sprague said. "One cannot lose sight of the fact that this, ah, Crocus List was conceived and financed entirely by – "

"We're talking about a bunch of *Britons*," Sir Nicholas said firmly. "Apparently intelligent men who went into this with their eyes open, acting in what they think is the best *British* interest. If Five wasn't allowed to catch them in this country when all they were doing was smearing Ettington and popping off guns in the Abbey, we can't expect Charlie to save our face when they go international."

Sprague looked mildly hurt. "Well, then I suppose our hopes rest entirely on Major Maxim. Although hopes for what, I can't say."

"And then," George said, "at least you'll be able to blame the Army as well."

West Berlin's prosperity stops well before the Wall itself, at roughly the point where the U-Bahn subway fills with Turkish immigrant workers and becomes known as the Orient Express. Beyond there, the buildings are old and shabby, the few modern ones standing aloof and uncomfortable, like guests at a wedding wondering what on earth sort of family their nephew is marrying into.

Maxim sat in a rather scruffy bar just out of sight of Checkpoint Charlie, stretching a Pils and feeling time pass with the east wind outside. But the wind was steady; he, and they, should be in the right place.

Sergeant Gower came in, wearing a uniform anorak and cypress-green beret. He ignored Maxim, went straight to a cigarette machine and bought a packet of Marlboros. The barman gave him a sour look as he went out again, turning right. Maxim waited two minutes, then followed.

In the car, Gower said: "It's in place," and told him the address. "And if you want transport over there, there's a green Lada taxi that'll be hanging round the Friedrichstrasse station. You call the driver Erich – shall I give you the number?"

Maxim repeated it carefully. "Thanks. I'll push on across, then. It's asking a bit, but if you could stick around here and be ready to grab the Volkswagen if it comes back – I'll try and be with it myself, but . . . I don't know if you've powers of arrest . . ."

"In Berlin, we can always work out something."

"Fine. And if I don't get back, could you signal George Harbinger at MoD?"

"You'll be back, Major." But it was the instinctive reassurance demanded on the eve of battle. Gower was torn – as Maxim could sense – between the common sense of letting him get on with his job and the feeling that nobody joined the Army to go into things alone. The Sergeant frowned through the windscreen and tapped his fingers quickly on the wheel. "I suppose I'm just the intellectual type, really . . . But there's something worries me. A Blowpipe's a good bit of kit, it did all right in the Falklands, I heard – but they shot off a lot more than they knocked down planes."

"Taking off, any aeroplane's a sitting duck. And they've been practising as much as they could."

"Civilians." The slow shake of Gower's head dismissed any civilian practice. "They've only got the one missile . . . it could have water on its brain or oil up its – I don't know about missiles – but one on one isn't a sure way. Then what? What's their back-up plan?"

"I don't know."

"Me neither, Major . . . but killing the Archbishop, I mean it's quite a big idea. If they were going to do it at all, they might want to get it right."

"They could be thinking of an assassination in London – only they don't stand a chance, now we're on to them."

"Yes. I just thought, if he's not going to fly over that Blowpipe anyway, if you'd gone along to guard him instead . . ."

"He's only half of it. If the Blowpipe brigade gets picked up – "

"They must have thought up some sort of getaway. I mean, it would bugger their plan if they got caught . . ."

"I don't want them to get away. I want to bring them back alive and talking."

42

The Wall that cuts Berlin in half, and makes West Berlin a landlocked island, brings a variety of emotions. It is nasty, but that is something you knew already. It is strange, a wall cutting across streets, at one place running down the centre of a street, pedantically following the boundaries of the prewar electoral districts – but just how strange only a Berliner could say, and increasingly only an older Berliner – although West Berlin is an old people's city. But perhaps strangest of all, it is old-fashioned: a Cold War attitude frozen in concrete, immortalising midnight deals in cigarettes, currency, people. It brings an exasperated demand: For God's sake, haven't things changed just a bit? The Wall is the answer, and the answer is No.

What it certainly is not is impressive. Barely twelve feet high, it could be scaled in seconds by trained men or knocked flat by a tank: of course, the Russians may well have thought of that. On the Western side it is covered in aerosol graffiti and occasional plaques where people have died trying to cross from the East, but graffiti dominates. Its strength lies on the Eastern side, in the no-man's-land of minefields, watchtowers, alarm fences, ditches, automatic guns and vehicle obstacles.

Yet even these are not very impressive as you walk past them at Checkpoint Charlie; or perhaps soldiers just get blasé about such things. Maxim noted them instinctively, at first pretending not to look, then gawping obviously, as he assumed a tourist would do. The pathway narrowed through wire fences and he found himself standing with a little group of real tourists on the wooden verandah of the long control shed, a dirty corrugated plastic roof overhead and a wire mesh gate ahead, waiting for his visa. And waiting. And waiting.

A single unarmed guard with a green-banded cap, chubby and pink-cheeked, strolled out among the cars on the widened roadway beside them, collecting and returning passports, lifting chain barriers to let a vehicle creep forward a few more yards to the next stage. From time to time he took a passport from a faceless window beyond the gate and held it up, open to show the photograph: a relieved tourist claimed it, was allowed through the gate to pay his five Deutschmarks, and vanished into the shed further along. The rest waited.

It became the timeless, mindless hospital hallway where you wait stripped of personality, because the real you is a clutch of paperwork being leisurely diagnosed behind closed doors; where the best news can only be that things aren't as bad as you are sure they are. Or that you will reach East Berlin.

It was a time for fears to grow. Absurdly, he began wondering if they had his photograph – Harry Maxim's photograph – on a file in that shed. They certainly had it on file somewhere behind the Iron Curtain, had had it from soon after he started work at Number 10, and he was a hundred miles behind the Curtain already. Or they were pulling the Winterbotham passport to pieces, spotting discrepancies and flaws he would never have suspected, that even Agnes . . . no, he didn't want to think of Agnes. She had nothing to do with Winterbotham. *I am Alan James Winterbotham, aged thirty-seven, born in London UK, hospital administrator . . .* But there's a photograph of Harry Maxim –

It was the guard holding up his passport.

Blindly, he took it. "*Danke schön . . .*"

"Five Deutschmarks."

He paid at the window, barely seeing the shadowed face beyond, walked the verandah, in through the door . . . There was a shelf scattered with small forms in different languages. He found an English one and filled out how much currency he was carrying, handed it to a middle-aged woman in uniform.

"Have you any books, papers?"

He half-pulled the unmarked map from his pocket; surely most tourists would carry that.

"A map." She waved him past. "You must change twenty-five marks."

He was ready for that. At the next desk he got twenty-five East German marks on a one-for-one exchange; the unofficial but real rate was four to one. And he was 'free' in East Berlin.

The first stage of the route was easy: straight ahead down the wide Friedrichstrasse. Even after the deliberate desolation behind the Wall, the street took time to revive, with buildings perhaps eight storeys high standing among empty plots; one of the buildings itself was derelict. The wind blew a fine dust out of the emptiness, bringing a weird reminder of Washington . . . *I am Alan James Winterbotham . . .*

At the broad Unter den Linden the new buildings began, stretching out in either direction. He waited for a green light; the traffic was far thinner than in the West, the cars smaller: Skodas and Ladas, many old and asthmatic, with dulled paintwork. The crowd thickened on the far side, as he neared the Friedrichstrasse station; there were a lot of uniforms – all East German: the overt Russian presence in Berlin is very small – with the officers all carrying briefcases that were as much a badge of rank as their epaulets.

He found the café easily, just past the three-level station complex and the Metropole Theatre. It was small and genteelly modern, with waitresses in white-frilled black uniforms weaving among tiny plastic-topped tables. He drank a coffee, black, and it tasted much as any coffee did, but he was no connoisseur; had the time-warp of the Wall made him expect something made from toasted acorns?

"Noch eins Kaffee, bitte." He could speak more fluent German than that, but Alan James Winterbotham couldn't. Most of the other customers were middle-aged ladies, seemingly well-dressed – he was no connoisseur there, either – chatting over an after-lunch coffee with perhaps a liqueur on the side. It was just . . . well, genteel.

When the coffee came, he stood up and looked around for the . . . er . . . The waitress pointed the way, past the rack of coats. He thanked her and moved off. Now he would find whether Sergeant Gower's visit had sparked any official interest. And if the middle-aged ladies suddenly turned into Volkspolizei agents and leapt on him as he lifted the plastic-wrapped pistol from the lavatory cistern, they would find out how Harry Maxim reacted. Not Alan James Winterbotham.

43

With a pistol nearly nine inches long and weighing over two pounds jammed uncomfortably in his waistband (but thank God it was November and the weather for his thick car-coat) it was difficult to feel much like Alan James Winterbotham. In fact, it was pointless, since no passport could explain that away. In a Marxist state private property has to be tolerated, but a private weapon is a denial of the state itself.

But *they don't know*, he told himself, trying to lighten his step.

It was nearly four miles through the streets to Pankow, so he walked back towards the station, looking for the green Lada taxi. It wasn't there, so he stood consulting the Berlin map – the agreed signal – until it cruised past, stopped and reversed: just a hungry taxi-driver looking for a tourist with West Deutschmarks.

"*Bist du Erich?*"

"*Ja. Herein.*"

He sat carefully on the uneven springs of the back seat. "*Nach dem Pankow S-Bahnof, bitte.*"

The Lada jerked away, and after they had gone a couple of blocks Erich held his hand over his shoulder with a snap of his fingers. Maxim dealt him two hundred West Deutschmarks, as agreed.

Erich wasn't entirely happy. "It is dangerous to drive you."

"Then drive carefully so that the police will not stop you."

"I have a wife, problems . . ."

"I have no wife, she was killed by a terrorist bomb. We all have problems." It was odd how crisply he could say that, a plain statement of fact. God rest you, Jenny, but I am alone in East Berlin.

Anyway, it shut Erich up. Maxim watched the streets settle down to a suburban evenness as they wriggled north, wondering for a while why the shops and office blocks seemed so drab, then realising it was simply the lack of advertising: neon signs and posters. Is *that* the alternative to drabness? he wondered.

The suburb of Pankow had been badly hit in the war, less by bombing than by the Russian drive from the north-east which had been bitterly opposed. But shells and small-arms fire don't knock down the solid Berlin apartment houses, just punch a few repairable holes and chip the elaborate carved stone around the windows from which boys hardly older than his Chris had sprayed Russian tanks with half-understood and wholly ineffective submachine-guns.

Even the children who had lived would be in their fifties now, the trees – which had probably suffered worse casualties – had grown again along the pavements, and Pankow was back to being stolid middle class again, the undefeatable enemy of the class war no matter how much of its fancy stonework you shot away.

"Drive me around," he told Erich. "Go left here."

Ahead, the tubby shape of a Boeing 737 rose against the western sun, silent as it turned because the wind delayed its roar. They were almost on the right line.

"I cannot just drive. It looks suspicious . . ."

"Another hundred." Maxim passed it over. "Keep moving, it won't look so bad."

"I am supposed to report what foreigners I take – "

"Let's hope they don't make me report, too, then."

Beyond the S-Bahn tracks, the suburb thinned out to parks, cemeteries and sports stadiums. They weaved through them; there were few pedestrians and fewer parked vehicles. Another airliner rose out of the west, behind them now.

"Go right," Maxim ordered, "and right again."

Something turned in behind them. Controlling his movement, Maxim looked casually back: a dark green van. The taxi shivered as Erich saw it. Maxim said: "Pull over and let them pass."

The van slid past, its windows blanked with venetian blinds. "Now follow," Maxim said.

"Follow *that*? Do you see the number?"

"No . . ." Then Maxim did. The van had Russian military plates. Until that moment, such plates had been abstract, part of his training, but a part that had sunk in. He felt a shudder of fear.

But surely it had been a Volkswagen – or was it a UAZ452? He tried desperately to remember from his glimpse. Russian military colour and plates, and the Russians could easily have commandeered a Volkswagen and painted it up – but that was the safest cover for the Crocus List, too; the Volkspolizei would think twice about stopping a Russian military van.

Whatever it was, the van turned off down a road through a park full of trees shedding leaves in gusts down the wind. Erich didn't turn. Maxim laid his pistol alongside Erich's ear. "Stop. Back up."

The Lada wavered to a halt, then reversed jerkily and turned. The van was stopping halfway along the park, screened by trees from the houses a couple of hundred metres away on either side.

"Right up behind him."

Erich brought the Lada to a stop. "You are going to take us to prison for ever – "

"Wait."

Somebody stepped from the driving seat of the van; he wore a dark leather coat and a fur hat and the pause when he saw the taxi behind froze him into an arrogant military statue. Then he walked towards them. Erich jammed the Lada into gear.

"Hold it!"

The man jerked open Erich's door. A second man, dressed the same way, was coming up on the other side. In accented German, the first man said: "Take this old thing away before – "

"*Ja, ja,*" Erich was in total agreement.

Maxim opened his own door. "Well, hello there, Mr Fluke. I don't know if you remember me from the Abbey – "

At that point, Erich and the Lada took off. Maxim

toppled on to the road, losing the gun and rolling to avoid Fluke's kick, then grabbing and twisting the foot so that Fluke cartwheeled over him and slammed on to the road-way. The second man was rushing at him, and Maxim sat up with the refound pistol and, with the slow motion that comes when you know you have just a fraction of a second on your side, shot him carefully in the leg.

In its way, it was a moment of victory. But Maxim couldn't think of anything clever to say, even if he had the breath to say it.

Fluke drove the van, wheezing and coughing from his own fall, and in the back Maxim bandaged the other man's leg. "It's going to hurt like hell until the medics get at it," he assured the man, "but it won't start bleeding again unless you begin dancing around, and I'm sure you don't plan to dance around. However, I'll take your passports, just in case."

With those, and their East German visas, in his hand, he had them nailed. They wouldn't last the night without identification. "So – I expect you've got some quiet place picked out where you can change the number plates back again? Fine, let's get there."

Fluke went no more than a mile, further north to where the houses petered out and there were whole blocks of allotment gardens, scruffy and deserted at that time of year. The Russian number plates came off in seconds and were dumped under a pile of compost. Then Maxim helped apply some colourful sticky-tape along the side of the van to soften its military look. That was the way they had brought it through the checkpoint, Fluke said, and Maxim accepted it. Nobody had anything to gain by getting held at the Wall.

Taking a last look around, he saw a small aircraft bend into a climbing turn a mile or so to the south-west, perhaps just over the Wall. Chubby fuselage, slender sharp wings, twin propeller engines . . . there could be two Jetstreams in Berlin that day, but it was a big coincidence in the timing: a glance at his watch showed just after three thirty. Ferrebee must have been stupidly trusting, or the Archbishop had overridden him or –

The aircraft's shape blurred with smoke that streamed away behind it for a moment, then it pitched nose-up, rolled lazily on its back and dived in a smooth curve behind the skyline of houses and trees. A mushroom of black smoke bubbled up.

For a dazed moment Maxim was back in the desert watching Jenny die in the bomb-torn Skyvan, wondering if that had really been a missile, then knowing it hadn't been, and neither had this.

"A bomb on board?" he demanded of Fluke, who was looking solemn. "A bomb? Was that your fallback? How was it fired?" He found he had the gun in his hand again.

"I was saying a prayer," Fluke said.

"For the Archbishop? I should keep it for yourself."

"For Jim Ferrebee."

44

Since 1945 the British Army's Berlin HQ has been in the 1936 Olympic stadium offices, although they have only recently got around to renaming the entrance road Jesse Owens Avenue, after the black runner with whom Hitler refused to shake hands. It was late evening, and the table had that late evening look: a litter of coffee cups, beer cans, half-eaten sandwiches, ashtrays and papers. The General had gone and the Brigadier and some colonels and the man from the Foreign Office and the man who was supposed to be from the Foreign Office but was Intelligence . . . just Maxim, Gower, and a balding bespectacled Major from Int Corps.

"I thought," the Major said, "that you told the General to piss off and mind his own business very politely – "

"I didn't tell him that."

"Of course you didn't, dear boy, but that was the message you intended and certainly the one he got. Anyway, your life is going to be one mad round of generals in the next few days." He lifted a signal form off the table. "I am to deliver you to the door of a Riff-RAF Dominie coming specially into Gatow in – just about an hour. Your own private jet: somebody up there on the sixth floor likes you."

"I'm not counting on it. You got a free ride to Tyburn Tree in the good old days, too."

"I don't see what more you could have done. Stayed with the Archbishop? You'd just be spread around a crater in the Gesundbrunnen railway yard as well – for the first time in your life, I dare say, indistinguishable from an Archbishop. Sorry: that wasn't in the best of taste. But you wouldn't have searched this Foreign Office chap's briefcase for a bomb, now would you? If you'd suspected him, you'd have done more than that . . ."

"I *should* have suspected him."

The Major cocked his head and looked at Maxim with a wry smile. "I really don't recommend a hair-shirt, old boy: not standard Army issue. Just remember that the Foreign Office in particular, and a lot of other government departments besides, have more to worry about right now than the future of one Army major. Particularly one who knows as much as you do."

Maxim nodded, numbly, and stood up. "Can I have a word with this man Fluke before I go?"

The Major slanted his eyebrows. "No rough stuff?"

"If I'd wanted to do that, I'd have done it before."

"I don't see why not, then . . ." He led the way. "We strip-searched him, as you suggested, and there's a guard in the room – I take your point about their predilection for suicide. D'you think you'll get anything useful?"

"Just one question."

"I can see why you'd like to take a little duty-free info back with you . . ." They walked across the lobby of the old Olympic offices, still with its full-frontal statue of some German runner where a military policeman positioned himself tactfully whenever an important woman visitor came calling. "You know, why don't you cross-badge to the Pansies? You seem to be doing our work for us already . . ."

The Intelligence Corps badge of a rose inside a wreath was widely interpreted as 'A rampant pansy resting on its laurels.'

"I'd like to try and make it at the teeth end."

"Very noble sentiment, come a war. Until then, as your experience may have taught you, Int Corps tends to get stuck with more biting than most."

Fluke's 'cell' was a spare room hastily fitted up with a cot and a large Military Police corporal. Too tired for formality, Maxim waved him out. "I'll guarantee him." He sat beside Fluke, who was stretched on the cot.

"What did the evening papers say?" Fluke asked.

"Just what you wanted: Russian missile from the East. It

seems somebody had rung the press agencies and warned about an attempt on the Archbishop – that would have been Ferrebee from the airport, I suppose. Pity it takes weeks to get a phone call across the Wall, or you could have called him and learnt I was in town; it might have saved your mate walking with a limp the rest of his life. They're fixing him up, he'll keep the leg. Yes, you got what you wanted in the papers, and tomorrow's – but after that, it all depends on me, much as anybody."

Fluke lifted himself slowly on his elbows. "Don't you want these talks on Berlin stopped? – what the Archbishop wanted?"

"I'm a soldier. I'm hired to defend a way of life, of taking decisions. I'm allowed my own opinions and my own vote, but no more. If I want more, I'm not supposed to take it . . . But I admit I did. My only excuse is, I didn't start it. Maybe Arnold Tatham did, but – "

"Who?"

"Tatham. The man who picked you up in St Louis. No" – Maxim shook his head wearily – "of course, he wouldn't give you his real name. But it was Arnold Tatham. Now you know. You can also know that even if the Prime Minister wants to hush you and the List up, I can still blow it."

"I doubt that would help your career."

"Seeing non-existent policemen at the Abbey hasn't helped it much, either."

"I'm sorry about that." Fluke smiled wanly. "But, you know, I do think it's all over now. What more do you want?"

"It's over when I say it's over, and I want to be quite sure the List never comes to life again. So write it down."

"Don't be ridiculous, man. Would you do that about your own colleagues in the Army?"

"I might, under the pressure I'm going to put on you. First, I can blow the whole scheme as a fake, undo everything you've done by sacrificing Barling, Ferrebee, the Archbishop and his pilot and a few others I don't think you even know about. That's One . . . where was I?" He shook his head with real tiredness. "Oh yes: your wife and children, of course. And Ferrebee's and that mate of yours in hospital here. You've given me the power to sacrifice them, brand them as the wives and children of traitors and murderers, since that's what you are. And finally, I want that List to take back to London, because you are not going to sacrifice *me*. So write it out." He stood up. "Oh – we identified one other, by the way."

"Who?"

Maxim shrugged. "I'm sure you'll include him, anyway."

"I must say," the Int Corps Major felt he must say, "that you sounded most convincing in there. Yes, of course I had the room wired; wouldn't you? Did you really have another name?"

Maxim nodded. "He's dead, but I don't think Fluke knows that."

"Quite splendid. Bluff from strength. It would be nice to have you among our select company."

Maxim leant against the corridor wall and scratched the badly-shaved area under his chin. "Right now, I'd settle for a nice simple World War."

"Noisy. Probably does frightful things to the roses, too. I think it's better kept to the professionals, but . . . Your transport for Gatow should be arriving about now, and I think Gower's got your bag somewhere . . ."

"When I've got that List."

45

"We failed," George said. "We simply bloody well failed. Not your fault, Harry, God knows, at least you got the List – "

"Now being mulled over," Sprague put in smoothly, "by our dear Prime Minister and the D–G of Security, in whose shoes I would not like to be at this moment. He was never up to the job, of course; I've said so all along. You haven't seen this List, George?"

"No," George growled, and Sprague looked relieved, since he hadn't either. "Harry got it classified Eyes Only and took it round to Number 10 himself. From which I doubt it will ever emerge. Personally, I'm not sure I wouldn't like it spread over every newspaper in the land."

"To what end, George? To tell the world it wasn't the terrible trigger-happy Russkies after all, but just a bunch of dedicated lay churchmen? I really think HM Government would rather see its policies frustrated by a Superpower than your little Crocus List; it maintains an illusion of scale. And truly, one would be swimming against the tide. The public now believes the Kremlin is a hive of cynical duplicity – which it is, the lie unmasks the truth – the Berlin talks are dead, it's inconceivable that we should go ahead now . . . Truly we are but pawns swept along by the tide of public opinion. Indeed, isn't that our function? Servants we chose to be, and servants we are." He sighed contentedly. "It'll be forgotten in a year – less, since one now doubts this government can last that long. Yes, George, I know foreign policy mistakes can't bring down governments these days, but a straw in the wind that lights upon the camel's back . . . And one thing that might interest you, Major: your colleague in illegal arms, Miss Algar, has been called home For Consultation, although I dare say most of the consultation has already taken place with the White House and Langley." He stood up. "I must away. No doubts or uncertainties? The tide, George, the tide, we are but servants of the tide." He went out with, as always, unhurried purpose.

"You have to believe," George said, "that there is more to the government of this country than *that*."

"I do. Has anything more been found out about Tatham?"

"Security's drawn a blank so far, but we have established a connection with Ferrebee. He was a member of a Bloomsbury arts club that Clare Hall rang a few times. Tatham to Hall to Ferrebee – don't they call that a double play, in America?"

"I wasn't there long enough."

"However," George went on, picking up a slip of paper, "the Director of a Church of England hospice in Suffolk wants to see me. That was another number Clare Hall rang. Care for a drive down there? I imagine your office can function without you for another day, since they probably wouldn't recognise you if you went in there anyway."

"I'd like to know when Agnes is getting in."

"Did you want to meet her plane?"

"I'd like to be there."

"Really?" George tried to hide his interest by glancing at the clock. "The overnight flights have all landed by now, it can't be until this evening or tomorrow – I'll find out for you."

"Please."

Now this is something I *can* tell Annette, George thought cheerfully, leading the way out.

There was nothing medical about the room, no hurry, no spilling paperwork, no white paint except on the ceiling and that was now a friendly pale brown. The furniture was dark and old without being very valuable, the few pictures were reproductions of Constable's harvest landscapes originally painted only a few dozen miles inland from there.

"Intimations of immortality," George said, looking round.

"Just so," the Director said, very pleased. He was a small chubby man with thick spectacles and an old sports jacket who bounced up and down in his desk chair as he talked. "Just what we try to offer our patients. A feeling of the seasons, rebirth as part of death. They all come here to die, all terminal cases. We try to relieve their pain – almost all are cancer victims – without turning them into vegetables. Give them the chance to die as human beings, and to come to terms with death beforehand. We find it is the old things that help."

George fidgeted in his chair, not wishing to come to terms with death just yet. "Yes, but you called us down here . . ."

"Of course. You must be very busy men." The Director bounced himself back in his chair. "We had a visit from your Security people yesterday, asking if we had an American patient or somebody who took telephone calls from America. I told them we hadn't – and how do you know if somebody's calling from America now, with this direct dialling? It could be just from the village, for all you can tell . . . But after they'd gone, I thought of a patient who'd lived some time in Canada, which had left him with something of an American accent, and a niece in Montreal – I tried to contact the people who'd come here, but I got put through to you . . . I do hope I'm not wasting your time."

"I'm sure you're not," George said. "So this man . . ."

"Joseph Adams."

Maxim handed over the photograph of Tatham that Agnes had taken from Clare Hall's house. "Ye-es," the Director said, frowning. "I think so. Of course, he's younger in this . . ."

"Can we see him?" George asked.

"Oh no." The Director was surprised. "He died three, nearly four months ago. His niece came over for the cremation service."

After a moment, Maxim said: "A tall woman, grey for her age, hair swept back over – "

"Yes, that's her. D'you know her? A charming lady."

George had been counting back. "Dead – all the time. From before the Russian proposals."

Maxim shook his head slowly. "He must have passed on the List, maybe when he knew he was dying."

"Did you ever think," George asked the Director, "that your Mr Adams might not be Mr Adams?"

"Mr Harbinger, Major – I imagine both your jobs put you in charge of other people. I am in charge of people who are going to die, within three months at the outside. I run, you might say, a crammer's course for death or eternity. It's not for me to choose which, I just help them come to terms with their own choice. Their future is so short, I can hardly waste time on the past."

He thought for a moment. "He talked of going on *missions*, I think he meant the wartime sort, and having to leave everything behind. He said that in the end, he'd left God behind. And had been looking for Him again. I know he's spent the last few years in various Church retreats around the country . . .

"People can become strongly religious in two ways, I find. Mostly it's a sense of the love of God, but sometimes it's hatred of the Devil. Such people really can spend their lives fighting evil, seeing it everywhere, in everything. I think it may be the Devil's subtlest temptation, because you devote your life to him. In the shadows."

"Mr Adams spent a long time in the shadows," George said evenly.

"I don't think I want to know more about him. But you mentioned a list . . . I hope this can be treated in confidence, although I'm not doing so myself . . ."

"Don't worry."

"Thank you. He gave me a letter for his niece – this was very near the end. He died of pneumonia, it was a bit messy . . . the envelope got stained and I took the letter out to put it in a new one . . . I shouldn't have read it, but all it said was 'Destroy the List'."

"Only she didn't," George said, speaking loud against the wind. "She sent the List to Ferrebee, I'd think, and told him to bring the clan together. Maybe posing as a cut-out for her father – I doubt we'll ever know."

The small plaque on the pine tree read: *Here are scattered the ashes of Joseph Adams* and the dates of birth and death.

Maxim shuffled a foot among the long grass of the over-grown churchyard.

"She couldn't put up a proper monument to him," George went on, "so she erected a bloody international crisis in his memory. Which he'd decided he didn't want."

The east wind was still holding, thrashing the nettles against their legs at the rickety lychgate as they walked back towards the hospice.

"If it had been him running it," Maxim said, "I wonder if we'd ever have caught them. He sounded better than us."

They had to pass the glassed-in verandah where a few well-wrapped patients sat staring out through the pines to the grey sea. They didn't look at Maxim and, after one glance, he didn't look at them.